The Vanity Project of Father Brendan Coglan

Judith Oliver

Stairwell Books //

Published by Stairwell Books
161 Lowther Street
York, YO31 7LZ

www.stairwellbooks.co.uk
@stairwellbooks

ISBN: 978-1-917334-20-4

Cover design: Susie Williamson

Dedicated to

Raymond Oliver

5th February 1940 - 6th February 1996.

Dad,

You loved me for the first twenty five years of my life. Your integrity, compassion, hopefulness and humour have guided me ever since.

Thank you for everything.

"The sacramental seal is inviolable; therefore, it is absolutely forbidden for a confessor to betray in any way a penitent in words or in any manner and for any reason."

Roman Catholic Canon Law

"I went to Catholic School. I got A Level guilt."

Billy Connolly

Prologue

He isn't quite sure how long he has been standing there, gazing down at the traffic as it streams underneath the bridge. Long enough for his knuckles, clenched around the cold steel of the railing, to turn white, anyway. Long enough for the vehicles beneath him to meld into a multicoloured blur; cars, lorries, buses distinguishable only by the pitch of their rumble. Long enough for the first withered petals to drop from the flowers he has tied to one of the rusty poles. He lets out a slow breath, closes his eyes and relaxes his grip, enfolded by a calmness more profound than any he has felt in a long while.

A very long while. Weeks? Years? He is no longer sure.

Now he's inhaling the odour of the traffic; feeling a strange compulsion to follow the waft to its source. The rhythmic whoosh from the cars below is hypnotic and welcoming; the mild morning tail breeze is propelling him gently towards the railing. Could it be that his senses and the elements are urging him to step over the ledge of the bridge and abandon himself to the merciful finality of the concrete road; the last decision he'll ever have to make?

God, it's a tempting notion.

He remains standing a while longer; listening, breathing, feeling. Not thinking; he's had enough of thinking to last him a lifetime.

Besides, what is there to think about? He has no trepidations about having to answer for his earthly crimes; nothing the afterlife could inflict upon him could possibly approach the horror of the maelstrom raging in his head. His parents? They may grieve for a while, but surely learning the truth will extinguish any lingering misplaced sorrow. Pain? That's no deterrent; he is

1

already in more agony than he can bear, and he knows he won't break any further; how can you break something that is already irredeemably shattered?

There is only himself, the road and the traffic below; the irresistible potential of absolute nothingness, the promise of no longer needing to feel anything at all.

2019

1.

When Father Jim McLean was seventeen, he had walked around with a broken leg for the best part of a week before seeking treatment, following a vicious rugby tackle. He had suffered a dose of malaria whilst serving as a padre in the first Iraqi war and refused to ease up on his counselling duties. He had undergone six rounds of radiotherapy for prostate cancer ten years ago with a not unimpressive degree of stoicism. It was a source of wry amusement to him, however, that the one malady guaranteed to catapult him back to the emotional state of a whiney six-year-old was a dose of the common cold. And the one from which he was currently suffering was a real humdinger.

He had coughed and sniffed his way through morning mass; a phlegm sodden handkerchief resting unceremoniously on a stool by the side of the altar. Afterwards, the handful of mainly elderly parishioners who had attended the 9:00 am service had almost all taken an involuntary step backwards as he stood by the door of St Jude's, throatily wishing them a good day. More than one kindly soul had suggested that he ought to be at home with a hot toddy and Jim could think of few reasons to disagree. Frankly, if he could have any wish in the world right then it would be to turn back time to when he actually was a whiney six-year-old, then curl up with his head in his mother's lap and his thumb in his mouth, with his teddy bear tucked firmly under his arm and his favourite blanket covering him.

His head thudded in time to his footsteps as he wearily trudged the ten-minute walk back to the parish house, the queasy roiling in his stomach quite banishing the usually pleasant anticipation of his post mass breakfast.

"AAAAA-Shoo!"

Jim tried but failed to stem the ferocious sneeze with his handkerchief; the contents of his nostrils exploded over the pavement and onto his shoes. The drizzle seemed to seep into his bones as he stopped to blow his sore, reddening nose and wipe his face. As he blew a thick wad of mucous into his handkerchief, a twinge above his nose gave him an indication that sinus trouble would not be far behind.

"Urgh," he said to himself; at least he thought he had said it to himself but could not discount the possibility that he had spoken aloud. "I really don't feel very well at all."

Christ, even his language was regressing to the range of a whiney six-year-old.

Jim quickly considered the remainder of his daily schedule. He normally put in an appearance at the Wednesday afternoon pensioner's club held in the church hall; however, he was certain that Pat, the club president, was perfectly capable of setting out the teas and biscuits and collecting the "voluntary" donations without his input. The bishop could wait another few days for the quarterly financial report – it was overdue anyway. That only left the evening confessions. Well, he was sure his new curate, Brendan would be willing to handle them. Brendan may have only been in residence for just over a month, but the young lad was as eager as a Jack Russell puppy to get stuck into parish responsibilities. This would be as good a learning opportunity as any. Right now, all Jim wanted was to hibernate in bed. As soon as he reached home, he stepped over the pizza delivery leaflets and Red Cross charity bag that had dropped through the letterbox and went straight into the kitchen. There, he rifled through the overhead kitchen cupboard for the Family Circle biscuit tin which housed the house's rudimentary first aid kit. Miracle of miracles, amongst the spilled plaster boxes and half-used paracetamol strips was an almost full box of Lemsip sachets and a bottle of Olbas oil still just about in date. A second rummage unearthed an even richer treasure – a hot water bottle, the existence of which Jim had completely forgotten. Jim thanked God unironically – although his face felt flushed, the rest of his body was beginning to shiver. Sod the common cold, this was more like flu. He put the kettle on and sent a text to Brendan whilst waiting for it to boil. Then he sneezed, filled the hot water bottle, sneezed, prepared the Lemsip and went to his bedroom where he sneezed, drew the curtains, sneezed again and sank onto the bed with a groan and yet another sneeze.

2.

"Father Coglan, why did Jesus cry before he raised Lazarus from the dead if he knew he was going to bring him back to life all along?"

"Well, what do you think?" Brendan was particularly proud of this go-to answer, which he had employed many times whilst helping with Mrs Smith's year 6 RE lessons.

The bell heralding mid-morning break cut off the discussion.

Wednesdays, which were spent helping at St Jude's Primary School were the highlight of Brendan's week. The fresh uninhibited innocence of the children, the potential each one of them held, never failed to move him. And the responsibility he, as a priest, would play in guiding them safely to adulthood was just beginning to scare him.

Brendan felt the buzz of Jim's incoming text in his back pocket and frowned as he read it over his mid-morning mug of tea. The text was brusque and to the point, rather at odds with his mentor's usual expansive forms of expression.

"I've come down with flu. feeling lousy. Gone to bed. You will need to hear the confessions tonight. Sorry, but not up to it."

Brendan felt a moment of concern for the older man coupled with a twinge of guilt that he hadn't noticed anything was amiss earlier. True, Jim had retired to bed early the previous night claiming exhaustion; and his snoring, never gentle, had been at the next level, causing Brendan to root through his bedside cabinet for his earplugs. Brendan also reflected that Jim had barely touched the lasagne he had prepared for their evening meal the previous night, but that could easily have been because Brendan had left it in the oven too long and burned the top.

"Something wrong?" enquired Mrs Smith, noticing the frown as she walked past, svelte in her grey woollen dress.

"I hope not. Father McLean has just texted to say he isn't very well."

"Oh, the poor man. Nothing serious I hope?" Mrs Smith paused to tuck a lock of silvery hair behind her ear.

"Flu, I think. Can't that be nasty in a man of his age?"

Mrs Smith laughed, years falling from her face as she did so.

"Don't let him hear you say that. He's younger than me, and there's plenty of life left in the both of us. I've known him to best people half his age in a chess match and he ran the Great North Run last year. Still, tell him I hope he's feeling better soon – flu can be nasty whatever age you are."

She gave Brendan a warmer smile than was strictly professionally necessary and headed off towards the photocopier. Women were always smiling at Brendan. Not in That Way of course. Even before his priestly aspirations surfaced, he had recognised that he was never destined for heartthrob status. But for some reason, any middle-aged woman he had known for longer than five minutes felt compelled to offer him cups of tea and worry whether he was feeding himself properly. He was sure he was regarded by many as a surrogate grandson.

Furthermore, he was aware that his loosely curling ash blonde hair, full lips, wide-set blue eyes and habitually earnest expression made him look substantially younger than his twenty-nine years. An Australian surfer dude with an identity crisis, was how his sister put it. He had tried to temper the image once by growing a beard, but even he had to admit that it had looked ridiculous, as if somebody had pasted it on hair by hair, with little regard for uniformity of length or colour. His slender frame, which had stubbornly resisted any form of bulking up exercises, did little to counteract the impression he gave of a skinny teenager in a black suit.

Brendan sent a short text back: "no problem, take care, hope you're feeling better soon."

He hoped that was sufficiently solicitous. He hadn't known Father Jim long but had grown fond of him quickly, as he did with most

6

people and, having worked as a carer for adults with dementia for a year before joining seminary, he was used to feeling a degree of responsibility towards those who were, however fleetingly, in a vulnerable position. *Not that he was comparing his mentor to a dementia patient,* he swiftly reminded himself. Apart from being in no doubt as to Jim's keen intelligence, he liked having his head attached to his shoulders.

The rest of the day passed enjoyably. Brendan led a class reading of "The Bear Hunt" and sent the children into fits of giggles over what he considered his rather splendid googly eyed bear impersonation, joined the teaching staff for an excellent butternut squash chilli for lunch (nicely mild; the school caterer obligingly accommodating the tastes of small children and culinarily unadventurous curates) and helpfully made up a pair for an uneven ball catching session during the afternoon's PE session.

Back at home, Brendan heard the salvo of sneezes from the foot of the stairs. He ran upstairs, tapped on Jim's door and opened it when he heard the grunted response. Jim was in bed; huddled over a Lemsip with a cardigan over his pyjamas and half-heartedly watching "The Repair Shop". His bulbous nose looked livid and scabby and two scrunched up handkerchiefs lay on the bed beside him. The room was fragrant with the piercing aroma of Olbas oil.

"How are you doing, Jim?"

Jim's voice was hoarse in reply.

"Absolutely terrible. I thought I was going to pass out when I got up to make a fresh Lemsip. My throat feels like I swallowed a box of razor bl –"

A sudden fit of coughing caused him to break off. He put down the Lemsip, spat into one of the handkerchiefs and examined the phlegm.

"Oh, that's sore," he groaned, rubbing his chest.

"Have you had anything to eat today?"

Jim shook his head.

"I could make you some soup before I go out, if you like?"

"I think there's a tin of chicken in the kitchen cupboard. I might be able to force that down. I couldn't face anything earlier. Are you sure you'll be okay tonight? There aren't normally many there and I'm really not up to doing confessions myself."

7

He punctuated his sentence with a gargantuan sneeze, which he stifled with his handkerchief.

"I'm sure I'll be fine. I'm here to help out with the workload, remember."

Jim sneezed again and blew his nose, then passed his cooling hot water bottle to Brendan.

"Could you see your way to filling this up for me? I can't get warm for love nor money today."

Brendan heated the soup and filled the hot water bottle. He would make himself a nice fluffy omelette when he got in afterwards. He liked to think of himself as a dab hand in the kitchen. Then it was time to freshen himself up in time for his first solo flight in the confessional cockpit.

3.

Since taking up his post at St Jude's, Brendan had been plagued by the memory of his seventeen-year-old self, learning to drive alongside an instructor with one hand on the wheel. Impatience for something to really stick his teeth into wasn't so much nibbling at him, as devouring him piecemeal. His mother's voice seemed to echo in his ear as he performed his evening shave. She had given him some strongly worded advice on his last visit home, along the lines of, "You can't expect to be running the show in five minutes flat, so shut up until you've learned something."

Not that he could fault his mother. Despite their initial shock when, at the age of twenty-two, he had first announced his intentions to join the priesthood, the support of his parents had been unwavering.

When Brendan chose to study history at University, his father had worried about his lack of clear ambitions. With good reason, Brendan had to admit. Bob Coglan had worked as an HGV driver most of his adult life, enduring a regime of getting up at around four every morning – sometimes not returning until nine at night – to provide for his family for over twenty years. A sudden redundancy from the large haulage company for which he worked, left Bob dependant on precarious short-term contracts arranged via poorly paying employment agencies. The family's never vast financial reserves thereafter veered between negligible and non-existent, occasionally dipping into negative with a narrow avoidance of totally buggered. His greatest wish for his two children was that they should live their lives with the luxury of financial security and stable employment. Brendan's sister Nicole, after a turbulent adolescence, had redeemed herself by studying nursing and securing a job in the busy A and E department of the local hospital. When Brendan had begun his priestly training, his parents had let out a joint sigh of relief, thankful that he had, at last, found a direction.

As Brendan let himself into St Jude's church, he was surprised to experience a sudden surge of trepidation. After all his "no problemo" bravado, what if he turned out to be – not to put too fine a point on it – completely crap at this?

What if he let Jim down in some way?

What if he upset a parishioner?

What if he forgot to lock up afterwards and the place got burned to the ground overnight?

"Enough, Brendan," he chided himself. "Time to focus!"

Remembering his breathing exercises, he blessed himself with holy water and knelt to pray before entering the confessional. He meditated in silence for some minutes, breathing in the heady scent of incense, aware of the distant hum of traffic as he prayed.

Heart rate nice and slow – check, breathing nice and steady – check, thoughts coming with a vague coherency rather than in firework like bursts – check.

Once Brendan felt sufficiently calm, he took a deep breath, opened the confessional door and got himself into position.

After the best part of an hour, Brendan was beginning to wish he had sneaked in a book. Of all the scenarios he had envisaged, the prospect of boredom had never featured. So, when he eventually heard footsteps tapping down the aisle, he mouthed a silent "Yesss!"

"Bless me Father, for I have sinned. It's been a month since my last confession. I'm absolutely mortified about this, but I think I've stolen something." Brendan caught a whiff of a sweet, floral perfume, and glimpsed loose curls through the grille.

Think you've stolen something? Either you did or you didn't.

"Would you like to tell me some more about this?"

Brendan was amazed at how composed his voice sounded. He could have been a veteran of fifty years' experience rather than a rookie making his first solo flight around the airfield. He nearly added "my daughter" but felt that this may be patronising. At very least it would be overkill. The woman who was speaking was probably – make that almost certainly – older than he was.

The woman cleared her throat and nervously began.

"So, I was in Aldi this week. I had the bairn's pushchair with me, and I put my few bits of shopping on the bottom as I went round. I thought I'd paid for everything but when I got home, I found a packet of pork chops that hadn't been scanned. I feel terrible, I'm not normally a shoplifter or owt. I didn't sleep last night through worrying about it. My husband thinks I'm barking. When I told him, he just laughed and said if I was going to go out on the rob, at least I could have lifted a nice juicy steak or something."

The woman did seem rather rattled. Brendan thought for a moment.

"Okay, well you've come to the right place. Let's get this sorted. Firstly, I'm not sure Aldi would expect you to bring the pork chops back again. How much did they cost?"

"Three pounds seventy."

"We've got a charity collection tin at the front porch. It goes to the local food bank. If you put the equivalent sum of money in there, we'll call it quits. Now for your penance say one Hail Mary, please. And next time you go shopping, maybe put the baby in a sling as you walk round?"

The woman gave an appreciative giggle.

Brendan absolved the woman from her sins and told her to go in peace. She thanked him and left. Brendan was sure that her footsteps sounded lighter on the parquet floor than they had on her way in. He grinned to himself, happy to have got the first one under his belt. It was another few minutes before Brendan heard a different set of footsteps, flatter and more ponderous this time, maybe suggesting a masculine presence.

10

"Bless me Father, for I have sinned."

The voice was deep and familiar. The grille which separated them was sufficiently wide spaced as to allow Brendan a glimpse of a face. He recognised Neville Tanner, a man whom Jim had introduced as one of his good friends during Brendan's first week at St Jude's. Neville was a retired painter and decorator who sometimes did odd jobs around the church; in fact, he had redecorated St Jude's almost entirely single handedly a couple of years ago. Jim had also mentioned that he used to run a club for underprivileged children and still delivered prescriptions for elderly neighbours.

So, another nice, easy one.

"It's been two years since my last confession. I need absolution from my sins, one in particular."

Neville sighed heavily. Brendan felt a rush of sympathy.

"Would you like to tell me what's troubling you?"

"I have certain images and videos on my computer. Some people may describe them as pornographic."

Brendan gulped. This was not what he had been envisaging. He tried hard not to feel shocked; but it was difficult when the closest he had come to viewing online pornography had been thumbing through a copy of "Loaded" that had been circulated throughout his sixth form common room. It had left him vaguely nauseated.

"Have you had them for long?"

To Brendan's concern, a tremor had crept into his voice and his palms had started to feel moist.

For fuck's sake Brendan, get a hold of yourself. So, the old gadgie's got a thing for Jordan. It's not going to make "Crimewatch" any time soon.

"The images feature children."

"Child pornography?"

Suddenly, Brendan felt his mouth going dry and his heart starting to race. He fought back the urge to leap up, sternly reminding himself of the vows he had taken. The very least of his duties was to hear the man out, however much his insides were backflipping.

"I suffer from certain compulsions. Not everyone understands them, how powerful they can be; how they torment me. The images bring me some relief."

Neville's sigh came from his boots this time.

"I've carried this terrible burden on my own for such a long time — at times it's been almost unbearable. I haven't hurt any children, Father. I have had the images for some time, and I think I'm going to delete them now. But I would like absolution first."

It was the matter-of-fact way in which Neville Tanner spoke that sickened Brendan. He might as well have been talking about having to cough up for a car parking fine he had unjustly received. Brendan's voice was considerably higher pitched when he next spoke.

"Are you intending to give the images to the police?"

"No, of course not," Neville Tanner sounded genuinely shocked at the notion. "Whatever would there be to gain by doing that? I haven't hurt anyone and going to the police would only lead to a lot of awkward questions, for my wife and daughter as well as me. I just need absolution."

Neville's voice had slowed as if he were consciously spelling out his plight; it was starting to take on a frustrated "What kind of idiot am I talking to?" quality.

Brendan breathed hard before making his next statement.

"I'm afraid I can't give it. Not unless you go to the police. Absolution is for people who show some signs of remorse." His throat was now so constricted that his voice had become little more than a squeak.

"Believe me Father, I am very remorseful."

For a remorseful voice, there seemed to be a lot of barely concealed anger.

"How can you say that, when you refuse to go to the police?"

Although Brendan was trying to sound as non-judgmental as possible, he was aware that he was probably falling short. With the back of his heel, he gave his shin a hard kick.

"The police wouldn't understand. They wouldn't care that those images are stopping me from harming children. All they would see is that I've broken some stupid law. At my age, I can't be doing with a police investigation. I came here to get absolution from God. Are you refusing to give me it?" He was no longer sounding sorrowful; nakedly aggressive was closer to the mark.

The walls of the confessional seemed overwhelmingly close. There was an unpleasant smell reminiscent of hard-boiled eggs emanating from the other side, although Brendan could not be sure whether he was imagining it. He was sweating by now, and mildly disorientated.

"Confession isn't some tick box exercise. You have committed a sin," he tried to explain. His voice was inaudible at first and he had to clear his throat and begin again.

"That requires repentance. Genuine repentance. But you aren't repenting. You say you haven't hurt anyone; but the images you possess, have you thought about where they come from? Some poor children will have had to do terrible things to bring them to you."

He paused, as much to force himself to take a strangulated breath as to let his message sink in. When Neville didn't answer, he went on; clutching onto the straw that he could somehow make Neville understand.

"Also, you have committed a crime. You haven't just offended God, you've offended society. You've broken the law. And you're more worried about inconvenience to yourself than about making things right. I can't absolve you from your sins under those conditions. It would be blasphemous."

Brendan realised that he was raising his voice and hoped that nobody could overhear him. He tried to modulate his pitch and ignore the hammering of his heart.

"Please, please go to the police. Own up properly to what you have done. Take whatever help they can give you. Then come back and I will gladly absolve you from your sins. But not like this. I can't, and I won't."

Neville's voice grew lower and even more menacing.

"Refused absolution; I don't bloody believe it. I have been a faithful member of this congregation since you were in short trousers, lad. I have done hours of unpaid work for this church. Whatever sins I've committed, I have more than made up for it in kind. And you are refusing me the sacrament when I need it most. Not a word of concern for any situation I could be in. No compassion for me or my family. Just 'Go to the police,' as if you were a mealy-mouthed proddy vicar. It's a bloody disgrace."

"I can tell that you're obviously in some distress and if you go to the police, I'll even come with you. And as soon as you've confessed to them, I'll grant you absolution but not before. It wouldn't be right. And," he added, almost as an afterthought, "You can't commit a sin like that and work it off by doing odd jobs. It doesn't work that way."

"Do you think I want these urges?" Martyrdom and aggression combined into a plaintive whine. "I never asked for them. They've been there all my life, constantly following me around. They have literally been my cross."

"Don't you dare compare your perversions to the cross!" This was the closest Brendan had been to losing his temper for a long time. "I'm sorry for speaking harshly, but I had to say it," he added.

"Do you have any idea what it must be like for me to live with my urges? The courage and self-control I need every single day of my life? Having to hide it from my wife because there's no way the naive bitch would understand? You haven't got a bloody clue what it's like. I'm as much a victim as any of the children on those images. And was it even that big a deal? They probably didn't even know what was going on. It was probably a fun day out for them, and they'll have got paid for it."

"No, no," Brendan was shaking his head, pleading, no longer able to articulate.

"I needed those images for my own sanity. Who knows what I might have been driven to do without them? Having them was the responsible thing for me to do. And not a word about the sacrifice I'm making in getting rid of them. No acknowledgement about the courage it's taken me to come here tonight. Well, I just hope you can live with yourself, because as it stands you are a disgrace to your profession, and any consequences are on you. Go to Hell, you bastard!"

There were tears in his voice. The eggy stench was stronger than ever.

The confessional door almost swung off its hinges as Neville stormed out. Brendan checked his watch. Just a few minutes remaining. He unclenched the fists he hadn't realised he had been making, surprised to see small crescents of blood appearing on each palm; swallowed down the bile that was sloshing in his throat. He hoped fervently that he would not be required to hear any more confessions that night; as it was, his head was spinning.

After an interminable amount of time, the hour was up. Brendan stumbled from the confessional, collapsing in the front pew. He gripped the front railing and paused. Then, in one deliberate motion he stretched backwards, swooped downwards and banged his head against it, welcoming the sharp pain that thwacked through him. As soon as the throb had eased, he closed his eyes and breathed slowly in through the nose and out through the mouth as he had been previously advised, trying to calm the tight pressure in his chest. Eventually his unsettled heart rate seemed to return to near normal, his hands stopped trembling and the church ceased whirling around him.

"Oh God, oh God!"

Brendan tried and failed to formulate a more coherent prayer. To refuse absolution was never an act to do lightly. In fact it was an enormity that Brendan had hoped he would never need to commit, but he felt as if he would have betrayed his own conscience to absolve a sin in those circumstances. Images of the children with whom he had spent such a pleasant day danced through his brain; the memory of their laughter and enthusiastic response to "Bear Hunt"; the fear (was "fear" too strong a word? Right then it certainly didn't seem so) that sometimes pierced his heart on seeing a trusting pair of eyes turn towards him: fear for their future; for childhood innocence that could be all to easily crushed; for lively spirits that could be demolished by one person's sick perversions.

"Oh God," he pleaded, hoping that God would eventually turn off the silent mode to which he had obviously set his hotline.

He waited for a few more minutes, locked up and began the walk home, hoping his legs wouldn't buckle on the way. For the first time in seven years, Brendan wondered whether joining the priesthood had been a monumental mistake.

2008

4.

When Brendan arrived at Leeds University, he had visions of getting
drunk and being wheeled around Morrison's car park in a trolley whilst
off his own trolley, preferably with a traffic cone on his head. His
recognition that this would have necessitate an almost total personality
dialysis did not dampen the fantasy in the slightest. He imagined
himself sitting in a smoke-filled apartment at three in the morning,
drinking cheap wine with a gang of earnest contemporaries and
holding complex discussions on the politics of various obscure
nations, some of which he had not yet heard or did not yet exist.
Maybe the gang would include some of those mythical creatures called
girls. Maybe he would even lose his virginity to one of them. That was
what he was supposed to be obsessing about, wasn't it? Getting his leg
over, rolling in the hay, playing hunt the sausage, call it what you will.
Maybe, once he had gone to the trouble of actually making the
acquaintance of some girls, his hitherto almost negligible sexual
curiosity would swell to a pitch that was socially acceptable. Or if that
was too big an ask, at least to a level that made him feel less like a total
weirdo.

The illusion lasted until the second day of Freshers' Week when he
strolled around the Societies Fair. Trestle tables lined up alongside
each other, staffed by eager second years loudly extolling the virtues
of their various obsessions. By the time Brendan had inched his way

through the jostling crowd to the end of the first aisle, he had been ambushed by members of the Ballroom Dancing Society – no chance, and the Real Ale Appreciation Society – no thanks, the organised pub crawl the previous evening had been a disappointing bore fest. If student life turned into one long round of shouting "Down in one," and playing "dodge the sick puddle" on the way home, he might as well pack his bags now. Also, on the "thanks but no thanks" list was the Historical Re-enactment Society; whilst Brendan freely admitted to being a bit of a nerd, you had to draw the line somewhere, didn't you?

The altogether quieter stand for the University Catholic Society shone out to him like an oasis of normality in a corral of shoving and shouting. A girl with neatly bobbed jet-black hair, round glasses and a small silver cross around her neck caught his eye and mouthed a shy "Hello." An acne scarred young man with soulful eyes and dark tousled hair offered a leaflet detailing mass times and prayer group sessions. Brendan practically begged for a pen to sign himself up on the spot. He had always found church rituals familiar and reassuring. Church was the one place where the anxieties that had been part of his life for as long as he could remember seemed to melt into insignificance. Unlike his parents and sister, Brendan attended mass every Sunday, as well as school masses.

Discussing his faith with his friends was a complete no-no. It was a truth as widely acknowledged as the fact that the world was round, that the proper topics of conversation at a boys' Catholic school were: football, girls, football, cricket, football, boners, football, wanking, football, ranking the female teachers in the order in which they would like to shag, football, slagging off parents, and football. Brendan could hold his own in a football discussion but when the topic of girls came around there was no disguising his lack of experience. He was sure he couldn't have been the only virgin in 6th form, but he was certainly the most obvious one, the one whose virginity was assumed without question. On the occasions when the boys' and girls' sixth forms joined for social events, Brendan would sit tongue tied, mentally miles apart from the uproar and guffawing around him.

Here, he felt accepted. LeedsCathSoc turned out to be a relaxed familial affair. There was a weekly mass in the University multidenominational chapel, which would be followed by weak tea and biscuits in the adjoining hall. Prayer sessions were held on a weekly basis, and these were often followed by a trip to the pub. Sometimes, the students were joined in the pub by Father "call me Martin," Johnstone, the avuncular priest, who would order a pint of beer, buy the first round and then leave before the group got too ebullient.

It was on one of these occasions that Brendan collided with someone on his way back from the bar. He gawped in horror as he saw a generous portion of his pint slosh down the black chiffon top of a girl he knew only by sight and heard an astonished gasp.

"Oh shit! I'm so sorry. I didn't see you!"

Brendan hastily averted his gaze from the soaked top, hoping his eyes hadn't lingered too much on the just visible cleavage.

"It's okay." The voice was calmer than Brendan would have expected. "Could I get a towel, please?" The accent was a delicate southern Irish. A bartender threw a tea towel, enough to rub the worst of the splash away, to Brendan's relief.

"There, nearly gone. But I think you owe me a white wine, though."

"Sure, go and grab a couple of seats and I'll be over in a minute. Least I can do."

He quickly backtracked. "Well, only if you want to sit next to me. I mean, you've probably got plans with other people."

"I'd love to sit next to you. It's Brendan, isn't it?"

A pair of huge dark brown eyes with the longest, thickest lashes Brendan had ever seen met his. As she turned and walked towards a table, Brendan noticed how the wide belt around her jeans accentuated her slim waist and curvy hips.

Too flustered to think clearly, Brendan ordered the wine and sat on the stool that had been pulled out for him. As he sat down, he had a proper look at the girl; petite with waist-length dark hair held back with a green silk scarf, an oval face with neatly proportioned features, and perfectly smooth, olive skin.

"Hi, err, nice to meet you properly, umm," came out so quickly that Brendan didn't realise until too late that he had no idea of the girl's name.

"Vicky," she supplied. "First year, fine art." She smiled.

"Great. Brendan, well you know that. Obviously! First year history, currently struggling with an essay on the French revolution."

Really, Brendan? Any more hints that you're a clueless idiot, while you're at it?

"Not that you're going to be interested in that," he added hastily.

"Nice to meet you, Brendan."

Brendan searched around for something to continue the conversation.

"So, are you enjoying Cath Soc, then?"

Of all the things you could have said, you just had to hit on the most nerd like comment in the history of mankind.

Vicky didn't seem to think so.

"I'm really enjoying it, makes a change from studying. And anything to get me out of the way of some of those bitches in my flat." The velvety eyes rolled.

Brendan tilted his head, hoping he was giving sufficient "tell me more" signals.

"Well, it's just one of them really."

Obviously, he was inquisitive enough.

"She's a vegan and lets everybody know it. She swore at me when she saw me eating a tuna sandwich yesterday. It was horrible, she called me an effing murderer, and she didn't even say effing; she said the whole word. None of the other girls said anything, I think they're all scared of her."

Brendan nodded with a bolt of sympathy, mixed with not a little rancour that anybody could be quite so mean.

"You should hear some of the things my sister comes out with," he said. "I dunno, since she decided she was an atheist she's under the impression that nobody else is allowed a point of view. Religion is an extension of the patriarchy, or something. She just about puts up with Mam or Dad going to church every few weeks or so but if I dare open my mouth, she's straight in there. Mam might pull her up if she goes too far, Dad doesn't do confrontation in any shape or form."

You go to church so often, Brendan, are you sure you're not sucking the priest off afterwards?

Why are you going upstairs, are you going to jerk off to a picture of the virgin Mary? were among Nicole's choicer insults. Thinking about them saddened him. He added, "Mind you, they did ground her when

19

they were called in to school after she had drawn upside down crucifixes on her RE exercise book."

He grinned, hoping he hadn't gone too far. To his relief, Vicky chuckled. Her laugh was deep and throaty.

"Catholic school?"

"Yeah, both of us. Mam and Dad insisted on it. Think it had more to do with OFSTED ratings than religion, though."

Just then, one of Vicky's friends tapped her on the shoulder and sat down to join them. Disappointment at the interruption of the tete a tete was mingled with relief that said tete a tete had been interrupted before he had managed to make even more of a fool of himself.

The next week, Vicky slid into the seat next to Brendan and asked about the essay he had confessed to having difficulty with the week before. She nodded sympathetically when he told her it was finished but didn't hold out much hope for a high grade. Vicky told Brendan about how much she enjoyed spending time with her Italian grandparents who had settled in Ireland in the 1950s and owned an ice cream parlour on the west coast.

Towards the end of the evening, Vicky sighed.

"Something wrong?" Brendan asked.

Vicky gave a half smile.

"Not wrong really. It's just that the latest Narnia movie comes out this weekend. I'd love to see it, but I don't know anyone to go with." Her Cupid's bow mouth formed a pout.

Was Vicky saying what he thought she was saying? Brendan was suddenly sitting bolt upright.

"Yes you do, I'd love to come with you."

"Really?" The Cupid's bow mouth curved into a smile and the eyes widened slightly.

"Really. I used to devour the Narnia books when I was younger."

Vicky's eyes met his directly.

"Thank you, so much. It's not a film I could have suggested to any of my flatmates or the girls on my course."

"Why not?"

"All the other girls I've met, they're all super stylish, they've seen the world, they're so confident with everything. And so cool. So cool you'd freeze over standing close to them."

20

As if to illustrate, she gave a shudder. "And sometimes, it gets too much. As if your choice of film or music makes you less of an adult, or something."

Brendan gave a sympathetic smile. Vicky was a sweet girl from rural Ireland, who liked to hang out in her grandparents' ice cream shop and spend hours painting the Kerry coastline. What would she have in common with a bunch of sophisticates from London or Edinburgh?

"Cool's overrated, if you ask me, like. And I can't think of a better way to spend a Saturday evening. Narnia, eh?"

They clinked glasses, then a bustling of stools being placed under tables and coats being donned indicated that the evening was drawing to a close. Brendan and Vicky hugged briefly and went their separate ways.

On Saturday evening, Brendan dressed carefully, ironing his favourite blue shirt and spending rather longer than usual trying to comb his hair into a vaguely fashionable style. Vicky met him outside the cinema, her usual jeans discarded in favour of a flowing paisley print dress. With her lack of makeup, she radiated wholesomeness.

"Hi," they both said shyly, before snickering at the sudden formality.

Brendan recovered himself and checked his watch.

"Err, we've got a bit of time before the film starts."

He started to flounder and covered it by asking, "Fancy some popcorn?"

"Salty popcorn would be lovely, please."

Vicky met his eye and they both started laughing again. Brendan hoped fervently that he didn't sound too nervous. He went swiftly to the concessions stand and bought two buckets of popcorn, sweet for himself and salty for Vicky. There was a moment of panic when after having been served, he looked around and could see no sign of Vicky. However, a quick scan revealed that she was sitting at one of the tables ranged outside of the Costa outlet.

"We've got time for a drink as well, if you like," he offered.

"Great," Vicky flashed a wide smile. "I'll have a cappuccino, please."

Brendan ordered a hot chocolate for himself and a cappuccino for Vicky. Vicky tentatively raised her cup.

"I hope I don't get froth on my nose," she giggled, wrinkling it.

"I'm sure you'll look lovely anyway, even with froth."

Was he getting the hang of this talking to the opposite sex business?

A couple of minutes silence followed. Vicky sipped her cappuccino while Brendan desperately tried to think of something that wasn't too obvious an attempt to stave off awkwardness.

"Ummm, I'm really looking forward to this film," was what he eventually landed on, hoping he didn't sound too feeble.

Vicky giggled again and twirled a strand of her glossy hair.

"So, what sort of films do you usually like?" she asked, dipping her fingers in the popcorn and slowly raising a piece to her lips. She was looking at him attentively now, as if she was actually interested in what he had to say

"Fantasy and comedy. I hate war movies or anything too violent, not for me at all."

So far, so good. He pushed a handful of popcorn into his mouth, hoping a) it didn't look too boorish, b) he didn't choke and end up spraying it all over Vicky and c) he could swallow it before it was his turn to speak again.

"That's exactly like me. I love a good romcom or just a pure romance. I like happy endings, true love. And it's so nice to meet a man who isn't mad for guns and people killing each other."

She delicately licked salt from her tapering fingers as her eyes met Brendan.

"I guess I just don't like to watch people hurting each other," Brendan mused, swallowing his popcorn abruptly and washing it down quickly before he choked. Then, before he could think, he continued, "I mean, it's bad enough that it happens in real life. Sometimes I feel the same about my course, history. So much of it is about fighting, dominance, people showing the very worst of humanity. I don't know, it gets depressing at times."

For fuck's sake! Where on earth had that come from?

Vicky nodded and her eyes widened.

"Maybe you should have chosen music or art, then you could have created something beautiful to look at instead of all that ugliness."

She placed the tip of her index finger on the back of Brendan's hand and traced a perfectly manicured nail along it.

"Yeah, well if I could draw a straight line or wasn't tone deaf, I'd consider it."

He examined the swirl across the top of his chocolate ruefully, until he felt the tip of a soft finger brushing the underside of his chin. He raised his eyes and gave a smile he wasn't sure he was feeling.

"It's so important to have something beautiful to look at, though, isn't it?"

Vicky tilted her head the slightest degree. Her face was inches from his and her voice had lowered to the point of huskiness.

"Err, yeah, I suppose so. Never really thought much about it, to be honest."

Brendan wasn't quite sure whether he registered or imagined a flicker of disappointment across her face. He frowned slightly, wondering why. Vicky drained her cappuccino and tucked her half-eaten bucket of popcorn under her arm.

"Come on, they'll be opening the doors in a minute."

She sounded short, for some reason. She stood up and led the way into the auditorium, barely waiting as Brendan abandoned his half-finished hot chocolate to follow her.

By the time the film had started, Vicky appeared to have recovered her previous good humour. She smiled at Brendan and reached for his hand. He returned the squeeze and Vicky leant her head against his shoulder. Brendan shifted nervously and tried to slow his breathing, not sure how he should proceed. For some reason he wasn't enjoying the physical closeness. Vicky's abundant hair was tickling his nose, and he pinched it to keep from sneezing. And the weight of her head on his shoulder was plain uncomfortable after a few minutes. Not wanting to appear rude, he stoically bore the discomfort until the film finished. When they left the cinema, Vicky grabbed his hand as they began the walk back to her student flat. Somehow, the sensation of her soft paw with the acrylic fingernails in his lean hand felt – disquieting. Try as he might, Brendan could not think of a more precise form of words to describe it. Not trusting himself to say or do anything, he stared straight ahead as Vicky chatted about the film, rotating his numb shoulder and grunting in a non-committal manner when a response seemed to be required of him. When they reached her block, she turned her face up towards him expectantly, those magnificent brown eyes locking with his.

Shit! What was supposed to happen now? Vicky didn't move, just stood gazing up to Brendan, her lips starting to pucker. Okay, so that was how the land lay. So why was Brendan wishing he was twenty miles away? He knelt over, and grazed Vicky's forehead with a quick peck, hoping it wouldn't be rude of him to make like a tree and leave. But Vicky seemed to have other ideas. She had taken possession of his hand again.

"Come up for a while. I've got something nice for us."

What the fuck? Is this really happening?

Brendan knew he had little – make that no – experience from which to draw. Flirting was something, that had normally been done to the better looking, sportier, funnier, more outgoing of Brendan's friends. In short, to anyone but Brendan. But a girl, however belatedly, showing an interest in him meant only one thing.

She squeezed his hand. "Come on!" Her meaning was clear.

It's time to man up, Brendan!

So, he followed Vicky to her flat. She opened the door, eyes tilted upwards displaying her luscious lashes.

"The others are all at an anti-meat vigil outside McDonald's. We've got the place to ourselves for the whole – well for as long as we like."

She led Brendan into the small lounge area of the shared flat. On the floor, a plastic checked tablecloth was spread, displaying bowls of chorizo, mozzarella balls, sundried tomatoes, humous and olives; what his mother scathingly called "middle class food". There was an open bottle of red wine and two glasses. Two large velveteen cushions were arranged beside the spread. Brendan sat cross legged on one of them while Vicky lit a series of candles which had been rammed into old wine bottles. She poured him a glass of wine, and he gulped a larger mouthful than he had intended, sending a pink splutter pattern over his shirt. Vicky knelt next to him, picked an olive from its bowl and pressed it against Brendan's lips. He bit into it, despite the fact that he absolutely hated olives, almost breaking a tooth on the stone which he removed. Not seeing anywhere to put the stone, other than the dish from which the olive had been taken – gross – he stuffed it down the back pocket of his jeans, which was probably just as gross. Honestly, what was wrong with sausage rolls? At least they didn't come complete with innards that needed to be spat out and disposed of. It took a sizeable sip of wine to rid him of the unpleasantly mucky taste. So far, so not too appalling.

Until Vicky put one hand on his cheek, turning his face towards her and kissed him full on the lips. Brendan tried to reciprocate and felt … nothing! Not the faintest of stirrings from his loins or from anywhere else in his body.

Vicky tried to kiss him again. The sensation of the moistness of her mouth against his own felt unbelievably intrusive. This time he shuffled backwards, his backside dragging the cushion with him. When he forced himself to look at Vicky, he could see the confusion in her eyes.

"Vicky, I'm sorry, I don't know what to say. I'm not sure I understand myself. It just feels … wrong," he finished weakly. "I mean you're lovely and everything but…"

"It's not me it's you, is that it?" There was a hint of challenge in her voice.

"Something like that. I tried, I wanted to feel something. You don't know how much I wanted something to happen. It's just …" he tailed off again. "Can't we just stay as friends?"

"Brendan," asked Vicky slowly. "Has it ever occurred to you that you might be gay?"

In fact, that was something that Brendan had considered in the past. He had attended an all boys' school, they had shared communal changing rooms and showers. He had never felt anything that could have remotely been described as a frisson of desire. He had lived with his sister through her various teenage obsessions and seen the Eminem and Robbie Williams posters proudly displayed on her bedroom wall. Nothing. One of his flatmates now was a buffed sports science student with a six pack that would make an Olympic gymnast jealous. Nothing. Based on the evidence of his whole lived experience Brendan had no reason to believe he was gay.

"No! Definitely not! I want to explain but I can't. Sometimes I wonder if I'm just not …anything."

Vicky stood up. A crimson rash was building under her chin.

"So, it is me then. You clearly don't fancy me."

She quickly brought her hands up to her cheeks.

"You think I'm a slut, is that it? Because I made the first move?"

Her voice was nakedly accusing now.

"You know, all my friends back home warned me about getting involved with someone from CathSoc. Why come to England in the first place if I was going to end up with the same kind of fucked up Madonna/whore complex, 1950s throwback arsehole I could have found in my own village? I could have joined theatre society or swimming club or climb up the bloody town hall naked held on only by a piece of Velcro society. But instead, I had to join the Catholic Society, hit on a bloody moralistic screw-up and totally embarrass myself."

Tears were streaming down her cheeks by now. The crimson had flooded her entire face. An acrylic eyelash (Brendan had heard of these but never seen one in action) had dislodged itself and gave the appearance of a spider crawling down her cheek.

"Fuck," she exclaimed, swiping it to the ground.

Brendan got up and reached out towards her, wanting to stroke her hair, do anything to offer some comfort. She put her tanned hand up, palm outwards.

"Don't you bloody dare! Just don't! Just –" she hesitated, looking as if she was searching for an appropriate turn of phrase before settling on, "Just… fuck off!"

And she picked up a dish of houmous and lobbed it at him. Brendan ducked to the side but not quite quickly enough. The dish of houmous landed squarely on his nose and stuck there. Brendan quickly removed it, but the majority of the houmous had clung to his face and clogged his nostrils. He absolutely hated houmous as well, and the sudden stench of garlic up his nose made him feel as if he were about to choke. Which he probably deserved. Seeing the fury in Vicky's eyes, Brendan hastily retreated to the door and left before she attempted to follow through with something heavier like the wine bottle. From the incandescence in her eyes, she probably hadn't ruled it out.

Brendan's breath came in wheezy gasps as he descended the stairs and let himself out. He sat at one of the picnic tables on the lawn outside of the block of flats and breathed slowly. He concentrated on the graffiti on the tabletop as he did so, tracing the grooves etched in by previous cohorts of undergraduates. After a few minutes his heartrate settled, the pressure in his chest eased and the high-pitched buzzing in his ears faded; his breathing slowed, and the sweat on his palms started to dry. Brendan used a tissue to hook some of the humous out of his nose and licked the rest off his lips, nearly gagging in the process – the coriander and garlic flavour was no less revolting than when it had nearly suffocated him. He was still shaking when he reached home.

5.

Brendan dreaded going to mass the following Sunday. Vicky had been so hurt and irate, she would likely lob a hymn book at him. Or perhaps she would sit masked in stoic dignity, determinedly ignoring him. Then again, she could catch one glance of him and succumb to a tsunami of tears. Brendan wasn't sure which would be worse.

But he had never envisaged the scenario that did come to pass: Vicky wasn't there.

"No Vicky today?" Brendan asked Katie, her best friend, afterwards, as they sipped tepid tea. He tried to keep his voice as casual as possible.

"Oh, didn't you hear? She's gone home for good. Withdrawn from her course and everything. She told me the other day. Her flatmates were all a bunch of bitches and then she got into a bit of bother with some boy or other. She wouldn't go into details, but he sounds a bit of a tosser if you ask me. It's a real shame. All the hard work in getting here and some pathetic loser screws it up for her."

The hard look she gave Brendan suggested that Vicky had gone into more details than Katie was letting on.

*

Three days later, Brendan was nervously sitting in the confessional.

27

"Bless me Father, for I have sinned. It's been two weeks since my last confession. Since then, I have been lazy sometimes, had unkind thoughts sometimes, I haven't always prayed enough or concentrated hard enough when I've been praying. Oh, and I think I may have ruined someone's life."

"Ruined somebody's life?" Father Johnstone's voice was soft from behind the grille. "That sounds like a heavy burden to be carrying. Would you like to tell me some more about it?"

"It was a girl I might have been going out with. At least I think we were going out. I'm not even sure. I've never really been out with a girl before. But she invited me back to her house. And she went to kiss me and …"

"Go on!"

"And I wanted to kiss her back. I really did but I couldn't. It felt wrong. She was lovely but I just didn't feel it physically. So she got angry. And she was upset. And now she's left Uni and it's all my fault. I've totally buggered, sorry, messed things up for her."

"Is that all that happened? You're telling me the truth now?"

"I promise that's all that happened."

"You do realise that people generally come and see me to talk about sins they have committed, not sins they haven't committed?"

"Yes, Father, but you don't understand. I must have really hurt her."

"So, she tried to kiss you, you didn't reciprocate and now you feel bad because she's left University. Would that be a fair summary?"

"Yes, Father."

"Have you considered that kissing her, when you didn't really mean it, would have hurt her more in the long run? You would have been lying to her, wouldn't you? Kissing her under false pretences. This way, she is free to find a young man who will want to kiss her back."

"But she's left Uni!"

"You think the world's entire population of eligible bachelors resides at Leeds University? Come to that, you think getting a degree from Leeds University is the only way to avoid messing up your life? And how do you know she wasn't thinking of leaving already? The student dropout rate within the first term of study is fairly high. The girl may have been struggling with her course or missing her friends and family. This event may have crystallized things for her, helped her make her mind up. You may even have done her a favour. She'll meet the right one someday. And so will you."

"That's another problem, Father. I've been curious, of course I have. Curious-ish anyway. But that sort of thing, you know, down there, I mean I'm sure I'm not gay, but I just haven't been really bothered."

Brendan's face was puce by now. He was sure he was generating enough heat to power the national grid for a week.

"I mean aren't men of my age supposed to think about it about a million times a day or something? But I don't. I mean I do occasionally, but I've never really been …aroused."

"Aroused?"

"In fact, I'm not sure whether or not I'm capable of feeling anything down there."

If Brendan hadn't known better, he could have sworn he heard Father Johnstone suppress a chortle. Father Johnstone cleared his throat before answering and he spoke slowly and deliberately.

"How old are you exactly?"

"Eighteen. I turned eighteen in July."

"So, at the age of eighteen, you're saying you don't think you're going to feel desire ever. Son, you've got a long time ahead of you. Don't overthink it, try and find some new interests. Perhaps you'll start to develop that way, perhaps not. Either way, you'll still be a valuable person, secure in the Lord's love. Does that help?"

Brendan had the distinct impression that Father Johnstone was starting to hurry things along now. Perhaps there was something he wanted to watch on television. Father Johnstone snorted and cleared his throat again.

"Now for your penance, say three Hail Marys. I absolve you from your sins, in the name of the Father and of the Son and of the Holy Spirit. Now go in peace and think about what we've talked about."

"Thank you, Father."

As Brendan walked up the aisle, he grinned, feeling lighter with every step he took. For the first time, he wondered what it would feel like to help ease another person's burden.

2019

6.

Despite the heavy drizzle and the darkening skies, Brendan felt an urgent need to go for a run to clear his head. He took a longer route than usual, pounding through the puddles with an uncharacteristic savageness, almost taking pleasure in the muddy splashes blemishing his calves, as he tried to outpace the unwanted adrenaline that had coursed through him since his encounter with Neville Tanner. Anger fought with anguish about his mishandling of the situation and so far, no clear winner seemed to be emerging.

"How dare he spoil my new life for me!" Brendan muttered, not caring about the petulance of his words, as he rounded a corner too quickly and almost took out a dog walker. The absurdity of the thought brought a bubble of manic laughter, twisting his mouth into a snarl. An elderly man gave him a nervous sidelong glance and crossed the street. By the time Brendan returned an hour later, he was exhausted, every muscle aching. The restless agitation, however, was as strong as ever, the prospect of settling to or concentrating on anything any time soon seemed about as likely as canoeing up the Amazon. On second thoughts, a few minutes googling travel companies could potentially result in him buggering off up the Amazon in a canoe by this time tomorrow. And the prospect didn't seem terrible.

After showering, he went to Jim's room. Brendan could hear that the portable television had been turned off and there was no sign of any light coming through the bottom of the door.

"Jim, are you awake?"

The only answer was a few doleful sniffs. Jim must be either sleeping or trying to. Brendan made himself an omelette which he ate without enthusiasm. Far from being the light fluffy creation of his previous imaginings, it had the texture of a gym mat. Afterwards, he prepared a short homily – probably crap, but he was past caring about that – for the next morning's mass, then went to his room where he tried to seek refuge in prayer.

"Lord, I think – no, I know – I messed up badly today. Lord, I was faced with a dilemma and was found wanting. I tried to act to the best of my ability, so why do I feel as if I have done something terrible? I failed to convince Neville to go to the police. I think I did as my conscience dictated, but should I have acted differently? Could I have made a difference tonight? Lord, please forgive me for not knowing how to react and please grant me some peace of mind."

Knowing that prayer has as much to do with listening as it has with talking, Brendan closed his eyes and tried to clear his mind. He sat in silence for some time, hoping some clarity would arrive. No such luck.

Brendan lay hot and sleepless in bed that night for a couple of hours before falling into a semi-doze.

It seemed that as soon as he had drifted off, he was awoken by the sound of a prolonged coughing fit. Brendan's phone displayed 2:15. Groggy from his half-sleep, he listened until the rattling and hawking was interrupted by a deep groan, the landing light was snapped on and rapid footsteps thudded across the hallway. Briefly, Brendan considered donning his earplugs and stuffing his head under the pillow, but the groaning had already intensified to an unignorable pitch. He found Jim in the bathroom, kneeling and retching over the toilet.

"You'd better have some water."

Brendan passed the toothbrush holder he had filled while Jim was bringing up the meagre contents of his stomach. As soon as Jim took a sip, he succumbed to another bout of violent retching, eventually spitting a mouthful of frothy bile into the toilet bowl.

"Can you pass me a cloth, please?"

Brendan soaked a facecloth in cold water and Jim wiped his mouth.

"Can you stand up?"

"Of course, I can bloody stand. I'm not completely decrepit!"

However, Jim clung onto Brendan's arm, swaying a little as they made their way back along the landing. He muttered half to himself and half to Brendan.

"Worst bug in years. Really not well at all. Don't think I'll be up to much for the next few days."

"Don't worry about anything, Jim. I can look after things while you concentrate on feeling better."

Brendan reckoned that it would have been cruel to say anything different; not to mention making himself look as inadequate as he felt. Had he really yearned for more challenges a few short hours ago? Or had that been a different idiot?

Jim belched hollowly as he sat on the bed and rubbed his chest, waving away the wastepaper basket that Brendan moved towards him.

"Nothing more to come up."

He unbuttoned his tartan pyjama top. "Hot now. I haven't been able to get warm all day but I'm roasting now. Might be running a temperature."

His face was covered in a sheen of perspiration. Brendan removed the duvet from Jim's bed and drew a sheet from the chest of drawers.

"This might be more comfortable for you, Jim. Is there anything else you need?"

Jim shook his head and curled under the sheet.

Brendan was spectacularly unrefreshed by the time his alarm rang at 6:00. He grabbed a quick mug of coffee, eschewing the decaffeinated brand he usually drank because of the euphemistically termed "nervous tummy" from which he suffered intermittently. Exam stress, pre-ordination nerves and the result of the 2016 EU referendum had all resulted in Brendan doubled up ashen faced on the lavatory, nursing a spasming abdomen whilst frantically spraying enough air freshener to make the ozone layer resemble a doily. He looked in the mirror as little as possible while he shaved.

Mass passed off uneventfully. Afterwards some of the parishioners asked after Father McLean.

"Not too good, I'm afraid."

"Oh, that did seem to be a dreadful cold he was starting yesterday. I told him he should be in bed with a hot toddy."

"I think he'll be in bed for a few days yet. It definitely looks like the flu."

"Well, be careful you don't catch it, Father Coglan. We can't have the two of you poorly."

"I'll be fine. I can't even remember the last cold I had."

On his way home, Brendan called at Sainsbury's to stock up on cold remedies. He added some jellies to the shopping basket, thinking they might ease Jim's throat. When he got back, he knocked on Jim's door and put his head round when he heard the answering cough.

"Feeling any better, Jim?"

Jim's voice was little more than a whisper. His eyes stood out like two red watery slits in his pale face.

"I feel like Mohammed Ali's punched me in each eye."

He attempted to blow his nose and emitted a loud honk. "Sinuses. I've been sick again as well. Barely made it to the toilet in time."

A bit too much information. A severe case of flu and an even more serious case of oversharing.

Brendan unloaded cough medicine and throat lozenges. Jim poured himself a spoonful of the cough mixture and winced as he swallowed it. He fingered a pair of swollen glands beneath his ears and unwrapped a throat sweet.

"Thank you," he croaked. "Are you sure you're okay looking after things for the next few days?"

"Absolutely fine, Jim. Don't worry about anything."

*

To Brendan's surprise, he found himself feeling more settled as the day progressed. He made scrambled eggs for him and Jim for lunch, and put one of the jellies on Jim's tray. When he collected it, he saw that Jim had eaten half the egg and left the toast but had eaten the jelly, which Brendan took to be a positive sign.

Next on the agenda: going off to visit a terminally ill parishioner. Thank goodness for his full schedule; there would be little time to dwell on matters today. Chatting with the elderly lady and gently holding her papery, bruise-blackened hand as she recalled her times in the WRENs seemed to bring her a measure of peace. Her memories soothed him almost as much as her.

"People don't believe me when I tell them how much fun we had, when we weren't on duty. The mischief we used to get up to, when we were on shore leave! The dances with the GIs! And I never wanted for a partner, either! I was the best jitterbugger in the company, though you wouldn't think so to look at me now."

"Oh, I believe it all right, Mrs Curtis. And I bet you can still remember the steps."

"Oh, I can all right. And the tunes. You can't beat a bit of Glenn Miller. I used to have all his records, but we had to get rid of a load of stuff when we downsized."

"Would you like me to bring some up on my phone? We can listen to them together."

"That would be grand, if you don't mind."

The lady's frail husband thanked Brendan as he escorted him to the door.

"I'm very grateful, Father. That's the calmest she's been in days. You don't know how much you've helped the both of us this afternoon."

"Don't thank me, I've enjoyed it. Anyone would find it fascinating."

And you have no idea how much better I feel now that I've been able to listen to a real-life person, rather than hearing Neville Tanner's voice echoing in my ears since yesterday. Let alone the Oversharer Extraordinare, but that's another story.

The man shook his head, as he supported himself against the doorframe.

"No, Father. Between you and me, it was always Valerie who was the religious one. Oh, I go along with it as I can see how much it means to her, but it's never really been for me. But this afternoon, when you were talking to her, asking her questions, listening to her stories, she forgot her pain for a while; and having someone who isn't a nurse or a social worker spend time with her, taking a genuine interest, I reckon that was a proper tonic. You see, lad, when you get to our age, and you get ill, you become a patient. A problem. A collection of symptoms to be managed. It's not often people remember you're a person, someone who's had a life and who's still got something of value to say. But you did. And for that, I thank you."

"That's very kind of you, Mr Curtis. I'll let you get back to Mrs Curtis now. And please call me when she's up to another visit."

Brendan then went back to the church, praying silently, thanking God for the easing of his own mind and waited in case any parishioners felt the need to enter. When he reached home, suddenly realising he was ravenous, he began to make himself a pan of spaghetti Bolognese. As he chopped and stirred, tension continued to ebb from him until he felt positively lighthearted.

If Jim made any noises during the night, Brendan was blissfully unaware. The lack of sleep had caught up with him and he slept heavily and dreamlessly. The next morning, he woke up energised and ready to face the day. After all, he had acted accordance to his conscience and, indeed, as his priestly duties required, with Tanner. Furthermore, he had helped somebody yesterday, hadn't he? And loved doing it. That had to count for something, didn't it? Brendan clung to that thought, repeating it several times throughout the morning like a mantra. As he shaved, he caught sight of himself grinning.

"Almost back to normal," he murmured. He offered up silent prayers of thanks as he said mass that morning. His homily was upbeat, and the congregation didn't *look* bored to tears.

After mass, it was time for the mother and toddler group. Brendan made teas and orange squashes, got toys out of cupboards and led the toddlers through a rendition of "He's got the whole world in his hands." Then, a pleasant walk homewards through the park was enhanced by a hot chocolate and a caramel shortcake at the coffee stand as he scrolled through the news on his phone. The illicitness of those few stolen moments, just for him, made the activity all the more pleasurable.

I can do this. No need to dwell on anything that's happened before, whether it was yesterday or twenty years ago. I'm not a waste of a life. I can do this.

7.

Two things hit Brendan the minute he arrived home. First, the reek of eucalyptus. Second, the sight of Jim sitting at the kitchen table in his dressing gown, a large towel over his head. For a moment, Brendan stared in fascination as Jim inhaled noisily, let out a rattling cough and spat into a wad of toilet paper torn from a roll sitting on the table.

"Jim, what on earth are you doing?"

Jim folded the towel back, revealing a Pyrex bowl full of hot water. His face was scarlet and his voice was croaky.

"Steam inhalation."

"What?"

"Steam inhalation. Ask your granny. I'm trying to clear my chest and sinuses. I need to pull myself together and quickly. I've got to go out after lunch."

He wiped the beads of sweat from his face.

"Oh Jim, do you really think you should? You're still not looking too good. If you need anything, I can get it."

"I'm not feeling too good either, but we had some dreadful news while you were out. It's Maureen."

"Maureen?" Brendan couldn't quite place her.

"Maureen Tanner, Neville's wife. Neville died yesterday. I don't know any details yet; the poor woman could barely speak for crying. She asked me to come round, and I couldn't very well say no. I've booked a taxi for 2:00."

He blew his nose with a squelch.

"That's a bit better now. I'm going for a bath, then could you heat me up some soup? I haven't got anything on my stomach, and I don't want to keel over while I'm at Maureen's."

"Yeah, no problem." Brendan was barely aware of speaking.

Mechanically, Brendan emptied the bowl of water, put the towel in the washing machine, scooped the pieces of used toilet paper into the bin and squirted bleach over the table. Then, without warning, an invisible fist punched him in the stomach, robbing him of breath. His knees buckled, he flopped onto the nearest chair and covered his face with his hands.

Neville was dead. And the last thing Brendan had done when he saw him was to refuse him absolution. The reassurances he had given himself suddenly felt hollow and facile. True, he had acted in accordance with his training but all the same, in effect he had damned him. Had he known Neville was going to die would he have acted any differently? He had all but begged the man to confess to the police.

Eventually he heard Jim's footsteps on the stairs and stood up, feeling himself tremble.

"Are you okay, Brendan? You don't look too clever yourself. In fact, you look like death warmed over. You're not catching my bug, are you?"

"I'm fine, just a bit tired. Shall I make us both something to eat?"

Jim nodded and sat at the kitchen table as Brendan heated vegetable soup and buttered bread. Jim ate without speaking. Brendan pushed the spoon around his bowl but left most of his meal.

"Do you want me to come with you, Jim?" Brendan was unable to bear the oppressive silence any longer.

"Not a good idea at the moment. There's bound to be a fair few people over, and besides, aren't you due to visit the retirement village this afternoon?"

At least the visit to the retirement village gave Brendan the chance to concentrate on something other than his own worries for a while. He was almost sorry when the warden chased him from the meeting room, tartly informing him that the local councillor was outside waiting to begin her surgery.

A few minutes after he reached home, he heard the rattle of a key. Jim's face had taken on a greyish tinge and the deep auburn of the few patches of hair which still retained their original colour stood out in sharp contrast. He raised a hand to fend off any questions.

"We'll talk later, Brendan. I have to lie down now before I fall down."

Once Brendan was left alone, anxiety began to snake unpleasantly through him, prickling his fingers, quickening his breath.

Go for a run; you need to move!

Brendan barely noticed the rain which soaked him or the puddles which muddied his legs up to the knees. He pounded hard down the street and around the park, several times, until his lungs burned and his feet were numb; not even pausing when he smooshed through a dog turd. Back home, he cleansed his trainers with antibacterial wipes and cleansed himself with a shower, turning the thermostat so high that he winced. When he came downstairs, Jim was sitting in the living room in his dressing gown again, nursing a mug of tea.

"Oh, Brendan, what a grim afternoon. Poor Maureen never stopped crying. I've never seen anyone so grief stricken."

Brendan nodded.

"Neville was only sixty-eight. That's no age these days. And as for poor Andrea, his daughter! She's getting married next summer. What's she going to do without her dad to walk her down the aisle?"

"How were you, though, Jim?"

"Well, I got through it without keeling over, which is something, I suppose. I'm shattered now though, and my throat and sinuses are killing me." He blew his nose. "Oh, I'm fed up of whinging."

"Don't worry about that. Did you find out how Neville died?"

"That's the worst thing. Neville hadn't come home before Maureen went to sleep Wednesday night, but that's not particularly unusual, not if he was at the CIU club, and he went there most nights. But he wasn't back by yesterday morning. That confused her so she came downstairs – no Neville anywhere in the house. So, she looked in the garage. He used to spend ages in there tinkering away on his own. Sweet Jesus, he was hanging from one of the beams. He'd climbed on a chair and kicked it to one side."

Brendan felt his stomach dropping as brutally as it had done the one time that he had ridden on a roller coaster. Luckily, Jim seemed oblivious.

"Brendan, it hadn't been quick. Poor Maureen, having to see him like that. Face purple, tongue hanging out, eyes bleeding. You know what was even worse, Maureen said? There were scratches around his neck as if he'd tried to fight it, like he'd changed his mind at the last minute but couldn't do anything to stop it."

Jim stopped speaking and took out his handkerchief. Brendan thought he was going to cough but realised with a shock that the reason Jim was wiping his eyes had nothing to do with flu. Jim drew in his breath and tried to speak but a sudden volley of sobs overwhelmed him.

Brendan took a step towards his mentor. At least that was his intention, but abruptly his hearing dulled, and grey spots gathered in front of him. He wobbled dangerously, stumbled and grabbed the door handle for support. Jim looked up.

"Sit down, Brendan. You've gone as white as a ghost."

Brendan heard Jim's hoarse voice dimly, as if from a distance. He dropped into the nearest armchair. Jim's voice became suddenly authoritative.

"Lean forward. No, lean forward properly. Head right between your knees. That's right. Take a few deep breaths. Good! Now, sit up again very slowly. You still haven't much colour. Are you sure you're not getting this flu?" Jim's tears had subsided as quickly as they had started.

"No, I never catch stuff like that. I must have stood up too quickly, is all."

"Brendan, you weren't sitting down in the first place. But I think I can guess what the problem is. I gave you a shock just there, throwing all that at you and then getting upset like that. But I had to get it off my chest. Hearing that horrible story, when I was under the weather to start with, really knocked me for six."

"Of course," Brendan mumbled. "Go on, please, if you find talking helps you."

"It does. Poor Neville! Maureen was breaking her heart. She told me he'd lost control of his bodily functions. Great pool of piss below him and he'd crapped himself as well."

"Maureen said that?" In spite of himself, Brendan was amazed at how many intimate details Maureen had divulged.

"She did, and she's normally so quiet. But she was just desperate to unload it all. She couldn't keep all that bottled up. But just imagine it! A strong proud man like Neville dying with no dignity at all. That's killing Maureen. Poor Neville! The mental torment he must have been in! Loving wife, well brought-up daughter, nice family, even a dog. And none of us ever had a clue what he must have been going through."

Jim coughed and wiped his eyes again. "Just so sad. I was very fond of Neville, you know. All the odd jobs he used to do around the church, and he would never take a penny for any of them. He wouldn't even let me pay him for materials. And he used to run that children's club as well until a few years ago when his arthritis got too bad."

Jim sighed. "It's going to be a tough few weeks. Maureen's going to need a lot of support in the run up to the funeral. I'm going to have to pray for guidance on how to see her through, because at the moment I'm truly at a loss. Losing a friend makes it so much harder."

Brendan's mouth felt very dry.

"Do you have any information about the funeral yet?" His voice came out in a squeak. But a question about the funeral seemed the most neutral thing to say.

"There'll need to be a post-mortem. I know it sounds stupid but it's still technically an unexplained death. Then the coroner will need to get involved. They'll want to see the report, speak to a few people."

"I know how a coroner's inquest runs."

Brendan's voice came out more sharply than he intended. Jim looked at him, an unmistakably wounded expression in his eyes.

"I'm sorry, that was rude of me. I didn't mean to sound so abrupt."

Jim nodded. "It's an upsetting time. They'll probably want to see some of his personal effects."

Like his laptop!

A sudden abdominal twinge sent Brendan bolting from the room. He managed to reach the toilet just in time for the violent evacuation of his bowels, then leaned, sweaty and panting against the cool tiles.

"Come on Brendan, you melt," he muttered. "Man up, won't you?"

He splashed some cold water on his face, and made his way downstairs.

"Sorry, bathroom. Couldn't wait." His voice sounded reassuringly level.

"It's okay. Anyway, we're probably looking at around three weeks before they release the body. Then Maureen will be able to plan the funeral. And the long hard business of putting her life back together. Brendan?"

"Yes, Jim?"

"Will you pray with me?"

"Of course."

The two men went through to the meeting room and sat at the oak table. Jim began.

"Lord, grant me the strength to overcome my own grief that I may support Maureen, who is suffering far more greatly, in hers. In Jesus' name, amen."

"Amen," Brendan echoed.

Jim went on, "And please be with Maureen at this time and comfort her and the rest of Neville's family. This we ask for Jesus' sake, amen. And please receive Neville's soul into Heaven."

This time, Brendan had to force the "amen" out of his mouth. He suspected that it would be a long time, if ever (an eternity, one might say) before Neville's soul could be received into Heaven. They sat in silence for a few more minutes. Then Jim announced he was going to bed.

Brendan sat at the table for a long time after Jim had left, mindlessly picking at an old scab – a remnant of an ironing accident the previous week – on the back of his hand.

Well, Brendan, if you weren't a hypocrite before, you certainly are now. Sitting there sympathizing with Jim when you know precisely what sort of man Neville Tanner is – was.

Yet he also knew that he was forbidden from making any use whatsoever of what he had heard in the confessional, and this included making judgments on Neville's character. But he could not unhear what he had heard, unknow what he had been told. And he had refused absolution.

Inadvertently, did you precipitate Neville's suicide? Did you even cause it?

The crime Neville had admitted to filled him with revulsion. Wouldn't it fill most decent people with revulsion?

But you're not most people, are you? You're a priest. And you're supposed to be following a man who believed in the value of all human life; who believed any genuine repentance could result in forgiveness.

But Neville hadn't repented. Had he? He certainly hadn't seemed bothered about the children whose images he had viewed. The conundrum spiralled; an out-of-control helicopter, each rotation driving Brendan ever further from certainty. When he had entered the priesthood, he had known, at the back of his mind, that he may at some point have to withhold the sacrament. But suicide as a result? This was not a possibility he had ever considered.

Feeling the need for something sweet, Brendan got up to make himself a mug of hot chocolate, ashamed of doing something to make himself feel better.

Almost immediately, he found himself clinging to the table for support. The dizzying notion had shot through him so quickly, he hadn't registered it until he heard the echo reverberating within his brain. And the echo screamed, "This isn't who I should be!"

2008

8.

Fresh from his disastrous experience with Vicky, and mindful of Father Johnstone's advice to find some new interests, Brendan signed up with the University Community Action volunteers. It wasn't long before he was contacted by the placement coordinator who proceeded to hit him with a barrage of information.

The Oluwu family lived in a bungalow in the outskirts of Leeds. Emmanuel (Dad) was a bus driver. Grace (Mum) was a full-time mother to eleven-year-old Timmy. Timmy had complex disabilities related to cerebral palsy. He couldn't speak, used a wheelchair, and was fed through a tube. He also had epilepsy. Brendan tried to take in the facts as they rained down on him, scribbling some notes as he listened.

"Anyway, it must all sound very dry listening to it like that. The only way to really find out if the placement will be a decent fit for you will be if you actually, you know, get to know the family? So, if you're still keen, I'll arrange an introductory visit next week."

Head reeling, Brendan agreed that would be a great idea.

The following Wednesday found Brendan sitting on the Oluwus' living room floor, mug of tea in one hand, chocolate brownie in the other, as Grace Oluwu chatted about Timmy.

"You know, the worst thing to come to terms with was the epilepsy," Grace said. "After the cerebral palsy and everything, that was one complication we could really have done without. Although,

43

thank goodness, we finally have a medication that has brought it nearly under control."

She was sipping tea while keenly watching Brendan as he sat cross legged next to Timmy, who was lying on an outsized beanbag, listening to a compilation of Disney songs. Timmy's face broke into a huge beam, as "I wannabe like you," began.

"You like that one? It's one of my favourites too," Brendan said.

"I'm the king of the swingers, the jungle VIP," he sang (badly).

Timmy made a high-pitched giggle; Grace grinned.

"Have you known any disabled children before?" she asked.

"A little bit. I mean, when I did A Level Health and Social Care, I helped out at a club for children with Down's once a week."

"Did you enjoy it?"

The wide smile on Grace's face made Brendan feel less like he was being probed. He quickly swallowed the mouthful of brownie he had been chewing.

"It was great fun. The kids were amazing. I'll tell you what, though, 'Old McDonald' does get monotonous after you've been through about twenty verses."

Grace chuckled. "I sometimes feel after we've had a Peppa Pig marathon that I want to make bacon sandwiches out of sheer spite."

Brendan was shortly spending an evening per week with Timmy, while Grace and Emmanuel attended bible study sessions. He read Timmy stories, drew him pictures and sang to him, which never failed to make Timmy giggle.

"Is my singing really that bad, Timmy?" he asked after Timmy had chortled a particularly lengthy time.

"Are you nodding? Really?" He opened his eyes in mock annoyance.

Brendan found the placement so enjoyable that he rapidly increased his visits, taking Timmy for walks in his wheelchair on his lecture-free Monday afternoons, often staying for evening meals. He soon discovered the outings Timmy preferred – the trip down to the lake throwing bread to the swans was a favourite. If Brendan wanted a reward, he had it in the excitement Timmy showed when he arrived or in the attempts Timmy would make to copy the animal noises Brendan made as they looked through picture books.

"The Lord blessed us when he brought you into our life, Brendan," Grace remarked on more than one occasion. "You certainly have a gift with Timmy. He's happier to see you than any other helper we have ever had."

"Have you ever thought about making care work your career?" asked Emmanuel one Monday evening as the three adults tucked into a hearty lamb stew. Timmy was sitting next to Brendan in his wheelchair, drinking from a covered plastic cup.

"I know that the pay is atrocious, but you would be excellent in a care role. You're patient, and you have a huge heart."

Brendan turned towards Timmy and wiped the corner of his mouth with a tissue.

"I love hanging out with Timmy. And I would love to help people, you're right there. But I'm not sure that I want it to be just in the physical sense. More like the whole person. Does that make sense or am I talking rubbish?"

Emmanuel grinned. "Do you mean help people spiritually?"

"Maybe." Brendan gave a half smile and retrieved the cup Timmy had dropped. "If I could know that I was doing something to make people feel better, feel valued, then I can't imagine that anything could be more satisfying."

Where did that come from? He had never even known he felt like that before now. Of course, it didn't help that he couldn't very well yak on about helping people spiritually without sounding like a hippy-dippy, where's my healing crystals, head case. But even so!

Brendan handed the cup to Timmy; Timmy immediately threw it on the floor again. Grace laughed.

Emmanuel nodded. "My brother is training to be a pastor. That is also a wonderful calling. I know you believe in God. Trust in him and pray to him for guidance and he will illuminate your path for you. Now, let us have some of the delicious looking blackcurrant cheesecake that I saw chilling in the fridge earlier."

9.

The placement with the Oluwu family lasted seven months, until the telephone call came. Brendan answered his mobile one evening; when he saw Emmanuel's name flash up, he fully expected that he would be asked to undertake an extra babysitting shift. However, this was a voice he did not recognise.

"Am I speaking to Brendan Coglan?"

"Hello, is that Emmanuel? I'm sorry, you sounded a bit different there."

"Brendan, I am so sorry to call you." The voice was heavy and serious, and heavily accented. "My name is Pastor Joseph Sibanda from Leeds City Evangelical Church, and I'm calling on behalf of Grace and Emmanuel. I am afraid I have some distressing news. Timmy died overnight. It appears that he suffered a seizure in his sleep. His mother discovered him in his bed this morning."

There was a pause. Pastor Sibanda clearly expected Brendan to make a comment, but speech had deserted him; his mouth seemed to have dried completely. The pastor waited a few seconds, then continued.

"Now it's important to remember Timmy didn't suffer. He wouldn't have known anything about it. His suffering in this life is over and he is with his heavenly father now. Brother Emmanuel and Sister Grace have asked me to tell some of the important people in Timmy's life. You were very important to Timmy. Sister Grace assured me that he loved you."

Brendan sat down, trying to take in the enormity of Pastor Sibanda's words. Even as he gripped the phone and tried to think of something – anything – to say to the kindly, disembodied voice, he could not quite believe that he would never see Timmy again, hear his chuckle, read stories to him, at least not in the present life.

It was weird, when you came to think of it. In real terms, very little had changed in his life. He would get up the next morning, attend lectures as always, go to the library as always, talk to his parents as always, eat, sleep, use the toilet as always, watch TV as always.

So why did he feel that everything had changed?

When Brendan eventually managed to speak, his voice sounded high pitched and foreign to him.

"I'm so, so sorry. I hadn't known Timmy long but … Oh God, his poor parents. I can't imagine what it must be like for them. Can I come and see them please, would that be okay?"

"Son, I can hear how distressed you are, but I must beg you to leave the Oluwus in peace for the time being. Grace's parents and sisters are there and are making sure they are cared for as well as possible. Please, at the moment, allow them to grieve together as a family. Later, they may welcome a visit but for now, privacy is what they need."

The voice was soft but there was an undeniable hint of steel underneath the velvet coating.

"What about, I would like to go to the …" the word "funeral" stuck in Brendan's throat. Talking about funerals for eleven-year-old children was just wrong. Eventually he said, "Memorial service. I want to go to the memorial service."

"The funeral will be held at Leeds City Evangelical Church, of course. We do not know the precise date as yet. We will need to allow time for Brother Emmanuel's family to travel from Nigeria. I will call you as soon as the arrangements have been made."

Pastor Sibanda excused himself, explaining to Brendan that he had several more calls to make. Brendan mumbled his thanks and went to lie on his bed; he needed to be alone for a while.

Knowing that it would be several days before the funeral would be held, Brendan decided to go back home to Sunderland for the weekend; if he were honest with himself, he felt the need for some parental comfort. Bob, his father, took him to see the match on Saturday and then out for a pint. Luckily, Bob didn't seem to be disconcerted by Brendan's lack of conversation and the companionable silence as they supped their bitter together felt almost cosy.

"It's the worst thing ever, when you see a parent lose a child," Nicole said to him that evening, before she left for work. "It absolutely kills you to see their faces. Shit, where's me right shoe?"

She bent over and retrieved a scuffed black loafer from under the telephone table.

"I can imagine. I can't say I'm looking forward to this funeral, but you know…"

"Brendan, nobody would think any the worse of you if you gave it a swerve. I mean, the thought of sitting in church, praying to a god who lets that sort of thing happen, ugh!"

"That's not the issue, Nic."

"Really? Not even a little bit?" Nicole checked her reflection in the hall mirror and re-tied her ponytail.

"Are you trying to make some sort of point here, Nic?"

"Just that anyone who can let innocent little kids suffer doesn't deserve worshipping. Shit, I'm going to miss my bus."

She cast Brendan a "This conversation isn't finished," look as she left.

*

On Sunday morning, Brendan went to mass and took comfort in the familiar liturgy, particularly the line "We look for the resurrection and the light and the life of the world to come." As always, he felt stronger after leaving church. At least he did until he got home, and Jackie, his mother, collared him.

"Brendan, I know you cared for this lad, but do you really think this funeral is the place for you? It's not as if you're family. You hadn't even known them very long. You wouldn't be missed. And after what happened the last time you were at a funeral, do you really think you can get through it on your own? This time, we won't be there to pick up the pieces."

"I'm sorry, Mam. I'll always feel terrible about what went on then. But I've got to go. The Oluwus have been a big part of my life for the last few months. And anyway," he resorted to the one argument which he knew his mother could not counteract. "It's not about me. They are the ones who are suffering, not me. If they can stand it, I don't have any excuse not to."

Jackie's look veered between pride and concern.

"Just hang on to that thought," was all she said, grimly.

Shortly afterwards Brendan and his parents sat down to Sunday lunch together.

"Where's our Nicole got to?" Bob asked, as he helped himself to roast potatoes.

"I'll give her a shout. Honestly, she knew we were nearly ready," Jackie shook her head. "Nicole, get yourself down here!"

Footsteps thudded down the stairs and the dining room door flew open. Nicole sat down with a thud and began heaping vegetables onto her plate. Although she hadn't yet spoken, Brendan remembered the unfinished conversation from earlier. He tried to screw himself up for the inevitable verbal pummelling.

"Good shift last night, Nicole?" Bob asked. He shook salt over his meat.

"Fucking terrible, if you really want to know. I had to look after some poor sod whose wife and baby had been killed by a drunk driver. Poor bloke, his whole world just gone like that."

She snapped her fingers.

"That must have been awful for you," said Brendan.

"Worse for him. But Brendan, I've got to ask. I mean, I genuinely want to know. Do you honestly still believe in God after that little baby died? And after that kid you were oh so fond of died as well?"

"Really, Nicole?" Bob asked.

"Yes, I do," Brendan kept his answer as brief as possible and gulped a mouthful of water.

"Seriously?"

"Yes!"

"After everything that poor family is going through, that hasn't made you ask any questions at all?"

"Leave off, Nicole. He's answered you twice," Bob said.

"Nicole, I still believe in God. Is that okay by you?" Brendan was aware of the petulance in his voice, but right then he couldn't have cared less. His knuckles were whitening with the intensity of his grip on the cutlery.

"I just don't get it. How can you possibly believe in a loving god who lets that sort of thing happen to an innocent child? Are you a fucking idiot or did you not even care that much?" She forked a carrot into her mouth and crunched it.

"Nicole, can you not try to keep a civil tongue in your head?" Jackie admonished. "At times, you've got a mouth like a Cullercoats fish wife."

Brendan had felt Nicole's words as if he had been thumped. He tried not to react, concentrating on pouring thick gravy over his roast beef.

"Brendan lad, that's going to spill over the top of your plate, if you're not careful," Bob advised.

"You're a nurse," Brendan protested, surrendering the gravy jug to his father. "Don't you ever see parents getting comfort from their faith when they have a sick child?"

Nicole put down her knife and fork, placed an index finger on her chin and glanced upwards, as if she were giving the matter some consideration.

"No, never!" she said.

Brendan doubted this was entirely true but couldn't find the energy to argue.

"His parents, Grace and Emmanuel, believe in God, and take comfort from this belief. It was their pastor who called me."

Brendan pushed peas around his place; the beef he was chewing seemed suddenly tougher, the gravy less tasty.

"Yeah, well a pastor calling people sounds a bit creepy if you ask me. Almost like he's wanting to keep outside influences away from them so he can keep on forcing his toxic doctrine down their throats while they're at their most vulnerable."

She picked up a Yorkshire pudding and took a substantial bite.

"For fuck's sake, Nicole," Brendan muttered under his breath.

Keep it cool, Brendan. Don't lose it.

"Oh, Brendan! Did I hear you say a naughty word? Come on, you are allowed to argue back, you know. You don't have to act like you're auditioning for sainthood twenty-four hours a day."

"Nicole," Jackie's eyes were narrowing now. "Much more from you and – "

Don't say anything. Be a good person. Don't let the mask slip.

"No, Mam, I'm serious here. Honestly, Brendan, do you never get tired of being too good for this world?"

"Nicole, can you not give it a fucking rest for five minutes? Just five, that's all I'm asking. Long enough to finish my fucking dinner. Then I'll be out of your hair again and you can find some other mug to torment."

Oh, shit, that's done it. Nice one, Brendan.

Brendan's knife fell onto the plate with a clatter as he dropped it. He fixed his eyes on the mound of cabbage, speckled with gravy; not wanting to acknowledge just how liberating it had felt to blow off a bit of steam.

"Right! I'm calling an end to this now, before this bloody dinner gets ruined for all of us," Jackie said. "Nicole, you're supposed to be a nurse, have some sensitivity!"

As she pointed a knife towards Nicole a blob of turnip slid off and plopped onto the tablecloth.

"I use all of it up at work. Like for that bloke last night. Or for the parents of the eighteen-year-old who got his brains caved in when he totalled his motorbike. Or the parents of the fifteen-year-old who's still in a coma after a bad ecstasy tablet. By the time I sit down with this sanctimonious prick, I'm clean out of empathy, sympathy, compassion or anything else you want to accuse me of not having."

"I haven't even mentioned religion all weekend. Go on, tell me just one time I've talked about it until you just asked me now!"

Brendan felt his cheeks flushing; temper threatening to bubble out of him. His guts were starting to bubble unpleasantly.

Not good, Brendan. Keep it inside. Don't upset anyone. Be the person you want to be.

"No, but where did you go this morning? Where will you go next Sunday morning? You might not say anything but it's there anyway. Just piss off back to Leeds and leave me alone!" Nicole stomped upstairs, taking her plate with her.

"Same old Nicole, zen as ever," Brendan, grimacing from the shooting cramps in his belly, couldn't restrain the sarcasm.

"Leave it, son, we've had enough for one day," Bob sighed.

The remainder of the meal was a strained monosyllabic affair. Nicole's parting shot was to bawl at Brendan from upstairs, "And don't bother coming back until you've gained a personality of your own, instead of one that's been drip fed into you for the last howeversolong. It's like living with a fucking cardboard cut-out."

Brendan was almost glad to be back on the train.

10.

Timmy's memorial service – even now he refused to call it a funeral – was like nothing Brendan had ever seen. The church didn't really look like a church, more like a repurposed conference hall that had been painted pale pink. There were no pews, but plastic stacking chairs were placed in neat rows with a wide aisle in the centre. There was a platform at one end, representing an altar, Brendan surmised; a pulpit and microphone at one side, a table in the centre and a piano at the other. "Know God, Know Love" was painted on the back wall in large blue letters and an oversized cross was mounted on the wall. There were easily two hundred people in attendance. Almost everyone was dressed head to foot in black – Brendan was beginning to feel out of place in his dark grey suit, purchased the previous year for his cousin's wedding, already pinching at the shoulders and displaying a substantial gap above his ankles.

Brendan was beginning to regret skipping breakfast; a vague light-headedness was hanging over him and he could feel the beginnings of a dull pressure in his temples. As much to give himself an escape route as to defer to the closer friends and relatives, he took a seat in the back row, close to a side door.

Timmy's white coffin, heartbreakingly small, had been placed at the front of the centre aisle. Emmanuel and Grace huddled together in the front row, arms wrapped tightly around each other, their respective families gathered protectively on either side of them. A small man with closely cropped white hair and steel rimmed glasses, who must have been Pastor Sibanda, spoke a few quiet words to the grieving couple before mounting the steps and turning to the congregation. Brendan was intrigued to see that he wore neither vestments nor a clerical collar; a minute cross on his lapel was the only indicator of his clerical role.

He could have been any age from sixty to eighty. His voice was melodic and clear as he began the service.

"Brothers and Sisters, today we are gathered to mourn the passing of our brother Timothy, but also to celebrate his life and resurrection into the company of Jesus. We remember his parents, Brother Emmanuel and Sister Grace, his grandparents, aunts and uncles, and we gather to pray that they receive the strength to go on and receive comfort from the love of God and from the love they receive from us.. Is anyone moved to begin?"

The service did not seem to follow much structure, Brendan thought as he tried to put his bewilderment aside. Various members of the congregation rose and either read passages from the bible, prayed spontaneously or shouted out numbers of hymns. There were a great many murmurs of "Alleluia" and "Praise Jesus," a lot of outstretched hands and upturned tear-streaked faces. Brendan was conscious of being one of the few dry-eyed people there. Tears did not come easily to him, and this occasion was set to be no exception. Despite his discombobulation, he went with the flow as best he could, joining in the few choruses to which he knew the words and saying "Amen," whenever somebody finished praying.

When Pastor Sibanda eventually returned to the dais, a hush fell over the congregation. Brendan was glad of the sudden quietness; the left side of his head was pounding by now and his unease was increasing with every minute. Pastor Sibanda read the passage from the book of Matthew which included the phrase "Suffer the little children to come unto me." Then he gently closed his bible and moved to the centre of the stage.

"This is the sermon no pastor ever wants to give," he began. "And last night I sat for over an hour, praying that the Lord would grant me the words to convey the message of his love in these sad, sad circumstances. And –"

He was abruptly interrupted as Grace rose and stretched her arms upwards. An anguished keening broke out from her, and her knees buckled. She would have hit the floor had it not been for Emmanuel steadying her. Pastor Sibanda gamely tried to press on with his sermon.

"And in the end, I asked God outright –"

Emmanuel held his wife with one arm and with the other hand he stroked her braided hair. His face was turned away, but Brendan could see the shaking of his shoulders and guessed that he too was weeping. Grace's father rubbed small circles on his daughter's back. Pastor Sibanda continued to speak.

"And as I closed my eyes, I reflected on –"

"Why, why, why?"

Grace broke free. She leapt to her feet fully this time, jerked her face upwards and screamed.

"Why have you done this to me? Why did you need to take my son from me? Was your own son not enough for you?" She collapsed into Emmanuel's arms and sobbed. Pastor Sibanda hastily gestured to the piano player and stepped down to embrace Grace and Emmanuel together.

Brendan felt an overwhelming need for fresh air. He slipped out of the side exit and leaned against the wall, resting his throbbing head against the rough bricks. He closed his eyes as he rubbed his temples, and on opening them saw that he was no longer alone in the small courtyard. A tall man was standing near the exit door, lighting a cigarette. He held out his cigarette packet towards Brendan.

"I don't smoke," Brendan said. "I just came out for a bit of air."

He suddenly felt very defensive, certain this stranger was about to tell him off for ducking out.

"Getting a bit much for you in there? I can't blame you."

Brendan ran his fingers through his hair.

"Seeing Grace like that, I don't know, it felt," he searched for the right expression, "it felt sort of wrong being there. A bit weird. Not sure why. But I needed to get out."

The man drew on his cigarette and exhaled slowly.

"I'm trying to give these up but right now the pull is just too strong," he said. "I'm David, Emmanuel's brother. I flew in from Abuja on Tuesday."

He had a stronger accent than his brother, was a little taller and wore glasses and a neat beard. Other than that, the family resemblance was clear.

David held out a hand. Brendan hadn't shaken hands with anybody since his final day at school when his Headmaster had wished him well. He hesitated a second, then took it, trying to mirror David's firm grip.

"Brendan Coglan. I volunteered with Timmy for a few months. I know it wasn't long, but I got very fond of him. Well, of all of them, I suppose. Yeah, all of them."

He gave an awkward half shrug.

"Really?" David's face opened into a smile. "When we Skyped last month, Emmanuel mentioned that a fantastic young man was volunteering with Timmy. Timmy's eyes lit up when Grace said your name."

Brendan was touched, but also felt sadder than ever. "I don't know how they're ever going to get through this. If they even can. They look so…" his voice tailed off.

David's voice grew more sombre. "The loss of a child is the saddest thing that can happen to a person. I'm a church elder in Abuja and I have known many families experience similar tragic deaths. This part never gets any easier. Without the Lord's help it would be almost impossible."

He took another long puff. Brendan didn't know what to say. Nothing he could think of seemed right under the circumstances. He snatched around mentally for an appropriate comment.

"Grace sounded so sad. And angry." It was the best he could grab.

David nodded. "For sure they are angry. Furious, even. Anger is a prayer. You see, prayer is all about communication with God. What sort of communication doesn't allow for anger? But they will get there in the end. I know they will. I know that God will be with them every step of the way."

David's eyes sparkled as he was speaking, and he emphasised his last sentence by making a fist and tapping his chest. Brendan couldn't help but feel impressed by his passion. He decided to risk a question.

"Do you think that will be enough?"

David grew even more animated. "Well, God will certainly need some help. But look at everyone they've got around them. So many wonderful people, the Lord acting through them all. Isn't that what we are all called to do? Allow the Lord to work through us for the benefit of others?"

He finished his cigarette and cocked his head, listening.

"I think they are nearly finished now."

Sure enough, there was a prolonged scraping of chairs, and four coffin bearers exited the main door of the church. A hearse and two funeral cars were parked in the main road to take the close family to the crematorium. Grace and Emmanuel slipped into the first car behind the hearse. Throwing his cigarette end into the drain, David hurried off to join the second car, grabbing the hand of an elegant lady who must have been his wife. Pastor Sibanda stood at the front of the church thanking people for coming. Brendan watched from the side courtyard and made to leave, hoping he would be unnoticed. However, before he had the chance to turn away, he felt a firm hand on his sleeve. Pastor Sibanda had caught up with him.

"Brendan?"

"Yeah, I'm Brendan."

"Thank you so much for coming today. Brother Emmanuel and Sister Grace will be touched to know you were here. I know the relationship Timmy and you had together gave them a lot of pleasure."

Brendan could only give a half-hearted shrug.

"No, I mean it," Pastor Sibanda insisted.

"Anyone would have liked Timmy."

Brendan was impatient to get away now, he was tired, wanted to be alone for a bit, take some paracetamol, rip off his suit and throw on a pair of jeans, and veg out gloriously in front of some mind-numbing daytime television.

Pastor Sibanda was not easily deterred.

"He was certainly a beautiful soul. But I believe that his parents will take a lot of comfort in knowing that his life was happy, and you played an important part in that, towards the end."

The pastor's shrewd eyes seemed to drill straight into Brendan.

"You should thank God that you had the opportunity to know the joy of making a difference to his life. And you should also pray for God to show you how you can build on the experience."

"Thank you. I will do," Brendan managed to articulate. Luckily, Pastor Sibanda was distracted by an elderly couple tapping him on his shoulder. Brendan gave a quick half wave before seizing his chance to escape.

That weekend, having mulled over his conversations with David and Pastor Sibanda, Brendan approached Father Johnstone and made his first enquiry about becoming a priest. If Father Johnstone was surprised, he didn't say so. However, his firm advice to Brendan was that he finish his degree first and gain some life experience.

"You're nineteen years old, only just finishing your first year. This is a massive decision for any man to make, least of all a lad of your age. You would need to be twenty-one anyway, before they would even look at you. A lot can happen in two years. Enjoy the rest of your studies. Enjoy your time with your peers. Make friends. Make a foray into the world of work. If you still feel the same way once you graduate, come and see me then and we'll have a longer talk."

Brendan followed Father Johnstone's advice as best he could. He studied hard. He engaged with the Leeds Student Action group again; this time helping to clear and maintain a local nature reserve. Brendan found he enjoyed the physical toil. His head never failed to feel clearer after a day's digging or rubbish removal.

He visited Grace and Emmanuel once after Timmy's funeral. Grace was taking a nap; Emmanuel said she was exhausted most of the time. Emmanuel embraced him tearfully and thanked him profusely for the help he had provided with Timmy. Brendan protested that he had enjoyed every minute and that it was he who should be thanking them. Grace's mother made him a cup of tea and handed him a plate of homemade biscuits. Brendan sat on the sofa with her and Emmanuel, answering Grace's mother's questions about his degree, asking about her other grandchildren and hating himself for not being able to offer anything more profound or comforting. Despite the amount of people around, the room felt unbearably hollow without Timmy's presence. Besides, without Timmy, what was he even doing there? When Brendan stood to leave, Emmanuel shook his hand and wished him well for the future. The gesture gave Brendan the impression of a final farewell, where everything that remained to be said had been said. He did not visit again.

2019

11.

The next few days passed in a blur for Brendan. He went about his duties mechanically, unable to concentrate on anything. He dropped the host while celebrating Saturday evening Mass and only just managed to stop himself from swearing. Afterwards, he couldn't remember any of his parishioners' names as he said goodbye.

"Time enough for you to start forgetting names when you get to our age, Father Coglan," said one gnarled lady, as she patted him gently on the arm.

Neville Tanner's face was the first thing he saw every morning, the last thing he saw at night, and Brendan sometimes found himself turning round if he was on his own, convinced he could feel a pair of eyes boring into his back. When this happened the first time he had to sit trembling on the edge of the bath, breathing slowly, until he felt able to face the world again.

And then there was Jim. He looked progressively paler and sounded progressively raspier over the weekend. On Sunday night, as Jim finished a particularly strident coughing bout, Brendan asked, "Do you not think you'd better get that seen to?"

"I'll give it a few days yet. I've got to get back into the swing of things. Starting with saying Mass tomorrow morning."

Brendan felt as if he ought to protest, but that it probably wouldn't be welcomed. So, he kept quiet.

If Brendan's anxiety hadn't kept him awake that night, then the constant stream of coughs echoing from Jim's room would have had the same effect. His ear plugs made no difference whatsoever.

He wasn't that surprised when Jim knocked on his door the next morning, white faced and barely able to speak.

"I'm sorry Brendan, I know I said I would say Mass today. I just can't manage it. I've not slept at all, my chest's worse than ever, I'm shivery and I can hardly stand."

He held the door handle tightly as he coughed and spat into his handkerchief.

"This green muck I'm bringing up is nobody's business."

It isn't any of my business either. But please don't let that stop you sharing details I really don't need to hear.

"I'm going to have to call the doctor this morning."

"Okay, no problem, thanks for giving me the heads up," Brendan mumbled through a yawn.

Jim coughed into his handkerchief again and examined the produce closely.

Oh heck, he's not going to want me to look at it, is he?

Luckily, Jim settled for shaking his head and rubbing his chest.

Brendan threw his clothes on, as Jim trundled back to bed. He was glad that the ritual was second nature enough for him to drift through on autopilot. The sermon might have been unusually short, but so what? The parishioners would probably be chuffed at the thought of getting out early and being able to get on with their day. At least, Brendan told himself they would.

He hurried back after Mass, to find Jim sitting warmly wrapped, waiting for a taxi.

"It's funny, usually you have to get quite stroppy to have a same day doctor's appointment. But as soon as I started to speak, she was fitting me in. I must sound worse than I thought."

Restless and nervous, Brendan embarked on a thorough clean of the bathroom. Once that was done, he swept the living room and kitchen floor and washed the kitchen cupboards. He was about to start washing the windows when Jim arrived back clutching a prescription. Jim removed his coat and threw himself onto the sofa.

"Nasty dose of bronchitis, she gave me a ten-day course of antibiotics, double strength. I could have a touch of pleurisy too; she couldn't be sure. Brendan, will you be able to cope on your own for a while? I've got the tablets, but she said that rest was the most important thing. I'm sorry to land everything on you, you've only been here a few weeks but there's no help for it."

A violent fit of coughing overtook Jim, causing him to bend forwards and rub his chest.

"Sure, Jim, anything you need me to do. Do you want me to get that prescription filled in for a start?"

"That would be grand. I can't even think of anything you need to do; my head is swimming. I'm pretty sure everything's in the diary anyway."

"Bed! Now! Don't worry about anything. I'll be fine. Haven't I always told you how keen I am to get involved?"

Brendan had a pretty good idea of Jim's schedule and a look through the diary confirmed it. Before hearing about Neville, he would have been excited at the prospect of taking over so many duties; now he second guessed himself over everything. He called St Jude's primary school to explain he would be arriving late on Wednesday as he needed to say Mass that morning and almost immediately afterwards forgot he had done so. He only remembered when he called up again a few minutes later and the secretary said how nice it was to hear from him twice in one day.

Then he went to collect Jim's prescription and walked out before it was dispensed; he was halfway home before he realised and needed to turn back again. As he was preparing dinner that night, he completely forgot to put the vegetables on to boil, so they ended up with lumpy shepherd's pie with no vegetables.

And the mental elephant in Brendan's mind was the Wednesday confessional session, which was building to the proportions of an unconquerable, fire breathing, snarling monster. By Wednesday, during his truncated day at the Primary School, he was almost paralysed with terror of the evening confession session. He tried to focus as best as possible; with the children he just about managed it but with the staff it was different.

"You must be very busy at the moment, Father Coglan, with Father McLean so poorly?" said Mrs Smith, as she buttered her jacket potato.

"Father McLean, oh he's still not right at all. Bronchitis, he's been told."

Brendan absentmindedly stirred his tea.

"Careful with that, Father Coglan. You're getting most of it on the table. I was saying though, you must have a lot of extra work to do."

"Oh, he's really worried about getting behind with his work. I've told him not to worry though."

Mrs Smith looked confused.

Why on earth was she looking at Brendan like he was standing on his head whistling "Singing in the Rain"? He had answered her, hadn't he? And in English? He glanced down at his teacup. Shit! Most of the tea had sloshed onto the table. How had he not noticed?

He would have to make a better fist of controlling himself that evening.

12.

At last, Brendan found himself in church before confessions started. He began by praying.

"Please God, help me not to be a monumental clusterfuck tonight," he whispered and this did not seem the least bit blasphemous. The walls of the confessional felt as claustrophobically close as they had whilst he was listening to Neville. For some reason he was sure he could smell the nasty eggy odour from the previous week and found himself wrestling with a powerful compulsion to leave and breathe in fresh air. Without thought, he started reciting prayers to himself as quickly as he could, as if they were nursery rhymes, hoping that every instinct would stop screaming at him to get the fuck out of the place.

The noise of the confessional door, when it eventually opened, made him jump.

"Father Coglan?" The voice was a child's. "Are you busy, you sounded like you were busy, but what would you be doing in here on your own?"

"I'm not too busy to talk to you," Brendan answered, rejoicing at the distraction.

"Oh, good. It's Luke. Hello, Father Coglan."

Luke? Luke! Tubby lad with hair like a bag of carrots in Mrs Smith's class. Always has his hand up. Nice kid.

"Hello, Luke. You know, you don't have to tell me your name if you don't want to."

"It's okay. I need to confess something, Father Coglan."

The child's voice dropped, and a wet sniff heralded an avalanche of tears.

"Well, you've come to the right place. What would you like to tell me about, Luke?"

"Last week during Mass, Father. Me and my sister were here with Grandma and Grandad. Grandma gave us both a pound for the collection but…"

"Go on!" Brendan urged.

Luke's voice had drained away, to be replaced by a bubbling sniff and the slurping of a sleeve being drawn across a nose.

"But I only pretended to put it in. I kept it in my pocket and just put my hand in. Then on the way back from school on Monday I bought a packet of Smarties. Mam doesn't let us eat them, because she says they're full of nasty stuff, but I think they taste nice. And when I was in my bedroom later my sister caught me eating them. She got really mad and asked why I hadn't got her some. And then she said it was probably a mortal sin pretending to put money in a collection plate and I'd go to Hell if I died, so I'd have to confess it. And," Luke's voice broke off into more sobs, "she said I had to tell you my name because you would probably have to tell Mrs Smith and Mam and Dad and everyone just so they would know what a thieving little scumbag I was. But going to Hell would be even worse.. I never slept last night, I was scared I would die before confession and go to Hell."

Safe ground! Thank you, Luke!

62

"Luke, in the first place, I could never tell anyone what you said here. No matter what you confessed to, even if it was terrible. Did you not know that?"

"Well, Mrs Smith said so once, but I thought she was just saying."

"Well, she wasn't." *You have no idea.*

"In the second place, although it's not great to pretend to give money to the collection, it's not really such a terrible sin either." *I can think of far worse ones, hopefully that you will never have to know about until you're much older.*

"And God would never send a child to Hell, never ever. God loves children. Didn't Jesus make a point of letting children come up to him while he was praying?"

Brendan could see Luke nodding through the grille.

"And in the third place, even though you were scared, you still came to see me. That was really brave. I think God will be very proud of you tonight, don't you?"

"Really?"

"Really. And the best thing is you don't need to feel bad now because I will absolve you. Do you know what that means?"

"Forgive?"

"Even better than that. It's like washing something and making it all nice and sparkling. As if it had never got dirty in the first place. You aren't going to pretend to put money in the collection anymore, are you?"

"No, Father Coglan. How many Hail Marys do I have to say? My sister said it would probably be at least a thousand."

"A thousand Hail Marys? I think we would probably run out of fingers to count them on. We'll make do with one. Shall we say it together? You can start."

"Do you feel better now?" Brendan asked when they had finished.

Brendan could see Luke answering him with an enthusiastic nod.

"Father Coglan? You weren't in our RE lesson this morning."

"No, I wasn't. Poor Father McLean isn't well, and he couldn't say Mass, so I had to, and I got to school after your RE lesson. As soon as Father McLean is better, I'll be back."

"I hope he's better soon, then. RE was well boring when you weren't there. And when anyone asked a question, Mrs Smith said,

'Why don't you ask Father Coglan when he comes back?' But supposing we forget what we were going to ask?"

"I'm sure you'll think of plenty of new questions. There wouldn't be much point in an RE lesson if nobody asked questions. Now, I think we're done here. You'd better go, it'll be getting dark soon and your parents will be worried."

"They think I'm out playing football on the field."

"Well, it's not a very good idea to lie to your parents either." *Brendan, what the fuck?* "In fact, you really shouldn't lie to anyone." *Better, Brendan, better.* "Now, go quickly and I'll see you next week, at school. And remember, I won't talk about this to anyone."

"Okay Father. Bye!"

The confessional door banged shut and footsteps sprinted up the aisle.

In spite of himself, Brendan chuckled. Maybe he could do this job? After all, at one point he had known without any further doubt that would never want to do anything else. And the moment of exact clarity had arrived as he himself had received absolution.

2009

13.

Sex! The final frontier! Brendan had never been troubled by the
unpredictable "boners" that had plagued some of his friends. It would
have been possible for him to count the wet dreams he had had
without running out of fingers. He had enjoyed sweaty sessions of
masturbation (under the duvet, into an old T shirt, don't let Mam hear)
but in the same way as he enjoyed a hot chocolate with extra
marshmallows or a Chinese takeaway; pleasant, certainly, but
something he could probably get by without, if push came to shove.
In fact, the prospect of a life without marshmallow-infused hot
chocolate would probably have upset him far more. But wasn't the
whole business supposed to be far more exciting if there was an actual
woman involved?

He knew that should he eventually join the priesthood, sex would
be out of the equation once and for all. So, his cherry was probably
destined to remain unpopped for the rest of his natural life. And, when
you looked at it, was that really such a massive deal? After all, he had
never travelled outside mainland Europe, had an operation (he very
much doubted whether the extraction of an infected molar counted),
ridden an elephant, got arrested, travelled in a hot air balloon, eaten
sushi, mooned in a public place, beaten somebody up, learned how to

play a musical instrument, gone skinny dipping, been stargazing, broken a bone, experimented with illegal drug taking, gone skiing, played strip poker, played any kind of poker, written his name in the snow with his own piss or marched in a political demonstration either, and he seemed to be able to get along perfectly well without ever having experienced any of those things. Did it really matter if nobody ever described him as a "man of the world", without a heavy side-order of irony? Would the failure to lose his virginity make much of a difference to his already unimpressive tally of life experiences?

But then came the party.

During Brendan's second year, he shared a house with two friends. Their neighbourhood was commonly described as a "student ghetto" which meant rows upon rows of semi-derelict back-to-backs – mould on walls and holes in ceilings coming as standard with no extra rental charge – where you could inhale enough marijuana to give you a pleasant high merely by walking along the street.

The side-effect of living in this ramshackle area was that complaints from the neighbours about late-night parties would be an unlikely prospect. Therefore, when his two housemates raised the suggestion of an after-we've-got-back-after-Christmas-and-everyone's-fucking-depressed-about-it party, Brendan knew that he wouldn't have a cat in Hell's chance of objecting. The guest list was typical of most student parties; invite everyone you know and hope they will bring along at least a handful of friends each. Brendan invited a few of his course mates, making the invitation as vague and unenthusiastic as manners would permit (he considered giving the wrong date entirely, but in the end his conscience wouldn't play ball) in the hope that they wouldn't turn up.

To Brendan's dismay – he had vainly hoped that an obliging hurricane, power cut or global pandemic would put paid to the proceedings – the night of the party arrived. Morrissey was whinging at a suitably anti-social volume; cans were stacked haphazardly on the kitchen table and Brendan was trying to melt into the corner of the living room, wishing the whole thing was over. He opened a bottle of red wine as he watched hordes of people, none of whom he recognised, stream into the living room. Wine was not something he often drank but if he was going to survive the evening, he would need to be wrapped in a twelve-tog alcohol cocoon at the bare minimum. Within half an hour the air was thick with smoke from tobacco and something more exotic, the living room was thick with bodies crammed together, laughing, drinking and copping off and Brendan was rapidly becoming thick headed with alcohol. He tried to fight his way to the kitchen. At least there, he could pretend to be washing glasses or fetching more alcohol. Or something.

"Brendan! Oy! Over here!"

Over the white noise of laughing, talking and Morrissey, he unmistakably heard his name. Being bawled by someone he did not recognise. Someone who was wearing skintight jeans and a strapless glittering top which exposed a jewelled navel ring glinting amidst an ample roll of fat. Hennaed hair was piled in a messy, top-heavy bun. Scarlet lipstick was making a perfect ring stain on the neck of the vodka bottle which she brandished. The stranger swayed unsteadily as she approached.

"Hope we're not too late. Me and Jack have just come from The Hyde Park. He's stopped off at Dominoes, but as far as I'm concerned, that's a waste of valuable drinking time."

She took in Brendan's puzzled expression, then burst into a raucous guffaw.

"You've literally got no idea who I am do you? It's Rosie, you moron. Jack's mate."

Jack was obviously someone Brendan knew, but beyond that he didn't have a scooby.

"Haven't seen you for ages, how are you doing?"

"Errr, fine."

"Me and Jack are house sharing now."

"Oh, how's that working out?" Brendan reckoned this would be a nice neutral response.

Rosie rolled her eyes. "It's a total fucking nightmare, actually. He's worse than my mum for moaning about rings round the bath and not emptying the bin enough. Anyway, we heard about tonight, so we thought we'd put in appearance."

Brendan raised his wine glass to his lips.

"Is that wine? What a lightweight. Here, put some of this in."

Rosie poured a hefty slug of vodka into Brendan's glass before he could protest. He took a small sip, shuddering at the bitterness.

"That's no good. You need to open your gob properly and glug it in."

Brendan raised the glass again. Rosie pressed her hand over the bottom and did not remove it until the glass was empty. Brendan narrowly avoided choking.

"That's better. Now have some more."

Rosie filled the wine glass. The vodka didn't taste quite as disgusting this time.

"That's right," Rosie appraised. "Let me catch up."

She drank deeply from the bottle.

"How's your love life?" yelled Rosie, in Brendan's ear. "Hope it's better than mine. I broke up with Connor last month."

Connor?? Who in the creation of crow's shit's Connor?

Brendan tried to nod sympathetically. Which, since his brain and his body seemed not to be working in tandem, was trickier than he thought. Rosie gave a dismissive wave.

"It's fine. He was a fucking control freak. He had the nerve to say I was being unreasonable whenever I went a weekend without texting him. Like we were fucking married or something. I've had it with clingy men. Actually, I've had it with serious relationships. Who the fuck needs to be tied down having cups of tea and reading Sunday papers at our age? He'd have had me buying ironing boards and vases given half the chance. I'd rather be dead. No, I'll stick to simple, uncomplicated fun."

Brendan was starting to feel hot and dizzy. He glanced at his feet and realised in horror that he had his slippers on. Rosie noticed too.

"Oh Brendan, slippers, really? Won't your grandad get jealous?"

She spluttered as she laughed. Brendan felt himself blushing. He took a large mouthful of vodka. Rosie topped his glass up.

"He'd have a hard job."

"Eh?"

"My grandad. He's been dead ten years."

Rosie looked nonplussed, then swatted Brendan on the arm.

"I'm only messing. You really need to chillax more."

She laughed again, throwing back her head and displaying a wobbling double chin. Brendan hastily gulped down the rest of the vodka and held out the empty glass. Rosie filled it.

"Easy, Tiger! Much more and we'll be onto your minging wine, unless we can nick something more exciting. Hey, what's that over there?"

She pointed towards the open front door and Brendan followed her sparkly blue nail-varnished finger. As he raised his head, Rosie dived in, smacked a kiss on his lips and prised his mouth open with her tongue. She had put down her bottle and Brendan found himself pressed with his back against the staircase, Rosie's hands squeezing his bottom. At some point, he had either put down his glass and the wine bottle or Rosie had removed them. Somehow, Brendan was running his hands down her back. Or was he clinging to her for balance? He felt so drunk he was glad of the wall for support. The noise of the party had assumed a humming background quality. Faces and bodies swarmed around him; the combination of smoky air and Rosie's body pressing into him threatened to overwhelm him completely. He wanted nothing more than to lie down and close his eyes and rest his spinning head.

Finally, Rosie came up for air. Brendan gasped. He could still taste her breath; the cigarette she had smoked on her way from the pub, the vodka, the garlic bread she had eaten with her lunch, the chewing gum with which she had unsuccessfully tried to disguise the garlicky smell. He could feel the greasy smear of her lipstick on his mouth. Brendan reached for the wine bottle and took a huge slug; it was that or throw up onto the floor.

"Where's your room? Come on!"

Grabbing the vodka with one hand, Rosie led him upstairs by the other, fighting her way through the crowd of people who had settled on the stairs. A girl Brendan didn't know protested as Rosie kicked her and her friend apart. Brendan mouthed the word "sorry" in their general direction.

"Well, which one is it?"

"The one on the left."

Brendan was dimly aware of his heart thumping as Rosie led him into his room. He felt a surge of embarrassment at his precisely stacked papers on the Ikea desk, the plain duvet over the neatly made bed, the bible on his small bookcase. At least there weren't any underpants on the floor.

"A bit beige, isn't it? Wait, no, serious, you actually have pyjamas?"

There was, indeed, a pair of Marks and Spencer pyjamas folded neatly on his pillow.

"Never mind."

She sat on the bed, patting the space next to her. Brendan plonked himself next to her and glugged another throatful of wine. Then inexplicably, he was on his back with Rosie scratching underneath his rugby shirt, fingers coming to rest at the zip of his jeans.

"God, I'm horny," she exclaimed.

Brendan groaned, looked downwards and saw Rosie unfastening his belt and jeans. He would never be able to decide whether he was too drunk or too shocked to protest. Or maybe just curious about what would happen next.

"Well come on then, do I have to do everything myself?"

Brendan blinked, not fully understanding.

"Get your bloody jeans down!"

Brendan lifted his pelvis and shuffled his jeans and boxers downwards until they were bunched around his knees. His breath was coming in short pants. Rosie tugged his jeans, and he lifted his feet so that she could remove them. She had to remove the offending slippers too and then, almost as an afterthought, pulled his socks off, wiggling one of his big toes as she did so. Naked from the waist down, Brendan was disturbed see a distinct lack of physical response to Rosie's ministrations. All he felt was ... drunk. Very, very drunk. Rosie bent over him blowing her smoky breath in his face. She ran her fingers through his pubic hair and began to stroke his penis. Brendan willed himself desperately to respond. He tried to think, hoping to buy himself a bit more time.

"My chest of drawers. Top drawer, next to the socks."

The university medical centre had provided students with a free packet of condoms when they registered, and Brendan had hung onto them because – you never knew.

"What are you on about? We don't need those buggers. I've been on the pill since I was sixteen."

"No, please let me!"

He sat up, ignoring his dizziness and attempted a winsome smile. Actually, he attempted a seductive smile, but even in his inebriated state he realised that "winsome" was the closest he was likely to get.

"I'm not sure I can do it without."

Rosie looked cynical.

"What are you gurning for?" she asked. "You look like you've got toothache."

"I've been itchy down there this week."

It was the best he could come up with.

"I might you know, have an infection or something. Wouldn't want you to catch anything off me."

Rosie looked even more sceptical.

"Because you put it about so much, is that it?"

But she obligingly rummaged in his drawer and threw the condom at him.

"Have it your own way."

Miraculously, Brendan caught it with one hand.

He turned his back to Rosie and attempted to stimulate himself by some surreptitious rubbing. When he judged himself sufficiently hard, he ripped the condom from its packet and began to put it on, eager now. It was actually going to happen. The big one. And petrified or not, he was determined to enjoy the experience. He may have begun the evening a boy, but, by golly, he was going to end it a man.

As soon as he had unrolled the condom up his penis, he felt himself explode.

"Shit!"

He looked up, stricken. Rosie had by this time removed her outer clothes and was bulging over the top of a tight lacy red bra. A thatch of pubic hair protruded from her thong. She regarded the sagging erection; a leftover prawn on the buffet table, and not even a king prawn, at that.

"Here."

She rolled back the condom, with a practised air. Brendan flushed with shame at the sticky mess which dripped out. Rosie threw it in the general direction of the wastepaper basket. It missed, leaving a trail of little white globs in its wake.

"Now, let me."

She stroked his penis again, with her moistened fingers, brought her face down and kissed it, surprisingly gently. Then licked it. Brendan felt himself grow harder.

"I've done this before; I know what will work."

She caressed his penis with her lips and the tips of her fingers. Despite himself, Brendan found himself starting to moan with pleasure or terror. He was no longer sure.

"Now, see."

She took off her thong and moved on top of him. Brendan stared at the ceiling, unable to move. His hands hung limply by his sides as Rosie manoeuvred herself expertly until suddenly, he was inside of her. He shuddered, groaned and his erection abruptly collapsed.

"Oh no, oh no!"

He pushed Rosie off him.

"I'm sorry, I'm really, really sorry. Maybe I'm tired or too drunk. This is the first time I've ever done this," he added. He stared dolefully at his forlorn penis which was now flopping as pathetically as a dying sardine.

"No shit, Sherlock!"

Rosie sounded as if she had lost patience. She grabbed her undergarments and began to get dressed. Brendan turned away from her, partly to allow her some privacy, partly because he was suddenly conscious of his own half nakedness.

"Well, that was a waste of time," she hissed furiously, as she fastened her bra. "Not to mention a waste of vodka."

She picked up the empty bottle and dropped it into the wastepaper basket, adding the sticky used condom as she did so. The clang reverberated painfully round Brendan's skull.

"You know, I had a bet on with Jack. He's said for months that you're in the closet. I was never sure. Now I know. You're not gay or straight. You're fucking frigid, man. All that bastard slurping and stroking just to coax a fucking semi out of you. And even that didn't last longer than ten seconds."

"I'm sorry," Brendan repeated feebly.

He turned to face Rosie, who was now wrestling with her glittery top.

"Please don't tell anyone."

"That I've just had the worst lay in my life by a country mile? If you can even call it a frigging lay, because, personally, I reckon the jury's still out on that one. Believe me, this is definitely not one I'm going to brag about."

"Rosie?"

"What?"

"How much was the bet for?"

"Fifty quid. Even if I'd won, it wouldn't have been worth it."

She left, slamming the door behind her.

The party was still in full swing. Brendan wanted desperately to shower and clean his teeth but knew that was impossible. He put on his beige pyjamas, turned the light off and pulled the beige duvet over his head before falling into a few hours of alcohol anaesthesia. Then a catapult back to consciousness.

14.

The party had obviously broken up as the house was silent. It took roughly ten seconds for the memory to hit Brendan and another five to realise how thirsty, sticky, sweaty, dirty and monstrously hungover he was. Fear of waking his housemates – and whatever stray bodies he might trip over on his way – stopped him from taking a much-needed shower. Instead, he drew his bony legs to his chest and lay, a nauseous, miserable bundle of humiliation, with his head under the pillow to block out the unusually bright morning light. At some point he used the toilet, the gush of urine echoing round his head like a thunderclap. For the first Sunday morning in years, he missed Mass.

It was well into the afternoon when he eventually dragged himself out of bed, the need for water and paracetamol finally overriding any other concerns. He plodded downstairs and stared in horror at the kitchen. Used glasses, broken glasses, empty bottles, spilled bottles, drying pools of sick and cigarette ends were everywhere. Brendan found an unused mug in the kitchen cupboard, filled it with water and downed two paracetamol.

"Bugger this for a game of soldiers," he muttered to himself, turning his back on the bombsite that had once been a kitchen.

You've got to live in it as well.

There were times that Brendan wished that the human species had evolved to no longer require a conscience.

"Not listening," he whispered.

That'll show Jiminy fucking Cricket.

And the landlord's doing an inspection tomorrow. And can you really trust that shower of shite snoring their mushes off upstairs to make the place habitable by then?"

"Okay, Jiminy. You win."

So, Brendan set about cleaning it up. His stomach lurched dangerously, and he gagged as he scraped the soggy cigarette ends out of the sink. When he had finished in the kitchen, he started in the living room and hall. There were bottles to throw into the recycling bin, vomit stains to scrub and finally the carpet to vacuum. It must have been a measure of how comatose his housemates still were, that nobody shouted abuse at him about the vacuum cleaner, which made an incessant, grating squeal because the bag needed emptying and nobody could be arsed to see to it. By the time Brendan had finished, it was starting to get dark.

Somewhat disappointed by the fact that nobody had yelled at him to shut the fuck up – he was just in the mood to punch somebody in the gob, should the occasion require – Brendan made a cup of tea and treated himself to an early night. Where his last conscious thought was, "Did that really happen?"

*

"Bless me Father, for I have sinned. I missed Mass on Sunday."

"Oh? Any particular reason?"

"No good reason, other than the fact I was hungover. I was at a party Saturday night and had a lot to drink."

"Well, that is something a lot of students do and you're only young."

"There's more. I had sexual relations. With a woman. At least I think I did. Technically, I'm not so sure."

"Oh?"

"Yes. I think we might have had" – Brendan dropped his voice to little more than a whisper – "sex!"

"Sex! With your girlfriend?"

"No, that makes it worse. I haven't got a girlfriend. I barely know her. I was drunk and she seemed to want it."

"She seemed to want it? Did you try to force her? If so, we are talking about a much   more serious matter."

Brendan was horrified.

"Father, I barely even knew what to do. I don't know much about girls, but I swear I didn't put pressure on her. At least I don't think I did. All I know is that it was a disaster and I hated it. Maybe I pressured her by being so rubbish she felt she couldn't give up on a bad job?"

"The way you are talking, I think we can rule out the possibility you forced her. Now tell me, how did you feel afterwards?"

"The next day I felt terrible. In the first place, for being so bad at it. I mean I didn't exactly give the girl the best night of her life. In the second place, for getting in that situation in the first place. I got drunk and I'm so stupid. I felt dirty, sinful. And I had a monster hangover. That's why I didn't go to Mass. I was cast adrift. How could I take the sacrament with all that on my conscience?"

A few seconds silence.

Oh shit! Here comes the lecture.

"Now, do you understand why the church proscribes sex outside of marriage? I know we come under a lot of fire for our supposedly outdated attitudes towards promiscuity. But there's far more to our stance than being killjoys. Did you really want your first sexual experience to be like that?"

"No, and if I could go back again, I would never have let myself get in that position."

"Well, you can't go back but you can take a lesson from it. Sex is a wonderful thing, when shared between a loving couple. But the act of love should never be abused or cheapened. I think you've just learned that."

"Of course, Father. I think I understand. I'm not normally promiscuous."

"I'm sure you aren't. But remember one thing. Whatever you have done you will always be loved by God. You will never be cast adrift. Now for your penance say a decade of the rosary and have more respect for yourself in future."

Brendan had never been so glad to receive the sacrament of absolution. He reflected afterwards that he could have saved himself some embarrassment by confessing anonymously to an unknown priest. But he felt that he owed it to God to confess to a man he knew. Anonymous confession would have felt like an act of weakness, avoiding the necessity of facing up to his transgressions in front of a familiar face. That was the moment when Brendan made up his mind that the priesthood would be his destination.

For the remainder of his time at University, Brendan prayed regularly, attended Mass regularly and spent hours in the Leeds Christian Society bookshop researching theological debates and testimonies of life in the priesthood. He kept up with his Leeds Student Action activities, so he could say that he had not closed himself off from life completely. After graduation (a respectable 2:1), he consulted with his diocesan vocations advisor and began the application process. Meanwhile, he took a job in a care home, working with dementia patients. He enjoyed it, particularly chatting to and getting to know the residents and looked forward to the day when he could be settled in his very own parish, dispensing spiritual care to people, comforting souls as well as bodies.

15.

It was a balmy summer Sunday afternoon, the first weekend of Brendan's visit home. The distant drone of one neighbour's lawn mower and the gurgle of the other's garden hose trickled through the open windows. Outside, Jackie Coglan's prized roses were a riot of colour splashes, and a flutter of butterflies hovered around the buddleia. Two woodpigeons nuzzled each other on the garden fence. So far, so idyllic.

The roast chicken had been eaten, the raspberry trifle had been praised and the dinner dishes had been cleared away. Bob Coglan, having finished the washing up, entered the living room with a damp tea towel still slung over his shoulder. He lowered himself into his favourite armchair – the one with the best view of the television – with a satisfied sigh, already anticipating his afternoon snooze. Jackie studied the Sunday Post crossword while Nicole, curled into the corner of the regency striped sofa, furtively texted on her phone. It was shaping up to be a drowsy non-eventful afternoon of comfortable family harmony.

Shit, I'm about to set the cat amongst the bloody pigeons here, aren't I?

Yup, but you can't put it off any longer.

Yeah, but does it have to be done right this very minute? I don't know if I've got the heart to spoil the afternoon for everyone.

So, what exactly are you planning to do, smartarse? Disappear for seven years and reappear magically in a stole and clerical collar? Yeah, that'd really work. Get on with it!

"Actually Mam, Dad, Nicole, I've got some news."

"Have you, now?" Jackie lowered her paper and removed her reading glasses. "Are we going to like it?"

Nicole smirked.

"I think we'd already guessed," she said, barely looking up from her phone.

Well, that wasn't the reaction I was expecting.

"Really? How come none of you ever said anything?"

"Well, it'd have been stating the bloody obvious, wouldn't it?"

"Well, I suppose that makes it a bit easier then. So, what do you all tink?"

"Son," Jackie folded her glasses and put them in their case, "it couldn't matter less to us. Did you really think it would change the way we thought about you? And it's the twenty-first century, for God's sake. Nobody needs to hide it these days, thank goodness. I can still remember all the hoo-ha about George Michael."

George Michael? What -

"These days, politicians, news readers, nobody gives a monkey's. I mean, look at Clare Balding. Or that historian that does all those programmes about the Tudors."

Oh, shit! They don't think –

"So, what's his name then?" Nicole finally put down her phone.

They do!

"That's not it. Nowhere near. What it is, is – over the past few months, I've been applying to join the priesthood. And I've been accepted. I start training in a month. It's going to take a long time, seven years actually. But at the end of it I'll be a priest. A real one," he finished, somewhat feebly.

Bob was suddenly erect in his chair.

"A priest? Well, you bugger, I never saw that one coming. But you won't be able to get married or have children or anything. Are you not a bit young to make that kind of a decision?"

"I'm nearly twenty-two, Dad. This isn't something I've decided overnight. There's been a long thought process involved. Lots of consultations. But I've been accepted, and I feel like I might have found my niche." His voice rose slightly. "Me and women, it was never going to work."

"Is that not what this is really about, son? You've just heard your mother. None of us care which end of the ballroom you dance at. You don't need to hide it by committing yourself to a life of celibacy."

"I'm not gay."

"I wouldn't care if you were. Is there anyone special in your life? A lad you'd like to introduce to us? If there is, we'd love to get to know him."

"Dad, I know you would support me if I did come out. But I'm not gay. And this feels so right. And I'll be able to minister to people, care for them. I'll still be part of the world. Just on a different path. And I'll still be your son, you know."

"It's a bit hard to get my head around, mind. Brendan, do you really think that lifestyle can make you happy?"

"It isn't just a matter of being happy, though, is it?"

"I would have thought it would have everything to do with being happy!"

"I know being happy and secure is all you wanted for me, Dad." Brendan leaned forward, running his fingers through his hair. "But this feels right. It feels like I've been travelling towards somewhere for the past few years and I've finally worked out where I'm heading. I feel better than happy. I feel at peace with myself."

"What about children, though? You'd be a brilliant dad. You're throwing that chance away."

Brendan shrugged. "I'll survive. And there's no guarantee I'd have had children anyway."

"Jackie, pet, what do you reckon to all this?" Bob's tone was almost imploring.

Jackie, for the last few moments, had been doodling on the margin of the paper. She looked directly at her husband.

"What I reckon is that, if it feels right to Brendan, then he should go for it. If it turns out not to be right, he won't make it through the training anyway."

She turned to Brendan. "At least you're on a definite path now. I was worried when you started working in that care home. We didn't encourage you to go to university to wipe backsides for legal minimum wage forever, you know."

"Mam, there's nothing wrong with –"

"I know, but half the owners of those places are no better than crooks, the way they treat their staff like bloody skivvies and their residents like bloody commodities. I'm amazed you stuck it as long as you did, to be quite honest. I'm just happy you've found something you really want to do. And," she paused and gave a dry half laugh, "at least you won't be getting a girl into trouble."

Without warning, Nicole leapt to her feet with a loud, "For fuck's sake," and grabbed the nearest object to hand which was the TV remote control. She lobbed it hard at the wall, above Brendan's head. Brendan jumped to catch it but timed his movement badly; the remote control smacked him on the side of his prominent nose, making him yelp, then thumped corner down onto the carpet.

"What the Hell! Nicole!"

"Is it broken?" Bob asked.

"Don't know. Hurts like mad, I know that much."

Bob picked up the remote control and experimentally turned the television on and off. "No, seems okay."

"Thanks Mam, I was wondering when you'd get a sly dig in," Nicole roared.

"Nicole, pet, your mam wasn't having a pop, you know," Bob said, once the remote control was firmly on the arm of his chair.

"Is someone going to tell me what the heck's going on here?" Brendan rubbed his injured nose.

"Well, it's up to Nicole, isn't it?" Bob said. "We weren't going to tell anyone just yet until the first three months."

"Three months of what?" Shock was giving way to confusion.

Nicole looked at her parents in turn then glared at Brendan.

"I'm pregnant, golden boy. No, I'm not married. No, I'm not getting married. So, are you going to call me a fallen woman? Or maybe you're going to go down the 'he who is without sin, cast the first stone' route. That would be right up your saintly little alley. Well, come on then! Let me have it!"

"Nicole, stop it!" This was from Jackie. "Not everything's about you, you know. Besides, you know your dad and I are thrilled for you and Gavin. And Brendan won't pass any comment about you not being married, will you?"

Jackie looked sharply at Brendan as she spoke; her tone was more forceful addressing him than it had been with Nicole.

"Of course not," Brendan fished in his jeans pocket for a tissue to stifle the trickle of blood which was emerging from his nostril. "Congratulations. It'll be nice to be an uncle."

He pinched his nose.

"Well, you won't be seeing much of the baby, will you? You've just told us you're about to withdraw from the human race, and I certainly won't be taking the baby to church. Anyway, I'm not sure I want you around it, full stop. Not now you're joining the kiddie fiddlers' brigade."

"Nicole! That's a terrible thing to say. That's your brother! And he's come to tell us the most important news of his life so far. And all you can do is insult him, for no reason whatsoever."

"Oh, come on, Mam. You know what they're all like. The Catholic church is full of it, they're all as bad as each other. And he's joining

80

them. Well, he's not going to be around any child of mine, that's for sure."

She turned to Brendan.

"Thanks, Brendan. Thanks a bunch. This was my time. First child for me, first grandchild in the family, all excited and everything. But now, you've managed to trump it. As always, it's all about Brendan."

"I didn't even know about the baby!"

Brendan's rapidly swelling nose was turning his speech into a whine. He blew out a blob of dark blood.

"Oh, just fuck off to Canterbury with peas in your shoes, why don't you?" Nicole stormed out, banging the door behind her so hard that it rattled.

Jackie sighed. With a weary, "I'll sort it," Bob heaved himself to his feet and followed Nicole, whose howls could now be heard from upstairs. Brendan examined the blood on his tissue and found a clean patch for his nose to drip into.

"Are you okay?" Jackie asked.

"I suppose so. What's she got against me, though?"

"She'll come round. She's under a lot of pressure. She and Gavin haven't been together that long. The baby is, let's say, an unexpected surprise. And she'll be very hormonal. I'm sure she didn't mean the half of what she said."

"She certainly sounded like she meant every word."

Brendan blew more blood out of his nose and pinched it again.

"Well, whatever, don't say anything back to her. Pretend you're in training already and turn the other cheek."

"I had literally not said a word when she chucked a remote control at my face."

"She never chucked it at you. It was just unfortunate you got in the way."

"Fair point! But I didn't have a go at her, anyway. She is okay, isn't she?"

"She's giving it the full tough cookie routine; you know our Nicole. But inside she's bound to be terrified. She and Gavin aren't even living together, for goodness' sake."

"Will he be a good dad, do you think?"

Jackie snorted. "Well, have you seen him around this weekend? I suppose it's possible that he could suddenly grow up and take responsibility for something for once in his life but, in all honesty, I'm not holding out much hope. Your dad and I are worried sick but we're trying to act as pleased as possible for her sake. It's all we can do. And," she added firmly, "while you're under our roof that's what you'll do as well."

Brendan tried to do exactly that. Once his nose had stopped bleeding, he washed his face and changed his T-shirt and tried to reduce the swelling by holding a bag of frozen sprouts over his face, in his bedroom, so as not to draw attention to himself. He was as solicitous as possible towards Nicole, making her cups of ginger tea – he had once heard that ginger tea was supposed to help with morning sickness – and giving her first dibs on the bathroom every morning. Although Nicole didn't exactly thank him, she didn't throw any more household objects at him; Brendan took that as progress.

Nicole tapped on Brendan's bedroom door the morning of his departure.

"I got you these," she said, holding out a bag of marshmallows and another of eclairs – two of Brendan's favourite sweets. "For the train. I thought it might be a while before you get anything else nice to eat."

"Thanks, Nicole. Thoughtful of you."

"I'm going to work in a bit. This is the last we'll see of each other for a while. Just wanted to say, sorry about your nose, and that. I was out of order."

Brendan shrugged. "It's okay. No harm done."

"I didn't mean for it to hit you or anything."

"I know."

Nicole started towards the door, then reconsidered.

"Brendan?"

"Yeah?"

"Good luck."

Nicole stepped forward and gave Brendan the briefest of hugs. "I hope you find whatever it is you're looking for."

Brendan returned the hug and Nicole planted a fleeting kiss on his cheek, squeezing his hand before she left the room.

That was seven years ago. Brendan's time in training passed peacefully and swiftly. He enjoyed each year more than the last, mentally appraising his spiritual growth and imagining the day when he would become a fully-fledged priest. As several of his contemporaries encountered doubts and ultimately abandoned their vocations, Brendan never wavered. He spent time on placements in hospitals and hospices where he felt privileged to support people at the most vulnerable moments of their lives. He spent long periods in silent prayer and reflection and was surprised at how little the time seemed to drag. He studied biblical teachings and felt more inspired with every passing day. The day when he lay prostrate in church and received the sacrament of holy ordination by the bishop was the happiest of his life. His parents attended, supportive as ever, if more than a little nonplussed by the rite.

Nicole did not attend, although Brendan had extended an invitation to her and her son, Teddy. He had visited Teddy shortly after he was born and peered into the Moses basket, stroking the petal-soft, downy head, marvelling that his gangly self could be related to somebody so miniscule and fragile. He shook Gavin's hand at the hospital, and refrained from calling him a tosser when he insisted on going on his regular Friday night drinking session with his mates the day the baby was discharged, despite Nicole being incapacitated by several Caesarean stitches. In fact, he hoovered the hastily acquired flat and cleaned the kitchen as their mother tackled a basket of ironing. He did, however, squeeze Jackie's shoulder sympathetically when she sighed "And so it begins," in the car on the way home. Within a year of Teddy's birth Gavin permanently absented himself from his and Nicole's lives. When Brendan heard of this, he surprised himself by feeling a quite unpriestly desire to storm round and punch Gavin in the face.

Brendan tried to maintain as much contact as possible with his nephew, sending money at Christmas and birthdays. Nicole would reciprocate with a polite thank you note and a photo of Teddy wearing or playing with what she had bought him. When he saw Teddy at family gatherings, Brendan observed him shyly from a distance.

"You can talk to him you know. He doesn't bite, well, apart from that one time at nursery," Nicole said, when Brendan was on a short visit to his parents.

Brendan looked at Teddy, fourteen months old and sporting a mop of flaxen curls, cramming a fistful of raisins into his mouth.

"It's okay," he said. "I don't want to scare him."

"Oh, for God's – goodness' sake!"

Nicole scooped Teddy from the floor and deposited him on Brendan's lap.

Brendan found himself looking directly into a pair of clear blue eyes, a replica of his own. As Teddy's mouth widened into a huge beam, Brendan gently tweaked his nose. Then Teddy stretched out a dimpled hand and Brendan felt a touch as delicate as a soft breath against his face, sparkling a thrill that travelled to his marrow. He gazed at Teddy, transfixed, for a moment; generations of Coglans reflected back at him.

Like looking at my younger self in a mirror.

Without warning, he stiffened, the connection broken, everything inside him screaming at him to relinquish the unsullied toddler.

"Can you take him, Mam? I'm desperate for the loo."

He hurried from the room, and leaned against the toilet door, shivering.

When he finished training, he received notification that he would be posted to St Jude's parish. He joked to himself that he had left one working class community in an industrial North East town to join another, barely ten miles away. Bob remarked that at least he would know how the land lay and that the community wouldn't come as a huge culture shock to him. Brendan was inclined to agree.

However, as he now trudged homewards, despite his enjoyable conversation with Luke, Brendan couldn't help wishing that he had opted for any other career in the world.

2019

16.

A week had passed. Jim was out of bed and halfway to stir-crazy. He grabbed the telephone when it rang on Wednesday evening.

"I'll get it, Brendan, it's high time I was getting back into the swing of things. Hello?"

Brendan went up to his room to allow Jim to finish his conversation in private. When he came downstairs, Jim was writing in the diary. He looked up as he saw Brendan coming into the room.

"That was Maureen." Jim finished writing, closed the diary and replaced the cap of his pen. "Neville's body has been released for burial. That will be an important milestone for Maureen."

"So is the coroner's investigation finished then?"

"Not yet. They've requested to see Neville's laptop."

Brendan gulped and willed his insides to obey orders.

"And they will want to speak to Maureen over the next few weeks. And Andrea, and Neville's friends. But now the postmortem's been completed the funeral can get underway. Maureen's asked for it to be next Thursday. You won't mind helping, will you?"

Shit!

"Me, Jim? Will that really be necessary? I'm not very experienced in funerals."

"Which is exactly why you need to be there. It can get tricky. You'd be surprised how many family feuds choose that time to rear their heads."

Cheers, Jim. You're not really selling this to me!

"So, you don't want be doing your first one cold, and I'm supposed to be mentoring you. Not that I've been able to do much of that lately. Besides, I considered Neville a good friend. I could do with the support if I'm honest. Will you do that for me, Brendan?"

Although the older man's words were mild there was a firm undertone to his voice.

"If it'll help."

"Great stuff. We'll go through everything later."

*

At Jim's insistence, he and Brendan arrived at St Jude's well before Neville's funeral was due to begin. Conducting the funeral was the last service Jim could do his old friend, and, by goodness, he was determined it would be carried out to the best of his ability. Brendan placed orders of service on the pews; there were at least a hundred. Maureen was clearly expecting a large turnout. As well she might, Jim mused; Neville had been well regarded in his local community. When Jim was satisfied that everything was in its proper place, the two priests proceeded to the vestry to change into their robes and purple stoles.

"Can we pray in silence for a while?" Jim asked.

They sat at the table and bowed their heads. Jim prayed for the strength to steer Maureen and the rest of the family through the procedure as painlessly as he could.

"Brendan," Jim said, tears spilling towards his cheeks. He took a long steadying breath. "Would you get me a glass of water please?"

Brendan filled a glass of water. Jim took a few sips then went over to the sink and dabbed his face with a wet paper towel. When he felt Brendan's hand against his shoulder, he said, "I'm okay, Brendan. It's going to be difficult but I'm okay. I've got to be okay for the family." He managed a smile. "Now do you see why I wanted you here?"

"It's all right, Jim. We've got this."

It was the first time Jim had heard Brendan speak that day. His words were calm, but Jim detected a slight tremble in his voice, and

Brendan seemed to be unaware that his hands were rapidly clenching and unclenching.

"They'll be arriving soon," Brendan's eyes flickered towards the clock.

"They will. Wait by the altar; I'll greet the family."

As Jim walked towards the entrance, he noticed that the pews were beginning to fill up; some people kneeling and praying, others shuffling uncomfortably as if they weren't sure what they should be doing. Men turned to acknowledge each other with nods and half waves; their wives tapped them on the wrists and hissed at them to keep their mouths shut, had they forgotten where they were?

St Jude's was almost full when a pair of headlights pierced the misty drizzle. Jim stepped forward. The first mourner's car arrived, bearing Maureen, her daughter Andrea and Andrea's fiancé, who stepped out first. He looked uncomfortable in his ill-fitting dark suit, as if his shirt collar were cutting into his neck. Maureen clutched his outstretched hand in a claw-like grip.

Jim had known Maureen for many years, but today she was almost unrecognisable. Grief appeared to have shrivelled her, etching prominent lines into her face, painting huge grey shadows under her eyes and stripping weight from her. Her brittle hair seemed to be lacquered to within an inch of its life. She stared straight ahead, as if she were barely aware of what was happening around her. Andrea followed, exiting the car with difficulty, hobbled by her tight black skirt. She was crying already, loud hulking sobs. Her fiancé put his arm around her, absurdly stretched between the two women. Neville's father stepped out of the second car, supported by his remaining son. His sharp-featured daughter-in-law hopped out behind them. She hurried to Maureen and Andrea, embracing each of them in turn before taking up position on the other side of her father-in-law.

"Maureen!"

Jim stepped over to her, taking both her hands in his. Whatever was left of Maureen was muffled by a cloak of blankness.

"Father McLean. What happens now?"

She might have been asking about the plot of a film. Shock must have settled in; Jim hoped it had numbed her sufficiently to make it through the day.

"Well, the coffin will be carried into the church. I'll bless it with holy water and walk in front of it. You and your family will walk behind. All your friends and relatives have already taken their places. Then, once you have sat down, we can begin the ceremony."

Maureen nodded. Jim sensed that the kindest thing he could do today would be to guide her through the process step by step.

"Now we will unload the coffin and it will be carried through to the porch."

Eight men, CIU club committee members, were acting as pallbearers. They were all smartly dressed in dark suits and black ties. Some of them displayed old military medals. All looked downcast. As Jim led the procession down the aisle, he could hear Andrea's high-pitched wailing interspersed with the uneven tap of Neville's father's stick against the floor. When the family were settled into the front pew, he announced the first hymn, "Lead Kindly Light".

Maureen was silent; still looking straight ahead, seemingly fixated on the tabernacle. Andrea's howls threatened to overwhelm the sound of singing. Jim could see her aunt nudging her from behind – *let it go Jean; the girl's just lost her father* – Andrea's fiancé turned to give the aunt a filthy stare and hugged Andrea more tightly. Neville's brother fiddled with the order of service, trying to help his father understand what was happening. The old man fumbled with his crotch; Andrea's aunt removed his hand and clung to his wrist. Jim caught himself expelling a sigh of relief when the hymn finished, and he could instruct everybody to sit down.

Jim's voice was starting to rasp. He was glad that he had asked Brendan to perform the gospel reading. Brendan's intonation was a little flat and hurried for Jim's liking, as if he were trying to race through as swiftly as possible. Jim would have to have words with him about that, later. When Brendan finished, turning away from the congregation without so much as acknowledging them (what was *wrong* with the lad today?), Jim stood, took a large swallow of the honey and water mixture he had placed on the altar table and started the homily.

"Ladies and gentlemen, we are here today to honour our friend Neville and commend him to God. I would like to start by..."

SLAM! Jim fell silent, thrown off guard, as several mourners startled and turned to see the cause of the sudden bang: a late arrival making

88

no attempt to avoid disrupting the proceedings. She wasn't dressed for a funeral; jeans, a silver puffer jacket and ankle boots loud enough generate a substantial clopping. She clutched a green document folder to her chest, as tightly as if she were carrying the crown jewels. What stood out most, however, was her utter focus.

Had she mistaken her destination? No, she was still striding up the aisle. A latecomer, then? But why was she not taking a seat? Surely if you had been disrespectful enough to arrive late to a funeral, the most appropriate course of action was to fit yourself unnoticed into the back row? But the woman kept on, right up to the altar, pushing past the coffin none too carefully and almost sending it flying. One lady almost dislocated her neck with craning, clearly her waning interest in the proceedings had been piqued.

"Would you like to take a seat?" Jim asked pointedly.

"Shut up!"

The words were a snarl. With one graceful swipe, the woman sent the framed photograph of Neville, reverently placed on top of the coffin by his brother, crashing to the ground. The glass shattered instantly, Neville's face landed upwards and was almost immediately adorned by a mouthful of spit. A collective gasp went round the congregation.

Somebody muttered, "Things are looking up here," just a bit too loudly. Jim mastered himself just enough to glare at her.

A second swipe sent a white wreath toppling. For the first time in his life, Jim found himself incapable of either speech or movement. The woman turned to face the congregation; several people glanced downwards, fidgeting awkwardly.

"Sorry to interrupt, but there's something you all need to know about Neville Tanner."

The woman's voice was at an unnaturally high pitch; she sounded one kick in the backside away from a complete meltdown.

"Neville Tanner! Worker, devoted husband, family man, deprived children's club leader, and all-round good guy. Well, you all knew that already, didn't you? But – and I bet you hadn't guessed this one – he was also a paedophile."

The woman's voice quivered as she spat out the word.

Maureen covered her mouth with a trembling hand and shook her head silently. Some men looked at each other as if to say, "Well is someone going to do something?" Others leaned forwards; studiously shocked expressions not quite managing to disguise their thrill. One man attempted to stand and was abruptly pulled back down by his wife; she was clearly relishing the unexpected entertainment far too much to countenance any attempt to get things back on track. Jim felt an irrational stab of anger towards her.

But he wasn't exactly doing any better, was he? It was up to him to act if he could only move; for a fleeting moment he entertained the totally sacrilegious thought that the woman had somehow cast a spell on him.

"How many of you knew? Did none of you guess? Or even suspect? Or even care? Because he was at it for bloody years. Did none of you even wonder about that fucking children's club he ran?"

Jim had no doubt that she would have continued, had it not been for Andrea shaking herself as if emerging from a trance and springing from her pew like an athlete out of a starting block, no easy feat given her solid build. She wrestled herself free from her fiancé's embrace and awkwardly climbed over the barrier in front of the front pew. Being short, she was unable to vault successfully, and the split in the back of her clinging skirt ripped, baring her stumpy legs to her buttocks. Not that she noticed, as she launched herself at the interloper and grabbed her shoulders, shaking her. Her face was an ugly contortion as she began to yell.

"You fucking lying bitch, Chloe Metcalfe. You fucking mental cow! You've always been a freak, an ugly lezbo freak. You were weird when we were at school and you're a complete psycho now. You're a lying cunt!"

She shook Chloe hard again and delivered a right-handed slap with some considerable force, sending Chloe staggering backwards towards the altar. The document folder dropped to the floor as Chloe's arms windmilled; she caught her heel on the step of the altar and landed hard on her bottom, swearing as she thumped down. The coffin, which had been caught by Chloe's elbow, rocked alarmingly. Andrea was over her in a second, straddling her and grabbing two handfuls of hair. She raised a mouthful of her own spit and deposited it with some force on Chloe's forehead.

"Get off me, you frigging slag!"

A booted foot came up and kicked Andrea hard in the stomach. Andrea let go of Chloe's hair and reeled backwards, crashing into the front pew, momentarily winded.

The crash brought Jim out of his paralysis. He went over to Chloe who was sitting rubbing her scalp where her hair had been grabbed. A good handful of ripped hair lay on the floor next to her.

"Young lady, I don't know who you are, but this behaviour is not at all appropriate. This is a house of God. Show some respect! And look at all of these people! They loved the man we are burying today. How could you bring further upset to them, with your ludicrous suggestions?"

Chloe stood up, wiping mucus off her face. She picked up her file and looked around as if only now aware of the impression she was making. She was sobbing now, standing over Andrea, and addressed her directly. She no longer sounded irate; just defeated.

"It's true. Sorry, Andrea but it's all true. Your father was a nonce. A great steaming nonce. If you say you don't know that, Andrea, you're either stupid or lying. He was a perv!" A pervert!"

Chloe's voice was starting to rise again. She waved her document folder.

"I've got it all written down here, exactly what the bastard's been up to. And that's just what I know about so far."

Andrea had recovered her breath and looked ready to mount a second assault.

"Brendan," Jim looked around. "Never mind sitting there like a tin of milk, I could do with some help here," he hissed.

But he saw that Brendan was very still, eyes closed. His face, whilst never high coloured, was the whitest Jim had ever seen it. He had one long narrow hand pressed to his chest. Jim's first thought was "What's he playing at?" Then he noticed the way Brendan was breathing, slowly in through the nose and out through the mouth, fully focused, pushing through the crowing that erupted as he inhaled. Jim finally understood.

Meanwhile, Andrea's fiancé had left the pew and was holding her – or maybe restraining her – in his arms and making crooning noises.

Maureen had, at last, collapsed in tears; her sister-in-law joined her in the pew to comfort her. Neville's brother took his father by the arm and, whispering something to his wife, led him away. When Jim had visited the old man, he thought he had recognised the first signs of dementia; now he hoped fervently that the man could not understand what was being said about his late son. To be fair, he looked completely oblivious, seemingly only interested in fumbling with himself.

"Please leave," Jim said to Chloe, his voice coming out more like a desperate plea, than a firm order. "Look at Maureen here. Don't ruin the last memory she's going to have of her husband. Besides, you are completely mistaken. I knew Neville; he was utterly incapable of those terrible things. Please leave and seek the help you need."

He laid a hand on Chloe's arm.

"Don't touch me, you patronising bastard!"

For the first time, Chloe seemed to notice Maureen's sniffles, Andrea's glare, the morbid fascination of the rest of the congregation.

"Oh, what's the use? What's the fucking point of any of this? It's obvious you've all made your minds up. Hysterical female versus local community stalwart. Fuck the sodding lot of you!"

She ran the length of the aisle, still clutching the folder. The echo of her keening reverberated as she crashed out of the church, leaving the double doors to swing behind her.

Andrea had recovered enough breath to yell, "Just because you don't even know who your own dad is, doesn't give you the right to tell lies about mine, schizo."

Jim looked behind; Brendan was grey by now, hunched over himself.

"Go and get changed, Brendan, then go home. I'll see you back there," he said quietly.

When he faced the congregation again, he saw that the wreath had been repositioned (now slightly squashed, a couple of flowers dislodged, but otherwise none the worse for wear), the photograph retrieved (pity about the glass shards every-bloody-where) and the coffin straightened.

"Right, that unfortunate interlude seems to have passed. Whoever the young lady was, she was obviously greatly disturbed."

Jim was painfully aware of how inadequate he must sound.

Neville's sister-in-law snorted. A man spoke from the back of the church, "Probably gatecrashed the wrong funeral."

A couple of people giggled nervously; the man's wife tutted and slapped him on the forearm. Several more people settled back in their pews, disappointed that the unexpected diversion was not set to continue.

Jim abandoned the homily and announced the offertory hymn, "Happy the Man". They were massively behind time now anyway; the drivers would be in a hurry to drive the family back home in time for their next funeral. The service limped along in a subdued manner. Neville's brother was supposed to have deliver a eulogy following communion, but he had left with his father. Of course, Jim could have asked if anyone else wanted to speak but why invite any more debacles? As Jim led the coffin to the churchyard for burial, he had a sudden fear that Chloe might be outside waiting to hurl more abuse at the funeral party. He was relieved to see the car park empty, apart from the drivers enjoying a sly cigarette and brushing sausage roll flakes off their coats.

Jim wanted to talk to Maureen as soon as the burial was finished but her sister-in-law had led her back to the car, and she had acquiesced without protest. Andrea had followed but her fiancé approached Jim, scratching his neck where it met his shirt collar.

"Andrea's Auntie Jean said to say thank you for the service. She said you handled it very professionally."

The lad was speaking as if reciting words he had been told to learn by heart.

"She said she hoped she would see you back at the house for a drink and a few nibbles."

"That's very kind, son, but I'm afraid I've got a lot to do here." This was only partly untrue. "Tell Andrea and Maureen that I'll call around to see them over the next couple of days."

"Righto, Father McLean."

"Oh, and tell Maureen not to worry; nobody with anything between their ears would believe a word that came out of that ridiculous woman's mouth."

Jim waited until the rest of the cars had pulled away before tidying up the church and getting changed. In truth, he wanted to catch up with Brendan. There was definitely something amiss with the young fellow and he intended to find out what it was, sooner rather than later.

17.

Back at home, there was no sign of Brendan. There was, however, a sickly reek of floral air freshener, tempered with an unpleasant, meaty undertone. Covering his nose, Jim went upstairs and knocked softly on Brendan's bedroom door.

"Come in," was the weary reply.

Brendan had closed the curtains and was lying on his bed, gently kneading his abdomen. He had removed his collar, and his top button was undone; his belt was also unbuckled.

"Sorry about the smell," Brendan's voice was a dull monotone. "Nervous tummy. Stress related, according to the doctor."

"Hmm. Are you feeling better now?"

"I'll be fine, Jim. Really. I don't know what happened there."

Jim sat in the chair by Brendan's desk and turned it to face the bed. He spoke gently, looking Brendan directly in the eye.

"You don't serve three years in Iraq as a padre without learning to recognise a panic attack, when you see one."

"I'm sorry." The words were whispered.

"It's nothing to apologise for. Have you had them before?"

Brendan nodded.

"None as bad as this one for ages though. Usually, keeping still and concentrating on breathing for a few seconds can hold it at bay," the unspoken words "without anybody noticing," hung in the air, "but this time, I don't know, was a bit worse than others. I'll be okay now."

"Hmm. You still haven't much colour. Was it that girl's outburst that brought it on? She was clearly deluded."

Brendan shrugged, "Maybe."

"How long have you been having them?"

"Since I was sixteen. The first one was at my best friend's funeral. But I don't get them loads. It's not a massive deal, really."

"Is there anything you would like to talk about?"

Brendan shook his head.

"I'm fine. Just really tired and a bit shaky. Is it okay if I stay here for a while? I think it's the best place for me at the minute."

"Most of them pass off perfectly smoothly, you know."

"I'm sorry?"

"Funerals. No matter what you see in the soap operas. Don't think I can't hear that Emmerdale theme tune from upstairs."

Brendan's mouth twitched, the faintest ghost of a half-smile.

"We'll talk through it all later and try and discuss what strategies we could use if anything like this ever were to happen again. Can't have you developing a mental block over funerals. Like it or not they're a big part of what we do. I'll go now. You need to spend some time in prayer."

Jim closed the door quietly behind him, leaving Brendan staring at the ceiling, sixteen years old all over again.

2006

18.

Whenever Brendan looked back, he was always struck by how innocuously the day had passed. He had spent most of it loafing in the park with a few friends; GCSE results were still an unthreatening four weeks away and the atmosphere in the group had been suffused with self-satisfied indolence. Footballs had been kicked, ice creams licked, jokes exchanged; the balmy heat providing a comforting backdrop. At home, things were uncharacteristically quiet; Nicole was on a girls' weekend to York.

When the doorbell rang, Brendan was experimenting with the kettlebells he had filched from under Nicole's bed – she'd never notice they were gone, and six packs don't grow by themselves – when the bedroom door opened.

"Brendan!"

"All right, Matt?"

Matt and Brendan had been firm friends since their mothers had met at a toddler group. During secondary school, they had spent many evenings holed up in Brendan's room – sometimes studying together or playing on Brendan's PlayStation, sometimes listening to music and not chatting at all. Overweight, unsporty and naturally shy, Matt, whilst not a bully-magnet exactly (even Brendan had to privately admit that Matt's soft reputation ironically provided some protection: few wannabee hard bastard kudos points were likely to be gained by reducing him to tearful shreds), had few friends. Brendan had always found his quiet demeanour made for easy company.

What was different this evening though, was that Matt had a large holdall with him. He flung himself on Brendan's bed and got straight to the point.

"I need somewhere to stay for a while, Bren. Do you think your mam and dad would mind if I dossed here a few days?"

Brendan put down his kettlebells and joined Matt on the bed, flopping tired and sweaty against the wall, hands cushioning his head.

"Can't see there being a problem. But why? Are your mam and dad going away?"

"No. I just need somewhere to crash for a little while. I'm going to get a job and earn enough money to get my own place or at least share a place. Please Bren, it's important."

"Get a job? You'll need more than a Saturday job to get your own place, you twat."

Brendan yawned, covering his mouth with the back of his hand.

"It's not going to be a Saturday job. They're recruiting for staff at Iceland. I'm not going to sixth form, I can't. I need to get out and getting a job is the only way I can afford it. It's not like I'm going to get brilliant GCSE grades anyway. I just need somewhere to stay for a while. I'll clean and everything. I'll chip in with food while I'm saving for my own place. I wouldn't ask if it wasn't important."

For the first time, Brendan noticed the lines of stress on his friend's chubby face, the threat of tears behind his bright blue eyes. Alert now, he sat up, drew his tanned knees to his chin and circled them with his arms.

"Matty, what's up? You've always got on great with your parents; have you had a row? I bet it's nothing compared to the ding-dongs Mam and Nicole have."

Matt shook his head and looked downwards.

"There hasn't been a row," he muttered. He put up a hand and wiped a tear from the corner of his eye.

"What then? You've not gone and got someone pregnant, have you?"

Brendan didn't really think this was likely; Matt was the only boy in his year whose sexual experience was blatantly as non-existent as his own. On the other hand, you never knew.

"Don't be a dickhead!"

Matt sounded too strained for Brendan to take offence at the "dickhead" comment.

"Are you going to come out then? Mate, if you are, it makes no difference to me and it won't to your mam and dad either. Your mam's well cool. Even if your dad did kick off, she'd take your part."

Matt remained silent.

"I mean, you'd still be the same, wouldn't you? I'd still trash you at Ultimate FIFA every time. Your Ali G impressions would be as shit as ever."

"I've not got anyone pregnant and I'm not gay," Matt mumbled.

Matt was looking down at his hands, picking at a loose fold of skin next to his thumb nail. Brendan had never seen him look more miserable.

"What then?"

Brendan laid his hand on Matt's wrist. Matt pulled away, shuddering.

"Okaayy! Are you going to tell me, then?"

Matt looked at him with red rimmed eyes.

"If I tell you, you've got to promise not to tell anyone, okay? Not your mam and dad, not a teacher, anyone. If you did, I'd have to leave. I mean really leave. London or somewhere."

"Okay, I won't. Just tell me what's up."

Brendan let his knees drop and sat cross legged. Matt wrapped his arms tightly around himself, looked at Brendan and took a deep breath.

"My grandad has been messing about with me."

"What you mean, really? Properly, you know?"

"It started about five years ago."

Matt's voice was dull and flat as if he were repeating something he'd gone over in his head several times.

"I was eleven. It was a year or so after Grandma had died. Mam and Dad were at the cinema and Grandad had volunteered to babysit. I was sitting on the sofa, next to Grandad. I remember Casualty was on the telly. Grandad put his arm around me. It was nice, but then he put his hand on the front of my pyjama bottoms and said, 'You're getting to be a big boy, aren't you?'"

"Matt! That's -"

"I was kind of grossed out but just sort of laughed. I guess I thought he'd done it by accident. I'm thick, that's why."

Matt wiped another tear away with the back of his hand and drew in a tremulous breath.

Brendan opened his mouth but couldn't find words.

"Anyway, I went to bed soon after. Mam and Dad came home, Grandad left and I thought that was the end of it. But a month or so later it was Mam and Dad's wedding anniversary, and they went out for a meal. Grandad was babysitting again. This time, I thought it would be all right. But."

Matt paused again. He sobbed a couple of times and wiped his nose on the back of his hand. A clear snot bubble sat there for a minute and then burst. Brendan pretended not to notice.

"He came into my bedroom and sat on the bed. He said how lonely he was without Grandma and how I could help make him feel better. He knew I'd want to help because I was such a good, kind boy. He was stroking my hair as he was talking. Then he he…"

Matt paused and wiped his eyes with the back of his hand.

"Mate, you don't need to tell me anything more, if you don't want to."

"That's when he …you know. Afterwards, he said I was a good boy, and we were sharing a special secret now. And he told me I could never tell anyone about it because nobody would understand how special it was and we'd both get into trouble. Mam would be really upset, and he could go to jail, and I'd go into a children's home. And Mam would hate me for causing so much trouble."

Again, Brendan did not know what to say. He laid his hand on Matt's arm and rubbed it, cursing himself for not being able to think of a less ineffective gesture. Matt shook him off.

"Don't! Please, don't!"

Brendan went back to circling his knees.

"Well, after that, Mam and Dad started going out one evening a month or so and he would babysit. Grandad said how much he enjoyed spending time with me, and that it was good for them to get out on their own sometimes. And it was always the same. Once I was in bed, he would come and do stuff. And it went on. A couple of times I pretended I wasn't well and went to bed before Grandad got there but it didn't do any good. He could tell if I was pretending to be asleep. When I was about fourteen, I told Mam and Dad I didn't need a babysitter anymore. But Mam said, 'Grandad looks forward so much to your evenings together. It would be unkind to stop them. We have to think of other people as well as ourselves, you know.'"

"Did you never think about telling anyone, a teacher or someone?" asked Brendan.

Matt looked wounded.

"After what Grandad had said? No. And he and Mam are really tight you know. She adores him and he still calls her his little princess."

"But, Matty, they're your *parents.*"

"Grandad said Mam may get so upset she could die. He said the cancer that killed Grandma sometimes ran in families and that stress would make Mam more likely to get it. And if that happened, Dad would really hate me."

"But that's bullshit! Stress doesn't make people get cancer. Everyone knows that."

"Would you take the chance? If it was your mam or dad?" Matt was looking angry now.

In spite of what he wanted to believe, Brendan knew he wouldn't.

"Didn't you ever try telling him you weren't going to do it anymore? You didn't need to tell anyone. Just refuse to do it."

"For fuck's sake, Bren. Do you really think I didn't?"

"Matt, I didn't mean that… Shit, I'm sorry."

Matt shrugged.

"I did try a few times, if you must know. Grandad said that if I really hadn't wanted to do it, I would never have done it in the first place. Then he said that maybe it would be for the best if we did tell Mam. She would hate both of us for doing it, I'd get sent to a home and everyone knows that homes would be full of staff wanting to do the exact same thing only worse. He'd go to prison. And we'd probably give Mam cancer. And I know it's mental, but I didn't want to hurt Grandad either."

Matt had two dripping candles underneath his nose now. He sniffed into the sleeve of his denim jacket.

"And I know this sounds sick, but it was like I almost got used to it. After a while, it was like, normal. So maybe there really was something in what Grandad was saying. Maybe I didn't really hate it as much as I thought. At first, when he stroked my hair, it felt kind of nice. That's the worst bit. Maybe I really am sick and twisted."

Matt drew his hands across his face, sending tears and snot spreading everywhere.

"Jesus, Matty," it was the first time Brendan had ever taken the Lord's name in vain since he found out it was a sin. "That sucks."

The words sounded useless even to him.

"And now, Grandad's getting on a bit. Mam says she would feel easier if he gave up his council flat and moved in with us. I can't stay there anymore. I need to get out. Please, Bren. I've never told anyone about this before. You can't tell anyone, you promised."

Brendan couldn't remember making any promises. But the sight of his friend's distraught face told him this was no time to split hairs.

"Okay, I'll ask Mam. She may be okay about it."

Seeing Matt's tear-stained face he added, "It might be best if you stay up here until I get back."

Jackie was ironing; a huge mound of freshly washed clothes piled into the basket at her feet. Not a great start, ironing always put her in a bad mood. Bob was still at work.

"Hi Mam, need any help with that?"

As she raised her head, Brendan noticed the patch of grey hairs mushrooming from her left temple; the crow's feet that were deepening around her eyes. When had all that started?

"What do you want, Brendan?"

The voice was tetchy. Was he really that transparent?

"Matt's upstairs."

"I know Matt's upstairs. I let him in."

Jackie adjusted the iron's temperature.

"Matt and I were wondering; would it be okay if he stayed here for a bit?"

Jackie took a blouse from the basket, shook it, and smoothed the collar on the ironing board.

"You mean tonight? I'd rather not, to be honest. I've got all this ironing to finish, and I don't have time to be looking out the airbed and blowing it up. And your dad will be knackered when he gets in from work. Can't you leave it until the weekend to have a sleepover?"

"Well, the thing is, I'm not talking about a sleepover, Mam. Matt's had sort of, like a row with his family. He needs somewhere to crash for a few nights, and I sort of told him he could stay here."

"Did you now? Well, you had no business doing that. In the first place, I don't know whether you've noticed but things are really tough at the moment. Your dad isn't earning much doing agency work. I've had my hours at the council cut *again*. And anyone who tells you that you don't notice one extra person is lying."

She banged the iron onto the blouse collar and pounded it vigorously. Brendan hesitated. He had tried not to notice the fact that crisps and biscuits had not been restocked as frequently over the past few months; that the bottle of Liebfraumilch his parents had used to share on Saturday evenings had gone the same journey as takeaways, videos and magazines, and that his mother had started taking sandwiches to work, instead of using the canteen. But maybe, he could use that to his advantage.

"How about if he got a job and chipped in with groceries?"

"You've thought it all through, the pair of you, haven't you?"

Jackie started ironing the sleeve of her blouse. "Well, in the second place, Di and I have been friends for years. Good friends. If there's been a row in the family, there's no way I would interfere with them sorting things out between themselves. It just wouldn't be right."

"It's not really a row," Brendan was skirting dangerously close to the truth.

"Well, is it or isn't it? Either way, the upshot is still the same. You're basically asking us to interfere between the Cassidys and their son and I'm not about to do that. And another thing. Nicole is on her nursing course now. What she doesn't need is a stranger -"

"Matt isn't a stranger; she's known him for years."

"Don't be a smart aleck. What she doesn't need is a male non-family member, if you want to be pedantic, bumping into her on the landing or knocking on the door when she's in the shower. Or making a noise when she needs to get to sleep if she's on an early shift. No, and that's final. Matt will have to work things out with his parents himself."

Jackie turned the sleeve over and started pressing its other side.

"Please, Mam!"

"No. And I don't want to hear another word about it. If Matt isn't getting on with his family, it's up to them to sort it out together. I can't be doing with getting mixed up in other people's affairs, I've enough stuff of my own to worry about. Like paying the gas bill and whether you're going to pass your GCSEs, and whether the car's going to pass its MOT and whether I'll still have a job by the time the latest round of redundancies has finished. When all that's sorted, then I'll worry about other families. Until then, don't harass me anymore."

She banged the heel of the iron on the ironing board as if to emphasise her point. Her voice had drifted dangerously close to a wobble.

Brendan saw there was no point in arguing. Matt was already standing up when he got back upstairs.

"Matty, I'm really sorry."

"It's okay," Matt managed a feeble smile. "I'll work something out. Thanks for trying anyhow."

"What are you going to do?"

"Haven't made my mind up yet, but I will do. Sorry if I've got you in bother with your parents. I'd better get going now, I'll see you around."

And then he did something he had never done before. He embraced Brendan. Brendan returned the hug.

"Thanks, mate, I mean it. You've always been a great mate, Bren. I could never have talked to anyone else like that. Most people would have thought I was making things up."

Brendan doubted that was the case. He dropped the hug but clung onto the sleeve of Matt's jacket. If he couldn't stop Matt's departure, maybe he could delay it.

"Matty, I don't want you to go. Not just yet. Please stay for a bit. We could go to the police together."

Matt shook his head.

"No, my mind's made up on that one. I'm off now, I'll call you soon, yeah?"

"Matty, please don't go. Where are you even going to sleep? On a park bench or something?"

He hoped the absurdity of the suggestion would bring Matt to his senses.

"I'll go back home for now. Tell Mam and Dad I want to get a job instead of A Levels. Then when I've got one, I can move out. I've got a few weeks to find something before Grandad moves in."

Brendan doubted that it would be that simple. However, any option being preferable to his friend spending the night on the street, he kept his misgivings to himself. Matt picked up his holdall and turned towards the door.

"Matty!"

Matt turned back.

"Take care, man!"

"I'll call you."

"Come over tomorrow; we'll work something out. Look at jobs together; put together a CV, that sort of thing."

"Yeah, tomorrow."

Matt sighed. His shoulders slumped like an old man's as he left the room, gently closing the door behind. He called "goodbye," to Jackie as he went.

Later, Brendan would ask himself whether he had been worried enough. Of course, he was concerned, but his friend had assured him that he was going to be safe, at least for that night. Hadn't Matt promised that he would call the next day? They had a couple of weeks to formulate a plan. He could maybe persuade him eventually to go to the police. Maybe, even, his mam would come round once things had settled down a bit. Maybe Matt's idea of renting a place wasn't too bad? He could even put his own sixth form plans on hold, and they could get a place together. True, he was planning to take A Levels but there were such things as apprenticeships, and you got paid for them. He would text Matt first thing in the morning.

Nevertheless, Brendan shivered. An amorphous, not-quite-memory was floating, just out of his reach; an image, smudged and blurred beyond all recognition, that Brendan did not care to examine too closely.

He needed something to take his mind off things. In fact, what he really wanted was a long soak in the bath and some music to help him unwind. He brought his CD player into the bathroom, playing it at full volume until Jackie yelled at him to "Turn that sodding music down, I can't hear the telly. And no running the hot water until it reaches your chin. That stuff costs money."

He finished his bath, and went downstairs to join Jackie. They watched television together until Bob came in and Jackie put the leftover fish pie in the microwave and gave it to Bob on a tray and Bob had some funny story about delivering some gear to an address that turned out to be the studio of a band he'd heard of, and the technician there had said, "None of them can sing a bloody note, it's all bloody smoke and mirrors," and they all laughed and shared a massive bar of chocolate afterwards – a rare treat, these days – and watched some more TV and then went to bed. It was the last time Brendan laughed for a long time.

19.

The text Brendan sent to Matt as soon as he woke up, "Call as soon as you can. Then come to mine," went unanswered. Again, Brendan was not especially anxious; Matt was not an early bird. He probably wouldn't even be awake until halfway through the morning, let alone out of bed and responding to texts. To pass the time, Brendan switched on his laptop and began to research apprenticeships, guessing that a concrete plan would help them sell the idea of leaving school to their parents. He wasn't worried when he heard Jackie saying "Hi, Diane," when she answered the phone mid-morning; they often called each other for a chat. He wasn't even worried when he heard Jackie mounting the steps and tapping on his door, entering without waiting for an answer.

But then she spoke.

"Brendan!"

Her voice was soft, her eyes moist, and her face ashen. And Brendan had the strangest feeling of knowing what she was about to say before she had uttered another word. He sat motionless as Jackie cleared her throat, knelt by his chair and took his hand in both of hers.

"Brendan, pet. I don't know how to tell you this. Something horrendous has happened."

A young man had jumped backwards off a bridge the previous night. He had been hit by a passing lorry. The lorry had braked as hard as it could, sending its trailer skidding over the next lane. But the boy had timed his jump perfectly. He had been killed outright.

"It was in the local news this morning, but they didn't say the name. I had no idea. But Di just rang."

In the pocket of his jacket was a wallet with a bank card and a brand-new provisional driving licence. "The police knocked on Di and Bill's door at two in the morning. They had to go to the hospital to identify him. Can you imagine anything more horrific?"

Matt had hit the front of the lorry from behind which meant that the front of his face had emerged relatively unscathed. The hospital had bandaged Matt so that the back of his head was concealed; presumably, a vain attempt to make the ordeal less traumatic for his parents.

"Di said that Bill actually thanked the nurses. I don't know how he didn't tear the place to bits."

Jackie shook her head.

"Bill and Di didn't think anything of it when he didn't come back home last night; they assumed he'd decided to spend the night here or with one of his other mates."

What other mates? Brendan thought. He didn't *have* any other mates.

"Or maybe that he'd gone out on the town for a spot of underage drinking, or something."

What? Matt was the least likely person that Brendan knew who would go out on the town for a spot of underage drinking. Did Di and Bill even know their son?

Jackie stood up and ran her fingers through her hair.

"Poor Di and Bill, they adored that lad. How could he do that to them? And do you know what? Di didn't mention a row. She said he'd seemed completely fine when she last saw him before he came to our house. I couldn't bear to tell her that he'd asked to stay at ours, and neither will you. They've got enough to deal with. And if they ask you if he seemed upset with them, don't say a word. The last thing they need is to start blaming themselves."

She shook her head again. "How could he possibly be so selfish?"

"Don't call Matt selfish!" Brendan almost shouted.

"Well, what else would you call it? He's left his parents with a lifetime of what ifs. And did he give a thought about the driver? That could have been your dad. The poor bloke could have been killed. As it is, he'll probably be seeing that boy hitting his windscreen every time he goes to sleep for the rest of his life. He might never work again. It's a bloody miracle there wasn't a huge pile up. He might have taken a dozen people with him."

Brendan was close to tears by now. "Matt wasn't selfish, you've got no idea."

"And what's that supposed to mean? Brendan, is there something you're not telling me? About why he wanted to stay with us? Because if there's anything you know of that would stop them torturing and blaming themselves, now's the time to say it."

She looked at him intently.

"I know I said not to mention if he was upset about something at home but if he was in trouble anywhere else, that's different."

Last night, Brendan had been willing, if not happy, to keep Matt's secret. When it would have been helpful for him to have spoken up. But now, what was the point of saying anything? Matt was dead, that was never going to change. Brendan had merrily sent him on his way, naively confident that they would be able to work out a solution between the two of them.

And Matt's parents might blame themselves, might even end up splitting up because of it. And it was true that Di was close to her father. A massive family row would, as his mother put it, be the last thing they needed.

"Nothing, Mam. Just please don't call Matty selfish. He wasn't, he really, really wasn't, not in all the years I knew him."

Jackie's expression softened.

"He was my best friend! Mam!"

Without speaking, Jackie opened her arms. Brendan laid his head upon her shoulder and clung to her, weeping silently as she stroked his hair.

20.

Matt's funeral was a few days later; Brendan couldn't be sure exactly how many. What he did remember was that it was unfittingly sunny. As Bob had been offered work that he could not afford to turn down, Jackie drove herself and Brendan to the funeral. Brendan sat in his parents' car wearing his new black tie, feeling that the picture-perfect sunshine was almost mocking him; surely rain or clouds would have been more appropriate.

Well, it is August, you plank! What did you expect?

Brendan pulled at the tie; he had thought on his last day of year 11 that he wouldn't have to wear one again until he was at least twenty-one, after Uni when he started a "proper" job.

His eyes were stinging with fatigue. He hadn't managed more than a couple of hours sleep a night since hearing about Matt's death, and none at all the night before the funeral. Every time he closed his eyes, he saw Matt begging him not to tell anyone. Brendan would clench his fists and concentrate on not crying or making any noises that could draw the attention of his parents.

"How are you doing there?" Jackie's eyes flicked towards Brendan, as she changed gear.

"Okay, I guess." Brendan tried to smile, and nearly managed it.

"Are you sure? You're very quiet this morning."

"Yeah, just knackered. I've been sleeping really crap lately."

Jackie took one hand off the steering wheel and laid it on top of Brendan's.

"I can see that, love, and it's not surprising after what's happened. It's going to take some time before you're feeling yourself again, you know."

"I'll be all right." He yawned rubbed his aching eyes. "Once I get a decent night's sleep. I feel like I'm walking around inside a big fluffy marshmallow or something."

Jackie gave a small chuckle.

"Marshmallow eh? That's not a bad one actually. Yeah, I think I get what you mean."

Brendan didn't say that he was almost grateful to the marshmallow fog; it was doing a sterling job of keeping everyone and everything at a comfortably numb distance.

"I'll be fine, Mam," he said, more for his own benefit than Jackie's. He was okay, he told himself. Well, no he wasn't, but he felt able to make it through the funeral without breaking down. That was all he was bothered about for now.

"Are you ready for this, son?"

With a shock, Brendan realised that they were about to turn into the church car park, just behind the mourner's car bearing Matt's parents and grandfather. He watched as the driver opened the door and the trio climbed out of the car and stood in a small circle, heads bowed.

Jackie pulled into a parking bay, turned off the engine, gave Brendan a small, tight smile, squeezed his shoulder and they both left the car.

The thunk of the car door behind him!

Brendan jumped and shuddered.

What the fuck? He'd heard a car door close before, hadn't he?

The sudden darkening of the sky as a cloud passed over the sun!

Hang on, five minutes ago it had been so bright, he'd had to squint to see properly. When did it suddenly get so overcast?

And the sight of a black clad figure laying a hand on Matt's grandad's back and saying, "We're thinking about you all, Eric."

And the sudden, blinding certainty that something was wrong. Very wrong. A fire alarm screeching within his head; a thousand flashing neon lights beaming "Danger" behind his eyes.

Almost instantaneously, a huge weight descended onto his chest, and he felt his heart start to gallop as it had never done before.

What the fuck?

Brendan tried to breathe in, and a loud crowing noise emitted. No air had come into his lungs. He tried to breathe again and this time the crowing was even louder. His palms haemorrhaged sweat. His heart rate ramped up several more gears. Tingles shivered throughout his skull. He tried to breathe again. Still no joy. Strangely, he felt as if he needed to move, to outrun the sensation of having the life squeezed out of him. But there was no way his legs could carry him further than a couple of steps. Dizzily, he leant against the side of the car and slid to his knees, still gasping, clawing desperately at his tie, trying to loosen it, his sweaty fingers losing their grip. The weight on his chest was unbearable, his vision clouded, and his heart hammered with a terrifying intensity.

Is this what dying feels like?

Knowing your body's shutting down from within, desperately trying to fight it, paralysed by the sheer force of what's going on inside you?

Am I dying?

"Brendan, BRENDAN!"

From a thousand miles away, he could just about make out Jackie's anxious voice, the vague outline of her bending over him.

A voice:

"Is he having an asthma attack? He's white as a sheet. I've got a Ventolin inhaler in my bag, if you need it."

"He's never had asthma in his life." There was no mistaking the fear in Jackie's voice. "I think he's choking on something."

"I'll call an ambulance," said another voice.

A thousand years or a few seconds later the ambulance arrived. Brendan felt himself being eased into a chair, the plastic of an oxygen mask sealed over his face, the motion as he was rolled into the back of the ambulance, the grip of Jackie's hand on his wrist.

"I'll follow in the car," she said.

Suddenly, Brendan was attacked by an alarming surge of nausea. He scrabbled at the oxygen mask, getting it off just in time before vomiting onto the ambulance floor, narrowly missing the paramedic's boots. She gave him a paper towel to clean himself up, then lowered the oxygen mask back over his mouth and nose. Her colleague began to drive.

"Leave that on for now."

She clipped a device onto Brendan's middle finger and peered at the flashing digits.

"Your oxygen sats are fine and you're getting a bit of colour back."

She took a stethoscope out of one of the overhead lockers, deftly undid Brendan's tie, unbuttoned his shirt and listened.

"Heart rate's rapid, but not breaking any records. Feeling any better?"

Brendan nodded. His vision was clearing and although his stomach was still ominously churning, the ache in his chest was starting to ease and his breathing was coming more readily. The curdled pong of undigested sugary milk and Weetabix was beginning to permeate the ambulance.

"Sorry about the mess," he managed to whisper.

"Don't worry about it. Trust me, we've had a lot worse in here."

The paramedic hunkered down next to him, neatly sidestepping the pool of sick. Her plait hung over her shoulder like a thick rope.

"They'll want to run a few tests once you get to hospital, but my guess is that you suffered a panic attack. I can see that you were about to go into a funeral. Was it someone close to you?"

Brendan lowered the mask.

"My best friend. It was a suicide." His stomach somersaulted and he gagged.

"I think I'm going to be sick ag …"

The paramedic passed him a cardboard bowl which Brendan filled. She silently removed it and replaced it with an empty bowl then passed him some more paper towels. Brendan gave a couple of dry retches, spat out the residue and wiped his mouth.

"I think once they've checked you over and made sure there's nothing more sinister going on, the best thing you can do is get yourself home and have a nice cup of tea and a lie down. A funeral on its own is bad enough, never mind a suicide. The mental health team may want to get in touch with you, give you some techniques to cope if anything like that happens again."

"Okay."

Not wanting further conversation, Brendan lay back and closed his eyes. The paramedic busied herself swabbing the floor with antibacterial wipes; Brendan could hear snippets of the conversation between her and her colleague; a debate regarding whether Dominos or Papa John's supplied the best pizzas. Brendan ignored them and tried to doze. At the hospital, he was wheeled into a cubicle, where he

111

waited for the doctor. Jackie sat next to him, stroking his forehead; by the time the doctor gave the verdict, she looked almost as wrung out as Brendan felt.

"A panic attack? Really? The way he looked and sounded I thought he was having a heart attack or something. Are you sure?"

"We've ruled out any immediate possible causes and as far as I can tell, there's no sign of any underlying problems," said the doctor. She gave an expansive yawn.

"I hope we're not keeping you up here, mind," Jackie's voice was tart.

"Sorry, I've been on shift since 4:00 this morning. A simple panic attack is by far the most likely explanation. Probably brought on by the stress of attending his friend's funeral."

She turned to Brendan, who was sitting on the hospital bed, panic now giving way to shame.

"Would you like us to make a referral to CAMHS?"

"I'm fine, honestly," said Brendan. "I feel much better since I threw up. I just want to get home. I haven't been sleeping too well since I heard the news."

The doctor nodded approvingly.

"Understandable. I'm quite happy to let you go. Take things easily for the rest of the day and the nurse will get you some leaflets with some self-help techniques in case anything like that ever happens again, and some details of support groups you might like to contact."

Her words were strangled by a second yawn. "If need be, you can contact your GP."

"Sorry about all this," Brendan said. "It feels like I've wasted everybody's time."

Jackie shushed him: "You've got as much right to be here as anybody else, son."

A nurse appeared with a selection of leaflets. None of them contained a section, "My best friend told me he was being sexually abused and I didn't say anything and now he's committed suicide."

Jackie's knuckles were white as she gripped the steering wheel whilst driving them both home.

"Well, we're not going to forget this day in a hurry, are we?"

Brendan didn't have the energy to protest that he hadn't chosen to suffer a panic attack just before his best friend's funeral.

"I wasn't overly impressed with that snotty doctor, mind. She could have at least looked like she was taking it seriously."

Brendan tried to zone out as Jackie rattled on.

"Poor Di and Bill, as well. A bloody ambulance in the church car park and the hearse having to move to let it through! I just hope the service wasn't disrupted too badly."

Di and Bill! With everything going on, Brendan had almost forgotten Matt's parents. He opened his eyes.

"I'm sorry, Mam. I don't know what came over me."

"Stop apologising, it was hardly your fault, was it? Scared me half out of my bloody wits though, I'll say that. Make sure you have a good read of those leaflets when you get back, so you know what to do if anything like that ever happens again."

When they got back home, craving solitude, Brendan pleaded a headache – he didn't have one but hoped that God would overlook one more lie – and went upstairs to his room. Jackie popped her head round the door at frequent intervals with tea and more tea, until Brendan felt like a sloshing waterbed whenever he turned over. At one point, he heard Jackie ringing Di to apologise on his behalf.

He whispered a silent apology to Matt, hoping he would understand. And, this time, he did promise never to reveal what Matt had disclosed.

21.

Brendan spent the next morning lying on the sofa, staring at the flickering television screen, with no idea whatsoever what the programme was. It could have been a cookery show; it usually was, on a Saturday morning. Jackie, unusually, didn't have a go at him for timewasting, or make any suggestions about jobs needing doing if he would only get his bloody finger out.

He was in a half doze when he was startled by the doorbell. Jackie opened the door, and Brendan heard her say "Di, come here," and pull her friend into her embrace. The living room door opened.

"Brendan, Di's here."

Brendan blinked himself into full consciousness, sat up and ran his hands through his unkempt hair. Jackie picked up the remote and turned the television off. Di sat down on the chair opposite Brendan.

"You weren't well at Matthew's funeral yesterday. I hope you're feeling better."

Her tone belied her compassionate words; her frown was one of bitter distaste, as if Brendan's very existence was objectionable to her after her own loss.

"I'm fine. Just a bit embarrassed now. Really sorry about it. Don't know what happened. I guess I just got a bit upset."

"Didn't we all!"

"It's kind of Di to come round to check you're all right, isn't it Brendan?"

Jackie was leaning against the closed living room door. She smiled at Brendan over the back of Di's head. Brendan noticed Di's expression rearranged   itself into something less sour, as she turned to Jackie.

"Jackie, I hope you don't mind me coming round, but I needed to ask Brendan something. I have to, or I'll drive myself mad wondering."

"Of course not, Di, if Brendan's up to it, that is."

"I'm sure he'll be just fine."

"Yeah, go on, Di!" Whatever Di was going to ask, Brendan hoped to get it over with quickly.

Di shuffled forward in her seat and leant towards Brendan. He noticed, with a shock, the mark that grief had stamped on Di's formerly attractive face. Her mouth was pinched, and her dark blue eyes were narrowed.

"Brendan, Matthew came to see you the night before he…the night before it happened. I need to know. Did he say anything that gave you a clue what he was considering? Did he mention anything he was worried about, anything at all?"

Brendan swallowed and shook his head.

"Anything? Really? I thought the two of you were close. Did he not give any hint? I have to know!" Beneath the anguish in her voice, Di sounded almost angry.

Brendan shook his head again, not trusting himself to speak.

"Please, Brendan. Give me something here. You must have noticed something." Di Cassidy's voice was starting to rise now. "For God's sake, tell me. You were supposed to be his best friend. God knows he wasn't exactly overburdened with them. Are you really trying to tell me you didn't have a clue what was going through his mind? Girls, boys, exam results, jobs? What the hell did you two even talk about?"

"Nothing really," Brendan mumbled. His belly was starting to gurgle. "We just talked. Football, telly, gaming, music, the regular stuff, you know."

"Are you sure? Think, for God's sake. What sort of friend were you? All that time you spent together, and you couldn't work out that there was something off?"

Without warning, Di grabbed Brendan's arm. Her sharp fingernails dug into his flesh.

"Think!" she commanded again.

Brendan shifted backwards and looked at Jackie for help as Di glared at him.

"Di, that's enough, pet! I know you're going through Hell, but Brendan's answered you. Besides, I've already given him the third degree; Matthew didn't drop any hints about what was going on in his head."

Di dropped Brendan's arm abruptly and covered her face. Brendan stood up, excused himself and raced, clutching his abdomen, to the toilet. Di had gone by the time he returned. White faced and trembling, he lay down facing the back of the sofa and tightly hugged a cushion over his contorting belly. Jackie stroked the top of his head briefly and left him to himself.

"She'll come round. We can't be too hard on her at the moment."

Brendan pretended to doze. After a while, he felt a gentle tug on his hair. He glanced upwards to see Bob looking down at him.

"Right, young'un. Your mam's decided she wants a couple of rose beds in the lawn, which means I need to dig a few deep holes. Fancy helping me?"

Without much enthusiasm, Brendan followed Bob into the back garden and together they marked out the spaces for the rose beds. Then Bob handed him a spade and told him to start digging. Brendan soon got lost in the work; he had always suspected he was stronger than his conspicuous lack of biceps suggested, and he found the physical labour exhilarating. After the holes had been dug, Bob managed to find several more jobs which appeared to require Brendan's immediate attention, and then hinted that the grass needed cutting. As Brendan dug, pruned and pulled, he forgot about his guilt and tiredness; his arms barely registered the scratches from the roses or stings from the nettle patch he cleared.

"Right, that's about enough for now," Bob declared eventually.

"Are you kidding? It feels like we're barely started."

Bob laughed.

"Have you checked your watch lately, son?"

Brendan was surprised to see he had been working for over three hours and even more amazed to realise he actually felt a little better. Later that afternoon, Bob walked to Blockbusters and came back with a copy of "Mission Impossible" and enough pick and mix for the whole family to share – a rare event these days, given the family's watching of every penny. Nicole gave Brendan first choice from the pick and mix bag, which was an almost unheard-of event and gave him a brief hug before they went to bed, an even bigger rarity. As they watched the film that night, Brendan felt a pang of gratitude for his family and the understated support they had shown.

Matt's death was mentioned when term started again, of course. The circumstances surrounding it were referred to obliquely by staff at a special assembly. Brendan's head of house offered his condolences and asked if Brendan thought he would benefit from some counselling sessions; he sounded relieved when Brendan replied that he was fine. The other lads talked briefly about Matt, then never mentioned him again. It wasn't as if Matt had been particularly friendly with any of them in the first place, and the beginning of sixth form was a much more significant occasion. Brendan found himself left on his own a great deal; he supposed the lads were afraid of intruding on his grief, or maybe just didn't know what to say. Either way, this suited Brendan down to the ground. He was quite content to keep his head down,

116

interacting with his peers just enough so as not to arouse the attention of the staff. He managed to keep it up all through sixth form.

2019

22.

Now, Brendan lay on a different bed, looking at the ceiling. There could be no doubt that he hadn't conducted himself as well as he could have done today.

At least you didn't end up throwing up all over a paramedic this time.

That had to count as an improvement.

And Jim doesn't appear to be holding it against you.

Which was another positive.

And this time, you don't have to keep schtum. This is something you heard in public, not in the confessional.

What? The notion threw Brendan off guard. His belly resumed its squirming, and a shudder ran through him.

You might even be able to be of some help.

Brendan pressed his hands against his temples.

You saw that young woman's face. There's no way you can possibly let that pass; risk your conscience a second time. You may have given your word not to betray Matt's confidence, but you haven't made any such commitment this time around.

Without any clear strategy, or even intention, he reached for his phone. He remembered that Andrea had called the girl "Chloe Metcalfe." It was as good a thing to go on as any. He typed Chloe Metcalfe into personfinder.com. The search yielded one hundred and twenty people with that name. He would need to filter it down. He selected the "filter by town option," to search for Chloe Metcalfes living in Newcastle. This time eighteen Chloe Metcalfes appeared.

Better, but still too many for any practical purposes.

How to narrow it down? Social media maybe? He googled the name "Chloe Metcalfe," and added UK. A list of Facebook pages for Chloe Metcalfes appeared. Brendan began to click on each one. The fifth entry showed a profile picture of a smiling mixed-race girl, with a Gateshead location. Her face was long and narrow, and her hair was loose, a riot of unruly curls. While Gateshead was not technically part of Newcastle, it may as well have been, lying just over the river. Could this be the correct person? Hard to tell for definite, but her face was certainly similar to the girl from earlier. Returning to personfinder.com, he typed the name in again but altered the "filter by town" option to Gateshead. This time one result was returned: Chloe Anne Metcalfe, 1 Marriners Wharf, Gateshead. Bingo! Suddenly excited, Brendan reached for a pen and paper –

And abruptly froze, hand in mid-stretch. What the heck did he think he was doing? He knew perfectly well that his priest status forbade him not only from revealing anything he had heard in the confessional, but from taking any action that could be remotely construed as resulting from having heard anything.

Would he be tracking this girl down based on the outburst she had made, had he not already heard Neville's confession?

This was a difficult one, for which Brendan did not have a ready answer. So, he knelt by his bed and prayed for a while hoping that some clarity would be bestowed on him. Unfortunately, not for the first time, he emerged from his prayers precisely not one jot wiser. If it wasn't wildly sacrilegious, he would have sworn that God was saying to him, "You're on your own with this one, kiddo."

But then, unbidden, he thought of Matt. Matt, who had thanked him for believing him. Matt, whose secret Brendan had kept even though he might have done better to betray it immediately. Matt, who had died as a consequence of his secret. But most of all, Matt, who had thanked Brendan for believing him.

And Brendan knew there was no way he was going to refrain from visiting Chloe. Help her if he could. He didn't need to mention Neville Tanner's confession. He could persuade her to do something, anything. He could support her, properly this time. Just because he had made a twenty-four-carat arse of the situation with Matt, didn't mean he couldn't redeem himself now.

He would say Mass tomorrow morning, and then help out at the playgroup session in the church hall. He always enjoyed the playgroup; and this time, it would bring the added bonus of taking his mind off what he was about to do that afternoon.

*

Jim studied his diary over breakfast the next morning. The afternoon was taken up by the prayer session in the retirement community, and he had earmarked the following day for admin catch up. This left the morning free, which was just as well. After the events at Neville's funeral, he didn't want to leave it a full day before visiting Maureen.

Jim had to ring Maureen's doorbell twice before he received any response, other than a deep bark. He wasn't too surprised; she had seemed like she was wading through life in slow-motion yesterday. Eventually, the door edged open, laboriously, as if the effort was wringing every ounce of strength from the person behind.

"Yes, hello?"

Jim couldn't remember the last time he had heard anybody sound so weary.

He was shocked by Maureen's appearance. Her shoulders were hunched, giving her the look of having sunken into herself still further since the funeral. Her normally tidy hair was uncombed and sticking out from her head at odd angles. In contrast to the smart black suit she had worn for the funeral, she was dressed in loose-fitting leggings and a hoodie that had clearly seen better days. The skin below her chin was sagging, as if there was not enough flesh to fill it.

Most disturbing was the lack of focus in her glassy eyes. Jim wouldn't have been surprised if she had failed to recognise him.

"Maureen!"

Jim hoped that there was enough warmth in his voice to disguise how startled he was at seeing Maureen's shrunken state.

"Father McLean, it's kind of you to drop by. The breakfast dishes aren't done yet. We weren't expecting company, you see."

She gestured vaguely towards the kitchen. But at least she knew him. That had to be something, didn't it?

"That's no problem at all. It's you I've come to see, not your kitchen. I've got an appointment this afternoon, but I couldn't let the day go by without coming to see you, especially after what happened yesterday."

"Of course, come into the living room and sit down, Father."

She waved in the general direction of the room. Her hand was as fleshless as a claw. Jim eased himself into a faded velveteen armchair. Maureen collapsed onto the sofa and covered herself with a crocheted blanket. Ralph, Neville's elderly chocolate labrador, moved stiffly towards her and settled himself by her feet.

"Jean was so kind yesterday," Maureen said. "She stayed and tidied everything away and vacuumed and washed up. Very good of her when she wanted to get back to her menfolk. Neville's brother took his father back to their house, there was no way he could let him sit through that terrible scene. He was going to come over, but the poor old fellow began to get distressed and asked why Neville hadn't been to visit him that week, so of course George couldn't leave him. His own brother's wake and he never got to go."

Maureen's voice tailed off. She stared into space, open mouthed before seeming to collect herself slightly.

"Would you like a cup of tea, Father?"

"I'm fine. Please don't go to any trouble on my account."

Just then there was the sound of a key in the front door.

"That will be Andrea. She's staying with me for a few days just until… well it's meant to be just until I get used to being on my own, but I can't see that ever happening. I can't sleep. Every time I close my eyes, I see Neville's face when I found him, all black, eyes bulging. He was so handsome and strong, and it feels as if I'll never be able to remember him that way again."

Maureen put her hands over her face and started to cry. Andrea hurried into the room. She was wearing ripped jeans, and her hair was scraped greasily back from her face into a ponytail. She dropped the shopping bags she was carrying and went to comfort her mother.

"I'll tell you what," said Jim. "I'll carry this shopping into the kitchen and make us all a cup of tea." Andrea started to protest but Jim waved her away. He carried the bags into the kitchen, and put the milk, cheese and ham into the fridge. While he waited for the kettle to boil, he loaded breakfast dishes into the dishwasher, filled the sink with warm water and washing up liquid, and ran a damp dishcloth over the table and kitchen surfaces. He made three cups of tea (luckily the tea bags were on display) and put them and the sugar canister on a small tray and brought it into the living room. Both women were crying now.

"Nice cup of tea. I won't pretend that it makes everything all right, but it certainly won't make anything worse."

"Andrea, biscuits," Maureen said absently and dabbed her eyes with a tissue.

Andrea ran into the kitchen and came back with a half packet of digestives. Ralph sat up, his ears pricking as soon as he heard the word "biscuits." Jim broke a digestive in half and whistled softly, tickling Ralph behind the ears as he chomped.

"Has the coroner been in touch yet? I'm sure you'll start to feel better once that awful business is over and done with."

"Someone from the coroner's office came round on Wednesday to collect Neville's phone and laptop. I handed them over and they said they'll have them back as soon as possible. Poor man, it feels like his death is becoming public property. He would have hated that."

Maureen's eyes filled with tears again.

"I can't sleep. All I want is some rest, black out everything for a while. And yesterday, that awful scene! That horrible girl! The photograph smashing – I can still hear it! Those disgusting accusations! Neville could never have done anything like that. Neville loved children, didn't he put all that effort into running that club? Neville was a good man. The best of men! How could anybody think anything else?"

Ralph, having finished the biscuit, took up his former position by Maureen's feet. Andrea broke in.

"That bitch Chloe Metcalfe was always weird, I said that yesterday. Like Dad would ever have done anything like that. I mean, apart from anything else, what about me? I'm his daughter. If he was going to go after anyone, it would have been me."

"Andrea, don't talk like that!" Maureen admonished.

Andrea rolled her eyes and gave a loud huff before saying, "Sorry, Mam, but it has to be said. After all that shit yesterday, I'm fucking raging. I swear on my life that he never, ever did anything bad. He didn't even like me walking around in my pyjamas when I was a kid, for fuck's sake. Went ballistic when he caught me wearing a strapless top once. And that schitzo bitch, did she really think anyone was going to believe her? Nobody will, at least they'd better not. And if anyone dares say anything, I'll swing for them."

Andrea's voice was rising steadily. Jim took a large swallow of tea.

"Maureen, Andrea, that young lady seemed very disturbed. She looked as if she didn't even know what she was doing. With any luck you won't hear anymore from her."

"What does that matter now?" wept Maureen. "Neville's funeral has already been ruined. Whenever anybody talks of him now, it will be 'Do you remember what happened at Neville's funeral?' And some people will wonder if there was any truth in it, that there's no smoke without fire. His reputation has already been tarnished. It will never come back. And what about my reputation? People will say I must have known something was going on, they'll say the wife always knows."

"Oh, Maureen, that isn't so. Nobody who knew Neville would ever think he would have been capable of that. When you're feeling better, you'll realise that all that silly girl did was to make herself look ridiculous."

"I'll never feel better, never again. Losing Neville to cancer or to an accident would have been bad enough. But to lose him the way I did? And now to hear all that? I'll never feel all right again. I can't sleep, you know."

She gasped as if a thought had just occurred to her.

"Supposing people think that's why he killed himself, because he had a secret he was ashamed of? And as much as I know that can't have been the case, it brings it back to me that I'll never know why he did it. I thought we were happy, Andrea settled with Tony, no real money troubles, he had plenty of friends. He wasn't much of a one for talking, but what man is with his wife? That's what his friends from the club were for. And none of them can think of any reason either. I just want to know so I can get some rest. I can't sleep."

Maureen sniffled into her blanket for a while. Ralph rested his grizzled head upon her knee and Maureen kneaded the top of his head with her fingers.

"Would it help to pray for a while?"

"I'm sorry, Father, not just now. I can't concentrate that long. I'm sorry. I need to get some rest, I can't sleep. Later Father, later I'll pray but I can't now."

Maureen wrapped her arms around herself and began to rock. Andrea gathered her mother into her arms and Marueen wept disconsolately. Jim discreetly cast an eye towards the mantlepiece clock.

"Will you be alright, Andrea? I don't like leaving you both like this, but I've got an appointment shortly."

"We'll be fine, Father. I'm going to call the doctor, see if they can't prescribe something to knock her out."

Andrea heaved herself to her feet.

"I can see myself out, Andrea."

"No, it's fine."

Andrea cast Jim a glance, then looked towards the door.

"I just wanted to say, thank you for your support, really, Father," Andrea said when they were out of earshot. "Also, to say sorry about the way Mam was today, but please don't let that put you off from coming again. Later, she'll be talking about how kind it was of you to drop round. But Father, one thing? You can come and pray with Mam if you like. She'll probably find it comforting. But don't expect me ever, ever to pray for that Metcalfe bitch or ever to forgive her. As far as I'm concerned, she's a fucking liar and if she's crazy enough to show her face round here, I'll spit in her face again. That's all."

The grating of a loud wail erupted from the living room. Andrea gave an exaggerated sigh. Jim thought he could make out a muttered "For fuck's sake."

"I'll be there in a minute, Mam," Andrea called. "I'm just showing Father McLean out."

They walked down the front path to the gate.

"So, you knew that girl before, then?"

"Oh, I knew her all right. She was in my year at secondary school. She was a right freak then and all." The ugly twisting of Andrea's features, as she almost hissed the words, disturbed Jim as much as Maureen's grief had done. He watched as she gave the garden wall a sharp kick, let out a substantial "Rraagh" and snatched a fistful of privet, which she started shredding. No way could Jim let her go back to Maureen while she was still in that state; she'd upset her even further. He would have to let her talk it out a bit more.

"I take it you weren't friends then?"

"Are you having a laugh? It was like she hated my guts on sight. If I sat down at a lunch table she was sitting at, she would get up and walk away. Literally. If ever I was called up to read or do a maths problem on the board, she would sit there giving me this filthy look all the time as though I was the one who had done something. No idea why. I never did owt to piss her off."

"Funny!" It was all Jim could think of to say. "I mean strange funny, not ha ha funny," he clarified as Andrea's brows knitted even closer.

"And listen to this! When I turned thirteen, I had this massive party. Mam and Dad hired a room in a hotel, I invited all of Year 8, including Chloe, though God knows I didn't want her mardy face there. But Mam said if I was inviting everyone, I couldn't leave her out, so it became a choice of putting up with her or just inviting a handful of people round for a crappy party at the house. Anyway, I left the invitation on her desk, she opened it and dropped it straight in the bin like it was dirty or something. Never said a word, just dropped it in the bin and went out of the room. Mental or what?"

"Did nobody else think her behaviour was strange?"

"Plenty of people did. I think a couple of her mates asked her if she had a problem with me, but she just said that I got on her nerves. I think even the teachers picked up on that incident though, because not long after we got one of those class lectures about how we all had to get on together and even if we didn't particularly like somebody, we had to cooperate with each other and work together for the sake of the whole class. You would have to have been a complete mong not to get the point."

Jim felt vaguely thankful that he didn't know what a mong was.

"Did you know why she was acting so strangely?"

"Like I gave a fuck! She was probably jealous. With her Primark shoes and her Asda backpack. And that stupid frizzy hair that she never got straightened. Her mam probably couldn't afford it. Let the charver cow get on with it! I had plenty of my own mates."

"Did any of the teachers ever get involved?" Jim was beginning to feel the cold air snaking around his neck.

"No, it's not like we were having actual fights or anything. And then a couple of years later she got even more weird."

The cold was beginning to seep upwards through Jim's thin soles. He was dangerously near the point of regretting carrying on the conversation. He reminded himself that it was better that Andrea got all this off her chest away from Maureen.

"In what way?" he asked.

"Well, for one, she never seemed to have a boyfriend, not that I would have really known, it wasn't like we were bezzie mates or anything. But a few other girls used to say that she never even seemed to fancy any of the lads. In the end we all assumed she was a lesbian."

"She didn't get bullied because of that, did she?"

"Like I'd give her the satisfaction!"

"I just wondered if she had been bullied, this could be some sort of revenge ploy?"

"Sick revenge ploy, if you ask me. And I've barely ever seen her since the day we left school. No, she's got a screw loose, that's all. But if I ever see her again, she'd better watch out. Trying to upset me is one thing, but coming after my dad when he can't defend himself and upsetting my mam when she's vulnerable? That's proper shan, that is."

Andrea shivered.

"Getting nippy," she said.

She bent to pick up the privet leaves she had shredded, then "brred" and rubbed her arms. Her face settled into its normal expression; her anger must be burning itself out for now. Jim gave a silent prayer of thanks.

"It is, and you haven't got a coat on. Get back inside and tell your mam goodbye from me. I'll be round to see her again in a few days."

"Thanks, I'll tell her. I'm going to call the doctor now and see if they can give her something. Then with any luck she may be a bit more with it when you're next here."

"God bless, Andrea!"

Jim turned up his collar as he walked, relieved that Andrea seemed calmer. He came home to find a scribbled note from Brendan on the kitchen table.

"Got a couple of calls to make. It might be late when I get back. There's enough left-over stew for one in the fridge, and I'll get something when I come in."

Jim opened the fridge, took one look at the dogfood-like sludge and chuckled. Brendan undoubtedly had many fine qualities but competence in cooking was not one of them. And the poor lad was completely unaware of the fact.

But if Brendan was out and about, he was obviously on the mend. And after the morning he had just passed, Jim would take little wins wherever he could find them.

23.

8:30.

Two hours and a half hours before Brendan could be on the way to Gateshead; he only had Mass to prepare and say and the playgroup to attend. At least he wouldn't to face Jim before leaving for St Jude's; he had an inkling his mentor would not be wholly approving of the visit.

9:00.

Two hours to go; Mass was due to start.

Concentrate, for goodness' sake, Brendan. The sacrament is the bread and butter — or should that be wine (hah bloody hah, no danger of your jokes showing any sign of improvement) — of your role. Give it the reverence it deserves. When did this visit become such a big deal in the first place?

10:00.

Mass was done, the parishioners hadn't run out screaming. It must have been okay, then. It had certainly felt like it was going okay and one of the regulars had commented, "Lovely homily, Father Coglan. It sounded very heartfelt." Definitely okay, then.

Why are you dumping all your eggs in the basket of this visit?

Well, that one was easy to answer. He was being a good, conscientious priest, helping a soul in distress, wasn't he?

10:40

Were the toddlers normally this noisy? And messy? Spilt Ribena, biscuit crumbs, Lego everywhere! Was something wrong with the clock? An arthritic tortoise could have moved more quickly than those pointers were. Would anyone notice if he started the tidy-up process a few minutes early? Maybe they could make a game out of it. If he started collecting cups and wiping benches, some of the parents might get the hint.

The clock eventually rolled round, the toys were tidied away, the children were zipped into anoraks and buggies, and none of them appeared to have been locked in the cupboard. No distraught howls of "where's my baby?" anyway. The parents had departed, the church hall locked, checked, checked again, and it was finally time.

Now, two buses later, Brendan was following the directions on his phone to Chloe's address.

This can't be right. I must have taken a wrong turn somewhere.

Brendan was looking at a row of smart, recently built riverside apartments in one of those spanking new, inoffensive to the point of blandness estates which are marketed to young professionals just about everywhere. Nicole called them "yuppy ghettoes". Bit harsh, but Brendan had to concede that she had a point.

Behind the apartments was an expanse of grass peppered by saplings in various stages of infancy, tethered to thick wooden poles. A freshly dug lake (or was it a pond?) housed a variety of colourful waterfowl. The path snaking through the grass was still sporting a newly pebbled gleam. Even the "no ball games" signs were pristine. Brendan had no idea what the going rate for one of the dwellings was, but was willing to bet his left kidney that they would be well out of his – or his family's – price range.

He checked the directions – he had, indeed, come to the right place – and chided himself for making stereotyped assumptions based on Chloe's outburst the previous day. What had he been expecting, a squat or something?

So, Chloe may be scarred, disturbed, mentally ill or a liar but she was clearly a fully functioning, solvent adult to afford to live in an

128

address like this. Which probably meant that she had a responsible, well-paid job.

Stick that in your pipe and smoke it, Jim!

Which led Brendan to another realisation: he had completely overlooked the possibility that she would not be at home, may well be out doing her responsible, well-paid job. There were benches around the lake/pond, but Brendan didn't particularly relish the idea of sitting there for the rest of the day, like a stalker. This looked like the kind of neighbourhood which would have social media groups for residents, only too eager to point out the presence of intruders "acting suspiciously". Besides, there was a distinct chill in the air.

I didn't think that one through, did I?

Oh well! If Chloe wasn't at home he would visit the nearest newsagent, purchase a pen and paper and push a note through the door, asking if she would like to contact him. As he approached Chloe's apartment, he saw that it was on the ground floor, with its own entrance, which at least eliminated the obstacle of trying to persuade another resident to let him in. Little wins!

Taking a deep breath, still with no clear idea of what he was going to say, Brendan walked up to the door: dark grey with three small glass diamonds, it had clearly cost a packet. The muffled sound of the first few bars of "Tubular Bells" rang out at his touch.

Here goes nothing.

But after a few seconds the door opened.

"Hello?"

The voice was wary. A face appeared round the door. More than that; the right face!

"Hello, do you want something?"

A touch of impatience. Brendan couldn't blame her for not wanting to be disturbed after yesterday's events, but he was here now; what did he have to lose by at least trying?

"Chloe Metcalfe?" The words came out in an eager rush.

She shrugged. "That's me."

"I'm Father Brendan Coglan." Chloe's expression immediately hardened.

"Brendan," he quickly amended. "We weren't introduced, but I was at Neville Tanner's funeral yesterday."

Okay, so this is the part where she slams the door in my face. And I haven't the least idea what to do next.

But against his expectations, Chloe opened the door wider. In contrast to her appearance yesterday, she was wearing a smart pair of camel trousers and a cream silky blouse. Her feet were bare, but she was wearing lipstick and mascara, and her hair was secured in a tight bun. Brendan could see that the skin around her fingernails was inflamed and raw, as if it had been bitten. She looked at him suspiciously, over a pair of reading glasses and took a step towards him.

"Look, if you've come to give me grief about what went on yesterday, you can turn around right now. And if you've come to tell me I'm lying, you can fuck right off as well, pardon my French. And if either of those two bitches have sent you to lecture me you can tell them from me that –"

Brendan threw up his hands in a gesture of surrender.

"Whoa! I haven't come to give you grief and I certainly haven't come to call you a liar. And neither Maureen nor Andrea Tanner know I'm here today. Father McLean, the parish priest doesn't even know either."

"The parish priest? What does that make you then? You look just like a priest to me, and you called yourself Father. Who exactly are you?"

"I'm the curate at St Jude's. Sometimes we're called assistant priests. I was ordained a couple of months ago."

"First job, eh?"

Could Chloe be softening?

"You could say so. There's a fair bit of learning the ropes involved. But I haven't come at anyone's orders if that's what you mean. Or to lecture you. Or even to criticise you. But I would like to talk to you."

"Talk to me? Yeah, right!"

So, not softening just yet then.

"Well, listen to you would be more accurate. I got the impression that maybe you might like someone to listen to you?"

"Maybe, but there was precious little sign of anyone wanting to do that yesterday. What's changed?"

Fair question! Here goes!

"As far as I'm concerned, nothing has –"

"I bloody knew –"

Brendan overrode her.

"What I meant was that I would have said the same to you yesterday. Only I never got the chance to speak to you. I would have liked to, but I couldn't."

"What was stopping you? And don't come over all 'You were overwrought, you poor little hysterical woman,' because if you do –"

"Nothing like that. Actually, I was the one who wasn't well."

"Convenient."

"No, really. You probably didn't notice, but–"

Chloe snapped her fingers, as if a chord had just twanged in her memory.

"Hang on a minute, you were that bloke sat at the back of the altar, hyperventilating."

"Trying not to hyperventilate, actually. Was it really that obvious?"

"Yup."

"I had a panic attack. I get them occasionally. That was a particularly bad one."

Chloe gave a half smile. Some of the hostility left her face.

"You might want to rethink your vocation if two hellcats going at each other hell for leather gives you the heebie-jeebies."

"There's a bit more to it than that, but that's not important right now."

Chloe raised one eyebrow.

"What's important is you. And yesterday, you looked like you were desperate for someone to hear you. And listening is part of my job description."

Chloe said nothing. Brendan risked a joke.

"I may not have been doing this job for very long, but I know that much!"

Chloe's eyes travelled up and down. She gave a half smile.

"Well, I wasn't expecting this. Fire and brimstone maybe. Or an army of men in white coats wanting to cart me off."

"Nothing like that, I promise. I honestly only want you to have a fair hearing."

Chloe said nothing for a while, but she looked at Brendan thoughtfully. She gnawed her bottom lip and her bony fingers tapped a thready pattern against the door. Brendan tried not to look away as he was given the once-over; he concentrated on keeping his breathing level and resisting the urge to kick a loose pebble into the grass. Eventually, Chloe gave an "ugh," and rubbed her forehead.

"What the Hell," she sighed. "How much worse can things get?"

She opened the door fully.

"You look sort of normal, I guess."

"Thank you! I aim to please." *Where did that come from?*

"I mean, not a creep or anything."

"Thank you again, I think."

"I'm probably going to regret this, but since you've come all this way, it would be rude not to offer you a cup of tea. Come in, but I warn you, if I reckon you even look like you might think I'm lying, I'll throw you out of the window myself."

Chloe led Brendan down a short dark hallway. There was an open door on the right-hand side leading to a small kitchen with dark grey units. It was attractive enough, but Brendan couldn't have swung a cat in there. There were two closed doors on the left and the hallway opened onto a generously sized living room. Three walls had been painted pale grey and one teal, and the floor was grey laminate with a dark teal rug. French doors opened onto a small, neatly kept courtyard. Next to them was a light wooden table, bearing an open laptop and a half-finished glass of juice.

Chloe gestured to a black leather sofa, and Brendan sat down, luxuriating at the squishiness. The sofa in the home he shared with Jim was a much older, lumpier affair, with winged backs and several throws disguising the worn patches.

"Tea, coffee? Something stronger?"

"Tea would be great, thanks. Just milk, no sugar. I'm –"

"If you say you're sweet enough I really will have to throw you out of the window. I'll be a minute."

"Sorry, old habit I picked up from my mam. You forget how annoying it is."

Brendan heard the kettle being filled and the clink of cutlery being moved around. Chloe appeared in a few minutes with a small tray holding two mugs of tea and a plate of chocolate biscuits. Brendan took a Kitkat. Chloe removed her glasses, put them on the edge of one of the two armchairs and sat down, tucking her feet underneath her.

"You're lucky I was in. I stupidly thought I'd be okay to go to work today. I work at one of the banks in town. But I couldn't concentrate for shit, so I said I had a headache and came home at lunchtime. I've just been mooching about since."

"Did you not have anyone who could have come round? Parents? A boyfriend?"

"Mum died a few years ago. Breast cancer. Dad's not part of the picture. No boyfriend."

"No friends you could ask round?"

"What, that I could say, 'Hi, by the way I was abused for years, found out he'd carked, went to the funeral, started shouting the odds and got into a punch-up with the grieving daughter' to? There's only one friend I would possibly talk with, and she's given me radio silence for the past week. That leaves my therapist and I'm not sure I'm quite ready to spill this latest development to her. That, and I don't have an appointment for another fortnight. Wait!"

A large ginger cat had appeared at the French doors and was miaowing insistently. Chloe hurried to let it in. When she did, Brendan noticed the doors opened onto a small, neat courtyard where four earthenware pots showcased varieties of hebes. Chloe sat back down, and the cat jumped on her knee and curled up, tail tucked tightly around itself. Chloe stroked it and smiled. "Meet Cleo! Yes, I know, I'm a crazy cat lady. Fulfilling every cliché, aren't I?"

Brendan reached over the glass coffee table and tentatively scratched Cleo's head. The cat twitched her ears but did not raise her head.

"That's a compliment. I've seen her hiss at people for taking that kind of liberty before."

"Is she your only one?"

"Yes. I may fulfil the crazy cat lady cliché but that doesn't mean I'm surrounded by them. Are priests allowed pets?"

"I don't think there's a rule about it but I'm more of a dog person and I don't think I'd have enough time to look after one properly. Maybe I should ask Father McLean about a parish goldfish."

They both laughed politely. Brendan sipped at his tea. Chloe continued stroking her cat, who had by now closed her eyes and begun a rumbling purr.

"You said your boss doesn't know you're here. Will you be in trouble when you go back? Consorting with the enemy or something?"

Brendan smiled but felt his guts twist slightly. Chloe may have spoken more accurately than she realised.

"It doesn't really work like that. But he might not entirely approve of me coming over without speaking to him first."

"Were you serious before, about wanting to listen to me?"

"Completely."

"And you won't call me a liar at any point? Because if you do, I'll …"

"Throw me out of the window?"

Despite her slight build, Brendan did not doubt for a minute that Chloe would at least try to carry out her threat.

"Something like that. Anyway, since you offered to listen, I'll talk. In fact, you've no idea how desperate I am to tell the world about that C U Next Tuesday. Let's face it, I was prepared to tell all his friends and entire family yesterday. But don't even think about judging me."

Chloe's words were firm but what struck Brendan was the almost childlike, pleading expression in her eyes, betraying a fragility that believed itself to be well buried. Brendan ached when he noticed it.

"Chloe, please believe me when I say that I will listen to you, and I won't betray any confidences. I know you don't know me from Adam, but I just want to reassure you that you can trust me."

Chloe managed a smile. "And I know it's absolutely crazy, but for some reason I believe you."

"Well, this job does have its advantages, that way."

"I was going to say, despite the dog collar. More the fact that you've gone to all this trouble and risked getting into bother to hear me out. And Cleo isn't objecting to you. And if you were going to give me a lecture, I expect you'd have started by now. So where would you like me to start?"

"The beginning works for me."

"Very beginning? Like 'Chapter One I Am Born' beginning?"

"Why not?"

134

Sitting on the comfortable sofa, crunching the biscuit and feeling the back of his head being pleasantly warmed by the stream of light through the window, Brendan felt himself begin to relax. He quickly reminded himself of his reason for being there, before he could start putting his feet up and reaching for the remote control.

Chloe leaned forwards and took a deep breath.

"Okay, very beginning it is. Mum and I moved here from London when I was a baby. Like I said, Dad was never on the scene. At least, if he ever was, it wasn't a scene Mum wanted to be involved in and certainly not one she wanted me growing up around. He ended up doing a twelve-year stretch. Drug dealing. Don't know when he's due out and I don't care either. That's Mum over there. Doreen, her name was."

Chloe pointed to a photograph on the wall showing Chloe, smiling in a graduation gown. Standing with an arm around Chloe's waist was a Black lady wearing a black and white turban. She shared Chloe's fine bone structure and almond eyes, which made the puffiness of her face and legs all the more obvious. Her smile was radiant with pride.

"It's not a particularly great picture of her, but she loved it. The chemo had bloated her out by then and she'd lost most of her hair. The NHS provided her with a wig, but she couldn't stand it. Said it itched non-stop. So, she started wearing that turban."

"She looks very proud. And happy."

Chloe nodded.

"Yeah, she was. The memory of that day got me through an awful lot of bad times."

There was another pause as Chloe gazed into the middle distance.

This was a mistake. It's too much for her. I'll apologise and -

"Anyway, back to the story."

Chloe slapped her hands onto her knees, all business now.

"Don't know how Mum ever got together with my loser of a father, although by all accounts he was a bit of a looker. Charm the birds out of the trees, you know. Well, Mum was eighteen and found herself knocked up. She didn't have much support. Her own mum had died a couple of years earlier, cancer again and her dad was a bit – well a lot – of a drinker. My dad had no intention of taking any responsibility and Mum's brother gave her a massive row about cheapening herself.

She never really spoke to him again, and I can't say I blame her. Mum was still living with Grandad, not that he was much use. Then, I was born and suddenly my dad started sniffing around. Mum allowed him to visit, but he would turn up stoned, his pockets full of drugs. One time he showed up with a holdall full of skunk and wanted Mum to stash it for him. Mum told him to do one, but he got nasty. I mean really nasty; the police had to be called. After that, Mum didn't hang around. She answered an advert for call centre staff in Newcastle and moved up here. I think it was the furthest away she could get and still be in England.

"It can't have been easy for her. Young woman on her own with a baby, in a new city."

"It wasn't. I was one by then. Her mum had left her just enough money for a rental deposit on a flat and she managed to find a childminder before she started her job. It was still hard for her though. You've got to remember that these were the days before tax credits and stuff. Single mums were at the top of a lot of people's hate lists. Especially Black single mums. And Dad never coughed up so much as a tenner. Well, Mum was great at the work, obviously, and got promoted fairly quickly, but still she was working full time and bringing up a young child, all by herself. No partying or Uni or boyfriends. Clothes from charity shops. But I was always fed, the rent was always paid on time and the bills were all paid. There may not have been much left over, but we did okay."

"She sounds a proper superstar."

Chloe's smile made her look far warmer than Brendan would have believed possible a few minutes ago.

"Looking back, she was pretty special. Of course, I never appreciated that at the time. She was just my strict mum."

Chloe blinked and began to pick at the skin around her fingers. The silence was only interrupted by Cleo's deep purrs.

"I'm sure she knew that you adored her."

Chloe tore a strip of skin from her thumb and wiped the bead of blood on her trouser leg. She sighed.

"Maybe."

"No, really."

"Do you want to hear the rest of this or not?" Chloe appeared to almost bristle. Cleo's purring came to an abrupt halt.

"Of course, yeah. Sorry. I just thought -"

"It's fine. Half the time I don't even know what I'm getting at. God, I've been rambling on for ages, haven't I? Don't worry, the juicy stuff's just round the corner."

Brendan tried not to stiffen too visibly. Chloe's hands flew to her face.

"Sorry, sorry, sorry. I don't know why I said that. I guess I was getting frustrated with myself for putting off getting to the point. You're not going to take off in a huff, are you? I promise I didn't mean to be a cow."

"You don't need to apologise, honestly." Brendan smiled in what he hoped was a reassuring way and forced himself to settle back on the sofa.

Chloe muttered, "Get to the point, Chloe," and resumed her stroking of Cleo. After a minute she began to speak again.

"Like I said there wasn't much money around. The estate we were living in wasn't the best and although drugs weren't anything like the problem they were in London, they were still around. Mum was worried about what I'd come across. I was nine by now, about the age when I was wanting to go off and do stuff, you know? Mum found out about a club for 'deprived' kids, whatever that meant, held at the community centre near my primary school. We went to meet Mr Tanner who ran it and then I started."

Chloe gave a deeper sigh and buried her fingers in Cleo's lush fur. Brendan leaned forward.

"Neville Tanner seemed really nice at first. Mum thought he was a lovely man, and he was really friendly and welcoming. Made sure I was settling in properly and never got left on my own. And the club was fun, you know? The first few months were great."

Chloe's voice had started to waver. Brendan swallowed hard. Knowing the direction Chloe's story was about to take didn't make it any easier to hear.

"Are you sure you want to hear this?"

Hear about a nine-year-old kid getting her life hacked to shreds? Not sure if "want" is the right word.

But Brendan knew there was only one possible answer.

"I'll listen as long as you want me to."

Even if it turns my stomach so much that I don't get off the bog for the next week.

"Okay, don't say you weren't warned. Everything was fine until Mum's hours at work changed, and they clashed with the club night. Can you believe, I cried when Mum told me? Stupid cow."

Chloe put her mug down and squeezed her thighs so hard it must have hurt. Cleo miaowed and jumped off her knees, taking refuge under the dining table.

Listening to the story was bad enough, but hearing Chloe part blame herself? That was off the scale.

"Please don't call yourself that!"

"It's how I feel!"

Chloe almost snarled the words. Brendan thought it would be wise to shut up. 'Please don't call yourself that' had to be the most pathetic response in the history of pathetic responses anyway. When Chloe had taken a few deep breaths, she began again.

"But then Neville Tanner offered to bring me back to his house. We could have something to eat together and then he'd give me a lift back home, just after Mum got in from work. Thursday night was when his wife took his daughter to dancing class, so it would be nice for him to have some company. He made it sound like we would be doing him a favour."

Chloe paused again, as if to gather her thoughts. She looked away briefly, as if she didn't want to meet Brendan's eyes.

"This is where it starts to get difficult. You might have to bear with me. The first few times were fine. We went back to his house, I watched TV on his massive telly for a while, he made fish fingers and chips or something like that and then he dropped me off just like he said he would. It was nice, you know? Like the kind of evenings I imagined dads had with their kids all the time. And I can't believe I'm saying that now!"

Chloe gripped her slender knees again; Brendan wanted to remove her hand; stop her from hurting herself. To distract himself, he thought back to evenings with his own family, rare times when his father had got home on time for a family evening meal and Nicole had decided to take a night off from being full on psycho. Nothing times, where they had chatted about naff all then gone on to play cards or watch some shit on the television; nothing remarkable would happen, nothing of earth-shattering importance would be discussed. Just simple, humdrum stuff he had always taken for granted. It was only when Chloe began speaking again that he realised yet another silence had passed.

"Sorry, it's just this bit is really hard to talk about. I know it's crazy, I mean I offered to talk to you, didn't I?"

Chloe's hands had started to tremble, and her eyes had become shiny.

"It's absolutely fine. If you want to leave it –"

But Chloe had taken another deep breath and begun again.

"Then one night, he told me he had something to show me upstairs. I didn't think anything of it until he pushed me into his bedroom and started to undo his trousers. I moved towards the door, but he got there before me. I just froze. I wanted to scream but it wouldn't come. Then he pushed me down on the bed with one hand and pulled my trackie bottoms down with the other. I could smell that horrible eggy stink on him, that I hadn't even noticed before."

Brendan remembered the stench from the confessional. He pressed his lips together to stop himself from saying something along the lines of "You smelled it too?"

Chloe seemed not to notice that she had begun plucking strands of hair from her head.

"I don't know how long it went on. Felt like ages but it probably wasn't. And then do you know what he said?"

Brendan shook his head, compelling himself to go on listening to this horribly familiar sounding story.

"He had a wooden floor in his bedroom. There was a loose floorboard in the corner, and he lifted it up. He said if I made any noise, he would kill me and hide my body underneath. And, if I ever said anything to anyone, he knew where I lived, and he would come into my house and kill me and my mum and hide us under the floorboards. Nobody would believe a little kid from a family like mine. And if I said I didn't want to go back to the club again he would kill us because he couldn't be sure I hadn't told Mum. And I know it sounds stupid, but I totally believed him."

Chloe was twisting her hands together by then, her slim fingers looked as if they were performing contortions. Brendan felt a sudden urge to fold them in his own.

"You poor, poor thing. Did your mam ever notice something was up?"

"I made sure she didn't. As far as I was concerned, we were both going to get killed if I breathed a word to anyone. For the best part of a year, once I week I would lie back on that stinking duvet and go to my happy place while he did whatever he wanted to do. I used to recite nursery rhymes to myself, even say my times tables over and over again, just so I wouldn't have to think about what was happening."

Brendan tried desperately to think of something to say.

"How did it end?"

Chloe shrugged.

"Mum got a better job at the other side of town, so it made sense to move. I don't know – all that shit going on, and it came to an end in the most mundane way imaginable. Seems inappropriate somehow. I was terrified that he'd be furious or that he would insist on keeping to the original agreement. But, looking back, I was ten by then, getting a bit taller, and starting to develop a bit upstairs."

Brendan felt himself redden. Luckily, Chloe didn't seem to notice.

"So, I was probably getting too old for him. But the last thing he said to me ~~that final time~~ was that he knew my new address and the threat still stood."

Chloe broke off here. Her breath was starting to sound ragged, and she was twisting her hands around each other even more.

"And Mum never found out. By the time I was old enough to realise it was all bollocks, she had started to get ill. So, there was no way I could tell her anything. She got better the first time but deep down I think we both knew that it was only a matter of time before it came back again. And it did in my third year of uni. That graduation photo – Mum died six months afterwards. I'd started work at the bank by then. I think she was reassured when she died that I was okay financially. And, and that..."

140

Chloe started to cry. The cat let out a series of disapproving miaows from under the table. Chloe wiped the heels of her hands across her face, smearing mascara across her cheeks.

"Sorry, Oh shit! Back in a minute," she managed between sobs, before getting up and hurrying to the bathroom.

In the absence of any better ideas, Brendan went into the kitchen and made two fresh mugs of tea. While he was there, he opened the kitchen window and stuck his head out, hoping Chloe wouldn't mind. After what he had just heard, he was desperate for some air.

The noise of the kettle was not quite loud enough to block out the sounds of Chloe's sobs. They came in rapid succession as if fighting to get out first. After a few minutes, Brendan heard the sound of a toilet flushing and water running in the sink, then a nose being blown three times; he hoped desperately that the worst part of the story was over now.

He carried the teas into the living room. Chloe sat down, wrapping her arms around herself as she did so. She had scrubbed away the streaks of mascara; her cheeks looked puffy and sore.

"Sorry about that. My therapist told me not to be afraid of tears. Emotions want to be felt, or so she said. Trouble is, it's not her who has to shed them. Who has them come at totally random moments like in the middle of Coronation Street. Or if *Isn't She Lovely* comes on the radio because that was Mum's favourite song. And who dreads crying, because each time I burst into fucking tears might be the time I can't ever stop and I just keep going forever. And who cries until in the end I don't even know what I'm fucking crying about whether it's Mum dying, or what that creep did or because I stubbed my bastard toe that morning."

The tears had started to flow again.

"Oh fuck!" Chloe sobbed. "Fuck, fuck, fuck!"

"Are you sure you wouldn't like me to go? I could come back to hear the rest when you're feeling better."

"You might be waiting a long time."

There was a hiccupping gasp between each word. Chloe disappeared into the bathroom again. The staccato of her sobbing lasted longer this time before settling. Cleo ran out of the French doors, with an indignant mew.

Chloe came back carrying a wad of toilet roll. She sat down and buried her face in it. When she looked up, she was trembling, and her eyes were bloodshot. Brendan waited in silence; more than ever, he didn't trust himself not to say entirely the wrong thing. She looked more vulnerable than anybody he had ever seen.

"I think I'm all right now. What can I say? It just comes on like that sometimes and there's nothing I can do about it. I've had to walk out of shops and all sorts. My therapist tells me it's part of the healing process. And I thought therapy was supposed to make you feel better. Ha!"

"Chloe, please don't apologise. After everything you've been through, I think you're allowed a few crying spells."

"Bloody inconvenient though."

Chloe shook herself, as if trying to shuck off her tears and managed a half smile as she blew her nose again.

"Anyway, now I've started I kind of want to keep going. You up for listening some more?"

"Of course, if it's not going to be too much for you."

Chloe blew her nose and wiped her eyes again. She sat twisting the toilet roll around her damp fingers.

"Too much for me? That's a good one. I didn't know priests told jokes. I lived through it, remember? Where was I? Oh, Mum and I had just moved. The new place was in a nicer area, which was a bonus. I'd changed primary school, and I was just starting to be able to breathe again when secondary school starts. And who should be in my year group but Andrea Fucking Tanner. I knew she was about the same age as me, but I'd never met her because we were at different primary schools. I knew her name though and their living room was full of photos. Even then, I'd thought what a smug little bitch she looked."

"That must have been horrendous for you."

"I couldn't believe it at first. I mean, what are the odds? It wasn't even a Catholic school. It got great results though, and nothing was too good for Andrea 'look at just how fucking amazing I am' Tanner."

"How on earth did you stand it? The constant reminder?"

Brendan's old French teacher had had the disconcerting habit of looking at his pupils as if he considered them to be a life form with the intelligence level somewhere below a gnat's. The look Chloe cast him now bore an uncanny similarity.

"And what choice did I have exactly?" The sarcasm was almost dripping.

"Sorry. Again."

"It's okay. I wonder sometimes myself. I thought about asking to be moved to another form, but the teachers might have asked why. There were thirty of us in the class, so it wasn't too difficult to avoid her. I couldn't stand the cow. She was always crapping on about how wonderful her dad was and all I could think was – you're so thick, you have no idea what a perv he is. Or maybe you do and you're just going along with it. I suppose I should have felt sorry for her, or worried. He could have been doing it to her for all I knew. But I didn't think of that."

"You were a child, Chloe. And you had been through some terrible things. Of course, you weren't going to be too concerned about Andrea."

"Thanks. To be honest, the way she reckoned herself, like she was God's gift, I probably would've hated her no matter who her dad was. There was one occasion, when she turned thirteen, she invited the whole class to some fancy schmanzy disco in an actual hotel. I found an invitation on my desk and opened it without knowing who it was from. As soon as I saw that, I started to panic because I knew that he would be there. I dropped it into the nearest bin and went straight to the toilet and washed my hands where they had touched the envelope."

"I can't imagine how horrible it must have been for you. I'm honestly in awe that you coped at all."

Chloe shrugged again.

"I guess I got used to it. I was in a higher set to her for most subjects; it wasn't that difficult to avoid her most of the time. I enjoyed school apart from her being around. I joined loads of clubs; computing, drama, hockey. I was quite good at hockey."

"Did you pretend the ball was Andrea's face?"

Chloe managed to grin.

"I might not have been able to stop at pretending. No, sometimes a cigar really is just a cigar. Then, Mum discovered a lump when I was sixteen. She had surgery and radiotherapy, and she was fine for a while.

143

But when I was in my final year at Uni, we found out it had metastasized. She had a few rounds of chemo until they decided it wasn't working and she'd be better off enjoying what time she did have left. I wanted to take a year out, but Mum wouldn't hear of it. She lived to see me get a first though. And then I found out that, years ago, she'd taken out a couple of life insurance policies. Typical of her. She'd never even buy herself a new handbag or anything, but she managed to put by enough for me to afford the deposit on this place. And with my job at the bank, I didn't have any bother getting a mortgage. Anyway, here's where it gets gruesome again."

Part of Brendan hoped that Chloe would tell him she needed a break. He wasn't sure quite how much more of this story he could take. But he suspected that this could be his one chance.

Chance for what, Brendan? What is it you're actually trying to achieve here?

Which was ridiculous. He was trying to help her. That was all there was to it.

Chloe gave a deep sigh.

"To be honest I'd rather get on with it, now that I've started."

Chloe shuddered and put her arms round herself again. She rocked back and forth a couple of times and then looked up. Brendan braced himself; he couldn't imagine how her story could possibly take an even more awful turn.

"After Mum died, I was fine for a while."

"Really?" Brendan doubted that "fine" would have been an accurate description.

"Well, I say I was fine. I was going through the motions, acting like a "fine" person would act. That went on about a year. But then…"
Chloe's voice trailed off and she stood up, looking away from Brendan.

Brendan twisted in his seat to watch her as she walked over to the French doors and stood with her back to him. He waited while she appeared to study the courtyard, seemingly oblivious to his presence.

"Chloe?"

Not for the first time, Brendan wondered if he had made a mistake in coming.

"Should I –?"

But then he saw that Chloe was unbuttoning one of the cuffs to her blouse and rolling up the sleeve.

"It's easier if I show you."

"Show me what?"

"Come over here. You'll see better in the light."

Brendan walked to where Chloe stood, and she displayed an upper arm that was criss-crossed with pink lines, some thready and no longer than a finger's width, others deeper and broader.

"Chloe, did you –"

Chloe nodded as she rolled down her sleeve. She returned to her armchair and sat down. Unbelievably, she smiled, as if she was trying to reassure him. Or maybe herself.

"It started one night while I was shaving my legs, I cut myself – accidentally, that is – and the blood started flowing. On one hand it stung like Hell, but on the other hand it felt so good to be feeling something again, even if I was hopping up and down swearing."

Chloe must have noticed Brendan' frown, because she added, "It's okay; I really don't expect you to get it."

"That's not just one scar though."

"I did it again the next night, on my upper arm this time. Pretty soon I was doing it three or four times a week. I'm not going to lie – it felt glorious. Just being able to have something physically real hurting; something to legitimately cry and swear about, you've no idea what a relief that was."

Brendan tried to imagine a scenario where he would feel better for deliberately hurting himself and failed. But coping with the death of her mother as well as all the crap she'd already been through? In that situation, all bets had to be off. Let's face it, the woman was a bloody hero just for being alive.

"But one night, around eighteen months ago, I cut myself lower down, just above my ankle. I got too enthusiastic and got a vein. It was deep and long."

This time Brendan was unable to suppress a gasp.

"Don't look so horrified!"

"Sorry, please tell me –"

"I know what you're going to ask, and no, I wasn't. This was purely an accident. Well, I mean the actual act wasn't an accident, but –"

"I know what you mean," Brendan finished, and managed a smile that he was far from feeling.

"Anyway, there was blood everywhere and it took me ages to stop it. Then when I was cleaning the mess up, I saw myself in the mirror, with my scarred arms and the blood drying all over me. And this time, I'd gone deep, and it hurt. Proper knacked, not just a sharp sting. And knew that if things went any further, I was going to do serious damage and next time I might not be able to stop it. What a wake-up call, eh?"

Brendan's mouth seemed to have dried; he could barely speak.

"Please tell me you got help." He was embarrassed at how useless he sounded.

Chloe shrugged.

"I went to the GP. Took ages to get seen but she was brilliant. Referred me as a high priority for counselling."

"That must have been a relief." It certainly was to Brendan, and he hadn't even been through it.

"You'd have thought. To tell you the truth, I was worried that they would be really insistent about going to the police and I didn't think I had the energy to go through a trial and be cross-examined. Plus, it was so long ago there probably wouldn't be any evidence. But it wasn't like that at all. She really listened. It felt good to finally talk about it. Eventually, she asked if I would be interested in joining a support group. Well, at the support group I saw someone I recognised, Frances, a year younger than me."

Chloe paused again and looked up, shuffling forwards in her chair. Brendan noticed, in surprise, that her eyes were alight now.

"She'd been at the club as well. At the end I caught up with her and we got talking. Turns out she had a similar story to mine. And get this, he started on her almost as soon as I had left. Fran had a disabled brother who took up a lot of her parents' attention, and they'd enrolled her in the club to have something to do for herself once a week. Well, Tanner talked to her mum and said he could see how difficult it was for her to get Fran there, and would Fran like to come and have something to eat at his house afterwards and then he could run her home? Sound familiar? You can guess what happened next, right down to the same threats that he would kill her and her parents and bury them under the floorboards if she said anything. Oh, he also said that

146

her brother would end up in a home where he would be chained to a radiator and sitting in his own shit all day. Nice, eh? Fran had it for two years until she got a bit too old for his taste."

Chloe took a mouthful of tea and put the mug down with a grimace. "Ugh, cold!"

"So did you, you know, give any more thought to going to the police?" Brendan felt he ought to ask, despite the depressing inevitability of the outcome.

"I wanted to, by then. Now there were two of us, I thought we would be a lot more credible, and they would have to take us seriously. But Fran wasn't so keen, and I didn't want to pressure her. I knew what she'd been through."

"Have you ever come across any other kids who went to the same club?"

"No. I'd moved to the other side of town, remember. Well, then I read in the Chronicle that he'd snuffed it. I told Fran and then she went kind of quiet. I thought, give her some space, she's got a lot to process. But then I got a bit worried about her. So I called her and she never answered. I've left loads of messages since, and she hasn't got back yet. The last one I left was Wednesday night, just before the funeral."

"To tell her what you were planning to do?"

"No, just to speak to her. I wasn't planning to do anything, until the last minute. But that morning I was all over the place. I just slung some clothes on, grabbed my dossier and jumped on a bus. I was too stressed to take the car, which is just as well. I'd probably have caused an accident. Anyway, in I strut like some demented old bag from a low budget soap opera, screaming the odds, just trying to make someone listen. Ha!"

"Chloe, this may not make you feel any better at the minute, but someone did listen. I listened." *And if I hadn't been sitting having a bloody panic attack, I might have been able to do something constructive.*

"Didn't feel like it at the time. Well once that bitch had tried to rip my hair out, reality hit. I knew I was wasting my time. I even heard someone laughing as I left. I suppose it might have looked a bit funny if you weren't involved. I made it back home before I collapsed on the bed and if you think I was blubbing before, you haven't seen anything.

147

Cleo buggered off into the garden and didn't come back until nighttime."

"I'm so sorry. I wish I had come over yesterday."

"Take it from me, you really don't."

"Fair enough. So what happens now?"

"I have to see Fran first before I decide anything. Seems like, since we went through it together, we should see it through together. I don't even know if there's a point going to the police though. It's not like either of us are going to get any justice, now he's croaked. I just hope that whatever finished him off in the end was painful and frightening. And I don't care if that sounds unforgiving, so if you're going to come out with some platitude or other, forget it!"

Until this moment, it had never occurred to Brendan that Chloe might not know the manner of Neville Tanner's death.

"I think he was probably in a lot of torment at the end. He took his own life."

"What?"

Chloe paled visibly and she stared open mouthed as Brendan went on, "He hanged himself. I'm so sorry, I hadn't realised you didn't know."

Chloe cupped her hands over her mouth and her shoulders began to heave.

"Chloe, I'm sorry, I didn't mean to upset you."

But when Chloe removed her hands from her mouth, she was laughing wildly; a shrill cackle, the kind that could turn into tears with minimal provocation. Brendan stared at the floor and tried not to react – mainly because he didn't have a clue what to say or do – as Chloe threw back her head and gave a guffaw that verged on a howl. Tears, anger, he reckoned he could have probably coped with but this? Ever more uncomfortable, he tried to keep his own breathing and heart rate steady, praying that he hadn't done more harm than good.

Luckily, before Brendan could succumb to his panic attack, Chloe's hooting laughter ended as abruptly as it had begun, and she sagged in her chair.

"So, the old bastard got there first, didn't he, deprived us even of that."

She wiped her eyes and shook her head, then thumped the arm of her chair.

"AAGH! So fucking unfair!"

She thumped her chair again, harder this time.

"Why the fuck should he decide how things end? It's just so fucking unfair."

Tears were brimming in Chloe's eyes again, and she stamped her bare foot onto the floor, hard enough that it must have hurt.

"Chloe, whatever you decide, he can't hurt you now. It's over."

At least this was a safe comment.

But Chloe's eyebrows knit together, and when she jabbed a scabbed forefinger at Brendan, her hand was shaking.

"You think? You really think?" The words were spat out, like something vile tasting. "How naïve are you actually? Can't hurt me? I see him around every corner. I see his face randomly in every crowd. I smell that boiled egg smell everywhere. Once I was in a café having a coffee and a croissant and somebody cracked open an egg for their baby. I only just made it to the toilet before I threw up; the smell brought me right back to that bedroom. And the nightmares! I wake up with my hand clenched in my mouth physically stopping myself from making a noise."

Chloe brought forward her right hand. There were unmistakably crescent shaped marks along the knuckles. Brendan couldn't stop himself wincing.

"So please don't tell me he can't hurt me anymore. Because when you sit up in bed, heart hammering in your chest, knuckles bleeding and silently screaming, it really doesn't feel like you've won some monumental victory. And you haven't even seen the worst of the scars."

Chloe shuddered and put her arms round herself. She rocked back and forth a couple of times and then looked up. Brendan ached for her.

"I'm sorry. I was being facile."

Chloe waved his apology away tiredly.

"No, you weren't to know. It just kills me that he's escaped justice. And please don't talk about getting his justice from God because, guess what – I don't believe in God. Or the afterlife."

Brendan didn't think it would be wise to contradict her.

"Did you say you were having a job getting hold of your friend, Frances?"

"Yes, she isn't responding to any of my texts, which is kind of worrying me a bit. I feel like I should go round there. I've left her alone so far, but now I'm starting to get really concerned."

"Do you think she'd talk to me?"

Chloe looked surprised. Which, Brendan supposed, she had every right to.

"I want to help as much as I can. I'll listen to Frances, if she will talk to me. And then maybe we can work out a plan of action. I know I'm probably being way too presumptuous but sometimes an outside viewpoint can be helpful".

Chloe eyed him.

"I guess you really are one of the good guys, aren't you? I mean you're taking me seriously, not just paying lip service. Whether Fran will speak to you is anyone's guess, but there's only one way to find out, I suppose."

"Would you like to go round now?"

Chloe shook her head.

"I'm absolutely knackered now. I just want to have a really long bath, cook myself some beans on toast and snuggle up on the sofa with Cleo if she ever comes back, watching something crap on the telly."

Brendan hoped he didn't look too relieved. Let alone Chloe, he'd had all he could cope with for the day.

"Tomorrow, though. Fran works shifts at a cab office. I know she works Friday evenings, so Saturday morning is generally quite a good time to catch her. She lives on your side of the river but it's probably easier if you come here and we'll go in the car. I'm not going to call her before, that's not getting me anywhere. We'll just turn up."

"Could she be on holiday?"

"When you meet her, you'll see why not. What time do you reckon you can get here by?"

"Well, I'm saying early morning Mass and then I'll have to tidy up. If I get a shift on, I can probably be here for around 11:00."

"Works for me, then we'll go and see Fran."

Chloe yawned and stretched her head back against her armchair. The movement was almost feline.

"I can see how tired you are. I'll go now and see you tomorrow."

Chloe did not try to dissuade Brendan from going. She got up and walked towards the front door. Before she opened it, she took a deep breath and blurted,

"Brendan, thank you for coming and listening. It means a lot to me. And for not minding when I got ratty with you. And thank you not for overreacting about the crying as well. The amount of people who see me cry and assume I need a big hug. Even complete strangers. And I hate seeming ungrateful, but that's really the last thing I want."

Chloe unlocked the door.

"Off you go, or your boss will be getting worried. Do priests have curfews?"

"We don't. But anyway, pastoral care is meant to be one of the most important aspects of our job so even if he did say anything, I have a cast iron excuse. Night, and see you tomorrow."

Brendan yawned continuously on his way to the bus stop and was pleased when he didn't have too long to wait before he was boarding the bus. He slumped into a seat, closing his eyes as he rested his head against the grimy window. As the bus thrummed and rocked, his thoughts faded in and out in a jumble.

Pastoral care, it was what he had come into the priesthood for. It was the most important aspect of the role, wasn't it?

Yes, Brendan. But are you sure this is just about practising pastoral care?

Suddenly he was wide awake. He sat up, with a start.

Of course it is. What other reason would there be?

The sidelong glance the old lady in the opposite seat cast him, made Brendan wonder whether he had spoken aloud.

I think you know, don't you? Or maybe you just don't want to know. Or remember.

Brendan didn't stop shivering until he arrived home.

24.

Brendan was relieved to find that Jim had taken himself off to bed by the time he arrived home, sparing him a potentially awkward interrogation of the "Whereabouts exactly did you disappear to today, Brendan?" variety.

It felt like ages since he had eaten anything other than Chloe's biscuits, and he was starving. Far too hungry to make himself a "proper" meal, he opened a can of beans. He and Chloe would both be having beans on toast tonight.

That night as he knelt by his bed and prayed, he asked God, "Please help me to help Chloe and please help me not to be tempted," without being quite sure what he was worried about being tempted by.

The next morning, following a restless night, Brendan scribbled a note to Jim, and left it on the kitchen table.

"I have a few calls to make after morning Mass. I may not be in until late afternoon." Then, worrying that it looked a bit terse, he added, "Hope you're continuing to feel better." Then, worrying that it looked a bit stilted, he added a smiley face. Then, worrying that it looked a bit childish, he threw away the note and went back to the original version. Then, he muttered, "Oh, sod it!" and sent a text instead.

Brendan tried not to hurry through Mass, and made sure to spend as much time chatting to the parishioners afterwards as usual. Even so, he was glad when everyone had left, all tidying up had been done and he was on the bus to the town centre.

Chloe looked surprisingly upbeat as she opened the door. She was wearing jeans and smart leather boots and had left her hair loose so that it bobbed around her shoulders. She shrugged on a khaki parka.

"Did you sleep well last night?" asked Brendan.

"Like a log, believe it or not. Not a single dream of any kind. Feels good to be sort of progressing things, you know."

Brendan could take her point. When he had blinked himself awake from a disturbing – he couldn't remember much about it, apart from a shadowed face looming at him – dream, he had consoled himself with the fact that this might be the day when he could actually do something without compromising his vows.

Chloe led the way over to a suite of garages behind the block. She grunted as she pushed up the heavy aluminium door to reveal a smart red Clio. She clicked the door open and gestured for Brendan to get inside. The car was spotlessly clean, not a sweet wrapper or discarded parking ticket anywhere. Brendan didn't know whether to be impressed or nervous; he hoped his shoes weren't trailing any unpleasant surprises.

"This is my pride and joy," said Chloe, as she adjusted the rear-view mirror. "I got it last year, second hand. After a particularly hard therapy session I thought it was time to treat myself to the upgrade on the clapped-out old Fiesta I'd been driving since I passed my test. Mum was dead chuffed when I passed. She'd never had the opportunity to learn."

Despite her chattiness, Brendan couldn't help noticing how her knee jiggled, and the slight stiffness of her shoulders. She was clearly more nervous than she was letting on. He hoped his presence in the confinement of the small car wasn't the cause of it.

"Are you all fastened in? Do you mind the radio on?"

Chloe seemed to settle as soon as she had manoeuvred the car onto the road. She was an excellent driver. Brendan could see her confidence as she negotiated her way through the heavy Saturday morning traffic, and her glee when she put her foot down on the dual carriageway. Whatever life had thrown at her, she was clearly a remarkably strong woman. He only hoped she could see that in herself.

"So, Father. What made you want to become a priest? Can't have been the pay packet."

"I've always loved the church – no, really. I always felt completely safe and at peace there. And when I was at Uni, I was involved with a family whose son died."

"Blimey, that wasn't the answer I'd expected."

"When I was at the funeral the kid's mam was screaming at God, really going for it. But then somebody told me that that was okay. Being angry was a form of communication, but that with God's help she would get through it."

"And did she?"

"We sort of lost touch after that. But I like to believe she did. And it kind of made sense to me. I wanted to help people communicate

153

with God; build their relationship with Him. I wanted to help people, I suppose."

"Didn't you consider social work or something, if you wanted to help people?"

"The Director of Vocations asked me exactly the same question. I'm not knocking social work; it's incredibly important and those people do an amazing job, but I wanted to help people spiritually. I wanted people to feel the sense of peace I did when they came into church. You see, I'd lost somebody once who didn't have that inner peace. And I wanted more than anything to help other people find it."

"What about relationships? You had to give up an awful lot on that score."

"I was asked that as well, several times. I've never felt it to be a particular issue. The idea of sharing my life with someone, with the level of intimacy that you know everything about each other – well on some level I guess I always knew that wouldn't be for me."

"If it works for you, that's great. Were your family okay about it? Sorry about all the questions, by the way. I just find it really interesting."

"No, it's fine! After they'd got over the shock, I think they were pleased I'd found something I was passionate about. I guess I'd been a bit aimless beforehand. My sister thought I'd finally completely flipped. I think she still does although I haven't seen her in ages."

"Not close then?"

"Not especially."

Brendan wanted desperately to avoid dropping the gut-spill that he had the impression his sister couldn't stand the sight of him; he was surprised to hear himself blurting out, "I've only seen her son a few times and he's seven now. I'm not sure she completely trusts me round him. I know there's been a lot of anti-priest publicity over the years, and I'm not sure she can see past that."

Chloe shuddered but did not say anything. She leaned forwards to change the radio station, flicking to a discussion about Scottish football that Brendan highly doubted held much interest for her Neither of them spoke for a while. They crossed the Tyne and headed west. Eventually Chloe spoke up.

"Brendan, I'm not sure how to say this; but, about Fran. You seem a kind person, not judgmental at all. Please could you remember that when you meet Fran. That's all I'm going to say."

Brendan got the message: Shut up!

They couldn't have travelled more than a few miles, but the housing estate Chloe pulled into might easily have been in a different galaxy from her own neighbourhood. Several high-rise blocks of flats crumbled into various states of disrepair; every single one of the windows of one block was boarded up. Chloe passed those and turned right at a halal supermarket. Around the corner, she drove past a cab office, a paint-peeled pizza take away belching out fumes of stale grease, a pawn broker's with one boarded-up window, a building that had once been a tanning salon and now wore a shield of forbidding steel shutters, and a betting shop, which was the only establishment that bore any sign of life. The car jerked its way over several prominent speed bumps and weaved through the traffic calming measures.

"There don't appear to be many people about."

"It's Saturday and it's not even noon. I'd be surprised if anyone was up yet."

She parked the car a couple of doors down from an off licence where a large handwritten sign advertised the presence of CCTV and the fact that no cash was stored overnight.

The shops had given way to a terrace of sagging houses, all of which had bay windows and small concrete outside areas behind dilapidated garden walls, from which a variety of weeds were sprouting. Not even the most determined optimist could have dignified the areas with the word "garden." Most of the front doors were crudely painted; windows were ornamented by badly hung curtains. Overflowing wheelie bins formed a guard of honour as Brendan and Chloe walked down the street. Brendan could not see a single paving slab that had not been broken into at least three pieces.

"We're at number 106, just there. Fran's got the ground floor flat. Mind the dog crap. And the broken bottle."

The two steps up to Fran's front door were badly worn. Her curtains were shut.

"Could she still be in bed?" he asked.

"Only one way to find out."

In the absence of any doorknob or bell, Chloe rapped loudly on the door with the palm of her hand, dislodging several blue paint flakes. There was no response. Chloe opened the letter flap and peered through.

"She's in. There's a light on in the hall."

"Forgot to turn it off when she went out?"

Chloe turned round and scowled.

"On Fran's budget you don't forget to turn lights out when you go out."

He really was being a complete div today.

Chloe hammered the door with the flats of both hands.

"Frances, it's Chloe. Come on, open the door!"

She opened the letter flap again and yelled through it.

"Okay Fran, I've given you time but I'm getting worried about you now. Look, I can see you're in and I'm going to stay here and keep on knocking until you answer. I'm not going anywhere."

She banged the door again, even more forcefully.

"You're not getting rid of me. If you want the noise to stop, you're going to have to let me in."

The next door along opened and a nervous looking face swathed in a brown headscarf peeped out.

"I don't care if I wake up every neighbour in the damned street," shouted Chloe, giving the door a kick for good measure.

There was a loud creak as the window belonging to Frances' upstairs neighbour opened. A shaven headed man, naked from the waist up, leaned out and shouted,

"Can you not keep it down for fuck's sake? It's only 12:00 on a Saturday. Some of us were at work until 3:00."

"Shut up, you lazy arsehole! This is an emergency."

"There'll be an emergency all right if you don't pipe down, pet."

Brendan felt it would be a judicious moment to open his jacket and reveal his clerical collar.

"Christ almighty, a bloody vicar! What the fuck are you doing over this end? Touting for business? You'll get no takers round here, mate."

"Leave him alone, you fat bastard. Anyway, he's a priest, not a vicar. Wanker!"

"Right, that's enough. I'm coming downstairs now, and you and Father Dougal had better be gone by the time I get down, else he'll be reading you the last rites."

Luckily, the door creaked open.

25.

A woman's breathless pant: "What the fuck were you shouting to Graeme? He's all right mostly, when he's not letting his staffie crap all over the street. You'd better come in before he sets it on you."

The door opened wider. The woman pressed up against the wall for Brendan and Chloe to squeeze past. Chloe hurried through to the living room straight away. In the light of the hall, Brendan got a clearer look.

Frances was nearly as wide as she was tall. She was wearing a brown velour tracksuit, the waistband of which was hidden by a white, flabby belly. Several rolls of fat were bunched under her chin. Her eyes and cheeks seemed oddly stretched as if the wideness of her face prevented them resting in their natural position. A stale, unwashed odour spoke of a body too cumbersome to fit into a bath or shower.

So that's what Chloe was getting at. You don't let yourself fall into that state unless you're at absolute rock bottom. Or several rungs below it.

Yet Frances's waist length auburn hair, though greasy, was thick and bright. Peeking through pouches of swollen flesh, her eyes were a vivid shade of green. She didn't speak to Brendan as he followed Chloe into the living room.

Brendan sank into the two-seater sofa next to Chloe, managing not to react as his bottom almost bumped the floor. The walls had been painted lavender at some stage and the paint was flaking off in places. A patch of damp was spreading from one ceiling corner. The fact that the heavy dark crimson curtains were still hanging was a clear defiance of gravity: there could have been no more than half a dozen curtain hooks holding them in place. Thick lines of dust decorated the skirting board and grubby finger marks covered the door; Brendan just about

157

managed to suppress an urge to run a bowl of hot water, grab a cloth and get stuck in. But the carpet had obviously been recently vacuumed and the glass topped coffee table was clear of smears.

There was however, a four pack of chocolate eclairs on the table, three and a half of which had already been eaten. Next to them was a Ventolin inhaler.

Frances lumbered into the room and heaved herself into an armchair under the window. As she passed, Brendan could see the crevice of her rump cheeks. The armchair creaked as Frances eased herself down. The cuffs of her tracksuit bottoms were riding up her pale unshaven shins; the flab on her legs obliterated any ankle definition that had ever been there. Her thick, pus-coloured toenails were overhanging like claws. Brendan hastily averted his eyes; he had a nasty suspicion that Frances attracted quite a few stares – she should be spared that indignity in her own home, at least. Chloe, on the other hand, immediately turned to her.

"Frances, babe, what's going on? I've been trying to call you for ages."

Her eyes lit on the open pack of chocolate eclairs on the table.

"Oh honey, what have you been doing, you were doing so well, too."

Frances reached over and took the final half éclair in her hand, grunting with the effort of stretching. Without giving the impression of much enjoyment, she defiantly shoved the last of the éclair into her chocolate smeared mouth.

"Oh babe," wailed Chloe. "What's happened? Talk to me, darling."

Frances swallowed the éclair without chewing and burped deeply, not bothering to cover her mouth.

"That's better. Who's he?" she asked, as if noticing Brendan for the first time.

"This is Brendan. He's a priest but don't worry about that, he's all right. He's come to talk to us about Neville Tanner. But first, do you think we could open the windows? Don't you find it stuffy in here?"

"If you don't like it, you know what you can do. I can't open the curtains. You can see the way they're hanging. If I try to move them, they'll bring the whole runner down and the landlord would probably charge me to rehang it. Anyway, why would I want to look out over this dump?"

Brendan found it hard to disagree. From what he had seen of the area, there was precious little evidence of anything with a cat in Hell's chance of lifting anyone's spirits.

"And what's with the cream cakes?" Chloe turned to Brendan. "Fran's supposed to be on a diet. She's been referred for a gastric band, but they won't operate until she loses two stone. She'd got nearly a quarter of the way there."

"Tell the whole world, why don't you? Anyway, what was the point? It isn't like I was ever going to reach it. It took over three months to lose half a stone. One step forward, two steps back."

"But the point is you were taking a step forward. Well, I'm not letting you slide back again. You can come and stay at mine. I'll make sure you stick to your diet."

"No, Chloe. Leave me alone. Honestly! Always with the nagging."

"If I nag you, it's because I care about you, babes. And if you'd answered my calls, I wouldn't have needed to be braying on your doorstep waking half your neighbours up. Please, darling, tell me what's going on. I know you must have got a shock when I told you Tanner had died. But we've got some decisions to make now. Like whether we go to the police with what we know."

"And what would the point of that be? He's dead, nobody can touch him anymore. And who would believe us anyway? The neurotic self-harmer and the lump of lard?"

"Don't talk about yourself like that. Hasn't that fuckwit taken enough self-respect from you, without you joining in?"

"Self-respect! Ha! What's that when it's got its knickers on?"

"If it makes any difference," interjected Brendan, "I believed Chloe straight away."

"No offence, but who the Hell are you? And don't say you're a priest. I may be fat, that doesn't make me stupid. Or blind. And, like I've already said about nine million times, what the Hell difference will it make now anyway?"

"Okay, point taken," said Brendan. "Look, we've only just met. But Chloe came to Neville Tanner's funeral and got a bit upset."

"Understatement of the millennium," Chloe said.

"Okay, a lot upset. And I felt I had to come and hear what she had to say. And when she said you had been through something similar with Neville Tanner, I felt I had to meet you as well. All I want to do is listen to you and help if I can." He fingered his collar.

"It's kind of what I signed up for. And about the police – it's true that you won't get retribution through the court and that honestly breaks my heart. But they will listen to you. And an unexplained death always goes to the coroner."

"Unexplained death? What was unexplained about it?"

"He topped himself," Chloe broke in.

Frances' already pallid face faded to milkiness, and she brought her hand to her mouth.

"It's true," Brendan said. "Which means that they will need to examine his computer and phone. If anything is on there, it will be found."

Brendan paused. He hadn't exactly broken the code not to allude to something he had heard in the confessional, but by Christ, he had sailed close to the wind. If he hadn't paused, Frances would have interrupted him anyway.

"Are you actually as naïve as you sound? You really think that the computer he kept on show at home, the one his wife walks past and has access to, will have anything dodgy on it? Or the phone that anyone could see him using if they walked by? He'll have had another device for that sort of thing. Which is probably lying at the bottom of the Tyne as we speak."

Each sentence Frances uttered was accompanied by a hissing wheeze. She took two puffs of her inhaler.

Brendan hadn't considered that possibility. Was he going to bring anything at all of value to this particular party?

"She's got a point, you know," said Chloe. "Really all the two of us have is our own testimonies."

Brendan shifted in his seat slightly.

"Okay, you've got me there. But if the two of you make a statement, the police would probably look into it further. There may have been loads of children abused by Neville Tanner. The police might be able to get records of children who attended his club, or contact neighbours, relations, that sort of thing. And I know Neville Tanner

160

can never answer for his crimes, but wouldn't it be some consolation to know that the world finally knows what a monster he was?"

"I thought you lot were all into forgiveness, not casting the first stone, God loves us all, never mind our sins, Jesus died for us blah blah blah."

"There's a bit more to it than that."

"What do you think, Fran?" asked Chloe. "We could make a real difference to people if we came forward."

"What do I think? I think the pair of you are living in cloud cuckoo land. And I'm thinking I don't want to put myself through that again. I've spoken to you, I've spoken to my therapist. How many more times do I have to relive the crappiest period of my miserable life? Just so some other poor bastard gets to do exactly the same. And any benefit I could have gained in the first place is well and truly gone now. There's no point in anything."

"No point? Fran, you are living with what that bastard has done to you every single day of your life. You can barely walk, you're stuck in a dead-end job far below your capabilities, you're hiding away in this flat. You never go out, except to work or buy groceries. You won't even open the curtains, let a bit of sunshine in. He's taken your health, your pride, your motivation. Fran, you have more to gain from making it all public than anyone I can ever imagine."

Frances ran her fingers through her greasy hair, digging them into her scalp. Then she clutched the overhanging flap of white belly and jiggled it.

"Speaking out isn't going to shift this, is it? Tell me, Chloe, what, exactly have I got to gain?"

"Pride in yourself, for a start! Maybe you could get out of this rut."

"Do you really think I like being like this?" Frances shot back. "Do you really think I like working in that stinking cab office for legal minimum wage, putting up with Mr Abdul's sarky comments because nobody else will hire a girl my size? 'Fran, can you work an extra three hours on Friday? Or do you have an exciting evening with a handsome man lined up?' snigger, snigger!"

She turned to Brendan.

"I did A Levels, you know. Got pretty good grades as well. Then I tried to get an apprenticeship. No, no, no, everywhere I asked. Tried

161

to get a job with a few prospects. No, no, no. One place even said to me that they couldn't take a chance on employing me because I would probably need too much time off for the health problems I was bound to have. Someone else said they wouldn't be able to find a seat to support my weight. Another time I was told that I didn't fit the corporate image the company wanted to portray. And that was to work in a bloody call centre. I reckon I only got the cab office job because I was the only mug desperate enough to apply."

"Isn't health discrimination illegal?" asked Brendan.

"And who would ever do anything about it, genius? Who would want to work anywhere under those circumstances anyway? As a matter of fact, I do have asthma."

Frances held up the inhaler she had been clutching.

"I had PIP until last year, when the ATOS assessment woman decided I was perfectly well and didn't need the money anymore. With the pittance I earn, I depended on that money to pay the rent on this dump. I'm in debt now, how do I go downwards from here? And that's only the start of it. I can't even leave the house without people making some comment. I get "Tinky Winky" or "Shrek" shouted at me most times I go out. I've had stuff lobbed at my head. When I go shopping, I get people peering into my trolley. Once I'd turned my back and when I looked round again someone was rifling through my food. And you know what she said? Not sorry or anything. Just 'I would cut down on the pork pies if I were you, pet.' And then she pointed to the salad aisle as if I was too thick to see it for myself. I can't get any clothes in shops; I have to order online, and they always bump the price up for large sizes. My legs chafe when they rub together; I get rashes; my back hurts when I stand or sit too long. I know that it'll be a race of whether a heart attack, diabetes or bowel cancer gets me first. So yes, I do understand what he has done to me. And no, I really can't see a way out of it now he's gone."

"I can see you have a lot on your plate," offered Brendan.

"On my plate, ha ha! That's a good one!" Frances' laugh was completely without mirth. "You know, I don't even like the food. Sometimes I feel revolted about what I'm stuffing into my body. I don't even enjoy the taste. I just feel disgusted with myself. And uncomfortable."

Brendan opened his mouth and listened in horror to what came out. "Do you ever, you know, make yourself, you know?"

"Make myself throw up, you mean? No need to be twee about it. Do me a favour! Do I look like Princess Di to you?"

A weighty silence descended and was only broken by Brendan clearing his throat. As if the noise had prompted her into speaking, Chloe said, "You see now what Fran's got to put up with?"

"I am here, you know, Chlo. You don't need to talk about me as if I'm not."

"Well, why don't you tell Brendan about it, then?"

"Because I don't know him?"

"Neither did I until yesterday but actually, he's not a bad listener. And he's said he wants to help us."

Frances still didn't look convinced.

Brendan took a deep breath.

"Frances, is it? You're right, you don't know me. And there's no reason for you to trust me. I get that. And if you like, I can walk away right now. But please don't shut Chloe out. If you knew how worried she was about you -"

"It's true, babes," Chloe interrupted. "I've been driving myself berserk since I haven't been able to get hold of you."

Frances threw up her hands and looked at Chloe, taking in her anguished expression. Something in her face softened, and she took a deep breath.

"Okay, you win, Chloe. I'll tell him, if it means that much to you. For a start, the ATOS woman was a proper moo. Basically, said that all that was wrong with me was my weight and it was up to me to sort it out. When I got home, I went into my bedroom, took all my clothes off and stood and stared at myself in the mirror, hating every square millimetre of my horrible podgy body."

"Oh babe, and you never said!"

"I'm telling you now, aren't I?

"That must have been horrible to go through," Brendan offered. "What happened next?"

"I had an asthma review with the doctor. As soon as I walked in, he could see I was having difficulty breathing. He said I met the physical criteria for bariatric surgery. I got referred for counselling to help with losing the weight, joined the survivors' support group, met Chloe -"

"Yeah, and you were doing so well at losing the weight. What's happened, Fran?"

"Are you telling this or me? I was raring to get on with the next chapter of my life. Lose the weight, get the surgery, get some more qualifications, get a half decent job and move out of this rat hole. Only then comes the difficult bit. Actually trying to lose the weight. It's mad that a habit you hate so much can be so difficult to kick."

"You're right, though," Brendan said. "I've lost count of the times my dad's tried to give up smoking. He knows it's a waste of money and likely to shave ten years off his life, and that Mam hates it. Still hasn't managed it."

Empathy, that was at least something he could give.

Frances's raised eyebrows, however, suggested that he had fallen short of the mark.

"Believe me, if it was just a habit, it'd be a whole lot easier. There's this little voice in your head the whole time screaming at you. 'Who do you think you're kidding? You can never do this. And why should you? You don't deserve to be healthy and happy. You deserve to stay in your hole for the rest of your hopefully short, unfulfilling, pointless, miserable life.' So, in the end you do give into it. And you know why? Because deep down, no matter what you tell yourself, there's a part of you that believes it. And that's what I hate most."

"Oh honey, why did you never tell me?"

"And while we were putting together our file about Neville Tanner, the voice got louder and louder. And the weight loss got less and less. And I couldn't see that I was ever going to get to the target weight. Which is why I did what I did."

"What do you mean, babes?"

Chloe's voice was still sympathetic, but her eyes had narrowed, and she was speaking more slowly.

Frances scratched nervously at her arms with blunt fingers.

"You're going to hate me for this, but I suppose you'll have to know eventually. And I'm past caring now. I looked up online the cost of private surgery. You can get it done for around £10,000. I had it in mind that I could go to a foreign clinic that may not ask too many questions about dieting. Turkey or somewhere."

Chloe gasped.

"Baby, do you have any idea how dangerous that would be? You could have ended up somewhere totally unlicensed. They could have butchered you or killed you."

"Didn't really care to be honest. Well, I reckoned I would probably need around £15,000 to cover it. Only thing is I don't actually have £15,000. But I could think of a way to get it. I hated Neville Tanner. And I reckoned he owed me."

Frances stopped speaking and began to pick at a loose thread on the arm of her chair. Brendan saw that her face had reddened and there were tears forming at the corners of her eyes.

"Are you saying what I think you're saying?" Chloe took one of Frances's hands in hers.

When Frances spoke, her voice was barely above a whisper.

"Please don't hate me, Chloe."

26.

A few weeks earlier

Of course, Frances can remember where Neville Tanner lives. After all, she's been there plenty of times, hasn't she? Two years of being taken there week after week in that stuffy blue Qashqai that always seemed to reek of whatever cloying perfume his inane daughter was currently spraying over her delicate little princess neck. Two years of being taken back to that house and letting him amuse himself on her as he saw fit until it was time for taking her back to her parents, who would always thank him and let him know how thrilled they were that she finally had an "outlet". An "outlet" for what, they had never made clear. They probably felt guilty about the amount of funfair visits or picnics that had to be curtailed due to Evan suffering a ginormous meltdown; or for the family holidays that had never been booked because Evan's routine was far too sacred ever to be tampered with.

Little do they know what really went on at Neville Tanner's house. Hopefully, they never will.

With any luck, tonight will be the beginning of payback time. She has no qualms about what she is going to do. Absolutely none. The bastard has it coming to him. She is doing this for herself; finally doing something for herself alone, and she can't quite believe how absolutely fucking wonderful it feels. Her only concern is whether she can pull it off. From a purely practical consideration, if he's moved, that's the whole plan (she gives a derisive laugh at this; even she finds it hard to dignify this half-baked, whole crazy notion with the word "plan") scuppered. Fortunately, an almost photographically imprinted memory of the events of that period has given her the knowledge of where and when he likes to go for a pint. Of course, it would be the local CIU club. There were enough pictures of him and the other committee members around his living room, weren't there? What better place for him to flaunt the cash and lord it over everyone else while keeping up the "I may have done okay for myself but I'm as grounded as I ever was, a real man of the people, me" schtick.

She's taken the bus and metro and arrived well before he could decently be expected to have gone there. The gaff doesn't even seem to be open yet. She's lucky that the bus stop allows her a decent view of it; hanging around at a bus stop is going to arouse fewer suspicions than loitering in a street. And, let's face it, with her humongous bulk and bright ginger hair, she isn't exactly going to be inconspicuous at the best of times.

A couple of hours into her vigil, now that it's fully dark, Frances is beginning to wonder why she has even started this course of action. She has seriously underestimated how big a strain standing in a bus stop, shuffling from side to side, would place on her body. Her feet feel like hot bricks in their £5 imitation Crocs and her spine feels as if there is a steel rod running up it. She leans against the iron bus shelter, grimacing. This so-called plan is feeling flimsier by the minute. She checks her phone, a cheap Nokia that she is embarrassed about taking out in public. Well, with any justice, a good tail wind and a couple of miracles thrown in she may be able to treat herself to an upgrade before she's very much older. The time is showing as 19:45. She'll give it until 21:00, if her back lasts that long, and then give it up as a bad job. So long, farewell, illusion. It was nice almost knowing you. She flexes her knees trying to get some relief for her back. The sharp twinge reminds her of why she is doing this. If she can afford the surgery, the resulting weight loss might reverse some of the damage she has been steadily doing to herself for the past however long. She closes her eyes briefly, tries to imagine herself somewhere else for a few minutes. Barbados would be ideal, but let's face it, even the skanky end of Blackpool would be a better bet than this graffiti ridden, cigarette-end littered armpit of a bus stop.

When she opens them, it takes her a few seconds to decide whether all her Christmases have come at once or whether she has finally flipped her lid. Neville Tanner is closing his garden gate and is ambling up the street in the direction of the club. Frances is suddenly mindful that he needs to pass by the bus stop. Shit! She can't exactly hide behind a lamppost, can she? This is where the whole thing could well derail. At least she may give him enough of a subliminal reminder for him to get a nightmare or two. Heart attack would probably be too much to ask for; although the redness of his complexion, and the irascibility that seems to shine through, even from the way he limps (Frances is glad to see that his hip appears to be giving him some discomfort) seem to suggest that a stroke may not be entirely out of the question. Frances ducks her head, as he struts along as cockily as he can, given his limp. Luckily, he stays on his side of the pavement. She looks up again once she's out of his potential field of vision; suddenly energised by the break she has just caught. He disappears into the scruffy club, leaving the iron door swinging behind him.

Frances briefly wonders what she is going to do until he rolls out again, but then she has a good look at the kebab shop over the road. She can see that there are stools perched in front of a plastic bench that gives a decent enough view of whoever is entering or leaving the club. She lumbers over and orders an extra-large doner and fries and a bottle of coca cola at the greasy counter.

"Enjoy," grunts the sulky teenaged server as she wraps it.

A tendril of dark hair has come loose from Sulkypants' hairnet and Frances notices a strand falling into the kebab. Both Frances and Sulkypants ignore it. Frances carries her meal to the plastic ledge, turning her back on the servers. She heaves herself onto the stool behind the chipped formica bench, feeling certain she can hear the other server sniggering from behind the skewer as the stool wobbles dangerously beneath her. She debates whether to turn around and say something sarcastic but decides against it. Nothing she hasn't experienced before, and besides she doesn't want to draw any more attention to herself than strictly necessary. The far bigger challenge for her is to make the food last. Normally, she shovels in meals as if she's been starved for a month, but tonight she wants an excuse to linger in this dive as long as possible. God knows, coming in here in the first place is going to look suspicious enough. Why would any idiot in their right mind voluntarily risk catching e-coli, when there's bound to be some perfectly good half eaten sandwich just begging to be scratted out of the nearest litter bin?

She chews the meat as conscientiously as she can, and makes sure she bites the fries at least once, instead of gulping them down as usual. The oil dripping from the meat disgusts her. Even the wilting lettuce and mushy tomatoes appear to be drowning in a scummy pool of it. If she hadn't made a conscious decision to make the meat last, the toughness of it would have demanded a lot of chewing anyway. The pitta is on the stale side and the servers have been stingy with the salt over the chips. In fact, the only vaguely palatable element of the meal is the bottle of Coke , and even that is warmer than it should be, making Frances think that the fridge probably isn't on its proper setting. Still, as hideous as the meal is and as rank as the smell is from behind the counter, it is still a considerable feat for Frances to pace herself. As she chews, she tries to remember the last meal she actually enjoyed and comes up with a blank. She is quite literally slowly killing herself for something she doesn't even relish: Here you go, Frances. Omit the pleasant drunken euphoria and proceed directly to the killer hangover, not forgetting to pick up the crippling sense of guilt on your way out. At least junkies experience the odd high as inadequate compensation for the damage they're inflicting on themselves.

To slow herself down, she picks up a discarded Metro newspaper and pretends to read it from cover to cover, whilst keeping a watchful eye on the club. Eventually the food is finished, leaving Frances bloated and uncomfortable. She sips the cola at a snail's pace. Few customers come into the shop and those who do are all in and out within five minutes. Conversation between the servers is in short supply, interaction with any customers, besides what is strictly necessary, is virtually non-existent. Once she has finished the tepid soda, Frances helps herself to a Styrofoam cup of tea from the clanking vending machine and adds three sugar sachets. It is as revolting as the rest of the meal, but at least it helps her kill some more time.

Despite Frances's fears that she will be stuck in greasy spoon Hell for ever, she eventually sees the door to the club open and Neville Tanner limp out. From her vantage point, Frances gets a clear view of the face that is unmistakably his. He is laughing with another man and slaps him on the *shoulder. This insouciance is all it takes to galvanise Frances into action. She slides off her stool, thankful for not getting stuck, and leaves the kebab shop without saying anything. It's probably apparent that she is following someone, but so what? What's anyone going to do, call the police? I'll see your cops and raise you an environmental health inspector.*

Frances follows the two men at what she hopes is a safe distance. Neville Tanner's dodgy hip is obviously causing him some pain; he keeps rubbing it and his limp is more pronounced now. Frances is glad of this; not just because seeing him suffer makes her heart soar, although this is true, but because it means Neville Tanner's walking pace is just about manageable. Even so, she is starting to wheeze; at one point she pauses to use her inhaler. Any faster, and she would be in serious difficulties. From her distance, Frances can't quite decipher the conversation between the two men, but she is pretty sure they are talking about football. She hopes fervently that the two men will part company soon, that Neville Tanner will not invite the other man back to his for a nightcap or something. When the streets fork off two ways, her prayers are answered. With a "See you the morrow, marra," Neville Tanner claps his friend on the back and they each follow a separate road.

"Hey, Neville!"

Frances's voice comes out, clear and strong. As she speaks, she realises for the first time that she has been worried about freezing or being paralysed by sheer terror and unable to get any words out. Ironically, the thing she realises is she has an absolute lack of fear. Maybe, in order to feel afraid, you need to have something worth losing. Neville Tanner turns around and Frances studies his face. Same dark mole on the left side of his nose sprouting wire-like hairs — obviously hasn't turned cancerous at any point, pity — same scrubby moustache, same gold tooth on the right side of his mouth. If it wasn't for a few more pounds (she, of all people, can't really judge him for that but what the Hell), and a couple of extra liver spots, he would have looked exactly the same. Frances feels a thrill of contempt and a wonder how this pathetic specimen could have had such a toxic effect on her for so long. She is surprised to feel vaguely insulted, that from his expression he doesn't have a bloody clue who she is. How mad, that after everything he's put her through, what's getting her goat is the fact that after howeversomany years, he doesn't even do her the courtesy of recognising her. Time to remind him, she reckons.

"Hey Neville, remember me? Franny Harrison from your old children's club?"

She tries faux-cheerfulness, for no other reason than she hopes that will unnerve him more. Does a vague flicker of recognition float across his face? Maybe, maybe not. Better prompt him some more, then.

"You should remember me. I spent every Thursday night at your place for two years. Don't you remember the games we used to play together?"

From the way his eyes start to dart from side to side and the way he's shuffling like he's desperate to get away, but with something is preventing him, he is definitely starting to cotton on. The intoxicating power Frances is feeling grows. Neville Tanner takes a step towards her and hisses, "Look, whatever you thought happened half a lifetime ago, you're mistaken. I took you back to my house, we had something to eat and I drove you back home. That's all."

Frances's euphoria is replaced by fury that this cretin who put her through so much shit is either in, or claiming, complete denial. She hisses back, just as venomously, "But it isn't all, is it? And guess what, there's not just me who says so either. There's at least six of us."

She has no idea whether or not this is true; it's a total bluff. But the widening of Neville Tanner's eyes and the way his face drains of colour tells her that she is probably not too far off the mark. He has also started to perspire. The ecstasy Frances feels at having an advantage, however temporary, over the scumbag spurs her on.

"The police may not have listened to just one of us but six, that's a whole other ball game. And when they investigate, how many more are they going to find?"

By this point, Neville Tanner's eyes are practically bulging out of his head.

"You'd better take a breather, Neville. I can see a vein throbbing in your neck. You might get an aneurism, only I could probably never be so lucky. Thinking about what all your mates are going to say, are you? Or how your precious little poppet Andrea is going to feel when she finds out her dad's a kiddy fiddler? Or maybe she knows already. Maybe she has personal experience of how vile a pig daddy actually is."

Frances briefly worries that this comment may have been a step too far. She is gratified to see that this doesn't appear to be the case.

"Please," he whispers. "No police. Anything that happened was a misunderstanding between us. Do you really want to make a mountain out of a molehill? Knowing how much is could hurt me? An old man, whose only ever tried to live a decent, Christian life?"

Frances would swear that she can see tears forming at the corners of his eyes but doesn't want to peer too closely at him. There is a lot of rancid kebab and possibly a hefty dose of botulism swishing round her stomach; she could easily hurl without very much encouragement. His self-pity nourishes her rage.

"You know you're talking bollocks and I know you're talking bollocks," she sneers, trying to keep her voice as quiet as possible. The streets are empty, but she doesn't want to take the chance that she could be overheard.

"But cool your jets, because it just so happens that this could be your lucky day. You see, I have a proposition for you. For £15,000 I can make the whole lot disappear. No more accusations, no more anything. I'll persuade the other girls that it's not worth the stress of putting themselves through a court case. If they contact the police, I'll be lying through my teeth, saying you were always a perfect gentleman whenever we were alone together. Win win. I can get on with my life with a bit of money to help me out and you can live out your final years in the bosom of your loving family, reputation intact. Seems like a fair deal to me."

"And suppose I don't have that kind of money? Apart from me car and me house I don't exactly have any assets. Certainly, no spare cash."

The very fact that he is puling like this gives Frances hope that he is seriously considering the deal. She is also aware that the adrenaline rush she felt when she saw him is fading. She wants nothing more than to wrap things up as quickly as possible. She shrugs.

"Your problem, not mine. Depends how much you think your marriage and reputation are worth. Cash in a funeral plan or something. Sell a kidney for all I care. Don't think about it for too long though, because I'm not going to hang around forever. Just be in that shitty kebab joint a week from today with the money."

She shuts up and stares at him.

"You wouldn't."

"Wouldn't I though?"

"A week today?"

"Yup."

"And it all goes away?"

"Every bit of it."

"What about them other little slappers?"

"Like I said, I'll convince them it's not worth the aggro. And I'll let them know that if they go to the police, I'll be there to say that they're lying. If

171

you're desperate enough, you can convince anyone of anything." She pauses and adds, "You should know that."

"And I know I can trust you, how?"

"Again, not my problem. Depends whether you want to take the risk."

Neville Tanner seems to be visibly shrinking. Had she not loathed the narcissistic bully so much, Frances could possibly feel sorry for him. She dismisses the notion as quickly as it arrives.

"How about £10,000?"

"You're trying to negotiate? Seriously? In your dreams! I said £15,000 and it is what it is." She shrugs again.

He deflates like the belly of a woman who has just given birth.

"Next week then, at Donna's Kebabs?"

He could have been arranging a coffee and catch up. Frances is careful to betray no emotion.

"I'll be there until 11:00," she says. "After that, all bets are off. Take it or leave it."

Neville Tanner turns around, as abruptly as his arthritic hip will let him. Before he does though, he leans towards Frances and whispers just loud enough for her to hear, eyes as malevolent as she can remember, "And if I ever see or hear from you again afterwards, one way or another, I will swing for you, you devious little bitch. And don't think I don't know people who could bust up that ugly face some more for you."

He hobbles away, as fast as his limp will let him.

Once upon a time, Frances would have been petrified of that growled threat. Now, her elation soars as she realises she finally has the upper hand. As she waddles back to the bus stop, she feels almost dignified.

27.

Brendan glanced at Chloe and could see the tears forming at the corners at her widening eyes, hear her sharp gasp before she interrupted.

"Are you completely brain dead? Have you got any idea of how much danger you could have been putting yourself in, you dozy mare?

He could have come to meet you with a knife or got some dodgy mates to duff you up or," she spread her hands out, "well, anything, really," she added.

Frances shrugged.

"Didn't really care, did I? And by then I had convinced myself that nothing would go wrong. That I wasn't poncing about cosplaying a pound shop Carmela Soprano. Well, next week came. I went back to the kebab shop, chucking out time came and no Neville. I was gutted but not particularly surprised. Looking back, the whole shoddy blackmail thing does seem a bit of a long shot."

"You think?"

"Keep it buttoned, okay Chlo? So, I resigned myself to dieting again. And then you called me to tell me he was dead. And I felt so stupid. And guilty. Not about him dying. He deserved everything he got. But I thought I must have stressed him into a heart attack or something, without him ever paying for what he did. And I hated myself for that. So, I ordered a sixteen inch pepperoni pizza and a whole tub of cookie dough ice cream and scoffed the lot. And since then, I've only left my flat to either go to work or go to buy food."

"Oh, Fran. I just wish you'd talked to me."

"And now you're telling me that he's killed himself. So I really have ruined everything. Me and you – we'll never have our day in court. And if there's any other victims then they won't either. And his family and friends are going to keep on thinking he was Mr Bloody Wonderful right until the end of time. Well, that's it. You can tell me you hate me and never want to see me again. And you," she continued, turning to Brendan, "can tell me I'm in mortal sin and am bound to go to Hell when I die. Which doesn't actually bother me because it can't be any worse than the Hell I'm living in now."

Brendan looked at Chloe. She was sitting with her hands steepled over her mouth and nose, not speaking. But he couldn't hold back.

"Frances, I would never tell anyone they were going to Hell. Believe it or not, that's not what Christianity is all about."

"Well goody goody."

"But even if your blackmail plan had worked, you still wouldn't have had your day in court, would you? As a matter of interest, what were you even going to say to Chloe? Just do a runner, never speak to her again? Would you really have done that to your friend?"

Once aired, the words seemed harsher than Brendan would have liked. What the heck; it needed to be said, didn't it?

"I don't know, okay. Yeah, you've got me, I didn't think about Chloe or anyone. So now I'm a selfish cow, on top of everything else. Got anything else to make me feel even worse about myself?"

Frances jerked her head in Brendan's direction and scowled.

"I'm sorry. That really wasn't my intention. But, Frances, don't you think you owe it to Chloe now to speak up? It may go some way to make you feel better for what you did."

Chloe gasped and covered her mouth. Brendan felt a moment's confusion before Frances spluttered,

"What I did? I might hate myself, but I'm not going to listen to an up his own arse, platitude-quoting priest judging me. Someone who probably has spent half his life in a church getting idolised by sex-starved nuns and the rest holding the hands of sweet little old ladies as they pop their clogs and doesn't know jack shit about what I've been through. So, you can fuck right off back to Rome, or Lourdes or wherever the Hell you come from, for all I care."

"I'm sorry. I just thought that…Chloe's been so brave, putting the dossier together, getting on with her life, speaking out at the funeral…"

"Brave as opposed to me, you mean? Sat on my fat lazy arse feeling sorry for myself all day? Well, let me tell you, Sunny Jim, when you've been gobbed on in the street, when you've been so low you can barely stand to go on living, when you can feel your life just swirling down this massive great big scummy toilet like a turd you can't flush, and people don't hold back in telling you it's all your own fault, then you can come to me and tell me how I should be behaving. And then come and talk to me about somebody else being brave because right now, it's taking me everything I have just to make it from one day to the next in one piece, so do not come swanning round here talking about what's going to make me feel better."

Brendan fell silent, chastened.

"I'm going to my room. Let yourselves out when you're ready."

Fran heaved herself upright and lumbered out. Brendan couldn't help noticing a surprising amount of dignity in the way she carried herself.

Chloe lowered her hands. She looked hard at Brendan. She slowly stood up and when she did, she was shaking with fury. She pointed an accusing finger at him.

"Don't you dare put this back on Fran. Just don't!"

"I'm sorry."

Chloe was having none of it.

"Doesn't it say in the bible not to judge someone unless you've walked a mile in their shoes? People do stupid shit when they're desperate; everything else goes out of the window. So, unless you can say something supportive, keep it zipped, all right?"

"I'm sorry," Brendan repeated. He knew it sounded inadequate but couldn't think of anything more helpful. "I've been worse than useless here, haven't I?"

"You said it!"

"Do you think we should leave?"

"You can bugger off if you like but there's no way I'm leaving until I'm sure Frances is okay."

A little of the accusatory hiss had left her voice, but not much. Anger continued to emanate from her like a miasma. She sat heavily back down.

Brendan and Chloe sat in uncomfortable silence for a few minutes, staring at the floor.

When Brendan could no longer bear the guilt screwing its way into his guts, he asked, "Do you think she's all right? Should we go and check?"

"I'll go. You wait there."

Brendan resumed his perusal of Frances's threadbare carpet. He'd well and truly buggered everything up today. He'd better go, give them both some space; he'd arsed the situation up beyond redemption anyway – but basic politeness dictated that he should let Chloe know. He made his way to the bedroom.

"Chloe –"

Chloe had her arm tightly around her friend's heaving shoulders, as Frances wiped her eyes. She ignored Brendan.

"Fran, don't feel bad about it, please don't. Two days ago, I was shouting the odds at his funeral. I just wish you'd told me about how much you were struggling. But don't listen to him."

The look Chloe cast Brendan could have shrivelled plants.

"He had absolutely no right to judge you. And neither does anyone else. If you don't want to go to the police, you won't hear another word about it from me. If I decide to go later on, I can keep your name out of it. But no, I won't put any more pressure on you to do something you don't feel comfortable with."

Chloe's anger was bad enough, but Frances's distress? There was no way he could go without at least trying to put things right.

"Frances, I'm sorry. What I said came out badly and it was a terrible thing to say. I hate that Neville Tanner got away with it. I hate what he did to both of you, how he messed up your lives. And what's killing me even more is that he's walking around with his reputation intact and everyone thinking he's some kind of Mr Nice Guy, when all the while we know precisely what he was capable of. It makes me feel sick, it really does."

Brendan stopped as he saw Chloe and Frances exchange seemingly confused glances.

"One thing he really isn't doing is walking around," Chloe said.

"Sorry, don't know why I said that. Must have been a slip of the tongue. Anyway, I had absolutely no right to speak to you like that and make you feel even worse than you did already. I failed." Brendan's voice was gentle, but even he was surprised at its intensity. Chloe looked at him, eyebrows raised. But did Brendan imagine a miniscule nod from Frances? Maybe not, because the next thing she said was,

"I'll do it, Chlo."

"Oh, Fran!"

"I'll do it. Not because of him," she gave Brendan a disdainful glance, "but I'll do it for you. For both of us. And you're right," she added reluctantly, addressing Brendan.

" If it gets investigated it's a chance to set the record straight. If nothing else his wife and daughter and all his mates will know what a low life perv he was."

Frances went on, her voice rising. "Why the fuck should I feel bad? I'm not the one who did something wrong, he is. If I can get people

176

to realise what a piece of shit Neville Tanner really was, then I can at least take a bit of pride from that."

She turned to Brendan again.

"You should know something. I don't like you. You're a sanctimonious tosser. You're not someone I would ever choose to be friends with, even though I don't have a lot of choice in the friends' department. In fact, I would be perfectly happy to go through the rest of my life never clapping eyes on you again. But you're right that I owe it to Chloe."

"You know, Fran, if you do that, I reckon you're strong enough to do anything. I reckon you could shed half your body weight without going anywhere near a surgeon." Chloe gave her friend a supportive squeeze.

"I think you're both incredibly brave," said Brendan. "Are we going to the police station now?"

"We?" asked both women simultaneously.

"Well, if you want it to be just the two of you, of course I'll leave now. But I thought maybe you would appreciate having somebody waiting for you after you come out of the interview rooms or wherever they talk to you. To stand at the foot of the cross, as it were."

Who on earth, apart from pretentious tossers, says "as it were" these days?

"What do you think, Fran?" asked Chloe. "Give the sanctimonious tosser another chance?"

Frances threw her hands up.

"He can come if he really wants to, I suppose. But we'd better go now, before I have time to change my mind."

28.

As they walked to Chloe's car, two cider-necking teenagers over the road started singing "Nelly the Elephant" at the top of their voices. Chloe started towards them, but Frances pulled her back.

"Leave, them, Chlo. As far as scumbags go, they're definitely second division."

177

Brendan adjusted his jacket to reveal his clerical collar and glanced as sternly as he could at the offenders. One had the grace to look shamefaced. The other yelled "Fuck off, Jovo!"

Seconds later, Brendan flinched as he felt an empty can hit the small of his back.

"You okay?" Chloe asked him. "You nearly jumped out of your skin there."

"I'm fine. Just got a bit of a thing about anything getting me in the back," he answered.

"Round here, you can count yourself lucky they didn't aim it at your head," Frances said.

Chloe clicked open the car and Brendan slid into the front seat. Nobody spoke during the journey.

It was mid-afternoon by the time they climbed out at the police station. Without speaking, Chloe and Frances reached for each other's hands. Brendan followed behind and took a seat in the reception area as the two women walked to the front desk. From his position, he could see Chloe leaning forwards and speaking in a low voice to the desk sergeant. He saw the sergeant gesture towards the seating area saying, "If you'll just have a seat over there, I'll get someone out to see you in a few moments." He then spoke softly into the intercom.

Chloe and Frances sat on either side of Brendan. He wished he could have taken both their hands in his, but settled for smiling in what he hoped was an encouraging way at each of them in turn. With obvious difficulty, Chloe returned the smile. Frances never lifted her eyes from the floor. A few minutes later, two plain-clothsed police officers approached them. A serious faced older man – Brendan couldn't shake the image of a strict but fair head teacher – asked Frances to accompany him. A younger woman in glasses, blonde hair tied back in a ponytail, smiled and escorted Chloe to a separate room. She looked like a teacher in her first term, Brendan thought.

"I'll be here waiting for you when you come out," he said, as Chloe picked up her handbag.

"You might like to go and grab a cup of tea or something," said one of the detectives. "We'll probably be a while. There's quite a decent café over the road."

"That'll do for me; I've just remembered I'm famished. See you both in a bit, yeah?"

Brendan crossed the road to the café, where he ordered a mug of tea and an egg sandwich, selecting a seat near the front window, so he could see the station door. Just in case Chloe and Frances finished earlier than suggested. One sniff of the egg was enough to obliterate Brendan's appetite, and he abandoned the sandwich after two small bites. He slurped the tea as quickly as manners and digestion would allow, not wanting to risk being late back. Even though he doubted that he had been much help at all.

He needn't have worried. As the detective had predicted, it was a good while before Chloe sat down next to him. Her eyes were moist, but she still managed to smile at Brendan.

"That's done. Intense, but done. They'll get in contact with social services, see if they can trace any more victims. They'll also contact his family. I suppose they're worried in case he tried anything with Andrea."

"How do you feel now?"

"Tired, more than anything, believe it or not. I'm worried about Fran though. She's so fragile. I don't want her to think she had to come forward just because she felt bad about what went on earlier."

"Are you sure you're okay about that?"

"Do I wish she hadn't done it? Of course I do. Do I wish I could see that cretinous face across a courtroom and cheer as he got sent down for years? Of course I do. But will I ever judge Frances? No, never. Anyway, I don't believe for a minute she'd have let me down. Even if he had come up with the money."

"That's very understanding of you."

"You needn't sound so bloody condescending. You're not off the hook by a long chalk. It was beyond tactless of you, to lecture her about needing to make up for what she'd done. I don't worry about money. Frances does. Nobody's got any business judging her, least of all you."

"Chloe, I wish you both knew how sorry I was."

Chloe leaned her head back against the wall and yawned.

"Just leave it, eh? I can't be bothered. Anyway, it's all water under the bridge now, I suppose. And whatever happens, he's dead. Frances

179

and I are alive. And who knows, maybe that was a better punishment than the courts could deliver."

She closed her eyes and they both fell silent. Brendan began a mental count of breeze blocks along the wall. Fortunately, he didn't have to endure the strained atmosphere for long before Frances emerged from a side room, a tissue held to her eyes. Chloe jumped up and ran towards her and they embraced tightly, holding each other in silence for what seemed like a long time. Then, with their arms still around each other they walked towards Chloe's car. Before they got into the car, Chloe spoke.

"Fran, you're coming back to mine for the night. You can sleep on my couch; I've got a spare duvet. I've got some smoked salmon and salad stuff in the fridge. Then tomorrow we can swing by yours and pick a few things up. You're staying with me for a while, until we both feel a bit stronger. I'll show you some of my mum's soup recipes, they're delicious and you wouldn't believe how cheap they are."

"You know," said Frances as she stretched the seatbelt around herself, "I was sort of thinking about going back to college next year. I could fit my shifts at the cab office round it. Maybe get my teaching assistant qualifications. That's got to be better than being stuck in that grotty office until I retire, listening to Abdul and his so called 'friendly banter'."

"Absolutely," Chloe said. "You should totally go for it, Fran."

As Chloe drove, she and Frances chatted, enthusiastically making plans. It transpired that Chloe had always fancied learning yoga, if only she could find somebody to go to classes with her. She had also thought about joining a walking group – "Loads of them are free and it's a great way of getting some gentle exercise."

Frances responded with the first hint of enthusiasm Brendan had heard from her in their short acquaintance. He was only half listening. Something told him that he was getting close to outstaying his welcome here, and the prospect inexplicably saddened him.

All too soon, the car pulled up outside Chloe's block. Chloe detached her house key from an overburdened keyring and gave it to Frances.

"Here, let yourself in and put the kettle on. I'm going to drive Brendan to the bus stop," she said.

"Sure, no worries, Chlo. I'll make a start on some food. See you in a few minutes." Frances didn't acknowledge Brendan as she waddled away.

Chloe started the car again.

"I'll drive you the next couple of stops," she said. As they reached the end of the street she added, "I just want to thank you, really. For listening."

Brendan shrugged. "I didn't exactly help much, did I?"

"About that – sorry for losing my rag with you earlier. And for having another go at you in the station."

"Not a problem. It's been a tense sort of day, hasn't it?"

"Besides, who knows? Maybe you did encourage Fran, just by believing her. I guess we'll never know for sure."

Chloe's car slid into a lay-by behind a bus stop. It was getting dark by now.

"Well, I guess this is goodbye," said Brendan.

"I guess so," replied Chloe.

"We could stay in touch if you like?"

Chloe smiled at him and took a deep breath. "Brendan, it's kind of you to offer. But I reckon Frances and I should take it ourselves from here. You seem like a sweet bloke, but you don't really understand what we've been through, do you? And we don't exactly have anything in common."

Brendan was about to protest, before thinking better of it. If Chloe noticed the slight hitch of his breath, she ignored it.

"No, thanks for everything but we'll be okay from now on. And even if we're not, we'll just have to work through it together. Now, are you going to get out? I'm clamming and there's a half made smoked salmon salad waiting for me at home."

"Are you sure the two of you will be alright?"

"There's going to be some bad patches. Well, a lot of bad patches. But so long as we look after each other, then we'll get through it."

"But you've seen for yourself just how fragile Frances is." Brendan was embarrassed to realise he was almost pleading.

"She is. So am I. But she was really brave today. I think she even surprised herself. Which goes to show she's much tougher than she, or any of us, thought. But whatever happens, we've got each other. Now, go, before I push the passenger eject button."

She held out her hand and Brendan took it. They shook, and Chloe leaned forwards and kissed him on the cheek.

"Hope that isn't a mortal sin," she grinned.

"Not even approaching one," returned Brendan. And he stepped out of the car, into the darkness.

*

After a nifty three point turn it didn't take Chloe long to drive back to her flat. The door was unlocked, and she pushed it open. From out of nowhere, Cleo appeared and began weaving figures of eight through Chloe's legs.

Frances was in the kitchen where two plates of salmon salad were on their way to being ready, and two mugs containing teabags were next to the kettle. Frances made the tea and brought the mugs into the living room. She handed one to Chloe.

"Thanks, mate. I needed that. How are you doing?"

"Surprisingly okay. Actually, better than okay. I feel like a weight has been lifted off me. Maybe a physical weight will be lifted off me as well."

Chloe smiled tiredly. "It won't all happen at once. There'll be bad times as well as good. But I'll be there for every single one."

"So will I. Anyway, what about Father Dishy? Do you reckon there could be something there?"

Chloe laughed out loud. "Between me and *Brendan*? Blimey, Fran, don't get carried away. No, apart from the fact that he's an actual priest, I haven't had those sorts of vibes from him. Besides, I sort of got the impression that he's got some baggage of his own. Don't ask me how, I just got that feeling. No idea what it could be. Not sure I actually care either – we've got enough to worry about."

"Yeah, I was picking up on that too, a bit. By the time you dropped me off, he was looking quite needy. I half expected him to ask for a cuddle."

"So, yeah, nice bloke and all that. But right now, we both need to be selfish. We can't afford to get drawn into anyone else's internal dramas." She paused, suddenly desperate for reassurance. "Does that sound terrible?"

"No, like you said, he might not be quite as much of a jerk as I first thought, but he's on the other side of the wall, isn't he? There's people who've been through this sort of stuff and there's other people. And he's the other half." She drained her tea. "Come on, want to help me chop some celery? I'll have mine whole. I've heard you can burn off more calories chomping at it than you consume."

After they had eaten, Chloe washed the dishes while Frances dried.

"Chlo?" Frances asked as she smoothed out her tea towel to dry, "Do you think I was a bit hard on the guy today? I pretty much told him I hated him. I think he might have felt a bit hurt."

"Brendan? He'll be fine. And even if he's not, we've got bigger things to worry about."

29.

It was pitch black by the time Brendan arrived home. His hopes that Jim would be in bed, leaving him to have some time alone, were dashed as soon as he saw the downstairs light on.

Jim was sitting on the sofa in his pyjamas, balancing the church laptop on his knees. He looked up when he saw Brendan.

"So, the wanderer returns. What have you been up to all day?"

"Oh, nothing special. Just a few calls I had to make."

"A few dozen, more like. Have you seen the time? Are you sure one of the calls wasn't to the Red Lion?"

"No, not at all. Just a couple of people in need of support."

"And could you give it?" Jim looked at Brendan more intently now. He was his mentor, after all.

"Let's just say, I get the feeling my work there is done. Listen, Jim, I'm kind of whacked. It's been a bit of a hectic day. I think I'm going to take a mug of tea up with me and turn in early. Do you mind?"

"Not at all. You've been flying around a lot lately. Just make sure you leave some space for quiet time and prayer before you go to sleep.

Parish work is all very well but you need to leave time for spiritual development as well. Are you happy to say early morning Mass tomorrow?"

Brendan knew this was a test. Saying "no" would suggest to Father Jim that his priorities were skewed.

"Of course, Jim." *Thanks a bunch, Jim. A couple of hours sweating over a homily for tomorrow. Just how I wanted to round off the day.*

At least preparing the homily would take his mind off things.

Off what exactly? Brendan was no longer sure. He studied the bible text and tried to hammer something appropriate into shape. At one point, he looked at his watch and found that nearly two hours had passed. Which would have been fine, had the majority of the A4 sheet of paper before him not been covered with an array of doodles, and precious little writing. A withering tree was being targeted by lightning bolts from a multitude of directions. What looked like the rolls of an ocean were threatening to submerge it from below. Brendan screwed up the paper, reread the text and discovered he had strung out a page of something which may or may not have been incoherent waffle, but it would have to do all the same. Maybe it would sound better when spoken aloud. Did anyone even listen to the homily anyway?

"Bedtime!" Brendan sighed, throwing down his pen.

But first, prayers! Maybe he would be able to find some solace for whatever was troubling him. He would, of course, first need to work out exactly what was troubling him, but baby steps and all that.

So, Brendan began to pray without knowing what he was praying for. He went through the motions of his usual prayers. He prayed for Frances and Chloe. He prayed to be delivered from temptation. "But what am I feeling tempted by?" he wondered aloud, and hoped Jim hadn't heard.

Chloe was attractive, feisty, obviously strong, and had shown tremendous compassion towards Frances. Frances was blessed with a pair of alluring green eyes, and she had shown huge amounts of courage, both in speaking to the police and confessing the blackmail to Chloe, who Brendan suspected was her closest, if not only, friend.

"Is it that I'm attracted to one of them?"

He pondered for a while and had to answer "no." If he pushed himself, he had to admit that the faint revulsion he had felt regarding sexual contact since the disastrous surrendering of his virginity was still there.

"Am I jealous of their closeness?"

He had joined the priesthood knowing and accepting the deal; that although he would still have friends and be an integrated member of society, the very close friendships that other people may experience would almost certainly not be part of the picture.

Besides, he had met Chloe a total of three times and had only become acquainted with Frances that day.

For fuck's sake, are you even listening to yourself, Brendan? As a priest, you're going to have to get used to helping people through moments of crisis and then being relegated back into the periphery of their lives. Agreed?

He tried and failed to think of any arguments.

So, this experience could be a useful learning experience. Now, all you have to do is pray for the grace to take what lessons you can from the situation and file them away for future reference. And job's a good un. Right?

Then he settled to sleep, which did not come for a long time; and when it did, Brendan woke on a nearly hourly basis. He was exhausted and ratty when he woke up in the morning, needing a cold shower to drag him into alertness before mass.

The sense of peace he had always felt in church was absent. Come to think about it, it had been absent more often than not ever since Neville Tanner had spilled his putrid guts. Brendan tried to relax himself by breathing deeply and steadily, but that didn't work either. The fly crawling along the altar rail, the cough of the bus outside sputtering into life, the scratch of a nylon label against his neck all seemed disproportionally obtrusive.

Unable to stand another second of stillness and failed concentration, he went into the vestry to change. Still no better. He greeted the organist, who was practising, and only just endured the whine of the instrument reverberating through his skull without screaming for respite.

By the time Mass started, Brendan felt so jittery that he had practically zero connection with any part of the mass. His homily sounded garbled and uninspired even to his own ears and he was sure he could see a look of boredom pass over some faces. He was so disengaged that the consecration and giving of communion felt almost sacrilegious, as if he was masquerading as a priest.

Then, miraculously: the opening bars of the final hymn.

Is it over yet? Please let nobody want to hang around and chat! A handshake and a few banal comments about the weather are pretty much my limit today.

Before he left, Brendan knelt and said an act of contrition, hoping that God would accept his apology for the shoddy work he had made of the day's Mass, and suspecting that Jim may not be quite as magnanimous as God.

Then, Brendan's feet walked home, Brendan's hands made lunch and Brendan's mouth exchanged a few pleasantries with Jim over the lunch table. Brendan's fingers toyed with his ham roll and threw most of it in the bin, then Brendan's bladder urinated in the toilet.

What am I doing?

You appear to be in the middle of a post-piss hand wash.

Yeah, but how the fuck did I get here?

Well, Brendan, I guess you can say your wheel's spinning but your hamster's well and truly fucked off.

The notion made him splutter even as it passed through his head. He stifled his near hysterical giggles with a towel, before concluding that he had better try to reunite body and mind, and pronto.

He went running, sprinting further and faster than he had gone in many years. He hurtled down the old wagonways and up to the Rising Sun country park, heading up hills and leaping over ditches until there was nothing but wind stinging his face, drizzle soaking him and uneven grass making his calves and ankles throb. Random song lyrics whooshed through his brain.

"I'll sing myself to sleep a song from the darkest hours," – *chance of singing myself to sleep at the moment would be a fine thing* – "secrets I can't keep inside all the day," – *wanna bet?* – "Hope that God exists," – *Okay, we're heading into dangerous territory for a priest now.*

He ran faster and faster as if speed could drown out the incoherent cacophony screaming within his brain. Thoughts and lyrics blurred into a kaleidoscopic white noise threatening to burst through his head. He ran harder still; into the wind, relishing the resistance against him.

He was unable to pray or sleep that night, either. The next morning, it occurred to him that this could be the day that the police contacted Maureen about the allegations.

He spent the entire morning pretending to work in his cell-sized room, one ear cocked for the inevitable phone call. He was halfway downstairs when it did come, clasping a bundle of materials for the confirmation class to his chest. He froze mid-step.

"Oh, Maureen, that's terrible. And were you on your own? And nobody stayed to support you? What a disgrace. No, of course I'll come round straight away. I'll be there in a few minutes."

Maureen! That's it then! This is where the brown stuff hits the fan!

"That was Maureen, in case you didn't guess," Jim said after he had hung up.

Brendan dumped his reading material onto the table.

"She's in a terrible state. A police officer's just been round and told her that some so-called 'credible allegations' had been made against Neville. That girl from the funeral must be vindictive as well as deranged. Can you imagine?"

Brendan shook his head; even if he had wanted to speak, the dryness of his mouth would have made it impossible.

"Maureen's absolutely distraught," Jim went on. "The officer told her they would need to speak to Andrea on her own. She even had to tell them where Andrea works. Poor Maureen! Brendan, I'm going to have to go round there. I don't know what time I'll be back."

Brendan was glad that Jim left before he needed to confess his part.

You can't put it off indefinitely, though.

Suddenly, Brendan's hands trembled and his heart accelerated.

Okay, this isn't good. Try to focus on something!

He tried to recite a litany of saints. His mind went blank.

Somehow, the house was closing in on him. It was oppressively stuffy, as if the oxygen was being deliberately syphoned off. Brendan dashed wildly from room to room, opening as many windows as possible. He removed his collar, suddenly feeling it to be unbearably constrictive. His throat was beginning to close. He tried to steady his breathing, but he was too far gone for that to help at all; his throat and chest were resolutely refusing entry to any air.

Shit! He took a desperate gulping breath, even though he knew this was probably the worst thing he could do. Nothing! His chest ached; he could feel his heart pounding a tattoo; his vision was clouded by small black dots.

Surely this was more than just a panic attack. This was going to be the day that his heart raced itself to extinction. He put his hand over his chest and strained fruitlessly for another breath. Then, he was dimly aware of his legs buckling before he hit the floor.

30.

"Father McLean," was all Maureen said when she opened the door. Her expression was stony.

Jim took a good look at her. Red rimmed eyes and smudged glasses suggested recent tears, but her hair was tidy today and she at least recognised him.

"How are you feeling, Maureen? Sleeping any better? Feel free to insult me if that's a stupid question."

"Andrea couldn't get me a doctor's appointment for the next two weeks, so she got me some stuff from the chemist. I wasn't expecting it to work, to be honest, but I've been out like a light ever since I started on them. I've no idea what's in them, Andrea can probably tell you. She said I can use them to tide me over until the doctor gives me something stronger. Go and make yourself comfortable in the living room while I make some tea."

Jim noticed that the living room had been dusted and vacuumed since his last visit, and that a Radio Times was resting on the sofa, with "QI" circled on Friday's page. Jim suspected that Neville would never have countenanced a programme presented by Sandi Toksvig being shown in his home. Brexit was one of the few issues on which he and Neville had disagreed.

Maureen shuffled back in, bearing a tray with two mugs of tea and slices of carrot cake.

"Not homemade, I'm afraid. I gave up baking years ago. Neville always said my scones would have made decent cannonballs. He was so funny like that, wasn't he? But Andrea took me shopping yesterday, and I decided to treat myself. I never used to buy carrot cake; Neville hated it. I'm so sorry, Father, I'm running on again. I keep losing track of things."

"I'm not surprised, with everything you're going through. I can't imagine how terrible it must have been today."

Maureen nodded and passed a slice of cake to Jim. If possible, she had lost even more weight over the weekend. The waistband around her trousers appeared loose and she kept fiddling with it. She sat down on the sofa. The labrador jumped up and snuggled next to her.

"It was the callous way they did it, as much as anything. Just said that some 'credible allegations' had been made." Maureen made an inverted commas gesture with her fingers. "Asked if I knew anything or suspected anything. You'd have thought it was me who'd been accused. And they were very insistent that they had to talk to Andrea straight away. That made me mad. As if Neville could ever have laid a finger on that girl. He never even spanked her. I was the disciplinarian in the house, he would have let her get away with murder." Maureen's hands twisted together in her lap.

"He certainly adored her." Said Jim. "I still remember that beautiful veil she wore for her first communion. And the fresh flowers in her hair. She looked like a little princess."

"That veil came from a proper wedding shop. I was just going to get something from BHS or somewhere, but Neville wouldn't hear of it. Nothing was too good for that girl. I suppose that was only natural after all the miscarriages. He wouldn't hear of her going to the local school – had to be the best in the area, even if it meant appealing to the council. That's just the kind of man he was. Never settling for second best. But I'm rambling on again. I'm so sorry, Father."

"Not at all, Maureen. You take as long as you like. You were telling me about the police visit."

"I was, wasn't I? Where was I? Oh, that's it! I asked them if they had any more details. I mean there must be a huge mistake. If they could just give me some details, I could point out what a ludicrous misunderstanding the whole affair was. But they said they couldn't.

Said they had to protect their witnesses. Protect the lying sluts, more like."

Maureen sniffed contemptuously. In spite of the trauma she was going through, Jim was pleased to see a sign of some spark. Come to think of it, he had never seen much sign of a spark in Maureen before.

"Witnesses? You mean there was more than one?"

"Two, apparently. That was the only information they could give me. The little whore must have had an accomplice. Though God knows what satisfaction they are getting from blackening the name of a decent man once he's dead and can't defend himself. They couldn't speak out when he was alive, could they? Oh, no. Because then there would be plenty of people to put them back in their box. No, attack the dead, that's what. Cowardly scum."

She twisted a small gold cross around her neck.

"Well, nobody in their right minds will believe them anyway," Jim said. "The truth will always come out in the end."

"Let's hope so," said Maureen grimly as she took a sip of tea. She suddenly brightened. "Oh, I know what I've been meaning to show you. I was looking through some old photographs over the weekend. I found a few of you and Neville together."

She went over to the bookshelf against the wall and withdrew a battered leather photograph album, which she handed to Jim. The labrador took advantage by stretching out full length on the sofa, snuffling loudly.

"Go on, have a look."

Jim opened the album to see a picture of himself and Neville standing together in front of St Jude's after Neville had helped with the big renovation project five years ago. Here was one at the club one St Patrick's day. Here was Jim posing with the family on Andrea's confirmation day, Neville with a hand on Andrea's shoulder, Maureen only just in shot. She'd been camara shy for as long as Jim had known her. It was pleasant to reminisce about his old friend, and Jim lost any sense of time.

In fact, it seemed like only seconds had passed when they were brutally interrupted by the slamming of a car door outside, swiftly followed by a loud hammering on the front door. When Maureen left him to open the door, he was amazed to see that nearly an hour had gone by.

Andrea flew in, howling, "Mam, you'll never guess what's happened."

"I think I know, pet," replied Maureen. "They were at our house just before and they wanted your work address. They told me they would need to see you as soon as possible."

"Could you not have sent me a text, given me the heads up? You have no idea how embarrassing it was. They came up to reception, showed their ID and said they needed to speak to me right away. We had to use a spare meeting room. But the walls were all glass, so any bugger could have looked in and seen what was going on. They could have been interviewing me for murder or anything."

"I'm sure nobody thought that," said Jim.

Andrea waved him away.

"And then they told me about these stupid allegations and asked me all sorts of questions about me and Dad. I think they were almost disappointed when I said he never did anything wrong. They kept repeating that it was okay, I would be listened to, they could arrange counselling for me. And in the end, I just jumped up and screamed, 'Counselling for what, you fucking morons? I've told you at least three times, my father never went anywhere near me. Now fuck off with your poxy allegations.' They probably heard me all over the office. Fuck knows how I'm going to hold my head up in there tomorrow."

"Oh, darling," crooned Maureen.

"And what's Ralph doing on the sofa? Dad would have gone fucking apeshit!"

She grabbed the labrador's collar and pulled hard. The labrador grunted and settled further into the velveteen sofa. Andrea gave a theatrical sigh and threw up her hands.

"For fuck's sake!"

"Well, I can see you need time to talk things over together," said Jim, suddenly relieved to be leaving. "I'll see myself out and we'll catch up again shortly. God bless both of you."

Without even pausing to brush carrot cake crumbs from his sweater, he headed for the front door.

*

When Maureen was sure she had heard the door click shut, she made Andrea a mug of tea with extra sugar, the way she liked it. Then she sat next to Andrea and took her French manicured hand in both of her papery ones. Looking down, Maureen noticed how loose her wedding ring was around her finger.

"Andrea pet, it's just the two of us now. No police, no Jim, no Chloe whateverhernamewas, nobody else. Just us. Andrea, I need to know if you're absolutely sure that your father never did anything to you. If there is, please tell me now while it's just the two of us. It can stay between ourselves – not even Tony will need to know. But I do. So, if there is anything at all in it, please say now."

Andrea looked horrified. She withdrew her hand from Maureen's grasp and inched backwards along the sofa, finally dislodging the labrador.

"Not you too, Mam. He never did anything like that. Never ever. Please, don't ever make me answer that question ever again."

And she shrank away as Maureen tried to hug her.

31.

"What in the name of all that's holy are you doing?"

Brendan winced as Jim's voice cut through the silence.

He had come round from – well, he supposed it was a faint – disoriented and with the beginnings of a substantial bruise sprouting from his right temple, but at least able to breathe more regularly. Shakily, he had dragged himself over to the sink and poured a glass of water. Then he had looked into the freezer, pulled out a bag of peas and held it against the rapidly swelling, already painful lump, mumbling "Ow, ow, ow," as he staggered towards the sofa. He had only taken a few steps when his abdomen spasmed and he rushed to the lavatory. Several sprays of air freshener later, he kicked off his shoes and stretched out on the lumpy sofa, closing his eyes, reflecting that with any luck there would be a special place in Hell for anybody who knowingly laid a hard wood floor. He was still in that position when Jim let himself in.

"Why's every window in the place wide open?" Jim went on. "It's like an ice box in here."

Brendan sat up, still pressing the frozen peas to his bruise.

"What's with the bag of peas? For goodness' sake, you're as white as a ghost. Did you disturb a burglar or something?"

Brendan's heart lifted marginally. If Jim was offering sympathy, his reactions to Brendan's revelations may be tempered slightly.

"No burglar, Jim. Just another panic attack. I didn't manage to clamp down on this one, though, and ended up hitting the deck."

"You mean you passed out? Brendan, we can't ignore this, you're going to need to get some help. Whatever your previous self-management techniques were, it's pretty obvious they're not as effective anymore."

"I will do, we'll talk tomorrow, I promise. I just want to take things a bit easily now. Ouch!" Brendan yelped; the effort of sitting up had intensified the pain in his skull to an excruciating level and sent waves of nausea rippling through him. He adjusted the position of the bag of peas. "Anyway, how is Maureen?"

"As you would expect. I don't know anything about that Chloe girl, but she must be seriously disturbed. And now there's another one getting in on the game. I just don't know how anybody could think such a thing about Neville Tanner, let alone say it. And to take it to the police. They have to be a pair of attention seekers. The sort who can't pass up the chance to create a bit of drama."

Jim removed his coat, draped it over the back of one of the armchairs and then sat down.

It was now or never.

"Jim, I need to tell you something, so hear me out for a minute. After the funeral, I was concerned about Chloe. So, I looked her up online, went to see her and met her friend, Frances. I listened to their

193

stories. And I believed them both. I'm the one that helped persuade them to go to the police."

Jim's mouth dropped open and he froze in position. It took him a minute to speak.

"But why? Have you taken leave of your senses, lad? I've been friends with Neville for years, you met that girl less than a week ago. You know nothing about her. She isn't even a parishioner here. What on earth possessed you? Is it because she was young and pretty? Did you get sucked in by the damsel in distress routine? You wouldn't be the first."

Any hope Brendan may have had for sympathy evaporated as Jim shook his head, expression hovering somewhere between incredulous and irate.

Keep calm, Brendan. Remember your vows. Remember not to let anything you heard in the confessional slip.

"No, that's not it."

"What, then? Did you not spare a thought for poor Maureen and Andrea? Have you no compassion, after everything they've been through? I expected far better from you, Brendan."

Brendan concentrated on not withering under Jim's fury.

"Jim, I did think of Maureen, but believe it or not my main concern was for the victims."

"Victims? Maureen and Andrea are the victims."

"I believed Chloe. And I didn't have a choice. My best friend was abused years ago, and I said nothing, and he committed suicide. And I couldn't live with myself if something like that happened again."

Jim stood up.

"Now we're getting somewhere. So, this great act of priestly concern was nothing but a half-baked attempt to assuage your own conscience over something that happened years ago. For crying out loud, Brendan!"

"It wasn't just that."

"Wasn't it? Because from where I'm standing –"

Shit! Watch what you say!

"Just, that what Chloe was saying rang true."

"Well, if that's what you thought – and I use the word loosely, because it seems to me that precious little thinking went on – you're

194

as deluded as she is. Call yourself a priest? You've tarnished the name of a perfectly decent man based on the word of a flake you met five minutes ago, just to make yourself feel better about a misjudgement you made way back when. I didn't think it would be possible for you to be so selfish. And to lack so much self-awareness. You must be a complete fool!"

Jim wasn't exactly shouting, but the tone of his voice was definitely first cousin to it. Brendan, head pounding, stomach still writhing, had had enough. He got up holding the back of the sofa for support; hoping wooziness wouldn't overtake him again.

"Jim, I'm perfectly happy to continue this discussion in the morning, if you like. But right now, I'm washed out and this bruise is killing me so, if you don't mind, I'm going to go upstairs and have an early night. You can carry on ripping me a new one tomorrow."

Jim puffed out his cheeks and blew, shaking his head.

Brendan regretted his impudence immediately. Jim may be misguided on the score, but he didn't deserve Brendan's truculence either.

"I'm sorry, Jim. I didn't mean to be so rude."

Jim waved the apology away.

"That's the least of our worries. I'm very angry, Brendan, no getting away from it. You should have come to me first before you jumped down that particular rabbit hole. God alone knows what damage you've caused. Go to bed now, if you're set on it. We'll talk more in the morning after we've both had time to calm down. Right now, I can hardly bear to look at you."

He closed the conversation by picking up his coat and carrying it into the hall, and adding, "I can't believe how bloody irresponsible you've been," before closing the door with considerably more force than necessary.

Brendan ran himself a bath before he went to bed, hoping it would help calm him down; and was not in the least surprised when it didn't work. This time when he lay on the bed he did not even attempt to pray; even if he had done, the thoughts whirling around his aching head would have rendered it impossible.

He had been so sure that he was doing the right thing. Truth to tell, he still felt sure. But Jim had been adamant, and he had been a priest for many years, far longer than Brendan.

Had he acted selfishly? Was he deluding himself that he wanted to help the girls, when really he only wanted to help himself by setting his own conscience straight?

No! I don't think so! Maybe! Could I be?

He realised he was no longer sure.

32.

Twilight cast an ominous purply hue over the churchyard as Brendan picked his way along. Before him stretched a multitude of mossy headstones peeking out from dense swathes of overgrown grass. To his right was an abandoned church; silent, boarded up, stonework blackened with age. Something about the building, whether it was the crows cawing from the rotting roof or the steady rattle of the bolted door, even though there was no discernible wind, repulsed him and he gave it as wide a berth as he could manage as he passed through the graveyard.

It wasn't the church that was calling him anyway; from somewhere beyond the yard, he could hear weeping – various voices combining into a discordant keening, drawing him inexorably. Trying to ignore the straggling weeds brushing against his knees, he pushed onwards. The thorns of a hundred spiky bushes snagged his robes as he walked.

Robes? For the first time he noticed how he was dressed; full gleaming white robes and a bright yellow stole, as if he were about to say Mass.

Brendan pressed on.

Moments (hours? days?) later, he fought his way through a dense copse of trees; the sun had now fully set but the moonlight shone brightly (too brightly; its brilliance was fierce), casting an eerie silvery halo over everything. Still, he kept going, completely immersed in his quest to seek out the source of the wailing. Everywhere, thorny branches seemed intent on relieving him of his eyes. He batted them away, bending almost double where they were too unwieldy.

He emerged from the thicket and suddenly found himself at the foot of a hill, at the top of which was a cross. A sentry in Roman dress was standing next to the cross, his face turned away. The cross was lit from behind; even the unnatural brightness of the shimmery moonlight could never have shone with such intensity. Brendan knew he should have been blinded by the brilliance, yet somehow his eyes were working completely well.

He had known since childhood that the cross represented salvation. So why was he certain that this particular tableau signified the exact opposite?

There was no question of not climbing the hill; no matter how much he dreaded what he might find at the top.

Brendan pressed on.

And then he reached the top.

He stared in revulsion at the man nailed to the cross, head bowed, blood gushing from his wrists and feet, forming a crimson pool at the base. He let out a horrified gasp, as the head suddenly jerked and met his eyes directly. A scream died in his throat as he recognised who it was.

"Matty!"

One side of Matthew's face was relatively unscathed, the other was a mass of maggots, bones and leaking cerebral fluid.

"Have you come to stand at the foot of my cross? Was it not enough for you to kill me before with your cowardice? You're doing it to me again with your hypocrisy."

"Matty, I'm sorry! I honestly thought I was doing the right thing. I don't know how I could have been so stupid."

"Oh, you know, Brendan. You always knew."

"Matty, I swear I didn't."

"And still you're lying. To me! To yourself! Years and years of lies. Nearly a whole lifetime."

"Matty! Please!"

But Matthew had fallen into shadows.

The moon was now illuminating the two kneeling figures as they turned to Brendan. One was Chloe, her pretty face scarred by hundreds of bleeding scratches which dripped over her clothes, down her nose, into her mouth. The other was Frances, so obese that her features had almost entirely disappeared into the bulges of her cheeks. Every part of her skin appeared stretched to bursting point, slits breaking out, black viscous fluid starting to seep through. The two women's voices mocked him in unison.

"Did you really think you would be welcome in our lives? You honestly thought you made a difference to us? How dare you presume to think that you could help us? You couldn't even save your own rotting soul."

The moonlight now glared over the soldier; Neville Tanner, face blackened, eyes a mess of broken veins, and the first mouldy patches of decomposition on his hands. He strode towards the cross and plunged a spear into Matthew's side. Blood spurted out, streaking down Brendan's robes.

The face that was, yet wasn't, Matthew's glared in undisguised hatred. Brendan tried to scream again but his mouth was covered by an invisible gag. The more he tried to scream, the thicker the gag felt. Brendan turned and started to run. He fled past the thicket this time, followed by jeering laughter.

"Run, run away; do what you do best. One day, you might even outrun yourself."

He ran faster, more swiftly than should have been possible, encumbered as he was by the priest's vestments. It was only seconds later (how?) that he found himself tearing towards another church: picturesque, intricate stained-glass windows and with a tall steeple, like he'd seen on a thousand Christmas cards. There was even a flurry of snow banking up against the walls, and the sound of carols echoing. No sight had ever been more welcome.

Brendan hurried towards the building. Even at the speed he was going, he noticed the bible text mounted at the church gate.

"Why do you see the speck in your neighbour's eye but do not notice the log in your own?" Matthew 7: 3-5.

Then he had reached the church door and slammed himself against it; already feeling the relief of sanctuary.

But the door remained closed. Brendan saw the wooden boards, like thick floorboards, nailed across it; the wood was vivid yellow and black bricks were filling in the spaces where stained glass windows had been just seconds ago.

From somewhere (where?) Neville Tanner's voice flooded his brain; whispering but as deafening as a shriek.

"We'll see each other soon enough. You'll join me where you sent me before long."

He felt darkness welling like an eclipse, whooshing towards him. In another second he would be swallowed. He slid downwards and closed his eyes, waiting to be obliterated.

And then, in a final burst of clarity, he realised the extent of his betrayal so many years ago. And he knew he could no longer stay at St Jude's.

33.

And then he was bolt upright in bed, drenched in sweat, yet shivering. His duvet was a tangled heap at his feet; he shook it and pulled it around him. Then, he turned his bedside light on and checked the time on his phone. 4:00 am. His hands shook so much as he sipped water from the glass on his bedside table, that he spilled half of it over his duvet.

The bruise on his head was throbbing more than ever. Brendan touched it lightly and immediately felt nauseous. He swallowed hard, took a couple more small sips of water and then lay back down, careful not to rest the bruise against the pillow. There was absolutely no point in turning the light off; sleep was the last thing he wanted now. But he was certain of what he needed to do.

He waited another hour and then got up, stripped his bed, neatly folded the bedding at its foot, went to the toilet, washed his face, shaved with his eyes closed and cleaned his teeth. He went back to the bedroom and opened the chest of drawers. The only items of clothing he possessed which were not part of the priestly uniform were his pyjamas and running clothes. He put on his running shorts and T shirt and added his nondescript grey hoodie. He slipped on some socks and squeezed his feet into his ageing trainers, then ran the brush over his hair. With any luck, he'd look like a regular early morning jogger, albeit one who had recently charged straight into a lamppost. When he decided what he was going to do with the rest of his life he could buy more clothes, should he require them.

What else would he need? His wallet, obviously, there was a small amount of money in his bank account. His phone? It was tempting to walk away with no means of contact whatsoever. But you never knew when a phone would come in useful. He grabbed the charging cable and stuffed it into his wallet.

He crept past Jim's room; he didn't think he had it in him to undergo a fresh confrontation.

You'll be leaving Jim to do everything on his own again, you know. How do you feel about that?

How did he feel? How would Jim feel would be the better question and, bearing in mind that Jim had handed him his arse on a plate not twelve hours earlier, Brendan suspected that his mentor would greet his departure by performing cartwheels and hanging up the bunting.

Even without that, Brendan's absence would be a temporary minor inconvenience at most. Anything he did, Jim would be able to do twice as well on his own and if the duties proved too onerous for him, another curate could probably be dispatched in a heartbeat.

But he couldn't leave without a word of explanation. At very least, he should send Jim a text.

"I'm sorry, I can't do this anymore," Brendan typed. "I am clearly not fit to be a priest. Thank you for everything and I'm sorry it didn't work out."

After this he switched his phone off, let himself out of the house and posted his key back through the letterbox. It was 5:20.

The late October chill hit him as soon as he stepped outside.

Okay, so what happens now?

He had absolutely no idea.

He started walking, letting his feet choose the direction, keeping his head down, oblivious to anything but the scrambling, swirling fracturing of his brain.

It was only the motion of his plodding feet that gave him any anchor at all; if he paused for a second, he would certainly disperse into a

200

million scraps of confetti. As he paced, he muttered, "Keep walking, keep walking, walk on with hope in your heart walkonwithhopeinyourheart walkonwithhopeinyourheart." until his feet came to a halt.

Brendan blinked as his surroundings rearranged themselves around him. Haymarket Metro, Boots, Lloyds bank. He had reached the town centre, then. A check of his watch revealed it to be 6:00.

So where do we go from here?

He started walking again. His feet appeared to be taking him in the direction of Gateshead, for some reason best known to themselves. What was in Gateshead? Chloe and Frances were. Would he be sure of a welcome from them?

Only one way to find out. He continued to let his legs set the agenda; still muttering to himself; the mantra now inexplicably, "Marshmallowsarenicemarshmallowsarenice, marshmellowsarenice."

Down the steep bank towards the Millennium Bridge, under the guano-encrusted Tyne Bridge, along the quayside, remembering happy Sunday mornings venturing from Sunderland to browse the market stalls (before the place had got all gentrified, when there was proper knock-off, dodgy as you like, tat to be found, to an eternal soundtrack of Foster and Allen) with his parents and sister. "OnceIhadabunchofthymeonceIhadabunchofthyme," was the refrain now. And it was just as annoying as it had been twenty years ago. Brendan kept on with it, regardless; towards Choe's estate.

It was around 7:00 when Brendan, thirsty and with aching legs, reached Chloe's flat. From a distance he could see that the kitchen blinds were still drawn shut. Was Frances still sleeping there? If so, who was taking the bed and who the couch? He suspected that Chloe would have had to sacrifice the bed; Frances's weight would have wrecked the sofa. In a last-ditch burst of energy, he sprinted towards the flat, lifted his hand to ring the bell, and abruptly halted.

What the fuck are you doing here?

Well, go on, then! What are you going to say? "Hi folks, surprise! I'm no longer a priest, now can I join your merry gang, please?"

And more to the point, what would Chloe and Frances say to that?

They would be bemused, probably hostile and even worse, distressed. The very fact that Chloe had ever confided in him had come from the fact that he was in a trustworthy position. Now he had voluntarily abandoned that position, what was left of him but a slightly unsavoury chancer? And even if Chloe were to allow him over the threshold, Frances would be there to deny him access into their inner sanctum. Give the girl her due, she had made no secret of her intense dislike of him. How had Brendan ever had the temerity to feel morally superior towards her? To accuse her of being a bad friend?

Like you set such a wonderful example of friendship with Matthew, you mean?

Brendan may be guilty of hypocrisy, but that was a charge that could never be levelled against Frances. He turned and this time jogged away. What now?

The word that immediately sprung to mind was "home". Not to the house which until nearly two hours ago he had shared with Jim, but to his old hometown of Sunderland.

And what do you think you're going to find there, Brendan?

I don't know. It's just where I want to be.

So he set off home.

34.

At 7:00 that morning, Maureen Tanner was padding downstairs, thanking God that the excruciatingly long night was finally over. So much for those fabulous, life-changing herbal sleeping tablets! Every single time she had been on the point of drifting into the comfort of sleep, the image of Andrea's angry face had jerked her back into full consciousness. Of course, Andrea had been appalled; how could Maureen ever have expected otherwise? She'd have to call her today, try to mend things. Falling out with Andrea would be more than she could bear.

She flinched at the memory of the fury in Andrea's eyes; the hurt she had felt as Andrea had abruptly stood and ignored Maureen's open arms as she left.

Why had she even asked the bloody question? She believed in her husband's innocence absolutely. Yet she had still asked the question. Make of that what you will, Maureen.

Tentatively, without really knowing why, she made her way to the door which connected the house to the garage, pushing against it until it opened. It had always been a little stiff. She stepped into the cold garage, bunching up her towelling dressing gown and fumbled for the light switch next to the door. The strip light fluttered unconvincingly for a few seconds then snapped fully on.

It was the first time Maureen had stepped inside the garage since discovering Neville's body, and it already smelt fusty from disuse. Against her will, she found her eyes drawn towards the hook Neville had used to kill himself. She was surprised to see that it looked like a perfectly normal garage roof hook, just like another one a few yards down, from which ladders were suspended.

A greater surprise was that when Maureen looked there, she did not feel particularly traumatised. She had feared she would see Neville hanging there in her mind's eye, his face black and his tongue protruding as it had been. But no. In fact, what grabbed her attention was the plastic garden chair he had used to stand on. It had been stood up again and pushed against the wall but whoever had done that had neglected to wipe the dirty print of Neville's trainers from the seat.

"Mucky beggars," muttered Maureen and nearly laughed at the absurdity. She was standing at the exact place where she had discovered her husband's body and she was more worried about a couple of footprints on a half-knackered plastic chair which, by rights, ought to have gone in the bin years ago.

Underneath the hook, a patch of concrete floor had been scrubbed so vigorously that the grey paint had almost worn away. She assumed this must have been Andrea or her fiancé. They could at least have made the effort to paint over it!

Maureen took a step forward, unable to shake the suspicion that she was trespassing. In her forty years of marriage, she had only been into the garage a couple of dozen times. Even Ralph didn't venture in, on pain of a whacked backside. What did she want to come in that filthy hole for, Neville had always wanted to know. If she had ever protested that she should sometimes give the garage a good clearing out, he

203

reminded her that mice were always getting in, she would be bound to get one running over her foot. This was usually enough to keep Maureen, who was terrified of mice, from pressing the issue further. Neville had always been considerate like that. He had built her a shed at the bottom of the garden for her gardening tools, so she would never have any reason to set foot there.

Once, she had entered the garage without him, that time she couldn't find the secateurs in the shed. It hadn't been long before she had felt Neville's breath on the back of her neck and his hand twisting her wrist. Naturally, he had been furious and called her an interfering, nosy old bag. She should thank God he had been good enough to marry her, because as sure as eggs were eggs, no other man would put up with any woman snooping around his own private territory. His eyes had been so hard that she had been afraid he was going to hit her, which was ridiculous, of course. He hadn't laid a finger on her for several years; not since she had learned not to complain about the amount of time he spent at the club. And never when Andrea was around.

He did turn her around and frogmarch her out, though. Later on, he had bought her a £5 bunch of flowers from Morrisons, and said, "Now see here, Maureen my little halfwit. You have your domain and I have mine. You don't find me setting foot in your kitchen, do you, unless you ask me to? That garage is my space. It's where I carry out my man stuff. And you can get that narky look off your face. I'm only thinking of you in all of this. You know how messy it gets in there. You're so clumsy you would be bound to hurt yourself on something. And the mouse problem in there is getting even worse."

Maureen hadn't thought it wise to point out that she hadn't seen hide nor hair of any mouse while she was in there.

She took another tentative step; Ralph's deep snoring from the hallway a reassuring lifeline to the world. She glanced fearfully behind, as if expecting to see Neville's accusing shape loom up large and furious. Nothing; of course, there was nothing there. She looked around. The garage wasn't particularly messy. Neville's Black and Decker work bench stood at one end, next to a shelf housing a few half empty, decades-old cans of paint, crusted around the lids. Cobwebs hung from every beam; Maureen's fingers itched to attack them with a feather duster. Andrea's old bike, complete with pink pompoms. A folded pasting table. No sign of any mice, though; no traps had been laid and there didn't seem to be any droppings.

Their old hardwood sideboard had been pushed against the opposite wall. When Neville had decided it was time to upgrade the living room furniture, he had told her he wouldn't throw it out; it would be perfect for storing his tools. Maureen had giggled as he awkwardly manoeuvred it from the living room into the garage, almost getting stuck in the door. How furious he had been about that! He had sulked for the rest of the weekend and then surprised her with another bunch of Morrisons flowers (£6 this time) when she had apologised sufficiently. Maureen smiled at the memory.

What would she ever do without him? She wasn't close at all to her own relatives; they hadn't cared for Neville. One cousin had even had the cheek to say that she had seemed "subdued" since she had met him, and nobody had said a word in contradiction. In solidarity with her husband, she had reduced contact with her family to Christmas cards. Their friends were mainly Neville's from the club. She was no longer in contact with any of her old work colleagues, not that she would really ever have described them as friends. She hadn't been in the habit of joining them on nights out; she had gone once or twice but Neville had been so disapproving that she had given up. When a man worked hard all week to provide for his family, he was entitled to expect his wife to want to spend their evenings together. Maureen's response had been that she would have loved to spend more evenings together, but he spent most of them at the club. Neville had called her a "manipulative, nagging bitch," among other things, and on that occasion, there had been no flowers from Morrisons, for any price.

Without knowing what she was looking for, if anything, Maureen made her way to the sideboard. There would almost certainly be nothing much inside, but a part of her had always thought it quite ridiculous that there was any part of the house to which she was forbidden access.

"What didn't you want me to see, Neville?" she murmured, then immediately frowned at her own disloyalty. Why on earth would Neville be hiding anything at all from her? He was completely innocent. Wasn't he?

Nevertheless, she slid the left-hand door along. A few hammers, spanners and a bag of screws and screwdrivers sat there next to a can of WD40 and a bottle of turps. So far, so mundane.

She could have closed the door there and then, retreated from the garage, made a cup of tea and put the expedition out of her mind.

But instead, she slid the right-hand door along, and found a large towel which had been bundled up in a huge ball. Maureen touched the towel. It was stiff, as if it had been dipped in starch. But why would Neville have dipped a towel in starch? She pulled the towel out and for some reason held it to her nose, expecting to smell turps. No turps but an unmistakable smell of... no, it couldn't possibly be. Could it? Underneath the towel there was a folded picnic blanket. Maureen hadn't seen that blanket for ages; she had once spent all afternoon looking for it, until Neville had reminded her that she had thrown it out because there was a hole in it. Why would he lie about something so trivial?

Less careful now, Maureen grabbed the blanket. There was something hard, heavy and flat wrapped in it. She pulled it out and uncovered a laptop. Why would Neville keep a laptop in the garage? He had owned a perfectly good one which, until the coroner had taken it, had lived on the bookcase in her living room. Neville had kept all the accounts from his erstwhile painting and decorating business on it. Why on earth would he have a second laptop and go to all this effort of keeping it hidden from her?

Maureen carried the device back to the living room and plugged it in. She tried the password for Neville's usual laptop: NevilleTanner1. Nothing. She tried NevilleTanner2. Nothing again. Maureen didn't know much about computers, but she knew enough to suppose that the third attempt would be the final one allowed, and if an unlocking code was sent to Neville's phone, then that would not be much good to her; Neville's phone also languished at the police station. She decided to leave the laptop for the time being and hurried back into the garage, not hesitating at all this time. At the back of the cupboard, behind where the swaddled laptop had nestled, there was a plastic Morrison's bag, well folded over. Maureen lifted out the bag and peered into it, at a large stash of photographs which looked as though they had been issued on a printer. Curious, she shook them out.

And immediately wanted to stuff them back in again.

A bunch of pictures were in her hand, more were resting on her lap, and Maureen's eyes were fixed ahead. Her curiosity had suddenly drained away. Suddenly, all she wanted to do was retreat from the garage – bugger the mess of the unexplored sanctum.

So why wasn't she moving? Why wasn't she locking the garage door, collecting Ralph and taking him for a walk as far away as possible? What was preventing her from either looking or moving?

She gave herself a shake. What, exactly was she afraid of? She knew Neville was completely innocent, so why not just look the printouts in the eye, find out that they were potential holiday destinations, or car maintenance guides, and then have a bloody good laugh at her own stupidity?

So, she looked.

And realised exactly what it was that she had dreaded discovering. Everything that she had so much hoped was a lie was, literally, in her hands.

Maureen shoved the damning evidence quickly back into the bag, ran out and scrubbed her hands in scalding hot water to which she added a squirt of bleach. She made a cup of tea and sat down; she needed to consider her options.

She could easily burn the horrific pictures and smash the laptop to smithereens. Nobody would ever be any the wiser. Not the police and certainly not Andrea. Andrea would be protected. Neville's reputation would be preserved. In many ways this would be the most attractive scenario.

But Andrea! Images of Andrea ran through Maureen's head. Andrea as a chubby, dark eyed toddler; Andrea proudly posing for a "first day at school" photograph in a too large uniform, pleated skirt practically grazing her ankles; Andrea aged eight in a bathing costume, building sandcastles in Torremolinos; Andrea dressed as an angel with a tinsel halo in a school nativity play, sporting a gap-toothed beam. Some of the children in the pictures were as young as Andrea had been at those times. Thankfully, there were no printouts of Andrea, which offered a miniscule amount of comfort. But how would Maureen feel if Andrea had been used in that way? The thought made her want to puke her tea into the sink.

Maureen had always believed herself to be a decent woman. Not too bright, as Neville had often pointed out to her, not much of a cook, not one for sparkling repartee. The person you would forget ten minutes after meeting them. But a fundamentally decent woman.

There had never been any question of Maureen doing anything even vaguely noteworthy in her whole life. She had been blessed with minimal intelligence, no particular sporting attributes, no artistic or musical inclinations. Had she lived a hundred thousand lives, the only way in which they would have varied would have been the names of her husbands, the type of dead-end job she had held or the amount of children she had birthed.

So, she had always known that her life would be small. Inconsequential. And, for the most part, she had been absolutely fine with that. She had never entertained dreams of witnessing the Northern Lights, gazing at the pyramids of Gaza, swimming with dolphins, watching whales from a boat in the middle of the Pacific Ocean, bungee jumping beside the Niagara Falls, winning Nobel prizes, writing a book or a song. In fact, since meeting Neville at the age of eighteen, the only ambition she had nurtured was to be a half decent wife and mother.

And her life had turned out every bit as limited as she had envisaged. She knew perfectly well that when she died, her earthly footprint would be negligible, to say the least. Truth to tell, there would only be Andrea who would mourn her. She had never run the Great North Run, baked for a charity cake stall, gone on a sponsored walk for Pudsey Bear. She had never joined a political party, signed a petition, saved a life, been a union member or raised her head above any sort of parapet in any way, shape or form. She could state with a reasonable degree of certainty that she had never inspired anyone.

But she had never intentionally hurt anyone either. Without knowing why, Maureen stood up and walked into the hallway, pausing at the square mirror. She stared at herself. A thin faced, greying (who was she kidding? Make that almost entirely grey), deeply lined woman stared back at her. Sixty years old and looking every day of it, and then some. Hair dry and brittle, sticking out and in need of a trim. Eyes with large dark shadows underneath. A top lip with a developing moustache. Amber-stained teeth. She reached out and touched the familiar image with a bitten nail, leaving a smear. It was by no means an attractive face. But it was the same face she had looked at for her whole life. She had looked proudly at her image the day after facing her relatives down after their criticism of Neville. Given her image a shy glance the morning of her wedding, hoping that Neville would be satisfied with what he saw. Smiled at her image when she had stood in front of the mirror with baby Andrea in her arms, laughing at Andrea's confusion as she stretched out her starfish hand and tried to touch her mother's reflection. And she was damned if she was going to spend the rest of her life unable to face the woman in the mirror.

A surge of something unfamiliar rose within her. Since Neville's death she had turned the circumstances over and over in her head; unable to sleep or eat. She had imagined Neville depressed, going through Hell on his own; thought a better wife could have imparted words of comfort or wisdom to him. And now it turned out that if he had been feeling misunderstood or lonely, then there was a damn good reason for it. All the time he hadn't shown any interest in her, had almost seemed repulsed by her, this was the secret he was hiding. And now the guilt had got the better of him – or maybe he had been threatened with exposure in some way – and he had taken the coward's way out and left her to clean up the mess. Same as he had done every night after tea; same as he had done whenever he dropped his discarded pants, complete with skiddies, on the bedroom floor; same as he had done when he had thrown a loaded plate at the wall because Maureen had put garlic in the mashed potatoes for a change.

"Well, this is where it ends, Neville. This is one mess I am not cleaning up for you."

Had she spoken the words aloud? Well, if she had done, who the Hell cared? Certainly not her.

The police officers who had visited the day before had left Maureen a telephone number in case she remembered anything or found anything which could be helpful to them or to social services. She called it straight away before her resolve had a chance to weaken. DC Calders assured her that "someone" would be round as soon as possible.

Andrea would have to be told, of course. But Maureen couldn't face doing that just yet. Let Andrea have a few more hours before the impression she had lovingly held of her father was so cruelly shattered.

Right now, Maureen needed the support of a friend. She telephoned Father Jim.

35.

A few weeks ago

So, this is how it ends. His whole life reduced to this. Bested by a morbidly obese monster, who had never troubled his thoughts for the past dozen or so years. The bloody state of her, to add insult to injury! He could barely fathom what charms she had ever held for him. He could only conclude that puberty could be a cruel master, converting doe-eyed budding beauties to full breasted or swinging hipped tarts. Or in this case, full-on monsters. And the beast in question well and truly had him by the short and curlies.

But hasn't he always suspected it would eventually come to this? He remembers a scene from a moronic cop show Andrea used to enjoy, where a corrupt police officer, on the point of being found out, sends a text saying, "Immediate exit required." The next second, all Hell breaks loose, as a posse of black-clad gangsters armed with more machine guns than you could shake a stick at storms the joint. Well, this is his "immediate exit required", his DefCon 4, the disaster plan he had hoped he wouldn't have to use but had prepared anyway. Did the scheming little cow really believe he would be able to conjure up fifteen thousand pounds out of thin air? He was a retired painter and decorator, not the bloody Duke of Northumberland.

True, he could burn the incriminating photographs, dump the computer and plead his innocence until the cows come home, but he is astute enough to know that if you throw enough mud at something, some of it will stick. And six of them! And that was just the current tally!

Once upon a time, a valued member of the community such as himself wouldn't have had any problem getting a bunch of vindictive little tarts dismissed as a group of hysterics; they'd have been laughed out of the cop shop, maybe even given a lecture about not displaying goods that weren't meant for sale. But now things are different. You can't get moved these days, for so called "feminists" spouting on about "mansplaining", "toxic masculinity", "me too". It's all about diversity, female representation, women-only spaces; you name it, those uppity bitches are Hell bent on it. And the upshot is that whinging females are now seen as victims, while decent men like himself get the shitty end of the stick and have their reputations hung out to dry for the world and his dog to scrutinise.

Maureen's opinion of him couldn't matter less, but could he bear seeing the devotion in Andrea's eyes clouded with suspicion every time she looked at him? And what about the club? God knows, it's his only sanctuary from his nagging wife. If his membership got revoked and he was forced to spend every evening in her stultifying company, even if he went straight to Hell now, it would be an upgrade. Not that he intends going to Hell. It's true that he had been disappointed by that holier than thou curate this evening. He supposes he can find enough generosity in his heart to be lenient though. The kid hasn't been in the job for longer than five minutes. Give him time, he'll learn what the trade-offs are. A bloke got a bit too friendly with some slappers from the children's club he ran, or with the little girl who used to live next door – who was forever flashing her knickers doing handstands in the garden, might he add – and then he did some work in the church, saved them a bunch of money or made a donation. In the olden days they had called it "buying indulgences", or something. Jim would have absolved him straight away, he was sure. True, he had never confessed to Jim, but he was a man of the world, he would undoubtedly understand that there were some things that may technically have been classed as a venial sin but could be disregarded. Especially when the poor bastard was trapped in a marriage as arid as his own. Besides, he had never had full sex with any of them. They would all have passed a virginity test afterwards, if such a thing existed. He hadn't even kissed them.

And so what, if he had done? When you looked at the backgrounds of some of the little fannies you knew it was a matter of "when" and not "if" they "knew" a man. Do-gooders love to talk about the corruption of innocence; well, within that brigade there was precious little innocence to be found, that was for sure. The way some of them paraded about in lip gloss or tight trousers that didn't leave anything to the imagination, well they deserved everything they got. As far as he was concerned, they were the ones who should have been grovelling in the confession, begging for absolution from the sin of leading him into temptation.

211

And he had never, ever gone near his daughter. Meddling with your own family was just plain wrong and somewhere he would never have dreamed of going. Surely, that had to count for something. In fact, you could argue that his secret stash and the little ways he scratched his itches could have kept him from looking at Andrea in that way.

But he has to deal with the situation as it is, however unjust it may be. And the fact is that tonight had been his last chance to receive absolution before pressing his immediate exit button. Okay, so he hadn't confessed to absolutely everything; but surely, he had admitted enough to keep God satisfied. Nobody confessed to absolutely everything, did they? He is sure God would have been proud of him for having the courage to admit at least some of his darkest secrets. And he is sure that, under the circumstances, God would accept a general act of contrition in lieu of absolution.

Only a few minutes now, before he's out of it all anyway. Truth to tell, he won't be entirely sorry to say goodbye to life. He knows he has taken every precaution to keep his stash and his computer hidden, but you can never be 100% sure of anything. The strain of concealing everything, coupled with the constant underlying worry that something like this could happen, have done nothing for his health the past few years. His body is starting to fall apart now, forcing him to give up the children's club, having to rely more and more on the pictures, and they are satisfying him less and less. He supposes he could try building a fake internet profile and messaging some likely mark, but the age group he prefers tends not to have access to social media as much as, say, teenagers. And even if he did hit lucky, he could never be sure that he wasn't being catfished (he's sure he's heard that term somewhere before) by some do-gooding vigilante group. And he knows that if he ends up being charged and found guilty, he'll almost certainly end up inside, something he has no intention of risking. Share a cell with some cretin who might well turn out to be a poofter, or a terrorist insisting on kneeling on the floor babbling away in some unintelligible foreign lingo? No, this way is by far the best.

Should he leave a note to Maureen or Andrea? Why bother, he's got nothing he wants to say to Maureen and nothing he can think of to say to Andrea. She's got her own life now, anyway.

Should he dump the photographs and computer? No. It won't affect him either way, will it? Let Maureen find it if she goes snooping. Maybe it will get a reaction of some sort out of her. Miracles can happen. He is almost sorry he won't be around to see her find the pictures. It might have given him a savage pleasure to witness her seeing what her shrivelled body, full length nightie, outsized briefs, stained teeth, bitten nails, dull conversation, saggy tits, utter predictability (two G and Ts on the rare occasions he had to invite her to the club for some do or other, mug of tea and digestive at 10:00) had driven him to. God, he's had the patience of a saint with that woman over the years.

It hadn't been too bad at first; Maureen's unbridled devotion and admiration had made a satisfactory mixture in the beginning. And she had been quite pretty in a mousy sort of way. But, Jesus Christ, it had worn thin pretty damn sharpish. Once upon a time she had, at least, argued back occasionally. That had been irritating enough, but her maddening passivity these days – she withers if he so much as gives her an annoyed glance – is even more aggravating. She still loves him, he is sure. Maybe she even thinks he still loves her. Well, finding the pictures might finally put her straight.

He fetches the rope from the sideboard. Luckily there's a hook in the ceiling already. He drags a plastic chair just below it. Congratulating himself on having thoroughly researched how to form an effective noose, he clears his throat and begins his own "immediate exit" strategy.

36.

At 7:00 that morning, Father Jim McLean was sitting at his kitchen table drinking a mug of tea before he got ready for morning Mass and ruminating on what a strange beast anger was. Yesterday evening, it had taken every atom of self-control he possessed not to add to his curate's tally of bruises. Now, though?

If he were to be completely honest with himself – and being a priest, he jolly well should be – he had to admit that a large part of him still felt betrayed, if that wasn't too strong a word. Brendan was giving a terrific impression of having swallowed hook, line and sinker every one of the deplorable allegations against his friend, and for the life of him, Jim couldn't work out why.

But he had known Brendan for a few weeks now, long enough to start to get the measure of him, and he was pretty sure that Brendan's actions must have been well intentioned. Yes, maybe he himself would not have acted that way, but Brendan did not have the years of friendship he and Neville had shared to draw on.

Brendan was clearly a kind young man – for goodness' sake, when he had been ill Brendan had looked after him with a patience many nurses would have found difficult to muster. And Mrs Smith, from St Jude's primary school, positively raved about him and how well he related to the children. The manager from the retirement community had said just the other day how much the residents looked forward to his visits and how much they appreciated the time he took to chat with them and show an interest in their lives. Did that sound like a lad with so much as a drop of malice in him? No, however skewed Brendan's actions may have been, they assuredly came from a good place.

Maybe he had been too harsh with Brendan yesterday? He had definitely let his temper get the better of him. He would need to mention it at confession this week.

He would, of course, also need to apologise to Brendan for his outburst. He slurped the rest of his tea and stretched towards the ceiling – his back was taking longer and longer to uncrick itself these mornings. He would catch him at the earliest opportunity – clear the air before it started to turn sour.

Now he came to think of it, why hadn't Brendan surfaced yet? It was unusual for him not to be up and about by now. After that whack on the head yesterday, maybe he should take a quick peek into Brendan's room just to check? A glance at the Brendan-shaped mound under the duvet would reassure him.

But, as soon as he opened Brendan's door, he saw that not only was the bed empty, it had also been stripped and the used bedding folded crisply at the end.

Not what he had hoped to find, but no need to form a search party just yet. There was probably a perfectly logical explanation – Brendan might not have wanted to risk waking him by turning on the washing machine; or maybe he had been going somewhere in a hurry and run out of time; or maybe he had… Anyway, the possibilities were endless.

He went to his own room and checked his phone. Straight away, the text message from Brendan flashed up.

214

"Oh, for crying out loud! The bloody great idiot!" Jim groaned. He immediately replied.

"I'm sorry, I should never have spoken to you like that. Please get in touch with me. You really don't want to be making any hurried decisions about this."

Was a text alone enough? Probably not, given the circumstances. He tried to leave a message on Brendan's voicemail but found it switched off. Of course, it was. Where on earth could he have gone and how on earth could Jim get him to reconsider?

But that was something he would have to think about later. There was no time to fanny around worrying now. His first responsibility was to get ready for morning Mass; and pray that some inspiration would come to him along the way.

37.

At 8:30 that morning, Brendan's metro clunked into Sunderland. It was getting busy now; the town teemed with commuters getting ready to begin work, bumping into each other, hurrying to their destinations. Well, not Brendan; he no longer had work to begin, or a destination to which to hurry.

He pulled his hood up as he walked through the town centre, not wanting to bump into anybody who might recognise him. He grimaced at the irony that although he was feeling more alone than at any part of his life, the last thing he wanted was to be near people. Especially people who were scurrying along like drones, not seeming to even notice, let alone take pleasure in each other's company. On the metro, heads had been buried in the free newspaper, faces had stared intently at screens. Brendan had barely heard one word of conversation, hadn't seen anyone look out of the window, or even demonstrate the slightest awareness of the world around them.

"Make a connection with each other!" he had wanted to scream. "You never know when everything's going to go tits up and you find yourself all alone at the bottom of a bloody great empty canyon, screaming as loud as you like because nobody is answering you, and you don't even know who you are anymore!"

Profound advice: pity it was of no bloody use to himself.

Quickening his steps, he headed away from the town centre. He had been walking for quite some time, still with no clear direction in mind, before he realised that he was heading towards the bridge from which Matthew had thrown himself.

Way to go, Brendan! Only thirteen years after the event! And as well as being late, you're empty handed.

There was a Tesco just ahead. He went inside, blinking in the harsh overhead light, and trying to tune out the tannoy. Along with a bunch of tired chrysanthemums, he picked up a can of coke – by now his eyes were heavy and stinging with fatigue, exacerbating the pain in his bruise. He was sure that the cashier gave him an odd look as he paid. She probably thought he had been in a punch-up with his girlfriend and was trying to make amends, with the world's crappiest peace offering. He could have used a self-service checkout but, as a rule, he avoided them like the plague, and he didn't see any reason to vary his practice now. Refusing to actively endorse a diabolical invention that had been created with the specific goal of the eventual redundancy of the human race (or so his father put it, and Brendan was inclined to agree), was the closest Brendan was ever likely to get to sticking it to the man.

Outside, Brendan downed the fizzy pop in one go and threw the empty can into the nearest bin. He belched loudly as the drink fizzed uncomfortably in his stomach, but he did feel considerably more wired. Buzzing, even.

He walked until he reached the bridge. A totally innocuous bridge, with nothing to distinguish it from any others spanning totally innocuous main roads anywhere else in the country. Brendan climbed the graffitied steps. *(BridgeofsighsBridgeovertheriverKwaiLinescomposed uponWestminsterBridgeBridgeovertroubledwaterLondonbridgeisfallingdown)*

The clanking of his feet on the metal echoed inside his skull. He reached the middle, grateful that the morning rush of pedestrians had finally quietened.

Brendan knelt and used the twine securing the flowers to tie them to the vertical iron railings. At some point, an advertisement for the

Samaritans had been riveted there. Probably in response to the suicides of people like Matthew; the only clue as to the anguish countless people must have carried with them.

Sorry, mate. I thought I was doing the right thing at the time. I just hope you can forgive me, wherever you are.

What did he mean "wherever you are?" Surely his friend was in Heaven. Brendan refused even to contemplate any other possibility. He stood there for quite some time, watching the traffic rumbling along below him, trying to imagine what it had been like for Matthew that night. Had he been worried about what he might face in the afterlife? Had he been afraid of misjudging the drop and surviving, but with life a whole lot worse than it already was for him? Or maybe, he just felt as if he had plain run out of options.

Standing there, right now, Brendan felt that he understood Matthew better than anyone had ever understood anybody. He knew without any doubt that what Matthew had craved was instant oblivion. Not to have to be concerned about what was going to happen to him ever again. Not to be tortured by the same thoughts whirling round and round in his head, like a washing machine stuck on a never-ending, repetitive cycle. No more worries or panicking, no more guilt or second guessing his motives. Total anaesthesia. Was he thinking of Matty's mindset now or his own? He was no longer sure. He was no longer sure about anything much.

The gentle murmur of the traffic below was strangely hypnotic. Brendan closed his eyes and gripped the rail, breathing in the fumy air.

Gosh, it was tempting, it was really tempting. Instant nothingness seemed very desirable. Just not existing here or anywhere else. Even considering it seemed to calm the clamour inside his brain. He leaned a little further forward.

"Excuse me, love!"

A sharp tap on Brendan's back brought him out of his trance, and he stiffened. The sensation of being touched from behind never failed to rattle him, sometimes to the point of feeling like he wanted to puke. He whirled round, ready to snarl at the intruder to bog off and mind her own fucking business.

"Are you alright there?"

Just in time, Brendan saw that he was facing an elderly woman who was pulling a Westie on a lead. She had a concerned face, with crinkles at the sides of her kind eyes and mouth. She could have been anybody's affable granny. And Brendan had been about to swear at her!

Nice one, Father Fucking Coglan! Just when you thought you couldn't sink any further, you almost rip the head off the sweetest person you're probably going to meet all day.

"Yeah, of course, yeah."

"Are you sure? You were ever so still."

"Yes, fine, honestly," replied Brendan, managing a faint smile. "Just taking a breather."

The old lady showed no sign of moving. Brendan gestured to let her past.

"No, you go first. I won't rest until I can see you're safely off that bridge. It wouldn't do to give an old lady nightmares, would it now?"

The old lady may have been slightly stooped, slightly built (Brendan hoped she never attempted the crossing during a gale force wind; she'd blow halfway to Oz) and slightly cloudy-eyed, but her voice was as firm as any Brendan had ever heard. There was no point in arguing; if he wanted her off the bridge, he would either have to push her or get down himself.

"No, I wouldn't want to do that," Brendan acquiesced. Easier that way, all round.

The old woman and her dog stood there like a pair of sentries until Brendan had crossed the bridge fully. Brendan could have sworn he heard the dog give an approving "wuff", but that was probably just him being stupid.

He was shaking as he clanked down the steps.

Get a grip on yourself, will you Brendan?

He didn't think that, even without the intervention of the old lady he would have followed in Matthew's footsteps. Would he? Surely not. He'd have moved eventually. Wouldn't he?

Nevertheless, he continued to tremble as he walked. Eventually, he came to a park, where he sat on a bench and listened to the collective shrieking of a class of school children enjoying their morning playtime. He reflected that he wouldn't be going into St Jude's Primary School anymore. The thought saddened him. Would he be letting the children down? Possibly, but he would be letting them down even further if he stayed. He was supposed to be a role model, wasn't he? What sort of a role model would a hypocritical coward (or cowardly hypocrite, insert insults as appropriate) be? It occurred to him that there was not one single aspect of his parish duties he would not miss. Even considering the short time he had been there, leaving felt like a vicious wrench.

He had been so clear that he was doing the right thing in refusing absolution to Neville; just as clear that he was doing the right thing in seeking out Chloe; just as clear that he was doing the right thing leaving St Jude's this morning. So why was everything such a blurry jumble now? Desire for oblivion was the only thing he was certain of.

38.

Jim could hear the telephone start to ring at the exact second that he inserted the key in his front door. He let out a string of expletives – some of which priests were definitely not supposed to know – whilst fumbling with his key, and grabbed the receiver just a second too late. Frustrating, but maybe just as well. Truthfully, Jim was more concerned about tracking down Brendan than anything else, at the moment.

He turned away from the phone, only to be overtaken by an inconvenient attack of conscience before he had even made it to the other side of the room. No matter how much he wanted to, he couldn't take the chance that the caller didn't need his help urgently.

Just as well, as it happened. Dialling 1471 revealed the number to be Maureen's; in all conscience, he couldn't delay returning the call immediately.

"Hello, Maureen. I'm sorry I missed your call. I was just coming back from Mass. What can I do for you today?"

"Father McLean," Maureen's voice sounded oddly determined. "I had to let you know myself, you've been so good to me lately. I couldn't let you find out some other way. I was in the garage this morning and I saw a laptop that I didn't realise Neville owned. There were some pictures there as well. Enough to convince me that the girl was not a lying troublemaker. In fact, she was probably speaking the truth. And if there are other allegations, they may be true as well."

Jim plopped into his armchair, before his legs could betray him.

"Father McLean, are you still there? You've gone quiet."

"Yes, yes I'm still here. You were saying there were pictures?"

"Oh, there were pictures, all right. They were bad, Father. Worse than bad. Sickeningly explicit. I would never have believed it if I hadn't seen them for myself. I've given them to the police. They just left half an hour ago. I think they believed me when I said that I had only come upon them today. I hope they did anyway. They must have done, because they didn't make me come into the police station or anything. Which is just as well, it's going to rain and they might not give me a lift back and I'm not sure how often the buses run and it's quite a walk back and if I leave Ralph alone for too long he might –"

"Oh, Maureen, God love you!" It was all Jim could think of to say, but he had to cut her off or she would gabble until kingdom come.

Its flow severed, Maureen's voice became tremulous. "After all the tears I've shed for him. All the years I was in awe of him, couldn't fathom what a wonderful man like him would see in somebody like me. All that time I've spent defending him. And all the time we spent at the weekend looking over old pictures of him. Now I don't even know who I'm grieving for. The man I thought I'd lost or the man I really lost. Does that even make any sense?"

"It makes perfect sense to me," Jim answered. He had drunk whiskey with Neville. Baptised his daughter. Received gifts of port from him at Christmas. And eaten sandwiches from Greggs with him, both of them cross-legged on dustsheets and covered in paint spattered overalls, the time Neville had decorated the church creche. The creche of all places!

"Do you want me to come round?"

"No, it's fine, Father. That's stupid of me! It's anything but fine, but I need to tell Andrea before anything else. She's got to be my priority now."

"Of course, she does. She'll be rocked by it all."

"I'm not going to lie, Father. I'm dreading it but I owe it to her to tell her face to face, as soon as possible. You know how she thought the world of Neville. And then I'll call Neville's brother. I only hope we can keep it quiet around his father, poor old thing. And after all that's done, I'm cancelling that expensive bloody headstone I ordered. I don't even care if I don't get the money back."

"Maureen, you've been very brave this morning. Probably more so than you realise. I'll let you go, and you can make your calls. But remember, I am still here for you."

"Thank you, Father McLean. I appreciate that."

"Not at all, Maureen. No matter what Neville did, you and he were still my friends, and nothing will take that away."

They said their goodbyes, then Jim sat with his head in his hands for a while.

He needed to get hold of Brendan. Let him know his instincts had been correct. He tried calling again. Same message saying the phone was switched off; Jim could cheerfully have cursed mobile technology at this point. What else could he do? He didn't know the numbers of any of Brendan's family. He could – maybe should – inform the Bishop of Brendan's moonlight flit but letting that particular genie out of the bottle was the last thing he wanted to do.

Good grief, he was fond of Brendan but at that particular moment he could cheerfully throttle him and feed his remains to the nearest crocodile piece by piece, for taking off like that.

But panicking wouldn't get him anywhere. For goodness' sake, it was *Brendan* he was thinking about. Mr Conscientious! Mr Keenie McKeen from KeenLand! No way could Brendan throw away his whole vocation, seven years of work and prayer, after one setback. He would just have to hold his nerve and sit it out until Brendan came to his senses.

That didn't mean he had to fanny around twiddling his thumbs, though. If he wasn't able to get in touch with Brendan, maybe he could take some action which might help restore his morale.

39.

When Brendan had first taken up residence on the park bench and sunk his head into his hands, he would have been perfectly okay with staying there until he sprouted cobwebs, and passers-by came to regard him as a piece of crap public art. What he had not imagined was that, even at the lowest ebb of his life thus far, the anguish he was experiencing would be no barrier to the sheer tedium of examining his palms indefinitely.

Turns out that there's a limit to how long a person can doggy paddle around an eddy of misery without it eventually becoming...well, boring. Who knew?

Plus, it was starting to rain; Brendan was not so weighted down by guilt and self-loathing that he was willing to risk a soaking while he had no clothes, other than those he was wearing.

And I can't believe that I was seriously – well semi-seriously – contemplating throwing myself off a bridge into a shitload of moving traffic, less than two hours ago. And now I'm worried about catching a chill from sitting around in my damp clothes. Irony is obviously alive and well and living in the heart of Father Brendan Michael Coglan.

His craving for blessed oblivion, however, was stronger than ever. He longed to be immune from any feeling, untroubled by himself and by the nonsensical intrusions *(intrusionscollusionsallusionsconfuckintusions)* polluting his brain, and the desire to bash himself over the head until the moronic refrains shut the fuck up. Even if it was just for a little while. In other words – and the idea thumped him over the head with all the subtlety of a flying donkey – he wanted to be as rip-roaringly drunk as a burrowful of skunks.

He started the long trudge back to the centre of town. His progress was slower this time; mainly because he had never felt so weary in his whole life; his calves seemed to shriek with the sheer effort of plonking one foot in front of the other. It was mid-day when he reached the town centre again.

He would need to choose his destination carefully. The pub would need to be quiet enough for him to be able to sit undisturbed whilst he slowly drank himself comatose, yet not so quiet that he was the only customer and therefore a likely source of interest for conversational bar staff.

In a grubby side street, he happened upon a venue which might well fit the bill. Even from the outside, the joint looked promisingly scruffy; and the inside boasted little to change Brendan's original perception. A solitary television broadcasted largely to itself, the images flickering, migraine-like, into the dinginess. Absolutely nothing in the way of quizzes, darts teams, or anything else that could possibly hint at a sense of community was advertised. The padded benches under the grimy windows were faded and the leatherette was torn in several places; springs were even poking out of some spots. Neither the floor nor the windows had benefited from a decent clean for several months, and the bar did not appear to have even a nodding acquaintance with a can of polish. This was a place beloved of absolutely nobody; clearly its only possible raison d'etre was to get the clientele blotto in as short a time as humanly possible, before they either staggered home or progressed to livelier places. Let's face it, there was bog all else to recommend the dive.

Brendan thought it was perfect.

Apart from two middle aged men who were deep in conversation with each other, he was the only customer. As he approached the bar, he saw that there was a rudimentary food menu – anything you like, as long as it's sandwiches or crisps – displayed. And if the state of the kitchen was anything like the rest of the place, they probably chucked a dose of salmonella in for free.

Although it must have been nearly twenty-four hours since he had last eaten – and that had whooshed pretty much straight through him – Brendan felt the exact opposite of hungry, as if a large stone had lodged itself in his stomach. Besides, eating would impede his goal which was to get gloriously, rip-roaringly stocious in as short a space of time as possible. He ordered a pint and hunched over it in a seat close to the television screen. If anybody approached him, he could pretend to be engrossed in Bargain Hunt.

Two hours and five pints later Brendan concluded that he was probably not cut out to be an alcoholic. In fact, he felt almost as sober as when he had walked into the pub. He had forgotten how great a strain beer placed on the bladder, as several trips to the toilet – which, with their stained urinals, tiny cracked squares of soap, non-working hand driers, broken bolts on the stall doors, suspicious crustings in the bowls and loose toilet roll shreds on the floor, did a sterling job of keeping the shithole chic theme running – had confirmed. Beer was clearly not going to have the desired effect on its own. So, he ordered a bottle of the cheapest red wine, gulping when the barman told him the price. The barman shoved a bottle and one glass in Brendan's general direction, not bothering to ask if he was expecting company. Brendan reckoned he probably wasn't the first sad sack who had wasted away an afternoon there. The door opened. A man in a suit walked in, ordered a triple vodka neat and immediately took refuge in the corner. He had probably just been fired.

The wine seemed to work a little better than the beer. After the first two glasses, Brendan started to feel pleasantly mellow. In fact, he even grinned at the barman who retorted, "This isn't that kind of place, pal."

Chastened, Brendan turned his attention back to the television and carried on drinking. By the time the bottle of wine was finished, the bar was a little fuller and the noise from the television was a blurry buzz round Brendan's ears, wrapping him in a secure little cocoon. Not wanting the sensation to end he walked reasonably steadily to the bar and asked for another bottle, his voice sounding reassuringly normal, at least to his ears.

"It's your funeral, pal," said the barman as he took payment before resuming his efforts to flirt with a terrifyingly raucous hen party of pink cowboy-hatted Glaswegians who were pre-loading at one end of the bar. It was starting to get a bit noisier now. This bottle didn't slide down quite so easily as the first had done. Maybe they kept their rubbish stuff for people who were already well oiled – a sort of Cana in reverse. Brendan ploughed steadily through it, even though his stomach now felt as stretched as his bladder had been previously, and the prospect of a deep, satisfying burp would have been a promise of Heaven.

By the time the second bottle was finished, Brendan was vaguely aware of the theme tune to the One Show starting up in the background. Unable to face another bottle of wine he asked for a double gin and tonic which he took back to his table, sloshing it a little on his way. Why had he not noticed how uneven the floor was until now? The gin and tonic was tasteless – at least Brendan couldn't taste anything. Nevertheless, he forced it down.

When he stood up again, he was suddenly aware of how hot it had grown. The bar was half full by now and Brendan felt, rather than heard, threads of conversation, now more irritating than soothing, wafting around him. The ground seemed to have graduated from uneven to positively lethal. Brendan's legs seemed unable to keep a straight line across the floor, it was so undulating. In fact, he narrowly avoided headbutting the television, which wasn't even in the same direction as the bar. And when he reached the bar, Brendan felt the need to lean against it to keep from sliding downwards.

"Another gin and tonic please," he enunciated, impressed with how coherent he must sound. After all, *he* had understood what he had said perfectly.

"I don't think so, pal."

"Are you ref-fefuging -refusing to serve me?".

"Yup. Pal, you're three sheets to the wind. You can hardly get your words out. Any more bevvies and I'll be scraping you off the floor come chucking out time. You've had a good session over there on your Jack Jones but it's time for you to go home and hit the hay now."

Brendan was about to protest but the barman drew himself to his full height, displaying biceps that Brendan would have wept for in happier times. Something in his expression warned Brendan that, even after five pints, two bottles of wine and a double gin and tonic, arguing was not a wise decision. He made his way to the door, bumping into a man as he went and sending half his pint sloshing over his hand. A growled, "Any more of that, mate, and I'll black your other eye for you," followed him.

As soon as he stepped onto the street, he was slapped by a blast of cold air. Not knowing where he was going, he saw a group of goths. He followed them for no other reason than reckoning they looked like the types who could easily root out another sufficiently seedy joint.

To his puzzlement, he didn't appear to be walking in a straight line. In fact, he zig-zagged from one side of the street to the other. He followed the goths for some time in this manner. Finally, he careened sideways into the front window of a KFC, ricocheted back into the

225

middle of the street, staggered three steps forward and ended up falling at full stretch onto the pavement, jarring his chin against the ground.

"Whoa! Incoming! Over here, quick!" Brendan heard the rush of approaching footsteps.

"Okay, mate, help's here! Can you look up for me?" Brendan had just enough awareness to recognise that the voice was male.

"I need you to look up for me," the voice repeated. Brendan raised his head and saw two blurry figures in red fleeces hovering over him. And heard an unmistakably female, oddly familiar voice saying, "What the living fuck? Christ almighty, I don't actually believe this."

Brendan felt a tug on his upper arm.

"Right, Mister, you're coming home with me. No arguments! Up, NOW!"

"What the fuck are you doing?" The owner of the male voice was clearly exasperated. "You know we don't take the punters home with us. You could be putting yourself in danger."

"I don't think so, with this one. Anyway, I don't really have a choice. Mam would kill me if I didn't make sure he was looked after properly. And I don't mean dropping him at A and E or pointing him in the general direction of a taxi either."

"Why on earth, though? I mean why would your mam give a monkey's about some random you found half comatose in the middle of the street?"

The faces of Brendan's rescuers chose that moment to gather into focus.

"Because he's my bloody brother, that's why."

Unmistakably, glaring back at him was the furious face of his sister, Nicole.

40.

Brendan was dimly aware of Nicole telling her co-rescuer that she was knocking off for the night. The man didn't bother protesting; if he had known Nicole for longer than ten minutes, he would have realised it was a fruitless exercise. Brendan tried to heave himself upwards but for some reason the ground had started spinning violently, making him feel as though he was at the centre of a playground roundabout. His stomach had also started to swirl.

"Right," he heard Nicole's voice again. "Can you grab him under his other arm, and we'll get him upright. Once he's standing, I should be able to get him back to my car myself."

"Okay, if you're sure." The man sounded doubtful. Brendan felt the world shift as he was hauled to his feet. The ground span faster than ever, his stomach tilted, and his legs lost all strength. He gripped Nicole's upper arm with both hands.

"Can you manage like that?" her colleague asked.

"Should be fine if you can whack his arm around my shoulder. I'll grab him by the waist."

Brendan stood unprotesting, as his rescuers manoeuvred him into a position suitable for being dragged across town.

"Right, off we go," Nicole barked.

Nicole set the pace, mouth set in a tight line, keeping Brendan firmly anchored to her side. She led the way to the multi storey carpark.

"It's a good thing I got parked on the ground level," she observed. "You can come home to mine and sleep it off. Tomorrow, you can tell me why I bumped into my priest brother dressed like he's about to start the Great North Run, only instead, he's lying kaylied in the middle of the town centre, with a massive bruise down one side of his head; making this officially the most surreal night of my life. Car's over there."

Nicole reached in her jeans pocket and took out a car key which she pointed towards small a grey Honda. She let go of Brendan and rotated her shoulder, saying, "Christ. You're heavier than you look."

Brendan teetered beside her.

He made it as far as the car, when the burp he had been craving forced itself out. He rubbed his chest, then watched in amazement as a gargantuan, claret-coloured flood gushed down his front and spilled onto his shorts and trainers. Another volcano-like surge followed hot on the heels of the first.

"Oh, fuck a doodle doo," groaned Nicole. "Kneel down and make sure you get it all up before you set foot in my car."

Brendan collapsed onto his hands and knees as it all erupted in repeated waves, splashing into a pool which spread until his hands and knees were paddling. Nicole crouched behind him and rubbed his back, until the paroxysms eased.

"Better?"

"Yeah, I'm good!"

Amazingly, despite the facts that Brendan had just regurgitated his entire nutritional intake from the past twenty-four hours and was now kneeling in a large pool of his own making, he felt remarkably enlivened. Terrific! Ready to take on the world! With bells on! Hangover, Shmangover!

"Up you get, let's get you into the car, then. Oh, shit, you're rancid. Your face is completely pebbledashed. Wait a minute. I'll get some wipes from inside."

With difficulty, Brendan struggled upright.

"Oh, fucking hell, Brendan!"

"Wha?" The word was followed by another belch, filling Brendan's mouth with acid. He spat pink bile into his hand and wiped it on his sleeve, feeling a sudden, inexplicable urge to laugh.

"Look downwards, you plank!"

"Oh!"

Vomit was apparently not the only fluid he had expelled. The crotch of his shorts was dark, and his inside legs were soaking.

"Have I really just –?"

"YES! You really have just."

"That's just … mental!"

Brendan succumbed to a fit of uncontrollable giggles. With a stony expression, Nicole handed him a packet of baby wipes. Brendan used one to wipe his mouth and hands.

"Don't forget your legs, oh come here, I'll do it." Nicole wiped Brendan's legs, non-too-tenderly. Brendan handed her his sick-saturated wipe.

"What the fuck am I supposed to do with that?" Nicole sounded like someone doing a heroic job of trying to hide her frustration. "Just drop it on the floor. I know it's littering but I'm really not too bothered about that at the moment."

Brendan convulsed again.

"I can forgive your sins if you like, remember? How many Hail Marys do you reckon?" Brendan wiped tears of laughter from his face. "I. HAVE. THE. POWER," he intoned with great solemnity, until laughter overtook him again.

Nicole ignored him. She opened the car boot, took out two Morrisons shopping bags and spread one across the passenger seat of the car.

"Sit on that," she said firmly as she pushed Brendan towards the seat. "Now, swing your legs round." Brendan obeyed, still laughing. Nicole leaned over to buckle his seatbelt and then handed him another shopping bag.

"Use this if you want to spew again."

She went round to the driving seat and opened both windows. "You stink, and I don't want you falling asleep and choking to death. At least, not on my watch. I hate paperwork at the best of times."

Brendan was beginning to understand about the smell. The ends of his hair had been soaked and were quickly drying in stiff peaks. His nose was feeling a bit clogged as well, maybe some sick had got lodged there. Thinking about it made him feel queasy and his laughter tailed off.

"Nic? I think I might have lied. I'm really not all right."

"You think?"

Brendan opened the Morrisons bag, just in case, and rested his head against the cool car window.

"Don't you dare bloody fall asleep on me!"

A half moan was the most Brendan could muster. Nicole turned up the radio.

"Not ideal, but better than nothing, I suppose," she said, as "Tragedy" belted out. "You're lucky it was me on tonight, you know. In case you're wondering."

Brendan was beyond wondering anything at this point. Nicole continued.

"I'm a night volunteer. Street pastor, you could say."

"Is it aff affy affel?" Brendan tried and failed to say "affiliated." He settled on "Churchy?"

"Is it shite! It's me you're talking to. It's mainly health service volunteers. Street pastor minus the religion, I should have said. I do a couple of nights a week protecting the drunks of Sunderland from themselves, making sure they get home safely, or get medical attention if they need it, that sort of thing. Teddy stays over at Mam and Dad's when I'm on duty. He loves it and, of course, they spoil him rotten. Tuesday's generally a quiet night, it tends to be the weekend when it all starts kicking off. Can't get moved for lairy gits starting fights in the kebab queue then. Anyway, I'm off work tomorrow so we can have a proper catch up then. No offence, but you're not exactly the world's best conversationalist at the moment, are you? Speaking of which, you'd better still be awake."

Brendan grunted to indicate that he was. Sort of, anyway.

"I'm assuming you don't want Mam and Dad to know about this little escapade?" Nicole went on. "I had imagined I'd be covering for you after a rough night out about twelve years ago. Better late than never, I suppose. How are you anyway, apart from completely rat-arsed? How's the priesthood shaping up to be?"

"I left today. Not going back," Brendan mumbled.

"Have you now? Well, I'll get the story out of you tomorrow." She gave him a sideways look. "Christ, you look like death warmed over. How much weight have you lost? And you're a terrible colour. Not to mention that bruise. And you're getting spots. Right, we're nearly home. We'll get you all cleaned up when we're inside."

The headlights of the Honda illuminated a newish, smallish brick house with a neatly cut front lawn. Nicole parked on the brick driveway.

"I'll open the front door and you can scoot straight in," she said. "And we're lucky; it's dark, so nobody can see your accident."

With difficulty, Brendan prised his eyes fully open, and Nicole helped him out of the passenger seat. When they were both inside, Nicole pointed upstairs.

"The bathroom is upstairs on the right. Get in the shower, you're minging. There's plenty of shower gel and shampoo. I'll get you some towels. Chuck your clothes on the landing and I'll put them through the washing machine." She glanced downwards. "Those trainers could do with a good scrub as well. I'll see to them."

She followed Brendan into the bathroom and pulled some blue towels out of the airing cupboard.

"There you go. I'll sit outside, in case you're feeling a bit unsteady."

"Yeah, thanks." By now, Brendan was feeling extremely unsteady.

"I'll get you some pyjamas as well. There's a pair Mam and Dad forgot, when they stayed over after their boiler conked."

She trotted off and chucked Brendan a navy Primark lounge suit, before taking up a sentry position outside the bathroom door. There was nothing that Brendan relished less than jumping in the shower, but something in Nicole's tone warned him that resistance would not be a good idea. So, he showered, hoping he was managing to remove the sticky clumps from his hair. His knees were filthy; Nicole's wipes hadn't removed much of the grime. They were also badly skinned. He leant over and dabbed them, until a sharp surge of nausea persuaded him to abandon the effort. Then he dried himself clumsily, not bothering with his hair, and put on the pyjamas. They were a little too short, finishing above his ankles, and were more than a little too wide, gaping around his midriff. He almost tripped over Nicole as he left the bathroom. She leapt up.

"Show me your hands!"

Nicole examined the scraped skin on his palms. "Now, let's have a look at your knees," she said, and gently felt them when Brendan pulled up his pyjama pants.

"They'll sting tomorrow. I'd best put some antiseptic on as well." She smeared cream over Brendan's knees and palms.

"You'd better use this," she said, taking a bottle of mouthwash out of the bathroom cabinet, "else you'll have a mouth like the bottom of a budgie's cage tomorrow."

Brendan sloshed it around his mouth, spat and repeated the process. Mingled with the recycled beer-gin-wine cocktail, it tasted foul.

"And use the toilet. I don't want you pissing in Teddy's bed. I'll wait outside, but don't think I won't be listening."

Brendan could well imagine the type of nurse Nicole would be. Her patients would have a hundred percent recovery rate. They wouldn't dare not.

"In there," Nicole pointed at a small room across the landing. At some point, she had turned the bedside light onto a low setting and turned down the duvet. A glass of water had been left on the bedside table and a bucket had been placed next to the bed. Brendan climbed gratefully in, slid under the duvet and lay on his back, careful not to disturb the bruise, which was now starting to throb again.

"Not happening," said Nicole firmly. "I need you on your side. Other side, please," she went on as Brendan turned to face the wall.

"My bruise hurts," he protested.

"Tough turds! If you vomit in your sleep, it needs to be able to run out, or you'll choke."

She pulled Brendan into a decent approximation of the recovery position. When she was satisfied, she turned the light out.

"I'll hang around outside for a bit, until you're properly asleep. We can fill each other in on everything in the morning."

Brendan felt his hair being gently stroked as his eyelids fluttered.

"Sleep well, Brendan. Whatever's up, we'll sort it out tomorrow, okay?"

A soft kiss brushed his forehead. Brendan had just enough time to wonder at the strange turn of events, and feel the relief of having someone look after him, before he passed out.

41.

It seemed that he had only closed his eyes for five minutes when the rattle of a million hailstones crashed into his skull, forcing him into wakefulness. He tentatively opened one eye and barely found the strength to groan, as a billion specks of lights as sharp as lasers bored into him. The hailstone din seemed to be coming from the bathroom; it abruptly stopped, to be replaced by a crash suggestive of a raging waterfall. That stopped too, and the bathroom door slammed shut. Brendan did not have words for the sheer volume of the bang.

As the room slid into focus, he saw that the lights were tips to what looked like a myriad of wands. He turned on the bedside light, shading his eyes from its vicious brightness. The wands were part of a repeated Harry Potter pattern on the wallpaper. In fact, the whole unfamiliar room was a homage to Harry Potter. Harry appeared on the curtains, rug, bedding and bedside lamp.

"It's like he's bloody stalking me!"

Next to the lamp sat a malevolent looking stuffed ginger cat, which Brendan avoided looking at. There was a Hogwarts dressing gown hanging on the back of the wall and what looked like a substantial collection of figurines on top of the chest of drawers. Brendan felt a moment's confusion before the events of the previous night came back to him, and he realised he must be in his nephew Teddy's bedroom.

The next thing he realised was that he was in excruciating pain. His bruise throbbed mercilessly down the full crescent of his face, his knees, hands and chin stung, his whole body felt stiff and jarred and there were a dozen different kinds of agony going on in his head. His stomach felt stretched and raw. Despite the mouthwash, his mouth was full of an acidic taste and his throat was parched. Making a supreme effort he raised his tortured head, picked up the glass of water, downed it in one swallow and immediately regretted the action, as his stomach clenched, protested and refused entry.

Brendan grabbed the bucket and retched. Unlike the painless eruptions of the previous night, this was a sweaty laborious business that stung his throat, strained his chest and intensified the pulsing behind his eyes to an almost intolerable level. The faint echo of recycled wine at the back of his throat increased his nausea, and he vomited again.

Nicole must have heard him, because she ran into his room, saying, "I see you've survived the night then. Okay, let's get you sitting up properly."

Brendan sat up fully, still hugging the bucket, like a long lost relative. After he had stared into it gasping for a few minutes, Nicole prised it from his arms.

"Okay, I think you're finished. Christ, you look like death gone cold now. I'll get you some paracetamol and some more water."

Brendan drew his hand across his mouth and lay back down, closing his eyes as Nicole removed the container. A laser display of sharp neon lines danced and zigzagged behind his shut eyes. It occurred to him that Nicole had been fully dressed. It must be well into morning, then.

Nicole came back with fresh water and two paracetamols, and the cleaned bucket.

"Take these and get bit more shut-eye. I'll be up with some tea and toast in a little while. Put a lining on your stomach." She paused then said, "Or I could do you a bacon buttie if you prefer."

Brendan gagged again and covered his mouth.

"Maybe not the bacon, then."

"Will you not talk about bac – shit! Bucket!"

Brendan heaved but all that came up was air. At least, he must be completely empty by now. Nicole passed him the water; hang on, was she smirking?

"You're enjoying this, aren't you?"

"Who me? I've never been so insulted. Take them tablets, I'll be back when they've had a chance to kick in."

She turned the bedside light out and closed the door gently behind her.

Brendan swallowed the paracetamol and melted into the soft pillow. He must have started dozing because the next thing he was aware of was Nicole's sing-song voice, dragging him back to consciousness.

"Wakey, wakey, time to sit up. Breakfast's ready."

Brendan rubbed his eyes and sat up gingerly. His stomach felt a little more settled and to his surprise, he realised he was hungry. The toast and butter smelt almost appetising. Nicole set a tray on his knees and he took a tentative bite of toast and chewed slowly, letting out a relieved sigh as it slid down without announcing any intention of performing an abrupt U turn.

Nicole sat on the end of the bed and waited. After a couple of minutes scrutinising her fingernails, curiosity appeared to get the better of her.

"Okay, when are you going to tell me what you were doing getting wasted in the city centre yesterday, looking like you'd been in a fight?"

Well, she was going to ask sooner or later. Brendan put down his half-eaten slice of toast.

"Not much to say, really. Only that I realised I'd made a serious wrong call joining the priesthood and decided to put it right. So, I quit."

"What do you mean, quit? I mean, have you put your notice in, talked it over with someone?"

"Well, I left a text for my mentor. He's probably got the message by now."

"And you can do that? Quit at a day's notice? Will I not get a crowd of handcuff waving cardinals banging on the front door?"

Brendan took a grateful slurp of tea; his throat still felt dry.

"It's not a prison, Nic. I can walk out when I like. I may be still technically a priest but so long as I don't want to get married that's not much of an issue. Besides, I'm making such a cock up of it they'll probably be glad to see the back of me."

"What sort of a cock up?"

Brendan shook his head. Ouch!

"Let's just say I supported some people who I thought needed supporting but my mentor thinks I called it wrong. And the people I supported would have got on just fine without me. So basically, by sticking my size twelves in where nobody had asked me to stick them, I've upset a load of decent people for nothing."

He rubbed his hands over his face, leaving a buttery smear.

"Whoa, let's get this straight. So basically, you pissed someone off while you were trying to help someone else."

"That's about the size of it."

"So, where's the problem?"

"That's just it. I thought I was doing the right thing. I sort of still do, I mean morally. But my mentor's convinced I didn't, so maybe he's right. And my motives for helping were probably selfish in the first place, making me feel better about stuff from yonks ago, which makes me a total hypocrite. And did I really even help that much? I don't even know. Personally, I think I made a gigantic arse of it. And everything just keeps going round and round until I want to whack my head off a brick wall."

Nicole slapped her hands on her thighs.

"Well thank goodness for that. For a minute there, I was worried you were going to come out with something over complicated."

Brendan ignored the maybe-sarcasm. And the fact that Nicole was now making the same sort of cough people make when they are trying to suppress a snigger.

"Does it make any sense to you? Because it sure as Hell doesn't to me."

"In all honesty, not really." Nicole abandoned the half-arsed effort to hide her smile. "I mean, as crises go, I've heard worse. I must admit I'm substantially underwhelmed. I was thinking girls. Or maybe boys."

"No and no. And don't even suggest altar boys, unless you want me to throw up again, right over Teddy's duvet."

Nicole grinned. "Wow, that sounds suspiciously like a sense of humour developing. Seriously though, if all that's worrying you is that you may have made a bad call, you're way overthinking things. You're a priest, your raison d'etre is to help people. You're going to arse a few things up along the way, so what? I spent my entire first nursing placement thinking I'd never get the hang of anything. And if you ruffled a few feathers in the process, well so much the worse. You think I never contradict the doctors when I'm on shift? I went right over the head of a junior last week, because he tried to fob someone off with Gaviscon. Just as well I did because she was actually having a fucking heart attack. Sometimes you have to speak out. And bugger the consequences."

And sometimes you want to speak out and you can't. And sometimes you should speak out and you don't. And sometimes, the consequences are too big to be buggered.

But Brendan only nodded and tried to smile. Things would only ever be black and white to Nicole.

Don't forget the fact that you're lying to her, as well. Like you've lied to yourself and everyone else most of your life.

Brendan took another bite of toast that was now starting to sag under the melted butter. He concentrated on chewing, trying to banish the nagging thoughts that were almost as troublesome as his headache. Okay, so maybe he hadn't told her the real reason for his near despair, but he was sitting cosily in her house, eating her food and accepting her comfort. He was still allowed to appreciate her kindness, wasn't he? Even if he didn't deserve it? And even if he still couldn't quite believe that they were sitting having a conversation like any brother and sister who didn't hate each other's guts?

Then Nicole did something Brendan had never known her to do. She leant forward and brushed a lock of curls out of his eyes.

"And if you really think your mentor wants you gone, you're dead wrong. Your phone fell out of your pocket as I was putting your clothes in the washing machine. I checked it in case anyone was trying to get hold of you. By the way, you seriously need to set a better passcode. 1234, really? There were at least twenty texts from someone called Jim, begging you to get in touch and let him know you were all right."

Brendan groaned.

"So, and please don't freak, I messaged him back and let him know you were safe and with me. He was going to get in a taxi and come straight round, but I rang him back and told him that really wasn't a good idea. So we chatted a bit more, then left it that I would return you tonight. Whatever you've done, he obviously doesn't think it's a career ending catastrophe either."

Brendan massaged his throbbing temples, as he struggled to digest the latest turn of events.

"Look Brendan, you worked towards this for years. Okay, so we've never been exactly close but I'm still your sister. Your big sister. And I'm not going to let you make the worst mistake of your life, even though half the time I want to throw you out of the nearest window."

Brendan picked up his tea and warmed his hands on the mug.

"Is that okay, by the way? I couldn't remember if you take sugar or not."

"It's great. But why do you even care whether I leave or not? Come to that, why are you doing any of this for me? I literally fall at your feet from out of nowhere, and you're immediately acting like my guardian angel when all my life you've absolutely hated me."

"Hated you? What are you on about? I've never hated you. Wanted to strangle you, yeah. Lots of times. But not hated."

"Nicole, you can barely stand to be in the same room as me. I hardly even know Teddy. What's changed all of a sudden?"

"Apart from the fact that last night and today you've seemed like an actual human for the first time in your life? Making real, actual human mistakes? Look, it was always going to be tricky between us. I was your typical angry-without-a-cause teenager. You were this pathologically well-behaved Peter Perfect. I can't ever remember you being in trouble with Mam and Dad once you were past ten or eleven. If anything, they used to worry because you weren't more rebellious or cheekier or something, like I was."

237

"Maybe they were glad of the rest, they probably reckoned they'd earned it."

Nicole pretended to swat him.

"Oy! Watch it! I mean, you totally lapped up the whole church thing when I had no use for it. They say Catholic girls go one way or the other. Once a few of us had decided that there was no such thing as a loving god who made people suffer, well that was it. We knew everything. And we were like, totally the first people who'd *ever* thought that, of course. And we weren't about to let anyone else forget it, especially anyone who disagreed with us."

"Like the time you removed all the religious Christmas cards from the mantelpiece because you said they were hijacking an ancient pagan winter solstice celebration?"

If Brendan remembered rightly, it hadn't just been the cards. The angel on the top of the Christmas tree had been replaced by a stuffed Pokémon, and the crib figurines had been substituted by Simpson characters. Jackie had insisted on Homer and Marge's eviction from the stable, but the Pokémon had reigned triumphantly until New Year.

Nicole nodded. "Most of the time, Mam and Dad were just like, 'Whatever you say, Nicole.' Mind you, they had bigger fish to fry, such as when I got brought home by the police that time I used a fake ID to try and get into the Blackie Boy."

"You got grounded for a month for that."

"So, the next closest target happened to be you, little bro. Looking back, I can see I probably came on too hard but, in those days, I just thought you were an annoying little goody two shoes."

"Sorry about that."

"You were a kid. We both were. One thing I will say though: you really did need to come out of yourself more. It can't have been healthy living in your own head so much. And you had that dodgy stomach, so if ever you got upset you would curl up, hugging your belly, having everybody fussing round you. You've no idea how aggravating that was."

"I didn't enjoy having those episodes, you know. They made me feel really poorly. And they were embarrassing. When they came on, I tried to sneak off and not draw attention to myself. Turns out, it's quite difficult to shit yourself discreetly."

238

That made them both laugh.

"Anyway, I was in trouble once with Mam," Brendan went on, feeling he needed to even things up a little. "She went ballistic when I had a panic attack in the middle of Sainsbury's. I was helping her with the Christmas food shop, and someone nudged a trolley into my back, and I started hyperventilating right in the middle of the freezer aisle. Nobody could get near the frozen parsnips. Nearly caused a pile up."

"Once! In all your adult life! And Brendan, she was scared. Have you ever seen anyone having a major panic attack before, apart from yourself? I've seen a fair few in A and E and they're not pretty. If you're not used to seeing them, you could easily think someone was seriously ill. Mam was probably just relieved that you were okay. The day of Matt Cassidy's funeral, when you'd got back from hospital, I heard her telling Dad how freaked out she'd been. The way you were grabbing at your chest, she thought you were having a heart attack."

"I hadn't ever thought of it like that."

"Don't beat yourself up. But the upshot was that, from my point of view, Mam only ever got annoyed with you because she was concerned about you, not angry. And then you announced that you were joining the priesthood right after I'd told Mam and Dad that I was pregnant by some radge I barely knew. Talk about the sublime and the ridiculous." She burst out laughing again. "Mam and Dad must have thought they'd gone wrong somewhere and never knew which one of us they'd gone wrong with."

"I wish I could have supported you more. You probably found it hurtful that I wasn't going to be around to play much of a part in the baby's life."

Nicole gave a dismissive wave. "I probably wouldn't have welcomed it. I don't think I could have handled a saintly brother around the place. In fact, I bloody know I couldn't. It didn't help when Gavin and I split up when Teddy was a year old."

"I knew it hadn't lasted, but I never got to hear the details."

"Not much to tell really. Turns out that sleepless nights, dirty nappies, clothes with puke on them, and no money aren't the world's greatest aphrodisiac. Gavin gave it a year before he took off with the little slag from the barbers. Last thing I heard, they'd emigrated to Australia together and are living the life of Riley. I only found out

239

about it when the maintenance payments stopped. Dad went apeshit. I, like a total fucking idiot, tried to defend Gavin, saying it was my fault for not making more of an effort with myself and not allowing more money to go on nights out and stuff. Well, Dad said the most tactless thing he could possibly have come up with under the circumstances."

"What did he say?" Brendan was beginning to enjoy the gossipy turn the conversation was taking.

"What didn't he say? The punchline was something along the lines of 'Understandable? Understandable, my arsehole! Do you think our Brendan could ever have walked out on a young lass with a year-old baby? Well, do you really?'"

"Ouch!"

"Ouch, indeed! I was raging. Because, of course, he was right. There's no way you would ever have treated anybody like that. You were always kind. I never valued that about you when we were kids, I always just found you a boring little prig."

"Thanks," said Brendan, but he smiled as he said it.

Nicole leaned over the tray and reached for Brendan's hand.

"But all that went on ages ago. And it would be nice to have a brother for a friend. So long as you never expect me to call you Father."

"I might insist on it once. To wind you up if nothing else."

"And it would be nice for Teddy to know his uncle. You'll meet him properly this afternoon."

"I would love that. You know I would never have … been a danger to him, no matter what you might have picked up from the big book of evil Catholics."

"I know. I was lashing out a lot at the time. I was confused and scared. And probably hormonal, truth be told."

"I should have been more understanding, I suppose. We'll be okay now though, won't we?"

"I guess so, St Brendan of All Pissheads. Come on, you've got to allow me one gloat. Think yourself lucky I didn't take a stack of incriminating photos and post them all over Instagram."

"Do you have an Insta account?"

"No, but right now I'm thinking it might be worth setting one up."

Brendan threw the hideous stuffed cat at Nicole, just missing her.

"Nicole, did you really not have Teddy baptised?"

"Nope."

"I could do it if you wanted. It needn't be a big thing. I could do it at the kitchen sink with a glass of water if you liked."

Nicole narrowed her eyes and threw Brendan a hard look. "Don't push it!"

42.

By mid-afternoon, Brendan was sitting comfortably in his freshly laundered clothes, awaiting Nicole's return from the school run. The front of his hoodie still bore a smattering of faint grey stains, where it had been soaked by red wine. Brendan found that he didn't care in the slightest. His running gear had definitely seen better days. Like himself, he supposed.

Not that this was strictly true. In fact, he felt remarkably refreshed, better than he had done for some time. Far better than he had any business feeling after yesterday's shenanigans. After he had finished his toast, he had slept again for a while, then showered, dressed and ventured downstairs, before Nicole went to collect Teddy from school.

"You'll love him. He can be a bit of a gobshite, so don't be scared to tell him to shut up if he goes on for too long."

Nicole's sitting room was cheerfully messy; one of her cardigans was draped over the back of an armchair and a collection of DVDs were haphazardly bundled into a coal scuttle. Now, curled up on Nicole's sofa with a half-finished mug of tea and a copy of Closer (who even were half of those people on the front cover?) within arm's reach, the radiator gradually clanking to life, and "Escape to the Country," playing silently on the television, Brendan wished he could stay there for – well forever, actually.

You can't though, can you? And tonight is when you have to face the music.

241

Brendan was spared from dwelling on that uncomfortable truth any further by the rattle of Nicole's key in the door.

"Shoes off, Teddy, before you go into the living room. Then you can say hello to your uncle."

There was a shuffling of shoes being removed and coats hung up, then the living room door flew open.

"Hello. Are you my Uncle Brendan? Mum said you'd come to visit. Do you like Harry Potter?"

"And that's the most important question he'll ask you today so be careful about how you answer it," laughed Nicole. She was carrying a lunchbox in one hand and a toy snowy owl in the other.

"I love Harry Potter," he said. This, at least, was true; both the books and films had always been a guilty pleasure of Brendan's.

Teddy nodded approvingly. Brendan took a long look at his nephew, drinking him in. It was like looking at an old picture of himself or Nicole. Same curling blonde hair which had been flaxen in Brendan's childhood, same clear blue eyes, same creamy complexion, same barely-there dusting of freckles across the nose. Teddy had evidently been more fortunate in the nasal department than either him or Nicole. Brendan's nose was long and almost witch-like, while Nicole's tended towards the snub. Teddy's was a perfect button. His face broke into an enormous grin, revealing adult front teeth slightly too large for his mouth.

"Wanna play Top Trumps? I've got a Harry Potter set."

"Sure, but you'll have to tell me what to do. I've never played before."

Teddy looked incredulous that a grown up should be ignorant of something as basic as a game of Top Trumps.

"It's easy, I'll get the cards."

"Take Hedwig with you when you go," said Nicole. She handed Teddy the stuffed owl. Teddy raced upstairs and shortly reappeared, brandishing a pack of cards.

"What's for tea, Mum?"

"Pizza. We need to have something quick because we're taking Uncle Brendan back to Newcastle afterwards."

"Yay! Are we having chips with it?"

"We are not. We're having salad. We're not having a dinner made entirely of junk food. But we've got some ice cream we can have with strawberries afterwards."

"Yay." Teddy lay on the carpet and performed a backwards roll, farting unashamedly as he did so. "Come on, Uncle Brendan, I'll teach you how to play."

Teddy dealt out the cards. He examined the pictures as he dealt, more than a card dealer strictly ought to.

"I like to get Dumbledore. He's the most powerful."

"And don't let him cheat!" Nicole called from the kitchen. "He will do, given half the chance."

"I think that horse has probably bolted by now, Nic."

Brendan and Teddy sat cross legged on the living room floor and played an involved game of Top Trumps for half an hour. Teddy won, maybe because he always made sure Dumbledore was in his pile. Brendan wondered for all of three seconds whether he should say something to the effect of "It's not nice to cheat, Teddy," before dismissing the idea. What was the point of being an uncle if you didn't occasionally get to be the cool adult in the room? Besides, who was he to judge anyone?

"Right, you two. Sorry to break up the party, but tea's ready. What do you have to do first, Teddy?"

"Uh, hands!"

"Get a shift on, then."

As soon as he caught a whiff of vegetable pizza, Brendan remembered that the only thing between him and his mammoth self-sabotaging session was a slice of toast. He couldn't remember when a pizza had smelled so delicious. It was all he could do not to pick up the entire slice and ram it down his throat in one swallow. Teddy started by attacking carrot batons, crunching them noisily.

"What did you do at school today, monster?" Nicole asked, when she finally sat down.

"I swung down the whole set of monkey bars at play time. All six of them. Konrad could only do three before he let go, and Anton couldn't do any at all. And at lunchtime, Konrad fell over, but he didn't cry, and Mrs Habib put a Mickey Mouse plaster on his knee."

"And how about the lessons?"

"Oh, them! Can't remember."

Nicole shared a conspiratorial eyeroll with Brendan.

"I guess I'll have to look in your school diary as usual then."

"What do you like best at school?" asked Brendan. "Apart from swinging on monkey bars at playtime?"

"Art," said Teddy, without hesitation. "I'm building a robot out of bits of cardboard and plastic. When it's finished, I'll paint it, but I don't know what colour yet. I might paint its legs one colour and its arms a different one. Do you think that would look nice?" He speared a cherry tomato.

"I'm sure it will, if you paint it with nice bright colours."

Teddy nodded. "And I like music too. I'm learning the recorder. Mum, can I play some tunes for Uncle Brendan after tea?"

"You can play while I'm washing up. Then we'll need to get going."

"Can we see inside Uncle Brendan's house?"

Brendan took a mouthful of water. "Well, it's not really my house. I live with an older gentleman called Father McLean. He's a priest as well."

Brendan had a moment's dread that the next question would be "What's a priest?" Luckily, Teddy had latched on to the other part of his answer.

"Is he really, really old? Like a hundred? Is he going to die soon?"

Brendan spluttered, then choked on a piece of pizza. Nicole had to thump him on the back and Brendan spat the pizza into his hand. Then everybody collapsed into fits of laughter, and Nicole ordered Teddy to engage in "Less talking and more eating."

As soon as Teddy had finished his last spoonful of ice cream, he slid off his seat.

"I need my recorder," he shouted as he ran upstairs. "And I need a poo."

"He's amazing," enthused Brendan, "but I bet you need a lot of energy."

"Oh yes! I wouldn't have it any other way, though. Now, you go into the living room and act like a willing audience while I sort out here, and we'll get off when I'm finished."

Teddy scampered downstairs again, clutching a recorder in one hand and a music book in another. Brendan sat and listened whilst

Teddy performed "Au Clair de la Lune", "Twinkle Twinkle" and "Mary Had a Little Lamb". Brendan applauded and then they had another game of Top Trumps, which Teddy won again.

"Right, monster," said Nicole when she had finished washing up. "I want you to go and have another wee and then wash your face. Then we'll take Uncle Brendan home."

Teddy obeyed without hesitation.

"Does he always do everything you tell him?"

"Pretty much, actually. He's always been an easy kid. I wonder who he could possibly take after? Not me, for a start. Right, have you got everything you came with?"

"Phone, wallet, clothes, yes that's everything."

"Good. Hey, monster, let's get into the car."

They all trooped out and Nicole buckled Teddy into his car seat.

"Have you got your postcode for the satnav? I don't trust your sense of direction."

"Mum, why does my bedroom smell so funny?" asked Teddy, as Nicole started the car.

"It's air freshener. Sometimes your room needs a spray." Nicole began to reverse onto the road.

Teddy gave an experimental sniff and wrinkled his nose.

"The car smells funny too."

"Well, I sprayed some air freshener in here, as well."

"Why?"

"Your mam brought me home in the car, Teddy," Brendan explained. "And I slept in your room. But I wasn't very well yesterday, and this morning. So that's why your mam needed to use the air freshener."

"What was wrong with you?"

"Teddy, manners," Nicole warned.

"Sorry," said Teddy quietly.

"I hurt my head," Brendan pointed to the still painful bruise down the side of his face. The deep purple now extended from his temple to his jawline, tempered with red and black patches. "And my hands and knees." He held up a scraped palm to Teddy. "And I got a nasty headache and an upset tummy."

"Were you sick?"

245

"Yeah, I was. That's why your mam needed to make it smell better."

"When I went to Flamingo Land with Konrad, his little brother was sick in the car, and it stank all the way back. Is that why you stayed here? So Mum could look after you? Mum looks after people for a job. She's a Band Six nurse so she must be very good at it."

Teddy's voice radiated pride.

"You know our next-door neighbour, Mr Singh? He fell over and hit his head last year. Mum covered him up and looked after him until the ambulance arrived. Which was more than either of his two sons managed to find the time to do."

"Teddy, who on earth said that to you?" asked Nicole.

"Grandma, when she came to look after me so you could go with Mr Singh in the ambulance. Anyway, Uncle Brendan. Did you come so Mum could look after you?"

"Partly, but I also wanted to meet you properly. And I'm very glad I have done."

"Will you come again? I want to show you my robot when it's finished."

"Yes, if you and your mam invite me."

"Can we, Mum?"

"I'm sure we can."

"Yay! Uncle Brendan? Mum says you can come and see us again."

"That's good. Because I can see that there's a large part of your education your mam has neglected."

"And what might that be?" Nicole sounded suspicious.

"How come there's so much Harry Potter stuff everywhere, but not a single piece of Star Wars memorabilia anywhere?"

"What's Star Wars?"

"Only the best movie franchise ever made. If you think a wand is cool, it's nothing compared to a light saber. And if you think Voldemort's scary, wait until you meet Darth Vader."

Teddy's eyes gleamed. "Will you come on Saturday, and we can watch it?"

"Well, maybe not this Saturday. I have work to do in Newcastle. But I promise I'll be over again soon, and I'll bring you a Star Wars DVD when I come."

"Cool, and Grandma and Grandad can come and watch it as well."

"Do you want to know a secret?"

Teddy nodded brightly.

"Grandad loves Star Wars too. He and I used to watch all three films back-to-back over Christmas. I bet he can't wait to introduce them to you as well."

"I take it Mam and I aren't getting a say in this?"

"No," Brendan and Teddy said in unison.

"Well, never let it be said that I would interfere in a male bonding session."

Nicole made a whistling sound as she eased the car on to the dual carriageway.

"Well, I never saw this one coming yesterday! One big happy family in one easy move. Mam and Dad will be happy, after they've got over being incredulous."

Brendan could see Nicole's grin reflected in the rear-view mirror.

"And what about you, Nicole? Are you happy?"

"Yes, I think I am."

"How long before we're at each other's throats again?"

"A couple of weeks."

"As long as that?"

"Probably not."

"Mum, why are you and Uncle Brendan laughing again?"

43.

The motion of the car soon lulled Teddy into a state of drowsiness. His head flopped against the side of his car seat, and his eyelids drooped. Nicole grinned.

"He always falls asleep in the car. He'll wake up when I get him home, though. I'll give him a warm bath and some hot milk and read him a few stories. That'll settle him. By the way, I think you're his new favourite person. I think you had him as soon as you said you like Harry."

"I can't wait to see him again. It won't scare him, seeing me all in black with a collar on, will it?"

"Brendan, his teacher's a goth. She wears black lipstick and DMs, for fu – fudge's sake. His teacher last year wore a hijab. He won't be fazed by a dog collar. Just make sure you keep in touch, yeah? It's been fun this afternoon. We'd – I'd – like to do it regularly."

Brendan tried to remember the last time he'd enjoyed himself so much and drew a blank.

"I'd like that too. Nicole?"

"Yeah?"

"Thanks for everything. You didn't have to help me last night. Or let me stay and meet Teddy."

"Like I'd have left you to marinate in your own pi – bodily fluids! Anyway, Teddy's loved meeting you and I've enjoyed having you around, even if it wasn't for long."

"I'm sorry we never got on properly before; I should have made more of an effort, especially when you were on your own." He added, "And you're doing an absolutely cracking job. You must feel proud every time you look at him."

"I'd ease up on the mushy shite if I were you, else I'll lock you in the boot." Nicole gave Brendan a warm smile though, before adding, "Apology accepted."

It wasn't much longer before they were back in Brendan's street. Nicole whistled as she pulled up in front of the red bricked detached house.

"Nice pad."

"Not mine. Jim and I live here grace and favour, courtesy of the diocese."

"Do you get your own cleaning lady? I'll be well jealous if you do."

"I wish. All kept in order by our own fair hands."

"You'd best get back in then. No sense putting it off, and I've got to get this one back before he's too far gone to have his bath."

"I'm not asleep," came a sleep-drowned voice from the back of the car. "Is Uncle Brendan getting out now?"

"Yes, I'm off now. But I'll see you again soon. Do I get a hug?"

Teddy opened his arms.

"You're privileged," said Nicole.

Brendan opened the back door of the car and leaned in awkwardly to hug Teddy. He breathed in the child's sweet, milky scent of shampoo and ice cream, felt the peach-soft skin against his own, wishing he could stay locked in that position forever. Despite the facts that being doubled over like a folded telescope was putting his back at a supremely uncomfortable angle, and that one foot was in a puddle.

"Bye for now, Teddy," he murmured as he disentangled himself.

"See you soon?" The words were barely distinguishable, through a gargantuan yawn.

"Try and stop me! God bless!"

Brendan could see Nicole's eyes narrow through the rear-view mirror. He quickly shut the car door, still feeling the warmth of Teddy's smooth arms around his neck. Brendan waved, took a deep breath, turned around and knocked at the door. Almost instantly, he saw a light being switched on through the door panel, and the door opened. There was no disguising Jim's obvious relief; if Brendan hadn't known better, he would have sworn the man was trying to restrain a hug.

"Thank goodness. You've no idea how worried I was. Why didn't you answer any of my texts?"

"I can only say I'm sorry."

"Well, thank goodness your sister had the sense to get in contact and put my mind at rest. Why have you never mentioned her? We talked for quite a while. She seems great."

"We weren't close for a long time. It was a sheer fluke, meeting each other last night. She is great though, I found that out last night and today. And my nephew is wonderful."

"Well, don't keep them to yourselves. Invite them round some time."

"Oh, I'm not sure – "

Jim held up one hand.

"Now, I know they're not religious, your sister left me in no doubt about that when we were chatting. But where's the law that says we should only be friends with people who agree with us? Now come into the back room, we need to have a proper talk."

The back room. Not a cosy chat over a mug of tea, then.

The back room was mainly used as a meeting room for visitors; Brendan felt a surge of trepidation, as if he were about to enter the headmaster's office. Nevertheless, he sat down at the formal oak table. The chairs were hard and not particularly comfortable, and the table sported a thin coating of dust. Jim followed with two glasses of water. He placed one on a flowered coaster in front of Brendan.

"I thought we'd better speak in here, given the things that were said the other night. I thought a more formal atmosphere might help us. And before we start talking, I think we should spend a few minutes in silent prayer."

"I'll try, Jim, but I've not been able to pray properly for the past few days. That's been part of the problem."

"Well, all the more reason to put that right now. Once we've talked, I'll hear your formal confession."

Brendan closed his eyes and bowed his head.

God, please grant me the strength and honesty to confess fully. To both you and to Jim.

But it was the memory of Nicole's voice, "Sometimes, you have to speak out and bugger the consequences," that answered him.

"Now," Jim began, interrupting Brendan's train of thought. "The first thing we need to talk about is the fact that you appear to have decided that you wish to leave the priesthood. Would you like to expand on that? Take your time, there's no rush, but I need some idea of how you are feeling."

"I don't know if I *want* to leave. It's more a case of whether I *should* leave. I've felt disconnected ever since – well, for a few weeks, anyway. I haven't felt the peace I normally feel. I haven't been able to pray. I've felt totally cut off, if I'm honest. From God. From other people too, until my sister found me last night."

"Well, that's a thing we've all felt at some time or other. Jesus Christ felt it whilst he was on the cross; he would be the first person to understand how you are feeling. And he would be the first person to remind you that at the end, he realised that God had not forsaken him, and never would."

"Jesus had honesty on his side, though. Father, there's something I haven't been honest about. I need to tell you before I go insane. Then you can decide whether I'm fit to remain here, or whether it would be best for all concerned if I were to leave right now."

Jim raised his hand. "We'll come to that. But firstly, do you honestly think you are the first priest ever to feel he couldn't carry on, when he first appreciates the full responsibility that a life of service to God and of service to others brings?"

Brendan expelled a whoosh of breath and ran his fingers through his hair.

"I don't know. I really don't. All I know is –"

Jim cut him off. "Well, I'm fairly sure that you could go to literally every parish in Britain and find a priest who at some point has thought the exact same thing."

"Yeah, well I bet it usually takes them longer than a month and a half to get to that point."

"Perhaps. But maybe experiencing this feeling early is no bad thing."

"How can it possibly be anything else? I'm supposed to be God's representative on Earth. And so far, I'm completely sucking – I mean failing miserably – at it."

Jim chuckled.

"God's representatives on Earth. Jesus's representatives. And you're coming up short. Seven years of seminary, and that's only dawning on you now? Have you any idea how arrogant you sound? You're beating yourself up because you're inferior to Jesus! As if you'd ever be anything but!"

In spite of himself, Brendan forced a half smile. "When you put it that way..."

"You need to accept your mistakes, forgive yourself as well as other people. Which brings me to my next point."

There's more?

Jim cleared his throat.

"I owe you an apology. I had no right to speak to you the way I did. You were doing what you thought was right and I was completely wrong in challenging you."

"Wha-what?"

"I accused you of being deluded. Yet I was the one who let years of friendship blind me. And it turns out you were more than just morally right. Maureen called yesterday."

251

"Ha – has she –?"

Jim's slow nod told Brendan all he needed to know.

"Brendan, I accused you of acting without compassion. In truth, you were displaying far more than I was. And so, I must ask you to forgive me. And I will also ask you to hear my confession when we have finished here. And now, I think it's time for you to have your say."

Brendan ran his fingers through his hair. He looked squarely into Jim's grey eyes, noting the remaining flecks of auburn in his mentor's busy eyebrows.

"Father, I need to confess something. Something I should have spoken about a long time ago. Something I've never told anybody about. It might help explain things. Or it might not. It might be just me. I could just be making excuses for myself. I mean I don't think I am but it's possible that –"

"Brendan," Jim's voice was gentle. "I think you need to get to the point. And if you pick at that T-shirt much more, there'll be none of it left. Lord knows, it's not looking too healthy in the first place."

"The point! Of course! Sorry! The point is, when Chloe first spoke up, I knew she was telling the truth. I mean obviously I didn't factually know, I'm not psychic or anything, I know that's all a load of bollocks. But I knew instinctively. And the reason I knew instinctively is –"

The words dried up. Brendan's mouth was suddenly very dry. He took a sip of water; his hand trembling so badly that he could barely set the glass down.

"Go on, lad."

Brendan swallowed. "The reason I knew instinctively is –"

Again, the words dried to a squeak.

"Do you need some more time, Brendan?" Jim spoke slowly and quietly.

Brendan shook his head and screwed up his eyes. He tried to speak again but no words came.

"Spit it out, Brendan. By the look of you, you've needed to say this for quite some time, haven't you?"

Brendan gulped some more water and cleared his throat. He thought of Chloe and Frances; tried to imagine them urging him on. Then he twisted his hands together and blurted out:

"The reason I knew instinctively, was that it happened to me."

2000

44.

"Down in a minute, Matty, then I'm gonna wop your arse some more."

"It's 'wop your ass', pillock! And besides, I'm gonna wop your ass."

"Don't think so!"

Ten-year-old Brendan hurries up the stairs at Matthew's house, regretting the extra glass of Sunny Delight he's drunk this afternoon. He almost doesn't make it to the bathroom in time; doesn't even have time to bolt the door behind him, although he manages to kick it shut before yanking down his shorts, plonking himself on the toilet and letting out a relieved sigh. At ten years old, sitting down to pee feels pretty undignified, but in a rush it was the quickest option. He knows he should have gone earlier, but he's having so much fun at Matthew's house on this epic summer afternoon, the hottest this year, he doesn't want to waste a single minute. They'd been running up and down the spacious garden for the past two hours firing water pistols at each other when Brendan's niggling need of the toilet had become an unignorable final demand. As Brendan catches his breath, he brushes away the loose blades of grass that are sticking to his bare chest. He abandoned his T shirt ages ago and he's slick with sunscreen.

Brendan is staying at Matthew's house for the weekend. It's his mam's 40th birthday and his dad has whisked her off to Edinburgh for the weekend. He surprised her with the confirmation of the hotel reservation last weekend – "Not quite Paris, the budget didn't stretch that far, but I've got tickets for Phantom of the Opera, and we'll have a great time at the castle and in the

253

shops." Brendan can't quite believe that they're going all that way and not going to the zoo. What's the point of going to a city where there are actual lions and tigers, and not going anywhere near them? Adults are weird. Nicole is on a residential trip with school this weekend, and when his mam asked what his dad was intending to do with Brendan, his dad's face broke into a huge grin. "You, son, are going to spend the weekend with your friend, Matthew. I've arranged it with Di and Bill. We'll come and collect you on Sunday afternoon when we get back."

So far, the weekend has been mega. Last night, he and Matthew scoffed pepperoni pizza and several bags of Haribo while watching "The Matrix" in Matthew's bedroom. This would never happen in his own home, where there is a strict "No food or television upstairs" policy, and where his pleas to rent "The Matrix" were met with an unnegotiable "It's a 15. That means it's not suitable for children." This morning, they went to the swimming baths and had coca cola and crisps in the café afterwards, another treat which would never have been allowed at home (where there is a strict no Coca Cola policy AND a strict no Sunny Delight policy to go alongside the strict no food or television upstairs policy. Too many nasty ingredients, is his mam's argument; Brendan would beg to differ).

Outside, Matthew's parents are washing off the barbecue, and they have been joined by Matthew's grandad who often comes over on Saturdays since his wife died a couple of months ago. He's pretty quiet, but otherwise seems okay.

Brendan's pee slows to a trickle and then stops. Good! So far he's winning the water fight and doesn't want to take too long and risk Matthew getting a second wind, even though he knows that's unlikely. Matthew may have the edge on the Playstation, but when it comes to anything involving physical ability, there isn't really much competition. He shakes, then flushes and pulls his pants up, before turning towards the sink to wash his hands.

Which is when everything changes.

It begins with Brendan being suddenly aware of a presence behind him. He doesn't know how he knows it, but the hairs on his arms spike and a shudder runs through him, like that time when he poured himself a bitter lemon thinking it was lemonade. Then he feels somebody's breath on the back of his head. Before he can look behind, a large warm hand is creeping down the waistband of his denim shorts, long nailed fingers roughly exploring and

254

searching. He freezes and silently grips the porcelain sink. The hand creeps further down.

A thousand spiders begin to dance on Brendan's skull, making him icy cold from the neck down and completely paralysing him; he couldn't have spoken if his life had depended upon it.

The fingers are still searching and exploring. Brendan hears a blissful moan.

He feels like he's floated outside his own body. The hand is still creeping. There's breath huffing warmly on the nape of his neck. Even so, he shivers; his legs are barely supporting him. There's a pressure on the small of his back, just above his shorts. It feels as if he is wedged against a doorknob or the handle of a screwdriver.

And the hand is still there.

The doorknob-pressure on his back increases, uncomfortably digging into him, driving him against the sink. His belly hurts as the rim of the sink bumps it. The person behind him is now panting heavily. There's a rough grunting sound and the pressure on Brendan's back intensifies briefly then releases. Brendan's back is sticky and itchy now. There is something warm and wet spreading down it.

The next thing he feels is a wet facecloth being harshly scrubbed over the sticky damp patch. It's cold enough to shake him out of his trance. He looks behind to see Matthew's grandad standing behind him, zip undone, face flushed, and smiling.

But it is not like a proper smile. Any fear Brendan may have felt before is multiplied as soon as he sees the sneery upward curve of that mouth, moist with saliva. Brendan can imagine the wicked witch in Snow White or the wolf in Red Riding Hood smiling the same way. And why is he thinking about fairy tales now? He's ten years old. He hasn't read fairy tales in, like, centuries.

Matthew's grandad kneels so that his head is on a level with Brendan. Brendan wants to draw back but the sink is behind him now, jutting into him; he is wedged against it, just as he had been wedged against the other thing a few minutes ago. He shuffles from foot to foot, not wanting to experience the pressing sensation in his back again. That was the nastiest thing he's ever felt.

Matthew's grandad carefully zips his trousers up and starts to speak. His voice is quiet, but somehow more terrifying than Brendan has ever known a voice be. Much scarier than Darth Vader, even scarier than Daleks, because lolling against his dad's side, saying "Exterminate" together – that's a fun scared.

This voice is pure threat.

"You're a nasty little brat, aren't you? Running around outside without your T-shirt and then leaving the bathroom door open like that. Showing your bits off. Inviting people to look. You must be completely depraved."

No adult has ever called Brendan "a nasty little brat" before. He doesn't know what "depraved" means but he can guess it's nothing good. He tries to shake his head, but he can't manage it. He opens his mouth to protest but his voice catches in his throat. A tear spills from the corner of one eye. Brendan brushes it away, embarrassed. Matthew's grandad gives a soft chuckle; some saliva has spilt from his bottom lip and is glistening on his chin. It's rank.

"Don't worry, I won't say anything. And neither will you, so stop crying like a sissy."

Brendan opens his mouth again. The words "I'm going to tell when I get home," form in his mouth but he can't force them out. Another tear falls.

As if he can hear the unspoken words, Matthew's grandad continues.

"We both know you're not going to tell. And we both know why, don't we?"

Brendan knows his mam and dad usually take the teacher's side if he or Nicole are ever in trouble at school (like the time when Nicole was caught with her headphones on during school Mass one day, listening to the Spice Girls- she might have got away with it had she not started singing "Who Do You Think You Are" during the consecration), but maybe something like this is different?

Matthew's grandad doesn't seem to think so.

"Because, if you do tell, you'll be in a lot of trouble. You've just done something very, very naughty. You made me do something naughty as well. And you didn't call out or try to stop me, did you? That proves you were enjoying yourself."

Does it? Brendan finally manages to shake his head and wipes away another tear with the back of his hand.

Matthew's grandad also shakes his head and looks at Brendan almost sorrowfully.

"You were loving it. Imagine tempting a grown up like that! That's far worse than anything else you could ever do. You'll be in serious trouble if you say anything. And it would serve you right."

"I didn't —"

"Everybody knows it's only grubby, nasty little boys that do that sort of thing."

Is he grubby and nasty? He feels filthy and horrible now. Maybe Matthew's grandad is right?

"You know, there are special schools for little boys who tell lies and who do dirty things. If you tell anyone about what you did, that's where you'll end up. You'll probably only be able to see your mam and dad once a month. They might visit at the beginning but sooner or later they'll stop coming."

They wouldn't, would they?

It seems that Matthew's grandad can read his mind.

"They'll stop coming because they'll be disgusted to have a vile little boy like you who runs around half naked. They won't let you live with them, so you'll have no home. Matthew will hate you too. So will your teachers if you ever tell them. They'll call the police and you'll be sent to a naughty boys' school straight away. You won't even have time to say goodbye to your parents. So, no, I don't think you're going to say anything are you?"

Brendan shakes his head again, silently. His shoulders slump. But he knows that he's not going to tell anyone, ever. It's just too risky.

"Good, I can keep a secret too, you know. I'll keep quiet about what you did today. Nobody need be any the wiser. You just need to keep your mouth shut."

Brendan tries to swallow but his mouth is dry. Even though he has just been to the toilet he feels the need to pee again already. His back's scratchy and raw where the facecloth has scoured him. Matthew's grandad rumples the crown of his head. For some reason, this gesture of conspiratorial camaraderie unsettles Brendan more than anything else. He wants to shake the hand from his head but is too terrified to move.

"So, we'll say no more about it. Then, you won't get into trouble. It'll be our little secret. Off you go and play and remember that this is your lucky day."

And he winks, before retreating, gently closing the door behind him. Brendan wipes his eyes again with a balled first and blinks back a final tear. He washes his hands more thoroughly than ever before. Then, he paints a fake smile on his face, grabs his T-shirt from Matthew's bedroom and goes back to playing in the garden with Matthew.

"Why've you put your T-shirt on, Brendan?" Matthew asks.

"I'm getting cold. Can we play something else now?"

"I'll get my Gameboy."

Matthew doesn't seem bothered to be stopping the water fight. He's looking a bit puffed anyway; he's probably had more exercise today than in the past month.

If Brendan's laughter sounds forced to his own ears, nobody else seems to notice. Matthew's grandad sits in a deckchair alongside Matthew's parents and opens a can of lager. He is shortly deep in conversation with them, paying no attention to the boys. Matthew's dad starts the barbecue up. The smoky smell, mingled with the caramelised onion burgers, normally so tempting, turns Brendan's already aching belly; he's starting to feel sick, and he seriously doubts whether he will be able manage any of it. Plates, buns and bottles of ketchup begin to appear. Matthew's mam brings out two glasses of lemonade for the boys. Her fingers must have been greasy because a glass slips out of her hand and smashes onto the floor.

"Bugger!" she exclaims and then bends down to clear up the glass. Then, "Ow," as a shard of glass pierces her thumb. She pulls it out and blood flows heavily, spilling onto the patio. Matthew's dad grabs a tea towel and wraps it round her thumb.

"That looks deep, Di. I think it's going to need a stitch. Come on, I'll run you down to A and E."

"You'll do no such thing. For a cut finger? We'll be there all night. And who do you think will look after the boys? Owww!"

"It's okay," says Matthew's grandad. "I'll stay with them. We'll have a lovely time together. You need to get that seen to, Princess. Let Bill take you down, we'll be just fine here."

So Matthew's parents depart for A and E. Matthew's grandad fills the boys' plates with burgers, sausages and bread buns.

"Looking good, lads. Dig in." His voice sounds completely normal, as if the events of the afternoon hadn't taken place.

Maybe it hadn't. Maybe Brendan had imagined the whole thing. Maybe if he lay down for a while, he would wake up and realise he'd been dreaming. As if to contradict him, the itch in his back suddenly intensifies. Brendan doesn't dare scratch it, Matthew's grandad might say something, and Brendan doesn't think he'll be able to magic up a response.

To look normal, Brendan nibbles half a hamburger, each mouthful nearly causing him to gag. Matthew more than makes up for Brendan's lack of appetite.

"Not hungry, Brendan?" Matthew's grandad is all cheerful now.

Brendan shakes his head, not trusting himself to speak.

"You had plenty of appetite earlier!"

What?

"You were walking into that Magnum. And filling yourself up with Sunny D."

"Sorry." Brendan chokes out the word.

"Never mind. I won't let on that you were greedy and spoiled your dinner. Our little secret, okay Brendan?"

Another wink. Every part of Brendan's skin is crawling, he wishes he could tear it off.

"Can I have your sausage if you don't want it?" Matthew asks.

"Sure. I don't want anymore."

"Cool! Then I'll get the tennis bats out, yeah?"

Brendan is glad to return to the bottom of the garden with Matthew, as far away from his grandad as possible. At one point Brendan returns to the patio area to pick up a stray ball. Matthew's grandad comes to the French doors and locks his eyes on Brendan. Brendan quickly turns away and scampers back down the garden to where Matthew is waiting. His fake smile doesn't budge.

Matthew's parents are still not back by bedtime.

"Wanna use the bathroom first?" Matthew is yawning heavily.

Brendan goes into the bathroom fully dressed, carrying his pyjamas with him. His heart hammers in his chest as he bolts the door firmly shut. He keeps one hand against it as he undresses and quickly puts his pyjamas on. Without looking away, he walks backwards towards the toilet, terrified that at any second the door handle will lift, and Matthew's grandad will appear, kneeling down and making that horrible not-smile. He's too scared to take a shower, even though he can almost feel the filth seeping through his pores. He sits on the toilet while brushing his teeth and washing his face, so he doesn't have to avert his eyes from the door. He tentatively raises his pyjama top and twists round to examine the sore, red patch in the mirror, running

259

his fingers over it lightly and wincing. His tummy still feels strange; he burps, and it tastes horrible and acidy. He leans over the sink and tries to retch, but doesn't bring anything up, so his tummy carries on bubbling and grumbling. As soon as he finishes, he picks up his dirty clothes and trots back into Matthew's bedroom, where the airbed is lying next to Matthew's bed. He dives straight into the sleeping bag and curls up in a ball, wrapping his arms tightly around his knees. He pretends to be asleep, when Matthew has finished in the bathroom, ignoring Matthew's shaking his shoulder. Matthew soon gives up and is asleep within a few minutes.

It's only when Matthew's snores settle into a gentle rhythm that Brendan opens his eyes. He tenses whenever he hears Matthew's grandad walking around downstairs. After a while, Brendan hears the front door opening, a few minutes of low chatter, then finally the closing of the front door as Matthew's grandad leaves.

Matthew grunts as he turns over in his sleep, the television comes on downstairs, someone goes into the kitchen and soon the smell of cheese on toast wafts upstairs. Nice ordinary smells and noises. Everything carrying on as normal.

That's what Brendan wants. To "take the blue pill," as they said in "The Matrix", and have "the thing" erased from his mind forever. To wake up as if "the thing" had never happened.

2019

45.

"So that's it, Jim. That's my story."

Brendan dared not look at Jim. The inevitable condemnation would be bad enough, he didn't have to watch as it was passed. Instead, he closed his eyes and concentrated on the ticking of the old-fashioned wood clock on the mantlepiece. The seconds seemed to tick by with an excruciating lack of urgency; maybe he was destined to spend the rest of his life trapped in this moment. Might not be the worst option. Then Jim spoke.

"Thank you for telling me, Brendan. That must have taken a lot of courage."

Brendan spoke before Jim could proceed to the "but" which must surely be about to follow. He didn't think he could bear to hear it.

"Jim, no. That's the last thing –"

"Did anything else happen that night?"

"Nothing. Like I said I pretended to be asleep, and it wasn't too long before Matthew's parents came back. So, nothing happened. Everything was fine."

"Are you sure about that, Brendan? I would have thought that in some ways, waiting for something that never came must have been just as frightening."

Brendan shrugged. He jiggled his leg so that his knee knocked against the tabletop. It didn't quite mask how badly he was trembling.

"Brendan, you've done a huge thing tonight. If you want to cry or scream or howl, that's absolutely fine."

Brendan closed his eyes, remembering a child curled over himself in a sleeping-bag, face salty from dried tears, biting his lip to stop himself from making a noise. His voice wavered when he spoke.

"It almost felt even worse; the worry that something was going to happen, and never did."

Jim nodded. "How about the next morning?"

Brendan shook his head and ran his fingers through his hair.

"You're going to think I'm nuts. Or lying."

"I can assure you I won't."

Jim's eyes were kind. For now. But Brendan had gone too far to rein back now.

"Okay then. By next morning it felt like I had imagined the whole thing. Even the red rash on my back had almost completely faded. By the time Mam and Dad came to pick me up I had pretty much convinced myself that nothing had happened at all. Crazy or what?"

"Not crazy at all, Brendan. Just terribly sad. That night – it must have been grim for you."

Brendan looked downwards, dragging out the last few dregs of the story.

"When Matt's parents went –." He dried up and started again.

"When Matt's parents went to bed, I fell asleep for a little bit, but I woke up through the night with a horrible pain and a runny tummy. I was scared to go to the toilet in case anyone heard me, so I didn't get there on time. I got some in my pyjama bottoms and had to rub it off with toilet paper. I was scared to cry in case I made a noise, so I screwed my face up and rubbed my tummy until the diarrhoea stopped. I couldn't get back to sleep because my tummy and bottom were still so sore, and I felt all shaky and cold."

Brendan let go of the T-shirt he had been unaware he was twisting in both hands, and drew his fingers across his cheeks, as if he was brushing away tears. However, he remained dry-eyed. He bit his bottom lip, hoping to stop its quivering.

"And you've suffered from stomach problems off and on, ever since?"

262

Brendan wrapped his arms around himself and looked down, nodding vigorously.

"My 'nervous tummy.' I never even considered that there might be a link."

So, he could add "stupidity" to his list of shortcomings; but it would have to take a back seat to "cowardice" and "hypocrisy" for the moment.

"It's difficult to make connections to something you've blotted out."

Brendan shook his head. He didn't deserve Jim's compassion. Why could Jim not see that?

"Did your parents notice anything was wrong?"

"They were buzzing from their weekend when they picked me up and I'm pretty sure I didn't act any differently. I may have been a bit quiet, but I can't say for definite one way or another. Either way nobody seemed to notice anything."

"And I'm guessing that the threats your abuser had hurled at you were enough to ensure you wouldn't tell anyone what had happened."

"That was only part of it. Like I said, for a long while it was like nothing HAD happened. It was there and then it wasn't there. Do you understand?"

Jim nodded. "I was a padre in Iraq, remember. I've seen how the mind can blot out traumatic incidents. Always seems to come back some time or another though."

With a huge effort, Brendan approximated the ghost of a smile.

"I wasn't in a war zone, Jim. What happened to me isn't in the same league as those guys."

"It was bad enough. And then a few years later, you had a friend who told you he had been through something similar."

"The friend was Matthew. And it was his grandfather. The same person."

This was the moment. This is when Jim would realise who Brendan really was. The kindness he had shown so far was about to smash into a wall. Brendan tried to meet his eyes.

"Now, do you get it, Jim? Matthew told me and I didn't say anything. He'd asked me not to and I got why he had. But I never told him what his grandfather had done to me. The one thing I could have

263

said to help him! And I didn't even say anything after he died either. When the police asked me afterwards whether there was anything strange about Matthew's behaviour that night or did he give any clues as to why he ended his life, I lied through my teeth and said that I didn't know anything. I lied to Matthew's parents as well. I lied, Father. Because when it comes down to it, I was too much of a fucking coward to tell the truth."

"I'm guessing as well, that by now you'd locked your memories in a place so safe and secure that it would do Fort Knox proud."

When was Jim's disgust going to show itself?

"It's like I'd painted over the memories and hoped they wouldn't break through all the layers. Telling myself nothing had happened until I believed it. Because I was a useless, weak, pathetic coward. Oh, I may have convinced myself over the years that I didn't want to betray Matty's confidence; didn't want to make things any worse for his parents, but at the end of the day it's a pack of lies."

"Brendan, it is *not* a lie. You said before, you got why Matthew didn't want to say anything."

"He was my best friend and I let him down. I even asked him if he'd ever told anyone or if he'd ever tried to stop it. I was practically victim blaming him. Matty looked so hurt. And I even told him his parents would believe him when I hadn't had the balls to tell my own, for the same reason."

"Brendan, you'd locked it away. You probably weren't even aware that it had happened at the time."

"Stop making excuses for me, Jim! I was the one doing the locking away. Nobody else! Why can't you see that?"

"What I can see is that you're judging yourself by what you know now. But you were an abused child then, not a priest."

"I was sixteen when Matthew told me." Brendan's voice was rising substantially now. "And it's not even as if I was tiny when it happened. I was ten. I could have kicked him or screamed but I didn't. Did that make me partly to blame?"

"No!" It was the loudest that Jim had spoken that evening. His eyes were glistening. "It was that monster's fault, nobody else's," he added, quieter this time.

I was ten.

264

"Oh, Jim! Matthew told me he was eleven when it started. Do you think I was his first? Supposing I gave him a taste for it? Maybe what happened to Matthew really was my fault."

Brendan covered his face with his hands.

Jim took Brendan's wrists and firmly removed Brendan's hands from his face. When he spoke, his voice was still quiet, but more insistent than Brendan had ever heard it.

"Brendan lad, listen to me now. Really listen. You were a terrified child. You are in no way responsible for what happened to you. Or to Matthew. And when Matthew told you, you were a sixteen-year-old boy who had never had the chance to process it. I'm not going to pretend that I understand how terrible it was for you. But as God is my witness, the only thing I feel for you right now is sympathy."

"I don't deserve it. All the church stuff, trying to be as good as possible? Based on self-serving lies, the lot of it. Lies and cowardice. And do you know what? In the grand scheme of things, one hand down a pair of shorts – it's almost nothing. Compared to what Matthew and the girls went through, well they would laugh their socks off if I described it as abuse. I feel bad even mentioning it in the same sentence."

"You feel bad because you weren't abused enough."

The baldness of the statement gave Brendan a hideous compulsion to laugh.

"If you like, yeah. How fucked up is that?"

"I was a padre, remember. I can recognise survivor's guilt when it smacks me in the face."

"And later, what did I do? I encouraged those girls to go to the police. To speak about the most horrendous moments of their lives and make them public. I made them do what I didn't have the guts to do. Literally didn't have the guts to do. Well done, Father Coglan! Your promotion to Pope is in the post! I can't blame them for hating me. And who knows how many people Matthew's grandfather has touched since?"

"Has touched since?"

"Yeah, he could have –"

"Brendan, you just said 'has touched' not 'touched'. Is…"

"...He still alive? Oh, yes. Alive and kicking and living his best life with his daughter and son-in-law. He must be ninety now. He's gone unchecked for all these years, just because I was too chickenshit to stop him. And that is on me, nobody else. Matthew's death is on me. I might as well have pushed him straight off that bridge."

"Brendan, what you experienced was abuse. It doesn't matter whether or not it was on the same scale as others have done. You said yourself that he has probably interfered with many children. Any one of them could have come forward. Why do you think they didn't?"

"I don't know, do I? I can only judge myself."

"They didn't, because abusers know exactly what to say to prevent that. They're experts in manipulation. And don't forget that Chloe and Frances had months of therapy behind them. Besides, even if you encouraged them to go to the police, you didn't compel them. The decision was theirs at the end of the day."

"I made Frances feel guilty. I told her she owed it to Chloe. That was cruel of me."

"Brendan, you couldn't be cruel if you had a gun held to your head. Perhaps you were misguided, but how did Frances seem afterwards?"

"She seemed relieved, but how would I know? How do I know what she was like afterwards?" Brendan rested his elbows on the table and cupped his head in his hands, only raising his head when Jim began to speak again.

"It won't be a straight road to recovery, that's for sure. But from what you said, the most important thing you did was listen to her."

Jim pointed to his ears. "You know, you have two of these," he pointed at his mouth "and one of these and you should use them in the same proportion. You seem to be gifted at that. It seems to me you were never afforded the same luxury. Is there anything else you would like to say?"

"Afterwards, I always tried to stay out of trouble, be good, if you know what I mean. And I always felt that church was one place I could relax, be fully at ease. That's part of why I wanted to be a priest. I wanted to help other people to experience that sense of peace. But, Father, what if it was all founded on lies? I've lied to myself and everyone about everything else. Why not this? Supposing my whole so-called vocation was just some massive great big vanity project? An ego trip? Am I being blasphemous even by calling myself a priest?"

Jim looked long and hard at Brendan. He laid one firm hand on Brendan's arm. When he spoke, his voice was infinitesimally gentle.

"Brendan, you said that you always felt peace in church. Has that changed?"

"Not until the past few weeks. I haven't been able to think straight or even know what I'm feeling."

"After what you've just told me, I'm not surprised. You said you wanted to help people feel the same peace that you did. You wanted to help people. Has that changed?"

"No, never."

"No, never, you say. Do you enjoy parish work?"

Brendan's face broke into a weak smile. "I love parish work, the school, the retirement village." His hands, which were tightly clenched together began to relax.

"That's the first genuine smile I've seen from you in a while. Mrs Smith raves about you whenever I speak with her. She says the children love you; you relate to them far better than any other priest that's been involved with the school." He chuckled. "I should feel insulted really, she included me in that category."

Brendan's smile was starting to look decidedly shaky.

"I'd hate to give it up. It's just that –"

"And what about Timmy, the boy you worked with while you were a student? I believe you built quite a relationship with him."

Brendan was taken aback. "How do you know about Timmy, Father? I don't think I've mentioned him to you."

Jim smiled.

"I took the liberty of getting in touch with Martin Johnstone from Leeds after you had done your moonlight flit. He and I go way back. I told him that you were finding life a bit difficult and could do with some encouragement. Martin told me about this family you had worked with and that they had been associated with an evangelical church. It didn't take much investigation to find it, I suppose the internet has some uses. I managed to speak to the pastor there and he agreed to pass on my email address to them. You must have made quite an impression, because Mrs Oluwu sent me an email by the end of the afternoon. Here it is."

Jim handed Brendan two sheets of printed paper. There was a long letter on one sheet. The second sheet showed Grace and Emmanuel, greyer, more lined but still recognisable. They were sitting on a sofa with two children between them, a boy resting his head on Grace's shoulder and a girl snuggled into the crook of Emmanuel's arm, gazing at him in a way that could only be described as adoring. Draped over the quartet was an extremely hairy, ungainly dog. Grace was in mid laugh as a mauve tongue swept her face. Emmanuel's head was thrown back as a whip-like tail tickled his nose. Brendan began to read.

> My Dear Brendan,
> Pastor Sibanda told us today that he had been contacted by your colleague. It was a wonderful surprise to hear some news about you. Your colleague had mentioned that you were somewhat demoralised and could do with some encouragement. This is something we are only too pleased to give.
> I remember you working with Timmy like it was yesterday. You may have only been with us a few months, but during that time you formed a wonderful bond with him. We had many helpers over the years, but I have never known Timmy look towards the door, eyes alight, when we told him who was coming until he met you.
> I am sorry I was not able to speak to you after Timmy's funeral. It was a long time before I was able to face the world again. If I had been strong enough, I would have told you that we took comfort in knowing how happy Timmy's short life had been; and that in the final months of his life, you played an important part in that. I would have said that memories of Timmy giggling as you tickled his feet or pulled a funny face consoled us during many sad times. I would have said that by allowing us the time to attend prayer groups and bible study sessions, you enabled us to strengthen our faith. Without that, we

might never have made it through the months following Timmy's death. So, we have many reasons to thank you. Sometimes I feel that we will never fully recover from Timmy's loss, and I have made peace with that. There are some things you never properly recover from. Maybe there are some things from which you should not fully recover. If I did not allow myself to mourn Timmy's death when I need to, I would be denying everything he meant to us and how much joy he brought us. Over time, I have come to realise that the secret is learning to live alongside the bad feelings, and to embrace the hope that things will not always be so bleak.

And we have known great happiness as well. Since Timmy died, I have been to university and qualified as a social worker. The additional income after I qualified meant that Emmanuel was able to reduce his hours at work and help me in the best job we have ever had – being foster parents. We have two children on a long-term placement with us – Blessing and Jacob. They bring us joy every day and we are hoping to finalize their adoption soon.

Pastor Sibanda informed us that you have become a Roman Catholic priest. I can think of nobody who would be better suited to this path. I know that you are feeling discouraged at present. This is something to which I can relate. There were many, many times after Timmy's death when I too felt that I had been cut off from God. It was only over time that I came to understand that God is with you even when you do not realise this, and He will continue walking beside you even though it may feel that He is far away. I feel His presence when Emmanuel and I pray together; I feel it in the strength of Emmanuel's arms when he holds me; in sad moments that are lightened by an unexpected memory of Timmy; in the love I feel when I braid Blessing's hair or feel the weight of Jacob's head on my shoulder.

It would be wonderful to hear back from you. Please remember that if you are ever in Leeds again you will find two old friends here, as well as two new ones.

With love and prayers,

Grace Oluwu.

It was only after finishing the letter that Brendan realised that Jim had left the room. He reread the email and saw, to his surprise, that there were two wet dots blurring the "wonderful" and "acquaintance". When put his fingers to his face, he realised that it was covered in tears.

Don't do this Brendan. Don't lose control. Keep it together.

Brendan bit his lip and tasted blood. He bit his thumb, feeling the rush of heat to his face and the constriction of his throat. When he opened his mouth a strange sound, part keening, part howl erupted.

I can't let this hap-

But Brendan couldn't hold back any longer.

It was so long since he had wept, he had almost forgotten the sensation; that each sob felt like a portion of his soul being painfully wrenched from him, each tear like another piece of himself melting away until he dissolved into a pool of his own anguish, the terrifying lack of control in surrendering himself entirely to his emotions. And worst of all, the horror of plummeting deeper and deeper into his worst memories.

A series of images flashed before him. Matthew's grandad kneeling in front of him; Matthew's anguished expression as he begged Brendan to keep his secret; Grace's grief-stricken outpouring at Timmy's funeral; the grille of the confessional with Neville Tanner's silhouette showing through; Chloe's anger; himself leaning over the bridge, a hair's breadth away from giving up. Each memory seemed to kick him squarely in the stomach.

From the kitchen, Jim heard everything. He nodded to himself, then rootled through the ironing basket for a handkerchief. Jim had no truck with paper tissues. They scratched the inside of your nose and after one good blow they were in shreds. With all the focus on the environment these days, he wondered why they were still used. Surely a nice cotton freshly ironed handkerchief was far more environmentally friendly, superior in every way, in fact. He knocked gently, not waiting for a reply. Brendan was at the table, shoulders convulsing, hands trembling, tears dripping through his bony fingers.

"Brendan," Jim said gently, placing a large hand on his shoulder.

Brendan removed his hands from his face. His skin was blotched pink and white, the ends of his hair were damp, and his nose was dripping thick streams into his mouth, a fact that he appeared not to notice. Jim passed him the handkerchief.

"Th-th-thanks," stuttered Brendan. Jim took one of Brendan's hands in both of his.

"Just go with it as long as you need to. I'm sure it's very overdue."

Jim rubbed Brendan's icy fingers, and, little by little, the sobs tailed off. Brendan released his grip on Jim's hand and blew his nose hard. He suddenly started to shudder violently and wrapped his arms around himself.

"I'm... I'm s-s-o c-c-cold." He sounded, Jim thought, utterly helpless.

"Come into the living room. We need to get you warmed up."

Jim wasn't surprised that when Brendan first tried to stand, his legs buckled; and that when he eventually got to his feet, he moved hesitantly, like he had no idea where he was. He placed a hand on Brendan's back and steered him into the living area, towards the sofa, pausing to turn the electric fire to its highest setting, then slipped a brown plush throw around Brendan's shoulders. He could see Brendan shaking underneath.

"I'll get you a hot drink."

Jim boiled the kettle, rejoicing that in his earlier illness he had happened upon the hot water bottle.

"That should help," he said, as he gave the bottle to Brendan when it was filled.

Brendan hugged it tightly and sipped the hot chocolate that Jim placed in front of him, almost spilling the mug on several occasions. Bit by bit, he became aware of the warmth of the hot water bottle flowing through him, the scalding sweetness of the hot chocolate as it touched his tongue, Jim's silent presence. Bit by bit, the shivers began to ease, and the tears cleared enough for him to see properly. But it was several more minutes before he was able to speak. His breath was still coming in dry heaving sobs.

"That's the first time I've cried since Matty died."

His voice felt hoarse and thick from unaccustomed weeping.

"That must have been over ten years ago."

"Thirteen. We were sixteen when he died. I've never shed a tear since."

His voice broke as he finished speaking. He sobbed a few more times, blew his nose and wiped his stinging eyes, then whispered "Sorry."

"Don't apologise. There must have been a great many tears stored up. There are probably many more to release, but at least you've made a start. How do you feel now?"

Brendan considered for a moment while he took another sip of his drink. "Wrung out and not myself, nowhere near, but clearer, I think. A bit clearer anyway. I feel like I want to stay, if that's any help."

"I'm pleased to hear it."

Brendan put down his mug and wiped away a few more tears that had formed in his eyes and started to spill onto his cheeks.

"Do-do you think I'll ever stop crying now that I've started?" He blew his nose again.

"Eventually."

"I couldn't cry after Matty's funeral. After I'd lied to everyone, I didn't feel like I deserved to. It's like I chose to keep shtum, I had to live with it. I've never even felt tearful since. Until now."

"The body can do strange things, that's for sure. But you've spoken now. There's no need for it to resist itself any longer."

More tears fell. Brendan heard the creak as Jim hauled himself out of the armchair and felt the warm hand stroking his back.

"That's good, Brendan lad. Let it come. It'll help you in the long run."

"I – think – I'm – broken." Brendan choked out the words between sobs. He was out of breath now, and his stomach was a giant pulsing knot. He kneaded it with his fist.

"For now, maybe. But you will mend. I'm quite sure of it."

272

"I'm sorry." Brendan whispered once the tears allowed him some respite. "Sorry about everything. I'll confess properly in the morning, but after mass, there's something I've got to do."

Brenda curled up on the sofa with the hot water bottle anchored between his knees and stomach and the throw wrapped protectively round him. Tears came again and he let them fall quietly into his handkerchief. Jim pretended to work on a crossword from his puzzle book ("At my age you need to keep the old grey cells in gear"), whilst surreptitiously observing him over the page.

Brendan was beyond exhausted by now; hollowed out and woozy, cheeks raw from the salt of his tears and head pounding. He rested his head against the arm of the sofa and let the various sounds wash over him; the rumble of a bus outside, the soft burr from the electric fire, the rustling of the pages in Jim's Puzzler. Presently, his eyes grew heavy. The familiar sights and sounds began to blur into each other.

"Come on. Getting a stiff neck won't help you," said Jim, putting his puzzle book down. "Get yourself off to bed now."

Brendan obeyed without comment.

46.

The next morning Brendan dressed properly, his collar feeling reassuringly familiar around his neck. His eyes were sore and bloodshot and the lashes thick with crust. Brendan bathed them in cold water, squinting at his reflection when he was done. Eyes a little red, face a little pale, but otherwise he hadn't scrubbed up too badly. Then he and Jim walked to St Jude's church together, two tall men, one solidly built, the other slim and verging on underweight, bending into the wind. They heard each other's confessions, which was more than a little awkward since neither wanted to give the other an overly burdensome penance. In the end they said a decade of the rosary together. Then, whilst Jim changed into his robes, Brendan lit a candle and dedicated it to Matthew.

"This is for you, mate. Sorry I took so long about it, but I think I'm ready now. I know what I've got to do. For me and for you."

Then he sat in the back pew and prayed for courage.

"Brendan, lad. I don't like to interrupt you, but we'll be starting in a couple of minutes. There's a couple of cars pulling in already."

Brendan started. How long had he been sitting there? A quick check of his watch told him; he had lost track of time. He stood up, stretched and inhaled deeply.

For the first time in many weeks, he felt completely at peace.

It wasn't long before the handful of regular attendees had assembled. Brendan sat bathed in the old sense of peace and calm; each response he uttered, a greeting from an old friend. At the end of Mass, he joined Jim in greeting the parishioners, some of them remarking how wonderful it was to see both men together. As the last parishioner departed Brendan caught Jim's eye, hoping to convey, "I'm off now." Jim's almost imperceptible nod told Brendan that he understood.

Brendan walked away from the church and down the street. He could have taken the bus or called a taxi, but he wanted to take his time. It felt like the action he was about to take should be performed in full consciousness and not rushed. He crossed the park, breathing in the chilly autumn air. There was a faint woody scent of bonfires in the air and Brendan passed through a pile of crackly dead leaves that had strewn across the ground. He had an incongruous impulse to kick them; swoop his arms under them and send the gold, brown and red scattering through the air as he had done when he was little, but resisted. He was sure there would be plenty of time to kick leaves in his life, hopefully with Teddy, maybe even with Grace's foster children.

As he walked into the wind, he felt his eyes begin to stream again, for reasons that had nothing at all to do with the weather. That was fine too. As Jim had advised him, there would be many more tears to come. Brendan did not feel bad about releasing them now. He didn't think he was naïve enough to believe that the crippling guilt about "not being abused enough" was gone for good, but he hoped that what he was about to do would help further him on the right path. Maybe, he would even be able to begin some sort of healing process. The drizzle was starting to fall now, fine pearls beading on Brendan's jacket and the ends of his hair.

At the other end of the park a long road stretched ahead. As Brendan walked, the lights in front of the police station grew brighter, a yellow haze peeping through the rain. Before he stepped through the gates, Brendan wiped his eyes and puffy face a final time and crossed himself. Then he walked into the forecourt, feeling more composed than he had done in a long time. He paused to let a car leave the forecourt and immediately sound the siren. As he walked into the station, he paid no attention to the collection of people slumped on the screwed down chairs. He walked to the desk and looked directly at the police officer seated behind the Perspex shield.

What he was about to do was completely irreversible. He felt bad for Di Cassidy, who would undoubtedly suffer, bad for his parents who would be crushed to learn he had not felt able to confide in them, bad for his sister who may feel that she had misjudged him in their youth. But he knew that he would feel far worse if he continued to remain quiet. He spoke quietly and clearly to the desk officer. His voice was steadier than he would ever have believed possible.

"I would like to report a case of historic sexual abuse."

The End

275

Acknowledgements

The biggest thanks are due to you, for being kind enough to read my book. I hope you enjoyed it and if so, I hope you'll continue to accompany me on my writing journey.

Thank you to Rose and Alan from Stairwell Books. Rose, you spotted the potential of my novel and took a chance on me. You have shown huge patience in guiding me, a complete rookie, through the process. Thank you to Georgia for your sterling editing work and to Suzy for the front cover illustration, which nailed the essence of the book better than I ever could have hoped.

Thank you to the members of Writers in the Evening group, in particular Will, Dave, Belinda, Sarah, Liz, Paul, Rebecca, Icy and Bella. Your comments and suggestions made this a far better novel than it would have been otherwise.

There is a team of people without whom I would great difficulty living, let alone writing. You are all amazing, and the work you do deserves so much more recognition than it gets. Special thanks to the grower of the world's most impressive beard and the person who is a much better team leader than he is a hairdresser.

Mum, you have inspired me in more ways than you will ever know. Your support, encouragement and unsurpassed radar for bull**** have helped make this book a reality.

Christopher, being your mother has been the greatest joy of my life. Thank you for always putting a smile on my face. You have given me so much, without ever realising it, and I love you more than anything.

The song that runs through Brendan's head is "Sit Down", by the band James. The lyrics were written by Tim Booth in 1988.

Other novels, novellas and short story collections available from
Stairwell Books

A Mind Prone to Evil	P S Lynch
Solstice	Ruth Aylett, Greg Michaelson
The Other Way	Victoria L. Humphreys
The Suitcase of Secrets	Julie Fearn
At Night, White Bracken	Gareth Wood
The Sunlit Pool of the Finished Image	David Hill
The Department of Certainty	S. C. Paterson
A Fistful of Ashes	Katy Turton
Widdershins	L.A.Robbins
100 Summers	Ali Sparkes
Skull Days	PJ Quinn
The Broke Hotel	Clayton Lister
Equinox	Ruth Aylett, Greg Michaelson
Not the Work of an Ordinary Boy	Victoria L. Humphreys
Black Harry	Mark P. Henderson
Eboracvm: Carved in Stone	Graham Clews
Down to Earth	Andrew Crowther
The Iron Brooch	Yvonne Hendrie
The Electric	Tim Murgatroyd
The Pirate Queen	Charlie Hill
Djoser and the Gods	Michael J. Lowis
Needleham	Terry Simpson
The Keepers	Pauline Kirk
Shadows of Fathers	Simon Cullerton
Blackbird's Song	Katy Turton
Eboracvm: the Fortress	Graham Clews
The Warder	Susie Williamson
Waters of Time	Pauline Kirk
The Water Bailiff's Daughter	Yvonne Hendrie
O Man of Clay	Eliza Mood
Eboracvm: the Village	Graham Clews
Sammy Blue Eyes	Frank Beill
Virginia	Alan Smith
Poetic Justice	PJ Quinn
Return of the Mantra	Susie Williamson
The Go-To Guy	Neal Hardin
Abernathy	Claire Patel-Campbell
Tyrants Rex	Clint Wastling
Border 7	Pauline Kirk

For further information please contact rose@stairwellbooks.com

www.stairwellbooks.co.uk
@stairwellbooks

www.ingramcontent.com/pod-product-compliance
Lightning Source LLC
Chambersburg PA
CBHW030650020726
47493CB00006B/1968